THE WITCHES OF PITFELDRY

By Harriet Smart

The Butchered Man: Northminster Mystery 1
The Dead Songbird: Northminster Mystery 2
The Shadowcutter: Northminster Mystery 3
The Hanging Cage: Northminster Mystery 4
The Ghosts of Ardenthwaite: Northminster Mystery 5
The Echo at Rooke Court: Northminster Mystery 6
The Fatal Engine: Northminster Mystery 7
The Witches of Pitfeldry: Northminster Mystery 8
Moonshine and Mercury: Northminster Mystery 9
Tarleton's Coffer: Northminster Mystery 10
The Wounded Oak: Northminster Mystery 11
Mummer's Night: A Northminster Novella
Carswell's First Case: A Northminster Novella
Emma Vernon's Northminster Ghost Stories
The Dolls at Heron's Reach
The True Value of Pearls
The Daughters of Blane
Green Grow the Rushes
The Wild Garden
The Lark Ascending
Reckless Griselda
A Tempting Proposal

THE WITCHES OF PITFELDRY

by

Harriet Smart

Published by Anthemion

First Edition

ISBN 978-1-907873-63-8

Made with Jutoh

Chapter One

April 1842

"You will think us extravagant," Mrs Carswell said to Felix, as she showed the room to him. "But these rooms have not been touched in twenty years."

"They look better for it," said the Rector. "Mrs McCroy was very wise to suggest we redecorate. I was not convinced at first, but the effect has been surprising."

"These printed cottons are much less dear than they were," Mrs Carswell added, tweaking one of the bed curtains to make it hang perfectly. "It was quite hard to choose, but after some debate we settled upon acorns and oak leaves."

"I see you have moved Lady Charlotte Brodie," Felix said, noticing the engraving after Gainsborough hanging above the mantelpiece.

"Yes, she looks quite well there, does she not?" said Mrs Carswell.

Lord Rothborough had given them the print, and the lady it showed was his own mother, the sixth Marchioness, and the heiress of the last Earl of Pitfeldry. He had instructed them to hang it in the nursery, and Felix imagined this must have caused some qualms in the hearts of the Rector and Mrs Carswell, who had parents of their own that they wished the child to honour. But in the end, the charming figure of his natural grandmother, dressed à la Van Dyck, had been allowed to remain.

Felix had occasionally speculated about what Lady Charlotte would have thought of her son bringing his natural child back to Pitfeldry to be made into a thorough Scotsman. Apparently she had been profoundly homesick for her home in Scotland, and had returned there as often as she could, notably for the birth of her youngest child, the present Lord Rothborough, in 1790. Having been delivered of the second boy she had long prayed for, as an act of thanks she restored the old chapel of Holy Trinity, Knocknaduh, which lay very close to the Castle of Pitfeldry, so that the handful of Episcopalians who remained in the district might have a proper place of worship. She also built a house nearby as a rectory. A neat, classical villa, fashioned from the dark stone of the district and eminently suitable for a clergyman and his family, it was here that Felix Carswell had spent most of his childhood. Whether she would have approved of this arrangement could never be known. Her smile in the Gainsborough print seemed benign. That was all that could be said.

"I do hope you will be comfortable, Miss King," Mrs Carswell said.

"How can I not be, ma'am?" said Miss King. "And the view – oh, my goodness, what can one say?"

Eleanor went and stood beside her.

"It's just as lovely as I said it would be, is it not?" she said.

"It is everything I expected. Thank you so much for bringing me."

"We could hardly have left you at home," said Eleanor.

"Now, Felix, you and Eleanor are in here, as before," said Mrs Carswell, going to the door and crossing the passageway, "but we have done a little sprucing here as well."

"By which she means she has run amok," said the Rector.

"It was necessary," Mrs Carswell said. "The old bed curtains fell to pieces in my hands, and there was no patching them. And as for running amok – it was your father himself who chose the paper. Birds of paradise, no less!"

Felix could not recall his father ever expressing any interest in anything as worldly as house-furnishing before. To find the guest bedchamber at the Rectory turned into an exotic bower for rainbow-feathered birds with curious expressions, was startling to say the least.

"I have been reading an interesting account of a mission to the Indies," said Mr Carswell, going to the bookshelf, taking down a book and handing it to Felix. "There was something in this pattern that made me think of it. It is an instructive volume. Ah, if I were forty years younger, I should, if God willed, have –"

And with that characteristic unfinished sentence he left the room.

"God might call us yet," said Mrs Carswell.

"On a mission to the Indies?" said Felix. This idea was more startling than the wallpaper.

"It has been quite a cold winter here," said Mrs Carswell, with a sigh. She turned to the bed, which was covered with an equally colourful counterpane formed of a mosaic of tiny hexagons and centred on a medallion showing a pair of parakeets. "And you see I have finished your coverlet at last. I have never taken so long about a piece of work. The light has been indifferent and I have been lazy."

"That scarcely looks like laziness," Felix said. "I'm glad you got Scott to test your eyes."

"Such fine work!" Miss King said. "I have heard of this technique, but I have never seen it."

"Do you like paper piecing, Miss King?" asked Mrs Carswell.

"Oh yes, but I am nowhere near this standard."

"Jenny is very clever with her hands," Eleanor said. "And she has even persuaded me to try it, and you know what a feeble needlewoman I am."

"And do you like it, my dear?" Mrs Carswell said.

"I do," she said. "But I'm only halfway through a pin cushion. Now, you must see the view from this window, Jenny, it is perfection!"

"Miss King is charming, Felix," said Mrs Carswell, drawing him into the passageway. "I did wonder at first, when you told me you were employing her, if it was wise to bring a stranger into the house, but she seems to be exactly what was required. How clever of Mrs Fforde to find her for you!"

"Do you really want to go and be missionaries?" Felix said.

"It is not a question of what we want, Felix," she said. "Now, I shall leave you to get settled. I am going to make some drop scones, so do not be long."

He went back into their bedroom. Eleanor and Miss King were still standing at the window, engrossed by the view, which was not without some merit, running as it did across the Glen of Pitfeldry to the mountains beyond, especially since all was cast in the velvety softness of a spring afternoon.

"And we shall go up there, up Ben Liath," Eleanor said. "You are a strong walker."

"The paths around Hawksby are all rather flat," said Miss King, glancing back at Felix. "A mountain is quite a different thing."

"It depends on the path," Felix said. "But the one we took last year – it is not arduous, if you take your time."

"We should go tomorrow," said Eleanor, "for you can never know if the weather will hold here. We should seize our chance at once!"

"Perhaps," said Miss King, with a smile, "if we are not too tired from the journey. It will be pleasant not to sleep in an inn tonight, I must say – not that the inns were uncomfortable, of course," she added carefully, remembering her place as a paid companion.

"Oh, Jenny, there is no need for you to be so grateful!" Eleanor exclaimed. "That inn last night was truly dreadful – we are all agreed on it. You are one of us, now," she said, hooking her arm into hers, and leaning against her. "You may complain as much as we all do. Now what was it Major Vernon said? Ah yes, complaining is part of the pleasure of travel."

"Very well," Miss King said. "I shall try my best."

It certainly had been quite a journey: three days in a procession of carriages from Queensferry to Pitfeldry, preceded by the steamer from Hull to Leith.

At this moment they were interrupted by Jacob and Johnny bringing in the luggage, of which there was a considerable amount. Johnny served as a general factotum at the Rectory, a good-hearted, brawny soul who had taught Felix how to trap animals for the purposes of dissection. Stevens, Eleanor's maid, followed with some of the smaller items.

"That bag is not ours, I think?" said Miss King.

"No, Miss, it belongs to Mrs Patton. I don't know how it got in with our things," said Stevens. "And she will be worried about it."

"I shall take it over after tea," said Felix. "I want to go and see how they have all settled in."

"Oh, then we shall come with you," said Eleanor. "It sounds like a charming walk –"

"No, no," said Felix. "Mrs Vernon will not want visitors just yet. In fact, I will go now while the light is with me. Better not to leave it."

He wondered then if he should simply have left Eleanor and Miss King with his parents, and carried on with the Vernons in their carriage across the Glen to old Mr Gault's house where they were to stay. Mrs Vernon's health had been precarious for some months: she had been troubled by lingering effects of the miscarriage she had suffered in December, suffering an intermittent exhaustion, the cause of which had been hard to diagnose. Her considerable will allowed her to make the best of it, but it was alarming none the less. Felix had done all he could for her, and with growing frustration had suggested that a change of air might be beneficial. It was an old nostrum, but it was often enough effective, especially after a dreary winter. Mrs Vernon had seized on the idea when it was discovered that Major Vernon was due a long leave, and the question of where they might go became a lively topic.

He and Eleanor had long planned to go to Pitfeldry after Easter, and Mrs Vernon expressed an interest in seeing Scotland for herself, and so the idea of a joint expedition had been formed. On enquiry, Mrs Carswell had revealed that Mrs McCroy, the lady who now owned old Mr Gault's house, often took in parties for the fishing and stalking and would be glad to accommodate the Vernons and provide all the necessary comforts at a sensible price. It was further reported that she had no fear of children, had an excellent cook and that the house was perhaps the nicest in the district, save the Castle. Indeed, Mrs Carswell hinted that she had wanted the Rector to buy it when it came on the market, and Lord Rothborough himself, who was the principal landowner in the district, had wanted it as well, but Mrs McCroy, by some means or other – witchcraft, perhaps – had got it from Mr Gault in the end.

Now, after the gruelling journey, Felix hoped that the house was as comfortable as promised and that Mrs Vernon was resting. She had looked most unwell in the carriage, although she had been attempting to make light of it, saying that her first glimpse of the mountains would surely cure her at once.

"So, Johnny, do you think the weather will hold?" Eleanor said. "We want to go up Ben Liath as soon as possible."

"Well, Mistress, I wouldn't know about that. The weather has been as good as you like, certainly it has, but it is strangely warm for the season and that often means it will turn again, and sharply. There is no knowing when a frost may come again."

"No!" exclaimed Eleanor. "No, do not say that! Please!"

"I've known snow in the Glen after Easter, many a time," Johnny went on. "You'll remember that, Master Felix. If Easter comes in March –"

"Old sayings are as often wrong as they are right," said Felix. "Here, Jacob, give me that bag. I won't be long."

He went down to the hall, and finding his hat, went to tell his father that he was going out. His mother was in the kitchen making the scones, a task she would never delegate.

"I'll come with you as far as the bridge," said the Rector, taking up his crook. "There is something I want to speak to you about, that you might wish to discuss with Major Vernon. It may be of some urgency."

They set out on the familiar path, accompanied by Amadeus, a lively young deerhound who was a recent addition to the household. He was ridiculously eager for the exercise and anxious to make friends with Felix.

"We shall have no peace for a day or two until he is used to you all," said Mr Carswell. "But I noticed Miss King had a way with him."

"He will want to sleep on her bed," said Felix, picking up a stick and throwing it to the dog, who obligingly set out to fetch it.

"He is never to go upstairs," said Mr Carswell. "And certainly not onto any beds. But she seems a sensible woman. I don't think she will indulge him – and neither will you, I trust," he added, watching as Felix stopped for a moment to caress the dog's head. "He has to learn his place in the order of things."

Felix threw the stick again and Amadeus rushed off. The dog had a beautiful energy in motion.

"I can't believe he was the runt of his litter," he said. "He is so handsome."

"Sandy McAllister is most discerning with his deerhounds," said Mr Carswell, referring to the farmer from whom he had got Amadeus. "Which is in our favour, is it not, sir?" he added, when Amadeus returned with the stick. "You get to be a pampered Rectory animal, with your bones and your blankets, eh?"

The dog panted appreciatively and ran off again after the stick.

"So, Papa, what was it you wanted to talk to me about?" said Felix, after they had walked for some minutes more, having left the extensive grounds of the Rectory to descend by the road down into the village. Holy Trinity lay to their right, its graveyard guarded by a pair of massive, stooping yew trees. Local legend claimed them to be more ancient than those at Fortingall, a story that Lord Rothborough liked a great deal. As a result the Castle employed a special man, grandly named the Steward of the Yews, to make sure no harm ever came to the trees. In reality, this was not an arduous task, and he was mostly employed keeping the graveyard tidy and helping in the garden at the Rectory. He lived with his family a little further down the road along which Felix and Mr Carswell were now walking. His wife was shaking out a rug as they passed, and naturally they had to stop and speak to her for a moment. This proved to be ten minutes, because in Pitfeldry nothing was ever accomplished in a moment. The children were called out of the house to be admired and inspected, and then Felix was implored to bring Mrs Felix down to the cottage before too long, so she could see the hens again.

Felix promised he would, and they walked on.

"So, Papa –" he began again, but this time Mr Carswell put his finger to his lips and said, "Not while we are in the village."

"As you like," said Felix.

"I have no wish to be overheard," he said as they turned into the lane lined with single-storey, white-painted cottages that formed the main part of the village on that side of the river. Only when they reached the stone bridge that crossed the river did Mr Carswell speak again, and then only when they had reached the centre of it. He stood looking downstream, holding Amadeus by his collar, and considered a while before he spoke.

"What knowledge do you have of witchcraft?" he said, at last.

"In what respect?"

"As an educated man."

"Not a great deal," Felix said. "Witchcraft – what exactly do you mean?"

"How it might present itself to one in your profession?"

"I'm not sure what you mean, Papa."

"You have read of cases of bewitchment and such like?"

"In old treatises, I suppose, but it is not something of which I have any experience. Do you think someone may be bewitched?"

There was another long silence as Mr Carswell gazed at the river.

"You know, of course, about the witches that were put to death here," he said.

"Yes, in the time of Charles the Second, and what a monstrous injustice that was! They were not witches, surely, but just poor souls that did not bow their heads sufficiently and found themselves in trouble for it."

"That is how it may be read, yes," said Mr Carswell, after another pause. "But they were educated men, who were not credulous by any means, and they firmly believed that the Devil was among them, and working through those women."

"Yes, but given the limits of knowledge at the time, with so many things unexplained, then perhaps things seemed to them to be –"

"But the Devil is real! And perhaps he was revealed to them in all his wickedness. After all, at the same time and across the Continent, and even in America, scores of witches came to light, did they not? Those creatures all confessed that they had had communion with Satan himself!"

"Confessing, no doubt, under extreme duress!" Felix put in. "They were tortured into it. People who are tortured will say anything. It is no use to any investigation to torture people

– they say exactly what the torturer wants them to say. Besides, even if they said Satan was there among them, it means nothing. There is no evidence that any such being exists. It is an act of faith to believe in Satan, as much an act of faith as it is to believe in God, is it not?"

This was a strong thing to say to his father, and he at once regretted being so blunt. But the topic and Mr Carswell's curious manner had unsettled him.

He began to apologise, but his father raised his hands to silence him.

"We will take this up later," he said. "We are not alone."

A young man, soberly and respectably garbed in the usual dress of a clergyman of the Church of Scotland, was coming across the bridge towards them. Amadeus began to growl as he approached and had to be swiftly told to hush by Mr Carswell.

"Ah, Mr Carswell, I thought it was you standing there!" he said. "Good afternoon! Is it not a glorious one?"

"Indeed, Mr Wallace," said Mr Carswell, struggling a little with Amadeus. "This is my son, Mr Felix Carswell. Felix, this is Mr Wallace, the new minister."

They shook hands.

"You are Mr Burnett's successor, then?" said Felix.

"Ah yes, yes, such an excellent gentleman. What great shoes to be filled, and as you can see, I only have small feet!" He pointed at his feet and laughed somewhat excessively at his own joke. "But much can be accomplished with small steps as well as large ones," he added, with great seriousness, "and indeed there is much to be accomplished here. I have just been with old Mrs Stewart. Poor woman, she is very tried by all her ailments, but she was comforted to see me. We read the psalms together."

Amadeus continued to protest.

"Please excuse my dog, sir," said Mr Carswell, tugging now at Amadeus' collar. "He has no manners, and I have kept him standing too long. We must be on our way. In fact, I shall take him straight back to the Rectory, Felix – he is altogether too restive. You carry on."

Felix nodded and began to cross the bridge.

"I am going your way, I think," said Mr Wallace. "May I come with you?"

"Yes, of course," said Felix, but not with any enthusiasm. He would have much preferred a solitary walk.

"I was on my way to pay my respects to Major and Mrs Vernon," Wallace said. "Naturally your visit has been all the talk here for some time. And Lord Rothborough is expected at the Castle soon, he tells me."

"Yes, at some point," said Felix.

"I look forward to knowing him in person," said Wallace. "We have corresponded, of course, quite extensively. He takes a great interest in parish matters here – it is only right and proper that he should – and he was grateful for my advice on certain questions which he could not settle for himself."

"I'm sure he was," said Felix.

"We had a most illuminating discussion of the Veto Act," Wallace went on. "And I was able to persuade him of the merits of upholding certain long-held conventions."

Felix knew nothing of this, and anxious not to pursue the matter, asked instead, "What is wrong with Mrs Stewart? If I remember her right, she was an energetic soul and always in good health. I hope it's nothing serious. Perhaps I should call on her. My father did not mention her being ill."

"It would be good of you, Mr Carswell, to take the trouble to see her. But I sense it is God's will that her time is coming fast, and the hope and truth that a minister of the Word can bring to the bedside must be the best medicine for her at present."

"If she is dying," said Felix, "there are many practical things that can be done to relieve her suffering. But then again, we must hope she is not, surely?"

"If it is God's will, then it is God's will," the young minister said, in such a lugubrious tone that Felix was very glad they had reached the gates of Mrs McCroy's house.

"You and Major Vernon will be glad of a respite from your unusual labours," said Mr Wallace. "I should not care for it! It seems to attract a great deal of attention. All those lurid newspaper reports, read by all and sundry. In fact, I fear they must fall often enough into innocent hands and have a tendency to corrupt."

"I disagree," said Felix. "The moral is always very clear, and if people are entertained by it, then let them be. They are more likely to learn any lessons they may need to learn that way. But most men are not inclined to murder, Mr Wallace. A newspaper article will not make them pick up an axe and murder their wives. It is always more complicated than that."

"I hope you are right," said Mr Wallace. They were at the front door now, and Felix tugged the bell with some force, hoping for a speedy admission and an end to this conversation.

Chapter Two

"What a shame to have to shut the shutters on such a day," said Emma.

"You are as impatient as the children," said Giles, having fastened the hook and then adjusted the curtains to make the room as dark as possible. "And having suffered a migraine or two in my time," he went on, going to the washstand and pouring some water into the bowl, "I know that this is the only way to deal with it."

She sighed. He soaked a napkin in the bowl and carefully folded it.

"It all looked so beautiful, and promising. I so want to go for a walk."

"It will all be there tomorrow."

"It will be raining tomorrow, no doubt, with my luck –"

"Stop complaining, Mrs Vernon," he said, laying the folded cloth across her eyes. "Remember what a miracle it is we even got here. There were several times on that road that I thought at least one of the wheels was going to part company from the axle."

"Yes, quite," Emma said. "And that is delicious. What a good nurse you are, Giles."

"I do what I can," he said, kissing her forehead. "Do you think you might manage to sleep?"

"I'm sure. I'm certainly tired enough," she said. "And this is such a comfortable bed. I hope Mrs McCroy has not given up her room to us. This feels as if it might be the best in the house."

"That is not worth worrying about," said Giles.

"No, but –"

"Hush," he said. "I'm sure she still has the best room in the house. It seems to be a big enough place for several handsome rooms."

"Yes, of course. Oh, why must I be silly just now, Giles, so stupid and useless? It is the worst part of this. The pain and the tiredness I can bear, but my mind is so –"

He kissed her forehead again. "You are none of those things. And you must rest. I will go and see if I can find that green tea for you."

He left her and made his way downstairs and into the dining room where he had left the children along with Greene, their nurse, and Patton, Emma's maid. Now he found those useful people had gone, and Sophy, Hamish and Sandro were instead in the charge of Mrs McCroy herself. She was sitting at the head of the table.

"I thought your servants would appreciate a cup of tea in the kitchen, Major Vernon. Jean will look after them," said Mrs McCroy.

"They certainly would," said Giles, astonished at how serene it felt. Sophy and Hamish were busy eating, but even Sandro, sitting in a high chair beside his hostess, was remarkably subdued. "Might it be possible for Mrs Vernon to have a pot of green tea?"

"I shall go and tell Jean," said Mrs McCroy, getting up. To Giles' surprise, Hamish even remembered to get up from his place, albeit with a slice of cake in his hand.

She left the room and when the door closed, Hamish said in an awed whisper, "There are four kinds of scone, Uncle Giles. Four!"

"That is more kinds of scone than I ever thought possible," said Giles, sitting down.

"And cake," Hamish went on.

"Seed cake," Sophy said, "and it is nice!"

"Truly?"

"Truly. Seed cake is usually horrid. May I pour your tea

for you, Uncle Giles?" Sophy said, bustling into Mrs McCroy's place.

"If you are careful," he said.

"How is Aunt Emma?" Hamish said, with his mouth full.

"Wanting to go for a walk, but I don't think she will be able. But we shall go out and find her some flowers. I think I saw some primroses as we came along."

"There were some outside the Rectory," Sophy said, pouring Giles a scant half a cup of tea as if she dared not pour more.

"We could go and get some of those," said Hamish, "and see Amadeus again."

Mr Carswell's magnificent young deerhound had profoundly impressed Hamish, even though he had only seen him for a minute or two.

"I don't think we had better go that far today," said Giles. "But tomorrow we will go and call."

"It's not very far," said Sophy, "back over the steep bridge and then along a bit. And we can get Patton's bag for her. It went in with the other luggage. She will not be able to sleep if she does not have her bag. It has her Bible and prayer book in it, and she cannot sleep without them by the bed."

"Ah, well, then," Giles said, "perhaps. A longer walk is perhaps not such a bad idea. I'm still rather stiff. Though I expect someone will send over Patton's bag before then. Might I have another cup of tea, Sophy – and which of these scones do you recommend?"

"The dark brown ones," Hamish said.

"No, no, the floury triangles," said Sophy.

This launched a debate over the merits of their respective candidates that was in danger of becoming unpleasantly heated, such was the competitive nature of the children, until, to Giles' relief, the doorbell sounded. Mrs McCroy brought in Carswell, carrying Patton's bag as well as his medical bag. He was accompanied by a pale-faced young man with lank, greasy hair. He was dressed in clerical black, with a high, stiff white cravat, and they soon learned it was Mr Wallace, the minister of the parish. Carswell excused himself at once to go and see Emma, leaving Giles and the children with Mr Wallace.

"I felt I must pay my respects and welcome you to the neighbourhood, Major Vernon," he said.

"That's very kind. I'm sorry Mrs Vernon is not here. You'll have gathered from Mr Carswell that she is not strong at present."

"Yes, I did – I was sorry to hear it," said Mr Wallace. He turned his attention to the children. "Ah, these must be the innocents that I hear you have so kindly sheltered, against the storm of their parents' wickedness. A striking act of Christian charity. I trust you are very good children and very grateful for all that is done for you. Do you say your prayers and study your Bibles?"

"My mama and papa are not wicked, sir," ventured Sophy. "At least I don't think so," she added, coming to lean against Giles. "Are they?" she finished, looking up at Giles with worried eyes. He slipped his arm about her, not at all liking that a stranger should have broached such a tender subject so carelessly in front of them.

"No, they are not!" said Hamish. "Excuse me, sir," he added quickly. "But –"

"Hamish," Giles said, "would you be so good as to take Sandro and find Greene? I think he is growing restive."

Hamish extracted Sandro from his seat and carried him out of the room without another word, with Sophy at his heels. Giles wished he could have gone with them.

"They will be in my prayers," said Mr Wallace.

"I don't know what you have heard, Mr Wallace," he said, "but my wife and I are only helping her sister and brother-in-law through their difficulties. It is a great pleasure for us to have the children with us."

"So they were not abandoned by their mother? I understood that was the case. I believe I heard it from Mr Carswell, no less."

"Yes, but it does not help them to hear their parents condemned."

"It is the truth, sir, is it not?" said Wallace.

"Yes, it may be, but it is not kind," Giles said.

"Do you think I ought to lie out of kindness, sir?" said Mr Wallace. "That is a fine thing to say to a minister of religion. Perhaps your profession has made you forget what is right."

"I'm not asking you to lie. To omit to say something is not a lie, Mr Wallace," said Giles. Feeling his irritation about to get the better of him, he changed the subject. "I understand you have not been long in place?" he said.

"We came here last November from Edinburgh."

"It must be a pleasant charge. I have heard Mr and Mrs Carswell speak very highly of the ordinary people here."

"There is a great deal to be done, I find," said Mr Wallace. "The Gospel is not so at the heart of affairs here as it should be."

"Does your family like the district?" Giles asked, not at all wishing to pursue the subject of his parishioners' lack of religious enthusiasm.

"My wife does, yes," said Mr Wallace. "But she is new to country living."

"So it still has all its charms for her," Giles said. "Long may it continue. You may find what is a novelty for her becomes a necessity. It must be a fine place to bring up a family." At which point, there came an appalling scream from the hall that could only be the work of Sandro. "Excuse me, sir," he said, and went out of the room to find Sandro lying face down on the flagged floor and howling in shock, having tripped on a length of carpet.

"There, my boy, that will teach you to run away from me!" Greene exclaimed. "Oh, do not take him up, sir, he will take it all wrong. He will not learn that way!"

"It was an accident," said Giles, taking Sandro into his arms. As was usual, this was enough to silence him.

"You are too soft on him, sir, that you are," said Greene.

"I'd rather he did not scream the house down," said Giles, "given the state of Mrs Vernon's head."

"I suppose so, sir, but I must take him back. It is time for the –" She saw Mr Wallace in the doorway and added in an embarrassed whisper, "Privy. Wherever it might be."

"Through there, in the yard," said Giles, pointing to the back door. "Now Sandro, be good!"

Sandro sniffed, and gazed mournfully over Greene's shoulder at Giles as he was carried away down the long passageway that divided the house.

Giles turned back to Mr Wallace.

"Perhaps I'd better not take up any more of your time, Mr Wallace," he said, going to the front door and opening it. "I hope I may bring Mrs Vernon to call on you and Mrs Wallace at the Manse when she is feeling stronger? It was good of you to come and see us. I shall tell her that you did."

"As you wish, sir. Good day."

Giles closed the door and turned back to see Mrs McCroy standing in the hall. She made an interesting figure – not wearing black, as might be expected, but soft red, with a long, picturesque jacket made from a bright print over it. He would have to ask Emma what she thought of this ensemble.

"Should I not have sent him away?" he said. "Did you want to speak to him?"

"No, not at all," she said. "I have sent the older children out into the garden, if you do not mind?"

"An excellent idea."

"They have noticed my cats."

"Sophy can never leave a cat alone. I hope there is no difficulty in that."

"No, they don't dislike children."

"Really, I do not think we could be better housed, ma'am," Giles said. "Tea was excellent."

"Thank you."

"I had better go up again," he said, indicating the stairs.

"Of course. I hope she is feeling better," Mrs McCroy said. "If you need anything, please just ask."

He went upstairs, and from the long stair window caught a glimpse of Sophy crouching on the grass making overtures to a large black and brown striped cat.

Carswell was just coming out of their bedroom.

"She's asleep now," he said, "and I didn't like to disturb her. In fact, I cannot offer anything but the usual prescription. Rest, and plenty of it. But at least she will be comfortable here."

"Will you thank Mrs Carswell for discovering this place for us?" Giles said. "Mrs McCroy seems to have everything so perfectly in hand. And there were four different sorts of scone. The children were lost for words – well, almost."

"Only four?" said Carswell with a smile. "Ah yes, scones are a great thing here."

They went downstairs together, and Carswell ran an appreciative hand along the finely carved oak bannisters. "I never knew this house was so well fitted out – I have never been inside before. Mr Gault was a strange old man who never saw anyone much. He let my father over the threshold from time to time."

"And you have never met Mrs McCroy before?"

"She came here after I went to Edinburgh, and I did not meet her last year, though I'm surprised, for she and my mother seem to be firm friends now. It is good for her – my mother, I mean – to have such a person in the neighbourhood. Her letters are full of her. She was the one who started them on the decorating – which is astonishing in itself. My father picking out wallpaper with birds of paradise on it! It must be seen to be believed."

"A man may give way to such fancies now and then, surely?" Giles said.

Carswell gave a nervous laugh.

"Yes, but you know what my father is like. Birds of paradise on a black ground? It must have cost a small fortune, and he hates to spend money. And he is making strange intimations, as I am sure Mr Wallace would put it. He is a pattern-book minister, by the by, is he not? I don't think I shall be going to listen to him preach, no matter what funny notions Eleanor has about the Kirk. It will be at least half an hour of dry meal without an interesting idea in it. No, ten minutes walking with him here was quite enough for me! I thought I might shake him off, but he was determined to see you."

Mrs McCroy came out of her sitting room.

"Would like a glass of wine, gentlemen?"

"No, thank you, I must get back to the Rectory, ma'am," said Carswell, shaking her hand. "It is very good to know you at last, though. My mother writes so much about you, I feel we must already be old friends."

"And she tells me a great deal about you, Mr Carswell, and of course you as well, Major Vernon. In fact, clippings from The Bugle sometimes find their way into my hands. Such exploits! You will be glad of a holiday."

"Yes, certainly," said Giles. "Now, I wonder if I can prevail on you both for some local knowledge. Where can I find some primroses for Mrs Vernon? I promised I would take Hamish and Sophy out to find some."

"There is a good crop down by the river, in the field beyond the garden there, in that clump of trees," said Mrs McCroy, opening the front door and pointing out the direction. "It is a bit of a scramble and rather muddy, but you do not look afraid of mud, and I'm sure the children are not."

"You have made your view much better by taking down that old elm," remarked Carswell. "I suppose you get more sun in the house now."

"I do. It felt wicked to take down such an old tree, and one that had been a sheltering friend to Mr Gault, who did not like the sunshine so much as I, but I have made some of it into a rustic bench. And as you say, the view of the Glen is much improved."

Carswell elected to show them to the primroses, as it was on his way back to the Rectory, and gathering up the children, they set out along the banks of the River Pit, which was heavily in its spring spate. Even here in the valley, it made an impressive show, rushing over the huge rocks that were scattered in the river bed, making perfect stepping stones. Both Sophy and Hamish looked longingly at them, for they presented a temptation to climb that Giles himself entirely understood. He was glad to seem them distracted by the excitement of the scenery.

"Wait until you see the Falls of Iolair, Hamish," said Carswell. "There is a bathing pool there, and rocks to dive from. For gentlemen only, I'm afraid, Sophy."

"No!" said Sophy. "How can that be, Uncle Giles?"

"I don't know. It's just the way of things," said Giles. "And the water will be extremely cold, I suppose, Mr Carswell?"

"It is. Perhaps that is why the ladies keep away."

"I don't see why ladies should be more afraid of cold water than gentlemen," Sophy said. "It does not frighten me."

She looked most aggrieved.

"Is there a bathing place for ladies?" Giles said.

"Well, there is the Witches' Pool," said Carswell, after a moment. "But –"

"Witches?" Sophy's eyes widened.

"So, you'd have to be a witch to bathe there," Hamish said. "Or is that where they drowned them? They did drown them, didn't they? To test them or something."

"The idea was if you were a witch you would be able to save yourself from drowning, and therefore that proved your guilt," said Giles.

"So, if you were innocent you were left to drown?" Sophy said. "And die?"

"Yes, I'm afraid so."

"But that is very wrong and – and very silly!" she exclaimed. "To let an innocent person die! How could they be so stupid? How could anyone think that was right?"

"I really don't know," said Giles. "I suppose they thought the innocent soul would go straight to Heaven."

"That doesn't make it any better," Sophy said. "It's still murder. You would arrest them for it, wouldn't you, Uncle Giles?"

"No he wouldn't," Hamish said. "He'd be the one doing the drowning."

"Hamish," said Carswell, "steady, now –"

"Brutally put, Hamish, but you have a point," Giles said. "Yes, it was those in authority who acted so unjustly. And if I knew no better, then I suppose I might –"

"No, no, you would never do such a thing!" Sophy said. "Because you *would* know better."

"It's a great puzzle," Giles said, "that men could find such things acceptable."

"Fear and superstition make us into fools," Carswell said. "Are those aconites down there as well as the primroses? Shall we get some of those? If we can get at them without ending up in the water."

"I'll get them," said Hamish, and went scrabbling down the bank, followed by Sophy.

"My father started talking about witchcraft," Carswell said. "That was what made me think of the Witches' Pool."

"Did they drown women there?"

"I don't know. But they did hang at least twenty poor souls in this parish alone." He exhaled. "Papa asked me what I knew about witchcraft. He wanted to talk to you about it as well. I did not get a chance to find out why he is concerned about it, for that wretched Wallace interrupted us, but I sensed that..." He shook his head and took a few steps down the muddy path. "How are you two managing?" he called.

"Look, look," said Sophy, coming back up the path. She was holding a single, tiny pink flower. "Look at this. Is it not beautiful? What can it be? I wish Celia were here, for she knows all the names. Do you know this one, Mr Carswell?"

Carswell took the flower and shook his head.

"Major?" Carswell said.

"No, but it is beautiful. Sophy, you must paint it and send it to Celia."

At that moment a sharp wind rushed about them and the clouds covered the sun. The little flower trembled alarmingly on its stalk.

"We should go back," said Giles. "We have had our luck with the weather today."

Chapter Three

Major Vernon was right: Felix only narrowly escaped a thorough soaking. By the time he returned to the Rectory the rain had come on heavily, and walking up the path, he saw that Eleanor was sitting on the window seat in the drawing room, looking out with a melancholy expression. He hoped, for all their sakes, that the rain would pass through the Glen overnight. She was pleased, however, with his gift of flowers, although the posy owed its charm to Sophy's skill in making up little bouquets.

They went upstairs to dress for dinner. It was curious to be again in the room where they had spent some of the earliest days of their marriage, but which was now quite unrecognisable. The birds captured in the wallpaper acquired a decidedly sinister mien as the dark light of an evening storm filled the room.

Jacob came in with a lamp and Stevens began to close the shutters. They both seemed a little perplexed about how things were to be managed without separate dressing rooms, having grown thoroughly used to the spacious luxuries of Hawksby.

It was evident that they had all settled into particular ways of doing things over the last few months. Felix, for his part, was acutely aware of how little time he had spent with Eleanor and how his work had seemed to capture all his attention and energy. He had been kept busy at the Infirmary: the dreadful weather had seen to that, with accidents and illness sending a flood of fresh cases everyday.

In the dreary depths of mid-January, Eleanor had lost a great deal of enthusiasm for life. Felix would come home late and find her staring out of the window. He had attempted to devote more attention to her, but there were always other calls on his time, and he found her sullen manner irritated him as much as it roused his sympathy.

At least her physical health was robust, and she continued to ride when the weather permitted, exhausting the grooms who went out with her. She bought several expensive horses, and Felix wondered if she might find pleasure in taking them hunting. He discussed it with Major Vernon, who occasionally indulged himself with a day riding to hounds and who would have been happy to accompany her. He went as far as to suggest this to Eleanor, but this provoked her fury. She gave him a long and harrowing lecture on the subject. Fox-hunting was an abomination, and the fact that Major Vernon and Lord Rothborough should care for it was a very black mark on their characters.

"If I were the Queen, I would have it banned!" she said. "It is utterly disgusting."

"Then perhaps you ought to write to her about it!" Felix had exclaimed.

"I might, though I don't suppose she is allowed to ban anything, which must be wretched! No, I should write to the Prime Minister."

He might have suggested she take that up as a cause, and then realised it would be extremely disagreeable to him if she did. He had no strong opinions one way or the other about fox-hunting, so long as he was not forced to do it, but to have his wife banging such a drum would make him feel foolish. It was not that he thought that wives and women in general should not have minds and strong opinions, nor do good and useful things in the world – quite the contrary. But the thought of being looked at askance by everyone, because his unhappy wife had taken up an unpopular cause, was too much to bear. It would be clear that he had utterly failed as a husband to make her contented.

It was Mrs Fforde who found the solution. She had heard

of a superior young woman, the daughter of a clergyman, who had been earning her living as a governess in a nobleman's family. She had fallen ill and resigned her place, feeling that small children were too much for her. She was looking for a position as a companion, and Mrs Fforde wondered if such a person might be of use to Mrs Carswell. Felix had been anxious that Eleanor would not agree to such a scheme, but when it was proposed she made no objections, even conceding it might be interesting to have someone about the house.

So, in February, Miss King came to them, and although Eleanor was a trifle indifferent at first, it was soon clear that Miss King had quietly awoken her curiosity. Miss King may have been plain, but she was certainly not dull-spirited. Her arrival coincided with the completion of some repairs on Ardenthwaite and there had been a few days of unusually good weather. He had left them there, walking together in the woods, which were carpeted with the first drifts of snowdrops; and when he returned two nights later, they were as close as sisters.

However much Miss King may have improved Eleanor's mood, he was conscious that it had not done much to change the uncomfortable state of affairs between them. They had scarcely shared a bed, let alone had relations. He felt that this holiday in Pitfeldry ought to be a test of the matter, but how he was supposed to do that, he was not at all sure. A bunch of primroses seemed like a poor start, and the birds of paradise were not encouraging him.

"No, Stevens, leave the shutters, I want to watch the storm," Eleanor said.

"As you wish, madam," said Stevens. "Your grey figured silk, madam? It's not too badly crushed."

"Yes, yes, but leave it there. Mr Carswell will help me. Go and see to Miss King, if you please. She needs help with her hair." Stevens left, and they were alone. "We went out into the garden and it all blew down!" Eleanor went on, unhooking her bodice front. "She said she wished she could crop it short. She finds it such a nuisance. Forty years ago it used to be the fashion for ladies to wear cropped hair – I have seen pictures." Now she walked over to the looking glass and gazed at herself. "Perhaps we should revive the fashion. I might suit it. Jenny certainly would."

"Please do not," said Felix. "Either of you."

"I would have thought you would like such a practical, rational idea," she said, turning back to him.

"I like your hair just as it is," he said. "I wish I could pull it down now," he added. The sight of her hair down in the past had never failed to rouse him, and he felt in need of such a stimulus. The situation ought to have been quite enough, but he found his physical instincts were dulled.

"And make Stevens cross with you?" she said. "Help me with this, will you? This tape is –"

He untangled the tight knot that was securing the skirt of her dress, and although this was the perfect moment to place a kiss on her bare shoulders as she adjusted her chemise for her evening bodice, he refrained, and instead continued to play the perfect lady's maid until she was clad in her grey silk, even to the point of handing her a shawl and helping her to cover those tempting bare shoulders.

She went to see that all was well with Miss King, leaving him to change his own clothes and wonder at his own wilful indifference.

They sat down to dinner. The soup had just been taken away, and Felix was eagerly anticipating the salmon trout promised in his honour, when the maidservant came in to tell Mr Carswell that there was someone at the door who would not be sent away, although it was dinner time. "And he wants Mr Felix as well," she added.

"Who is it, Grizel?"

"It's Jackie McPherson, Westerlochan's man, sir. He says –"

"Yes, yes, of course," said Mr Carswell rising. "Excuse us, please, my dears, but this must be attended to at once."

He motioned for Felix to follow him. They went out into the hall where a broad-shouldered young man, dressed in the rough clothes of a farm servant and soaked from the storm, stood with his sodden bonnet in his hands.

"It has happened again, sir, just as I told you before, but this time, the littlest girl as well, wee Agnes. Putting up an awful commotion she was!" he said, shaking his head.

"Did Mr Murray send you to fetch me?" asked Mr Carswell.

"Nay, but I could not leave it, so I came down the Glen to fetch you – I have Mr Murray's gig, though, so you'll no' have to walk."

"He'll not be pleased to see me, if you don't have his permission, Jackie," said Mr Carswell.

"I could not have stayed there, truth be told. It fairly scared me out of my skin."

"I am sure Mrs Murray will be glad to see a medical man," said Mr Carswell. "You'd better fetch your bag, Felix."

"No disrespect, sir," said Jackie to Felix. "But it's a man of God that house needs – a real man of God, I mean, no' yon man Wallace –"

"Your employers are still Christians, Jackie," said Mr Carswell, "whatever church they choose."

"Aye, but that milksop Wallace," said Jackie, "he'd no' be able to see off the Devil! And if I lose my place for this, sir, then that'll be a lesson to me for going to work there in the first place. I should have gone up to my Uncle's in Logie as my mother told me."

"Do not speak of Mr Wallace so!" said Mr Carswell. "That does not become you."

"I'm sorry, sir, I'm sure," said Jackie, but he did not sound very repentant.

"Who are these Murrays?" Felix asked, when they went

outside to the gig. It was not a name he recalled in the neighbourhood.

"Murray took over Westerlochan last autumn," said Mr Carswell, climbing into the gig and wrapping his shepherd's plaid about him in expert fashion against the rain. Felix had no such useful garment to hand and climbed up reluctantly beside him.

"He's no' from the Glen," said Jackie. "Ayrshire," he added.

"He has a fine way with cattle, that you must concede, Jackie," said Mr Carswell.

It was a tedious journey up the Glen, as the rain lashed the imperfect covering of the gig. The pony was tired and Jackie did not urge him on. It felt for all the world as if they were making a pleasure excursion to admire the scenery, not an expedition to confront the Devil himself – if that was what this was.

At last they passed through a clump of beeches and in through a stone gate that marked the entrance to the farmtoun of Westerlochan. Through the thickening murk of the sodden evening, Felix could just see that the farmhouse was a white-harled building of moderate size and plainly constructed, surrounded by the usual utilitarian buildings. There was at least some hope of a good fire and a reasonable welcome inside. It was in the nature of Pitfeldry to be hospitable.

As they approached, a boy came running out, and rushed to catch the pony's bridle.

"Is it all still goin' on in there, Ned?" said Jackie, jumping down.

"Aye, it is, and the master was asking where you'd gone with the nag because he wanted to get Mr Wallace, so I said you'd gone down for Mr Carswell."

"We had better go in at once," said Mr Carswell.

Felix noticed that on the threshold he blessed himself, and that Jackie did likewise. This struck him as extraordinary, for usually his father reserved this action for the execution of the liturgy, and he stopped for a moment. There was the sound of screaming and a sash being opened, and he looked towards the upper windows of the house.

A girl with wild hair was struggling at the window, attempting, it seemed, to throw herself out of it. She was leaning over the sill and howling. Unseen hands appeared to drag her back and the window was slammed shut.

Felix ran into the house. The staircase lay ahead and his father was already halfway upstairs. The girl's otherworldly screaming continued.

A huge man stood at the top of the landing, barring their way. He was in his shirt sleeves with disordered hair and he had the air of the master of the house about him. Felix assumed this was Mr Murray.

"Westerlochan," said Mr Carswell, addressing him by the name of his farm, as was the custom. "You'll forgive me coming unbidden, but it seems needs must. May I see your girls? Jackie has told me they are afflicted – indeed, I can hear that for myself –"

Murray glanced at Felix and said, "You're the surgeon, then?" Felix nodded. "Do what you can – if you can do anything!"

He stood back and let them pass. Felix hastened into the room and saw that the girl was struggling to escape the restraining embrace of an older woman, perhaps her mother. She was obviously determined to head back towards the window, and in a moment had succeeded in getting free. Felix intervened to stop her, and found himself in a full-on wrestling match. At the same time, she kept up her shrieking. She was furious and surprisingly strong.

He managed to drag her to a bench by the wall, and sat down there with her clamped in his arms, hoping he might be able to calm her, for he was worried that she was having some sort of respiratory attack. She submitted to this, but only just, and then suddenly – after a particularly piercing shriek – she fell into a dead faint in his arms.

For several minutes she was utterly unresponsive, despite his efforts to revive her, and then she started into consciousness again, and gazed at him in astonishment. She had large, prominent blue eyes and the effect was disconcerting, as if being stared at by a living doll.

"Where am I?" she said.

"You're in your room at home, Janet," said Mr Carswell, coming forward. "And this is my son, Mr Felix Carswell. He's a doctor and has come to help you."

"A doctor?" she said. "Why do I need a doctor? I'm no' sick, am I?"

"You are not right," Mr Carswell said. "Surely you know that?"

"I don't know..." She looked about the room, which was in utter disarray, with the mattresses and clothes pulled from the beds, as if from some violent earth movement. There was a broken chamber pot on the floor, and it looked as if its contents were decorating the walls. "What happened?"

"Can you no' remember what you did, Janet?" said the woman.

"Of course she can!" said Mr Murray, striding in the room. "And if you deny it, there will be hell to pay, you filthy wee bitch!"

"But I don't know what happened," Janet said, cowering a little in Felix's embrace as Murray loomed over them. "I swear it! I don't remember anything. A minute ago I was kneeling down with Jess and Agnes to say our prayers, and then I was here..."

"How can you not remember it?" Murray said. "All that commotion and screaming? How? You threw the pot at the wall!"

"I don't know," said the girl, with a sob. "All I know is my head aches and I am prickling all over." She began to scratch herself.

"You had better get into bed," said Felix. "And then I can examine you properly – with your permission?"

Janet nodded, but Mr Murray suddenly dragged her up by her forearms and thrust her across the room into her mother's arms.

"With my permission, sir!" he said. "She's my stepdaughter. And you are too young by far to making free wi' a young woman. We will get Mr Hamilton from Dunkeld to come over tomorrow. He is a sound man. Yes, Mary?" he added.

"If you'll excuse me," Mary said, with a respectful nod at the Rector, "I've heard shocking things about young doctors left alone with young women."

"Might I point out, ma'am – Mrs Murray?" Felix said, inferring from her age and dress she was Westerlochan's wife, "that to send for Mr Hamilton would take two days. Your daughter – she is your daughter, I take it –?" The woman nodded. "She is in a dangerous state, and sound though Mr Hamilton is, this case is not an ordinary one. He would be the first to agree with me on that! And as for the question of it being improper or immodest, that is a slur that I will overlook, given that you are in the midst of a distressing business. My advice, if you care for it, is that you will let me look to her properly. I understand that there has been some trouble with your other daughters?"

Mrs Murray nodded and seemed about to speak, but Murray interrupted with a mutter, "Given who he is –"

"That is unnecessary," said Mr Carswell, mildly enough, but Felix knew he felt the insult as much as he did, perhaps more. "But as my son said, you are in the midst of distress –" He went over to the girl, who was standing trembling in her mother's arms, and laid his hand on her forehead. "The Lord bless you and keep you, my child. Oh, how cold you are –" Janet began to sob at this.

"I strongly advise you to get her to bed," Felix said, "and

if you will not accept my help, let me at least tell Mr Hamilton what I observed here tonight."

"Perhaps you should let him look at Aggie," said Mrs Murray to her husband. "She's not strong at the best of times and –"

"Oh, as you like, woman," Murray said and left the room, banging the door behind him.

"He does not want the expense," Mrs Murray whispered. "But Aggie, that is his own girl, his only girl, and he is daft for her. But you must be expensive, sir and we have very little to spare at present."

"There will be no fee," said Felix. "Please, will you just let me help you? Since I have come all this way?"

"Yes, yes, but we will pay what we can. Otherwise –"

"Let that conversation come in its season," said Mr Carswell, who had begun to straighten the bedclothes. "This child needs the peace of her bed."

So they busied themselves getting the distressed and exhausted Janet into her bed. Mr Carswell surprised Felix by being an expert bedmaker, and showed signs of being an equally good nurse.

"I'd better get this cleared up," said Mrs Murray, and went about gathering the broken shards. There was a book lying spine-up on the floor, near the debris. It proved to be a Bible, and in a sorry state, with pages falling from it.

Janet gave a sudden howl as her mother picked it up.

"I remember now!" she said. "I had to throw it from me, for it was burning my hands."

She looked down at her hands uncomprehendingly as if she expected to see marks upon them.

Felix caught his father's eye for a moment. He looked troubled, and then, as if taking care not to look so, turned back to Janet, and fixed his most kindly gaze on her.

"Would you like to pray with me for a while, my child?" he said softly. She nodded. "And my son will go to see your sisters.”

Chapter Four

The two girls, Jessie and Agnes, had been taken into an adjoining chamber, probably the best bedroom judging by its curtains and furniture. Agnes, the youngest of them, was asleep in her father's arms as he sat by the fire in an old wing chair, while the other girl had curled up on the bed under a red coverlet. It was a curiously serene picture and Felix had no inclination to disturb them. There were no dangerous signs about them as far as he could see. Whatever it was that had occurred had clearly exhausted them, and seemingly their father as well, for he was dozing when Felix and Mrs Murray came in.

Mrs Murray lifted the child from his arms and put her into the bed next to her sister.

"God willing there'll be peace until morning," she said. "Janet is quieter now. Stay there and sleep yourself," she added.

Murray rubbed his stubbled face.

"I won't leave them," he said.

"Then I will stay with Janet," Mrs Murray said.

"How many times has this happened?" Felix asked, when they were in the passageway again.

"Three times. Tonight, though – this was something new – Agnes was there. She begged to share with them. Usually she is on the wee bed, in with my husband and me, but she wanted to be with her sisters. So they all went up to say their prayers together. Janet is very religious, and a good girl, although my husband would say she's thrawn, and I suppose there's some truth in that. She's of that age –" She sighed.

"How old is she?"

"Fifteen. Well, nearly sixteen."

"And the others?"

"Jessie is twelve, and Agnes is eight."

"And those are your only children?"

"No, I have a little lad, but he's out to nurse. I could not feed him," she added with a sniff. "I'm hoping to wean him soon and bring him back, but with all this... nonsense – that's what my husband calls it – I don't like to. Janet is so –"

"Would you say it was Janet who is affected most?" Felix said.

"If you'd asked me this morning, I should have said so," said Mrs Murray, "but the littler ones tonight – they were just as bad. It was like nothing I've ever seen. Screaming and wailing and dancing around, saying that they were on fire. Mr Murray dragged them out of there and gave them a good scolding, which seemed to have some effect, but Janet was deaf to everything, even though she got a fair few slaps from us. You saw for yourself how she was." She shook her head and wrapped her arms about her. Then she asked, "What do you think we should do? Have you ever seen the like of it before?"

At this moment Mr Carswell came out of Janet's room, closing the door gently behind him.

"She's sleeping," he said.

"Thank you, Minister," said Mrs Murray.

"I will come back tomorrow," Felix said, anxious for sleep himself now. "And examine them properly, if you do not mind? There can be no progress here until that is done." She nodded her assent. "Try and get some rest yourself," he said.

"Sound counsel," said Mr Carswell. "Now, Mrs Murray, we will leave you, but remember that God and His saints are guarding your girls. Commend yourself and them to His care and all will be well."

"Yes, sir, I shall," said Mrs Murray.

They walked back to the Rectory as the storm had passed over, rather like the girls' fits, and the night was not so dark. A lantern showed them the way, and although very tired, Felix felt the benefit of the exercise. However, he noticed that his father's pace was a little slower than previously. They walked in silence for a while, and then Felix asked, "Do you still keep a note of the weather, Papa?"

"Yes, of course," said Mr Carswell. "Why?"

"It would be interesting to see if there is any correlation between those episodes of fitting and storms such as we had tonight."

"Is that an established phenomenon?"

"No, it is absolute speculation. Well, not quite. I have read a paper on something similar, but I cannot at this moment recall where. I am so tired, I feel I must be dreaming it. It seems like a preposterous notion, yet animals are acutely aware of changes in the weather, I think."

"That is true," said Mr Carswell.

"And as we are animals too – however, there are many other causes, that are not obvious at first glance, that may be at the root of it. It is simply a question of eliminating all possibilities."

"Simply?" said Mr Carswell. "I do not see anything simple about this case."

"Remember when Major Vernon and I were poisoned by mushrooms? That made us behave like madmen. Perhaps these girls have eaten something – but then, the timing of the incidents –"

"Each time it has been provoked by prayer," said Mr Carswell. "They knelt down to say their prayers, and –"

"It seems most unlikely to me that that has anything to do with it. It is merely a coincidence. Trust me, Papa, there will be some specific, natural cause to this. We certainly need not ascribe it to witchcraft. For that is what you have been thinking, is it not? When you spoke to me on the bridge, this was what you wished to tell me about, yes?"

Mr Carswell did not answer for some time. They were negotiating a rough piece of track at the time, and the darkness had suddenly become profound, as the moon, such as it was, was obscured by the clouds, and Felix was obliged to lift the lantern higher so that they should not stumble. Once they were on the better path that led to the Rectory, and the lights of the house were in sight, Mr Carswell broke his silence.

"I pray you are right," he said. "But I cannot help thinking that there is something wrong here. There is an account of what happened here two hundred years ago and it does not make for comforting reading. There were two young sisters who fell prey to convulsions, and they were certain they had been bewitched."

"Papa, really, that cannot have any bearing on present circumstances! That was a period of wretched ignorance and superstition, and such accounts cannot be considered to be anything but heavily biased by those who wrote them. If you look for the Devil, you will see him!"

"And why should he not be there, Felix?" said Mr Carswell. "I know he is there, hiding, like the moon behind the clouds. He is always with us, tempting us away from the right path, and I feel his power gaining on us, day by day. There is something amiss, here, I feel it in my marrow, and I shall pray to God that he makes you feel it, sooner rather than later. If those poor children are bewitched then we must help them, by whatever means necessary."

"What on earth do you mean by that, Papa?" said Felix, but Mr Carswell held up his hand to silence him, for they were now at the back door to the Rectory. He opened the door, and Amadeus came rushing out to meet them.

Mrs Carswell was waiting in the little sitting room for them, with supper laid by the fire. This cheerful, normal domesticity was a welcome sight.

"Everyone else has gone to bed," she said, embracing him. "Goodness, how cold your hands are. Where were your gloves?"

"I don't know," said Felix. "Papa, you should sit down

and drink a glass of wine and eat something," he added, seeing that his father was on the verge of leaving for his study.

"Yes, indeed, James," said Mrs Carswell. "You have missed your dinner."

"I only wish to look out a few papers for Felix, my dear."

"That can wait until morning," said Mrs Carswell. "Come, now, I will not have you neglect yourself."

"As you wish," said Mr Carswell dutifully.

When grace had been said, they sat down to eat. Felix noticed that his father's appetite was not all it should have been, and Amadeus was handed more scraps than were perhaps good for him. That Mr Carswell was deeply uneasy about what they had witnessed was plain, and Felix struggled to think what he might to say to console him.

He did not wish to accuse him of outright superstition, but every argument he formed seemed to involve a direct repudiation of the actual existence of the Devil and all his alleged minions, including witches, and that would take them into uncomfortable territory indeed. To confess to him that he believed the Devil to be an invention to stop men from misbehaving, implied too clearly that he also had little faith left in the existence of God. If his father was worried already, then that information would send him into a paroxysm of anxiety. So Felix held his tongue and ate his supper, while Mrs Carswell told them of the delightful evening she had spent with Eleanor and Miss King. They had had an orgy of talk on paper piecing, it seemed, and nothing could have pleased her more. This provoked a brief smile from Mr Carswell, before he got up from the table and excused himself. Amadeus trotted after him.

"Don't sit up too long," said Mrs Carswell.

"I might say that to you two," said Mr Carswell. "You will sit and chatter all night." He raised his hand in a gesture half of farewell and half of benediction, and then came back into the room and kissed his wife and Felix in turn, muttering that it was good he was home. It was evident he was headed for the cold corner of his study that served him as an oratory, and Mrs Carswell sighed when the door shut behind him.

"I'm glad you are here, as well," she said, reaching out and laying her hand on his knee. "And your father is right. We must go to bed, even if he will not."

Felix was glad to obey, and took his candle and went upstairs, reminding himself as he did to go to the guest bedroom instead of his old quarters. He opened the door gently, fearing to wake Eleanor, and discerned two bodies under the covers, and two night-capped heads on the pillows. Miss King must have joined her, no doubt to continue their evening conversation in the comfort of bed, until they had fallen asleep by accident. He was sure it was not intentional and that Miss King would be mortified at having usurped his place. He was amused by it, however, and certainly could not bring himself to disturb them, and so went to sleep in Miss King's bedroom. The bower of oak leaves suited him better than the birds of paradise.

Chapter Five

When breakfast had been cleared away, Giles commandeered the table and spread out a large and beautifully detailed map of the Glen of Pitfeldry, which had been sent down from the Castle at Lord Rothborough's special request.

"How kind of Lord Rothborough," said Mrs McCroy.

"My husband likes nothing better than a map, Mrs McCroy," Emma said. She was sitting by the fire, and Giles thought she looked brighter already. She had declared herself very willing for a walk.

"I have often bored Lord Rothborough on the subject," said Giles, scanning the map. "But he is very tolerant."

"He likes them as well as you do," Emma said. "They have been agitating for the General Survey to be better funded. And something is being done as a result."

"It is only common sense that it should be," said Giles.

"All due to the power of your wonderful letters," said Emma.

"Which you edited so effectively," he said.

"I have been good for something these past months," she said, with a smile.

"Certainly you have," Giles said. "Now, here is your house, Mrs McCroy."

"How wonderful!" she said, fixing a pair of glasses to her nose and examining the map closely. "There is my summerhouse! I never would have imagined that would be on a map. Oh, and there is the avenue of trees leading up to the Castle! That is a lovely walk – one of my favourites in the winter, because, of course, the road is well made and one does not get so muddy. It is quite flat too. You ought to go there this morning.

I suppose you will be going up there to dine soon enough, for I understand his Lordship is coming home soon. They have been opening up the Castle."

"He is hoping to be here at the end of the week," Giles said. "But he has business in Edinburgh. Hamish, come and look at this. Are your hands clean?"

"Yes."

"Let me see, Hamish," said Emma. "You must not spoil Lord Rothborough's map with honey."

The inspection finished, Hamish came to look at the map.

"See if you can find us," Giles said.

This took him no time.

"Where are the waterfalls Mr Carswell was talking about?" he asked.

"I cannot remember the name. Mrs McCroy?" Giles said. "He mentioned a bathing pool for gentlemen only."

"Oh, he must mean the Spouts," said Mrs McCroy.

"The Spouts? What a prosaic name for something as lovely as a waterfall," said Emma, laughing. "I hope we women may go and look at them, even if we may not bathe there."

"Nobody ever bathes there," Mrs McCroy said, "at least not if they have any sense. The water is always cold, even in the height of summer."

"Mr Carswell said he went swimming there," Hamish said.

"He must be a hardy soul, then," said Mrs McCroy with a shudder. "But I do not advise it, unless you are fond of cold baths."

"Swimming is different," said Hamish. "I shall not mind." He turned back to the map, searching for the Spouts. "This is it, is it not, Uncle Giles? If you follow the river northwards, yes?"

"Yes, perhaps. It does not say the Spouts but – no, I cannot make that out. Is that Gaelic, ma'am?" he said.

"Ah, yes, it will be," said Mrs McCroy. "Eas iolair-bhuidhe. The falls of the golden eagle."

"Now, that does not sound prosaic," Emma said. "What was it again – eas iolair-bhui – ?" Mrs McCroy repeated the phrase and Emma attempted it again. "Oh dear, I cannot say it at all. Hamish, you must try."

Hamish did and was not unsuccessful.

"Do you have the Gaelic?" Mrs McCroy said. "Your pronunciation is excellent."

"Some," said Hamish, beaming at the compliment. "My father sometimes speaks it to me."

"Ah yes, he is from Drumgordon, I think you said?"

"Yes," said Hamish. "And we are going to go there, if it can be managed," he added, turning to Giles and Emma with appeal in his eyes.

"Your grandfather has still not replied to any of my letters," Emma said. "We cannot go where we are not invited, Hamish."

This had been a vexing business. Captain Gordon's family were the proprietors of a small estate at Drumgordon, sixty miles north of Pitfeldry as the crow flies. How many days journey it would take mere humans to reach it, and how they might do so, was a matter that Giles had not yet determined, so they had decided to keep the children's expectations of seeing the place severely in check. Emma had written several charming letters to Mr Gordon, their grandfather, to inform them that the children were now in their care in Northminster. The continued lack of response made it feel as if they were suspected of mercenary behaviour: that Mr Gordon feared a horrible bill for boots and books and therefore had failed to engage on the matter. Of course, there may have been a great many reasons why he had failed to answer Emma's letters. It might be that his own son had told him not to. However, that seemed unlikely, given that Captain Gordon had not answered any of the letters they had sent to him either, much to the disappointment of the children. It was perhaps a family failing never to correspond, but that was so curious a failing that Giles could not quite put that as the cause of it. In short, it was a puzzle that they had not yet solved. From Hamish's petulant expression, it was clear that it needed to be resolved. He dreamed of seeing the home of his ancestors, and their patient explanations as to why this might not be possible were wearing thin. Sometimes Giles feared that he might set off to Drumgordon of his own accord. It was the sort of stupid thing he would have attempted at that age, had he been in such circumstances.

"I'm very sorry," Emma added, but Hamish still looked miserable.

"There may be a letter yet," said Giles. "He knows we are here and where to direct them. Perhaps he will prefer to write to a Scots address. One can never know."

This was sweetening the matter somewhat, and was most unlikely; Emma frowned at him for saying it, but Giles had no wish to spoil the holiday mood with unvarnished truths. He wanted Hamish tractable and good-humoured. It seemed to do the trick, and Hamish went back to studying the map, measuring the distance to the Spouts by means of his thumb and forefinger.

Jean, the maid, came in and announced that Major Vernon was wanted.

"By whom, Jean?"

"Mr McDonald, his Lordship's factor," Jean said.

"Send him in," said Giles.

"Nay, sir, he wants to speak privately with you," Jean said. "He's outside."

Giles went out to the hall.

"Mr McDonald, how may I help you?"

"I am glad to find you here, sir," said Mr McDonald. "I should have been to call about the fishing soon enough, of course. His Lordship wrote to me himself to see you about that."

"But this is not about fishing?" Giles said. He could tell the man was distressed, and he went and shut the dining room door so they should not be overheard.

"No, it is not, sir," said Mr McDonald. "One of his Lordship's foresters has found a body – a woman, God rest her soul."

"And you suspect she did not die naturally?"

"You had better come and see for yourself, Major Vernon. I have a pony for you."

~

"We'll be better on foot from here," said McDonald, dismounting. They had been climbing a fairly steep track, still muddy from last night's storm, and it had been heavy going. Ahead of them were some tethered ponies and with them, three men standing smoking their pipes.

"Are we in the Forest of Pitfeldry now?" Giles said, dismounting also. He was trying to match the landscape to the map he had just been studying, and the route that they had come. Below him the Glen of Pitfeldry spread out, with the flash of the curving river visible here and there in the bright morning sun.

"Yes," said McDonald. "And it extends beyond Ben Liath yonder. If you carry on up, you reach the shealings."

"That's the summer pasture?"

"Aye," said McDonald.

"But an inhospitable spot at this time of year?"

"Yes, they don't go up to graze until May, as a rule."

One of the pipe smokers came down to take charge of their horses.

"Mr Felix is here now, Mr McDonald," he said. "And he

turned her over and it's Mrs Gowans."

"Bel Gowans?" said McDonald. "What was she doing up here?"

"That's a question, aye," said the man. "Is this yon Major Vernon then?"

"It is indeed, McPherson. Major Vernon, this is Davie McPherson, one of his Lordship's foresters."

"Was it you that found the body, Mr McPherson?" Giles asked.

"No, sir, it was my nephew, Sam."

"And what was his business up here this morning?" Giles asked.

"I sent him up to mend a wall," said McDonald. "If I hadn't, then I don't suppose she would have been found. Mrs Gowans – are you sure, Davie?"

"Aye," said Davie.

"She keeps the shop down in the village," McDonald said.

At this moment the sun was obscured by a cloud.

"I'd better have a look," said Giles, "before the rain comes on again."

A few more minutes' climb led them to the body. It was a beautiful spot, full of gorse and picturesque rocky outcrops, where an artist might happily settle down to sketch the glen below. Carswell was sketching, of course, but he was not drawing the scenery. He was making his usual careful record of the circumstances.

"She was found face down," he said, by way of greeting.

The body had been covered by a dull-covered plaid. Giles stooped to lifted it and frowned. A woman in her thirties, handsome – despite a mud-stained face – with a mangled bonnet and a crushed lace cap. Her expression was not peaceful. About her neck was a bright silk fringed scarf, incongruously cheerful in yellow and red.

"Dear God," he murmured, gently replacing the plaid again. Presumably it was her own shawl that now covered her.

"Poor soul. Did you know her?" he said to Carswell.

"Yes," he said. "You know she keeps – kept – the shop? A very respectable body, as they say."

"How long has she been here?" Giles said.

"I am guessing since last night," said Carswell, "for she is stone cold, but there is no sign of any real decay yet, and the animals have not begun on her, thank God. But the storm has taken its toll."

"Why did the man who found her assume foul play?" said Giles.

"Because of this," said Carswell, and flipping back a page, handed his sketchbook to Giles. "Five stones lying on her back. I have put them over there. I thought you might like to see them. They could not have got there by chance. They had been placed very deliberately."

"Stones?" said Giles.

"Carefully chosen flat ones," Carswell said. "I have numbered them, naturally."

"Yes, I see," said Giles, examining the items for himself now. "Perfect for skimming." He looked about him. "Do you think they were gathered here?"

"Here or nearby," said Carswell. "If you go higher up there are plenty."

"It is extraordinary," said Giles. "What was the cause of death?"

"Asphyxiation," said Carswell. "She was strangled with the scarf she was wearing."

"That suggests an opportunistic assault. Was she robbed, I wonder? Or assaulted in any other way?"

"I cannot say until I have examined her properly."

"We need to get her moved as soon as we can. This Highland weather – where do you think might suit?"

Carswell thought for a moment.

"We should go down to the Castle, to the Factor's offices. They will serve as well as anywhere."

"And what is the procedure here? To whom should I write?"

"The Sheriff in Perth, in the first instance. I hope he will take the entire matter out of our hands."

"Yes, quite – we must not be seen to be trespassing on anyone else's turf. We can only do what needs to be done and no more. Stones or no stones." He picked one up.

"After all, we are supposed to be on leave," said Carswell. "Although –"

"Yes?"

"I have already been called to a strange case. It was the business my father wanted your opinion on. I should be there now, in fact. It was somewhat unsettling, all in all. As is this – stones! I could scarcely believe it when I saw it. Have you ever come across anything resembling that?"

Giles shook his head and gathered up the rest of the stones. He put them in his handkerchief and tied it up carefully.

"I will go and speak to Mr McDonald about moving her. And then I will talk to the fellow that found him – Sam McPherson, is that right?" Carswell nodded. "It will be best to get a statement from him while his memory is still fresh."

Chapter Six

Having seen to it that Mrs Gowans' remains were safely lodged in the shelter of the Factor's offices, Felix made his way back to Westerlochan Farm. He was nervous at what he might find there. The discovery of the body, with those five stones so carefully placed on it, had unnerved him, he could not deny. It went contrary to the usual pattern of things in the Glen.

He was relieved to find the two younger girls in the yard in front of the house, feeding the hens. It was reassuring to see them behaving just as country children should. At first sight, they seemed to be in perfect health with bright complexions.

He introduced himself and admired the hens. He was glad that they did not seem inclined at once to run inside for their mother, for he wanted to talk to them alone. Aggie, the youngest, was clearly the poultry-fancier and on his inquiring, told him the names of the breeds and how much they laid, while Jessie held up her own particular favourite for him to inspect.

"She's not a good layer at all," Jessie said, "but she's much the prettiest, wouldn't you say?"

"They are all so pretty I can hardly choose," said Felix. "Those black and white ones – my mother has some like that, but not nearly so fat."

"She needs to give them buttermilk," said Aggie. "Does she?"

"That I don't know," Felix said. "I will ask her. I'm glad to see you are both looking well. Your parents were worried about you last night. What do you remember of it?" Aggie looked at Jessie and Jessie looked at Aggie, and Felix wondered if it would be best to speak to each alone.

"Perhaps you should tell your mother I'm here, Jessie," he

said.

Jessie went obediently into the house and Aggie said, "I don't remember it at all. All I remember was I woke up in Ma and Pa's bed this morning."

"And you haven't felt ill at all?" he said. "A headache or stomachache, perhaps?"

"No, sir."

"Are you sure there was nothing from last night that you remember?"

"There was the itching," she said after a moment.

"Itching – what sort?"

"Like nettle rash." She gave a shiver as if recalling the effect. "Like a lot of nettle rash."

"I see. And did your skin come up in bumps too, like nettle rash?"

"No, but I wanted to scratch my skin off. It was very sore. I wanted to run out and throw myself in the water trough."

"Was it anywhere in particular, this itch? On your back, your arms?"

"All over," she said. "And it was hot, you know, like a burn. That's why I wanted to get in the trough."

"And when did this start?"

"When we were saying our prayers."

"Are you sure about that? It didn't start earlier? You didn't feel unwell earlier at all?"

"No, sir. It just came on when we knelt down and Janet started 'Our Father'. The itching and the burning. It was right queer."

"I'm sure it was. But you feel quite well now? You haven't felt anything similar today?"

"Nothing, sir. And that's all I remember, being so hot and so itchy, and then –" She shrugged.

"I'll speak to Jessie now, if I may?" he said. "Can you go in and send her out without your mother?"

The girl went, and Jessie returned, scooping up her hen as she did, as if she wanted the comfort of it under her arm.

"You wanted to speak to me, sir?"

"About last night."

She sighed and petted the hen.

"Aye, sir," she said.

"How old are you, Jessie?"

"Twelve, sir," she said.

"And what do you remember from last night?"

She glanced about her, took a step closer to him, and said in a whisper, "It was the Devil, sir. He came in the minute Janet said 'our Father'. I felt him in the room wi' us, looking at us in our shifts, and he made me feel I was on fire and I could not keep still, as if he were making me dance."

"You believe the Devil was in the room with you?" said Felix.

"I know he was, sir. I would not lie about such a thing. He was there. I know it."

"Then what happened?"

"I must have passed out. I thought I was going to be sick and I know I was screaming my heart out, because my throat is sore today, and I ran out of the room looking for my mother and – but then –" She shook her head. "I don't remember anything else, except that he was in my dreams as well."

"The Devil, you mean?"

"I don't think he went away until the sun came up. He was in my head all night. He came at the sound of a prayer – that's what he does."

"Where did you hear that?" said Felix. "I've never heard that notion before."

"I don't know," she said. "But that's what brought him."

"I don't think it was the Devil," said Felix. "And you should not let yourself think it might be that. Don't let old stories frighten you."

"But what else could it be?" the girl said, earnestly.

"Given that Effie Haynes brought him up because Janet was sharp with her."

"Brought him up? Do you mean she summoned him?"

"Aye, sir. She has him as her lover. Everyone says so, for why else would she live all alone like that in that dirty wee place?"

"Effie Haynes?" Felix said, trying to place the name, but he could not. "Who is she?"

"Her sister keeps the shop – Mrs Gowans," Jessie went on. "She's gone over to your father's Kirk."

"Effie or her sister?" said Felix.

"Mistress Gowans," said Jessie. "Mr Wallace was telling my stepfather of it the other day, and he wasn't too pleased about it. He wanted my stepfather to talk to her – he's an elder, you see."

At this moment, Aggie came out of the house with Mrs Murray.

"Thank God you're here, sir," she said. "It's Janet. She cannot move herself."

He ran upstairs and found Janet lying on her bed, on her back and in tears.

"I can't get up," she said. "I keep trying but I can't."

In some respects it was a relief to deal with a merely physical crisis after listening to Jessie's rather febrile account. He took his time to calm Janet, and then gently but thoroughly examined her. There was no obvious physical cause, as far as he could tell, and curiously she seemed to feel no pain. She described the sensation as being chained down, that her limbs were like lead and she could not lift them. Yet she could speak and her breathing, if a little shallow, was not impaired. Her pulse was also raised, but that was to be expected given her evident anxiety. Could it be superstitious fear that had induced this state in her? It was extremely perplexing, and the worst of it was that he could not bring her any immediate relief. He suggested to his mother that she rub her legs and arms with almond oil, thinking perhaps the action would stimulate her reflexes.

As he turned to leave the room he saw that Jessie and Aggie were lurking in the passageway.

"It's all Effie Haynes' fault, sir," Jessie said, grabbing his sleeve. "She said she would and she has."

"If you are accusing this person of something," Felix said, "you must be straight about it. But think before you speak. It is no small thing to do."

"No, sir, I know that, I would not say anything if she had not said it to Janet. We were all there. Aggie heard it too, didn't you?" Aggie nodded. "We heard her curse Janet. We heard her!"

~

"I take it," said Giles, "that throwing around accusations of witchcraft is not commonplace in these parts?"

"No, it certainly is not!" exclaimed Carswell. "I have never heard such nonsense before. But these girls are not from here. According to my father, Murray only took over the tack last year."

"The tack?"

"The lease on the farm," Carswell said. "They must have learnt these stupid ideas elsewhere."

"And Effie Haynes is the sister of our dead woman," Giles said.

"Yes, and there is another detail I forgot to mention – according to the girl, Mrs Gowans had joined my father's congregation."

"That's interesting," said Giles. "Did her family go with her?"

"I don't know. My father will be able to tell us the long

and short of it."

"Does that happen often?" said Giles. "Leaving the Kirk for the Episcopalians?"

"I have never heard of it here," said Carswell. "People here are usually settled in their habits."

"And do you know anything of Effie Haynes?"

"No. I don't recall Mrs Gowans having a sister. She must have gone away when she was young and has only come back recently."

The door opened, and Jean came in and asked if she might lay the table for lunch. At the same time, Emma, the children and Mrs McCroy could be seen through the window returning from their walk.

"Mrs Vernon is looking well this morning," said Carswell.

"Yes, she is," said Giles. "Shall we go and meet them?"

"We have extraordinary news!" said Emma, as she passed through the garden gate. "We met with Mrs Maxwell, the housekeeper at the Castle. Lady Rothborough is apparently en route for Pitfeldry. She will be here tomorrow."

"Good God!" said Carswell. "Excuse me, but her Ladyship detests Scotland. She has only ever been here once, as far as I can recall. What is she about?"

"She has a German prince with her," Emma said. "Apparently he wanted to see Scotland, and so she has brought him to Pitfeldry."

"There must be more to it than that," Carswell said. "Anyway, I had better get back to the Rectory."

He made his farewells, and the ladies and the children went into the house. Giles waited a moment to speak alone to him again.

"I take it your father will visit Mr Gowans this afternoon?" he said.

"I should imagine so," said Carswell.

"I'll go with him. I should like to see the man for myself."

"I thought we were surrendering the conduct of the investigation to the Sheriff?"

"It can't hurt to assemble a little more information, given we are on the ground," Giles said. "It would be negligent to do otherwise. And I can't help finding these accusations from the girls rather interesting."

"What? You can't believe there is any truth in them?"

"No, but there has obviously been some bad feeling. Effie Haynes has made herself unpopular. That's interesting in itself, given the manner of her sister's death."

"But the two matters can scarcely be connected, surely?"

"Most probably not, but I should like to settle the question for myself."

Carswell smiled and shook his head.

"This was supposed to be your furlough, Major. And Mrs Vernon will not –"

"I know," said Giles. "But you must admit that the circumstances demand our attention, to some degree? I promise I shall not let it get out of hand. There will still be plenty of time for the scenery."

Chapter Seven

Felix arrived back at the Rectory just in time for lunch. Eleanor was arranging various posies of wildflowers about the dining room as he came in.

"Jenny and I had the most enchanting ramble," she said.

"I wish I could have been with you," he said. "I'm sorry."

"There will be other times, I'm sure," Eleanor said, placing one final vase at the centre of the table. "And that poor woman – she kept the shop, I hear?"

"So all the news has got here?" Felix said.

"Was she murdered?" Eleanor said.

"It seems likely," said Felix, pouring himself a glass of wine.

Eleanor shook her head in sympathy, but her attention was all on her flowers. "How does that look? I can never do it as well as Jenny. She is so clever."

"It looks very well," said Felix. "Did you hear anything about Murray's daughters on your ramble?"

"Those are the girls you went to see last night?"

"I was there again this morning. The eldest of them –" He broke off, for his mother and Miss King had come into the room.

"Oh, how charming," Mrs Carswell said, seeing the flowers. "Ah, there you are, Felix," she added, greeting him with a kiss. "I thought I heard you come in. Your father has been anxious to speak to you. You went up to Westerlochan again, I understand?"

"I did," said Felix. "And Miss Agnes Murray tells me you should give your hens buttermilk. Do you know them, Mama – the Murrays, I mean?"

"Not well. But those girls are nice creatures and always properly respectful when we meet them. It is a pity that they should be troubled." She gave a sigh. "And now poor Mrs Gowans is dead! This is all most unsettling," she added, laying her hand on his arm.

"It is fortunate that you and Major Vernon are here to deal with it," Miss King said.

"It seems almost providential," said Mrs Carswell.

"I hope that I shall have nothing more to do with it," said Felix, "nor Major Vernon. For one thing, we have no authority here. The Sheriff will not thank us for interfering."

"I should think he will be grateful," said Mrs Carswell. "He can hardly have much experience of this sort of thing. He will want justice served, and who better to see to that than you and the Major?"

Felix drank some wine and said, "It's probably a simple matter and he will not need us to do anything."

"Do you truly think so?" said Mrs Carswell. "Why would anyone wish to murder Mrs Gowans? She was a truly good woman."

"Are not women usually murdered by their husbands?" Eleanor said.

"That is the common pattern, yes, unfortunately," he said.

"It cannot be so in this case," said Mrs Carswell, sitting down at the table, "for Mr Gowans is a gentle soul. Poor man."

"When it comes to murder, people often act entirely contrary to their usual habits," Felix said.

"Are we speaking of Mrs Gowans?" said Mr Carswell from the doorway. Felix glanced behind him and nodded. "She has been murdered, then?"

"It seems so," Felix said.

Mr Carswell went to his place at the head of the table.

"You might have waited until we had given thanks," he said, indicating the wine glass in Felix's hand. Felix put down his glass, annoyed to be reproached for such a trivial matter. The worst of it was that it evoked an instinctive flush of shame at being caught doing something of which his father disapproved. It was as if he were sixteen again.

"Then say grace, my dear, and let the poor boy eat," said Mrs Carswell. "He has been hard at work all morning."

Mr Carswell did not omit to commend Mrs Gowans' soul to God's keeping, as well as the usual business, and took his time about it, so that Grizel came in fretting because the soup had gone cold.

Lunch over, Felix escaped into the garden, hoping to smoke a cheroot, but Eleanor and Miss King joined him, and so he was frustrated in this. The talk was of the afternoon's activities.

"Do you have to go and see that girl again?" Eleanor asked.

"Yes, she's in quite a serious state," said Felix. "She is paralysed."

"How terrible," Miss King said. "Did she injure herself?"

"No, and that's the puzzle of it. I wish I had my books with me!"

"Can you not use the library at the Castle?" Eleanor said.

"That may not be possible. That is the other news: Lady Rothborough is coming to the Castle tomorrow, just to crown matters!"

"But she never comes here," said Eleanor. "Why is she coming now?"

"She means mischief, I'm sure," Felix said. "She has a German prince with her."

"How intriguing!" said Eleanor. "I have never met a prince. Have you, Jenny?"

"No, of course not," said Miss King.

"And you are hardly likely to meet this one," Felix said.

"Why not? Surely we will go and dine there?" Eleanor said.

"I very much doubt it," said Felix.

"She may choose not to receive you, Felix," said Eleanor, "but she cannot refuse to see me. After all, I am her husband's ward, and surely your parents always dine there when Lord Rothborough comes to the Castle."

"No, they do not dine out," said Felix. "And why on earth would you wish to see her? She is an impossible person and she has caused a great deal of unnecessary grief, as you know quite well!" He noticed that Miss King was looking somewhat confused – if not shocked – at the warmth of his tone. "I know I sound unkind, and really, I would respect her, if she merited it. But she does nothing but cause trouble."

"I should like to meet her," Eleanor said. "I cannot believe she is as bad as she is painted. And a German prince sounds most interesting." She dropped a deep curtsey to Miss King. "How do you do, your Royal Highness? Or should it be Serene Highness? We must look it up. I should not like to get it wrong."

"They have dozens of tin-pot principalities over there," Felix said. "He is probably an utter nobody."

"Then why would Lady Rothborough have taken him up?" Eleanor said. "Perhaps she wants him for Charlotte, now she has broken with Dunbar."

"God forbid!" said Felix. "No, I do not think that even she would think of that."

"If a German prince is good enough for the Queen, then surely one would be good enough for Charlotte?" said Eleanor.

"If that is her intention, then it is absolute wickedness on her part," Felix said. "Lord Rothborough has told me how unhappy Charlotte is. If she is intent on clumsy matchmaking then it would be rubbing salt in that wound! Not to mention how it will affect him! I wonder if she cannot be sent away."

"How can she be?" said Eleanor. "That would be outrageous."

"Deflected, then. If she were to hear there was a murderer about, that might make her turn tail. If my presence is not enough to upset her, of course!"

"You must excuse my confusion," Miss King said. "I don't quite understand why Lady Rothborough will not receive you, Mr Carswell."

Had she, despite living with them for over two months, not realised the nature of his relationship to the Rothborough family? He was surprised that Eleanor had not been more to the point about it. He wondered if she was embarrassed about it. He realised that they had never really discussed the matter.

"I hope it is not impertinent of me to ask," Miss King added.

"It is because of who he is," said Eleanor.

This did not help Miss King much, and Felix was forced to say what he never liked to say directly: "I am Lord Rothborough's natural son. I was adopted by Mr and Mrs Carswell."

"Oh," was all Miss King could manage. She coloured and looked away. "I'm sorry," she added. "Perhaps I should have guessed."

"Why on earth should you?" said Eleanor. "You might have guessed if you had seen Felix and Lord Rothborough together, but you have not met him yet. There is very little guessing to be done."

"Oh," said Miss King again, and then after a pause, she turned to Felix and said, "I imagine it must be very hard for you. The world is so unkind about these things."

"I've been lucky," said Felix, touched by her sincerity. "And most of the time, it scarcely bothers me. But it is not pleasant for Eleanor. You are right, Eleanor – Lady Rothborough ought to see you! In fact you should insist on it."

"I certainly shall!" said Eleanor. "And perhaps I shall marry dear Jenny off to this German prince. You would suit a small crown, Jenny. Someone called King ought to marry a prince, don't you think?"

"No," said Miss King. "I can't agree. I would rather stay a plain King than be a princess. I do not think crowns, however small, and robes and so forth, would suit me at all. I'm quite happy as I am."

"Can you not allow yourself to be tempted?" Eleanor said.

"Never," said Miss King.

"Then let him be madly in love with you and blow out his brains when you refuse him!" Eleanor said.

"He is more likely to fall in love with you, Eleanor," said Miss King.

Felix left them in the garden and went into the house. Major Vernon had just arrived with the children. The Major was stooping down to let Sandro down from his shoulders, but Sandro seemed reluctant to relinquish his perch, and it ended a moment later after an undignified struggle with Major Vernon sitting on the floor and the wriggling infant in his arms.

"Again!" Sandro said. "Again."

"You know that word too well," said Major Vernon. "Hamish, will you get him off me?"

Hamish extracted him efficiently but abruptly, and Sandro screamed in protest. Now on his knees, Major Vernon took him back, and looking him in the eyes, said to him: "If you could manage to be charming while you are here, Sandro, we would be very much obliged. Yes?" He tapped the boy on his nose, which astonishingly seemed to silence him.

Now Mrs Carswell came out of the drawing room.

"Ah, Miss Gordon and Master Gordon!" she said. "Not to mention Master Sandro! Thank you for coming. And thank you for bringing them, Major Vernon!"

"A pleasure, ma'am. It was good of you to ask them."

"We scarcely had a chance to become acquainted yesterday, did we?" said Mrs Carswell, crouching down and putting out both her hands to Sandro. "And the Rector would like

Amadeus walked, if you do not mind, Hamish? And I should like some help with my hens, Sophy. Then we must teach Miss King and Mrs Carswell to make pancakes. Hello, Sandro," she added softly, drawing the child a little closer to her. "What a handsome little man you are! It quite reminds me..." She broke off and glanced up at Felix, who realised she must be remembering his own arrival at the Rectory, though he doubted that Lord Rothborough had brought him in on his shoulders.

"May I really take Amadeus out, ma'am?" said Hamish.

"Yes, it would be a great help to Mr Carswell if you would," Mrs Carswell said. "He has his calls to pay, and sometimes Amadeus is not welcome."

"Truly?" Hamish said. "Why not?"

"He is young," Mrs Carswell said, "and it is not always appropriate to take a lively dog when a family has suffered a death."

"Oh, do you mean –?" he said, and Mrs Carswell nodded.

At this moment, Mr Carswell, accompanied by Amadeus, came out of his study. He gazed down at the sight of his wife, crouched on the floor with Sandro.

"Is he not bonny, James?" she said.

"You must not wear yourself out with him," said Mr Carswell.

"No, no, I shall not. And Eleanor and Miss King are here. And I have got Grizel to bring down Felix's old toys from the attic."

"You still have them?" Felix said, surprised they had not been passed on to some needy family.

"They did not seem quite right for the village children," she said. By which he supposed that they had been expensive toys purchased by Lord Rothborough and therefore had a mild air of corruption about them. He had only been allowed to play with them sparingly himself. There had been a high shelf in the nursery press where they had been kept.

"Major Vernon, do you have a moment?" Mr Carswell

said.

"I was hoping to speak to you, sir, so yes," said Major Vernon. "And you, Carswell."

"Shall I take Amadeus for his walk now, sir?" said Hamish.

"Perhaps you'd better," said Mr Carswell, "for it looks as if the rain will come on later."

So everyone went their various ways and Felix followed his father and Major Vernon into the study.

"I take it you want to talk about Mrs Gowans, Major," Mr Carswell said when the door was closed.

"I understand she had joined your congregation recently."

"That's true," said Mr Carswell. "She wished to become a communicant."

"Did that surprise you?"

"Perhaps. It's not the usual way of things here. And of course I do not encourage such defections. That would be unconscionable. But she approached me after morning prayer and asked for my guidance. She said she was lost and was looking for peace. So we talked of God and His grace and she seemed consoled by it – no, indeed, she was encouraged. Then she began to come on Sundays and seemed anxious to learn all she could." He sat down. "I pray earnestly that her soul is now with God, for she was a good woman – humble, yes, but blessed with a fine perception of the Divine. It is not often one meets such people." He gave a great sigh and rubbed his face. "You are certain that there is some wicked person behind this? That it cannot be an accident?"

"No, unfortunately not," said Major Vernon. "What can you tell us of her family? She has a husband living?"

"Yes, a nice enough fellow, but simple. There was none of the zeal for self-improvement that she displayed. But he will be broken by this."

"There was no trouble between them as far as you know?"

"None at all," said Mr Carswell. "And that sort of thing is never concealed here."

"And her children?"

"A little girl of ten. She helps in the shop. A very good little soul."

"And she has a sister, I believe?" said Felix. "Euphemia Haynes?"

"Ah yes, Effie," Mr Carswell said, and gave another great sigh. "Effie Haynes. Indeed."

Felix wondered if he should mention the accusations made by Jessie Murray, but stopped his tongue. His father looked distressed enough. Accusations of witchcraft could wait.

"Where does she live now?" he asked instead.

"In a bothy at the edge of the Forest – you know the one, Felix. Just off the track up to Ben Liath," said Mr Carswell. "She should not be there. I fear she has an immoral arrangement with one of the foresters." He rubbed his face. "A source of great distress to Mrs Gowans, of course."

"Which of the foresters?" Major Vernon said.

"Angus Lowndie. I have spoken to Mr McDonald about it, of course, and I dare say Mr Wallace has too. He is nominally one of his flock, but he prefers to drink on a Sunday morning."

"Was he there this morning?" said Major Vernon to Felix.

"I don't know," said Felix.

"You would not know him. He's new to the Forest," said Mr Carswell. "Mr McDonald only took him on a year ago. He is exceptionally skilled, though – he was up at Glen Barr for some years, I understand, in Mr Stewart-Campbell's service, but his character is not all it should be."

"We shall have to talk to him," said Major Vernon. "And to Mrs Haynes."

Felix frowned. It was clear that Major Vernon had the bit between his teeth.

Chapter Eight

Any self-respecting shopman in Northminster would have been puzzled by and possibly contemptuous of what passed for a shop in Pitfeldry. There was nothing to distinguish the Gowans' establishment from the other single-storey cottages that lined the main street of the village, except for a bench under the front window. Whether this was for weary customers to sit upon or would normally be used to display goods, Giles could not guess. The shop was closed, the shutters fixed tight.

Mr Gowans had emerged from his gloomy interior in his shirt sleeves and did not seem surprised to see the Rector.

"May I come in, Mr Gowans?" the Rector asked.

"Mr Wallace is here, sir," said Gowans. He glanced at Giles.

"This is Major Vernon," said Mr Carswell.

"I see," said Gowans. "You'd best come in, then."

They passed through the shop, such as it was, into the kitchen beyond. Here there was some light from a generous peat fire on the hearth. A young girl was sitting on the floor, wrapped in her shawl, looking pale and distressed, while Mr Wallace sat at the kitchen table, the family Bible open in front of him.

"A sad day, Mr Carswell," he said, getting up. "A very sad day."

"Aye, it is that, Mr Wallace," said Mr Carswell. He went to the girl and laid his hand on her forehead for her moment. "God be with you, Mary. Your mother is with Him now."

"Is she?" she said, looking up at Mr Carswell. "What if she is not one of –"

"She is with Him," said Mr Carswell. "How could she not

be? Such a good, loving woman. One of His own."

"Are you sure, sir?" Mary said.

Mr Carswell took her hand and nodded solemnly.

"She said I was to talk to you if anything bad happened," Mary said.

"My door is always open," said Mr Carswell. "And that of Mr Wallace, of course," he added, indicating the young minister.

"Will you take a cup of tea, sir?" said Mr Gowans.

"No, no," said Mr Carswell. "I am only passing by to tell you both that she will be in my prayers and to offer my deepest condolences, Mr Gowans. Whatever I can do to help you and your family, I will, of course, do. Your wife was a rare creature, and the manner of her death –" He broke off with a shake of his head.

"It is as well you are here, Major Vernon," said Mr Wallace.

"I assure you, Mr Gowans," Giles said, "that everything will be done to make sure this deed does not go unpunished."

"Thank you, sir," said Gowans.

"Perhaps I might take a few details from you, about your wife's movements yesterday? Any details you can give me will be of great assistance."

"As you like, sir," said Gowans, indicating a rough stool. He sat down at the table, with a certain heaviness.

"Mr Wallace, will you walk with me a little?" said Mr Carswell. "There are a few matters I should like to discuss with you."

"Of course, sir," said Mr Wallace.

The two clergymen took their leave, and Giles was left with Mr Gowans, his daughter and the spitting of the peat fire.

"So she will go to heaven, Pa," said Mary. "If the Rector says so."

"I don't know," said Mr Gowans. "I don't know about anything any more." He pressed his hands to his face.

"Mother said to trust what the Rector said. That he had the truth of it all," said Mary. "Not Mr Wallace."

"What did Mr Wallace say to you, Mary?" Giles asked.

"That we could not know she was saved. It was only for God to say and it was all decided at the beginning of time, whether we were damned or saved, and there was nothing we could do about it. Ever. But mother said that –"

"Hush, hush," said Mr Gowans. "I cannae bear all this talk! Go and tidy the shop. That is what your mother would have said as well, yes?"

"Yes, Pa," the girl said, and went away.

"So?" said Gowans to Giles.

"When did you last see your wife, Mr Gowans?" Giles said, taking out his notebook.

"Yesterday at about five," said Gowans. "After we had closed up the shop, she gave us a bit of supper and then said she was away to talk to her sister."

"That would be Effie?"

"Aye," said Gowans. "Effie."

"And she lives on the other side of the village, on the edge of the Forest?"

"Aye, she does now. She was here a while, but we could not stand it."

"Why was that?"

"She is a wild one. She likes to drink, and she's bone idle. I would not have had her here – Bel felt she ought to help, but she was soon at the end of her tether wi' her. Funny how it is with sisters, sometimes."

"So you asked her to leave?"

"She was supposed to go away and get work somewhere. She talked of getting a job in Glasgow. She'd been there before, been married there to a sailor, or at least as good as married, if you know what I mean. Anyway, he got tired of her, which is no surprise, and she came back, thinking that Bel and I would look after her. And we said we would, if she helped us, but she never did."

"So you told her to leave?"

"No, although it nearly came to that. No, she went, saying she'd found a place of her own. We didn't think it would be that bothy though, and then we heard that Angus Lowndie had said she could have it for her own, which left us thinking –"

"That they were lovers? Was that the talk?"

"It was more than talk. He is always bragging about it, having her and so forth. She is a handsome quean, like her sister, and he would marry her if she'd have him, but I don't think she would. Or perhaps she cannot, for that sailor may be her real husband for all I know. But Bel wanted it all made respectable, of course, and they had words about it, many a time."

"Is that why she went up there last night?" said Giles.

"I suppose it was," said Gowans, scratching his head. "But Bel had so many notions in her head these days I can't say for certain. Yon Reverend Carswell had given her all these books to read and they made her half daft, to tell you the truth. I told her I wanted her to bide here last night, but she said she must go and talk to Effie, and now –" His voice broke and he looked away, stifling his tears.

"And this was at about six o'clock?" Giles said after a moment. Gowans nodded.

Giles judged it best to leave him at this point, and went out to the shop where Mary was dutifully sweeping the floor, or rather dragging a broom about in a lacklustre fashion.

"When did you last see your mother?" he asked.

"Just after supper last night," she said, with a sob. "She said she would be back in no more than an hour. We were going to read together."

"I'm very sorry," Giles said, leaning against the counter.

"She had a nice book from the Rector. By Mr Keble. Wi' lovely poems in it."

She burst into tears and ran out of the room, leaving

Giles in the empty shop, feeling all her desolation as if it were his own.

It was all very well for people to observe how fortunate it was that he was here, but he felt he had brought a curse on the place, as if his very presence had unleashed the murderous instinct in someone. That was ridiculous, of course. Murder struck unexpectedly. The only comfort was that he might be able to catch this person and bring some sense and order to the bald facts of Bel Gowans' death; but he had no power to bring her back to her daughter. Mary would have to read Keble alone, and mend her own heart.

~

By the time Felix arrived back at Westerlochan, Janet had discovered the use of her limbs again, but despite a great deal of questioning, he felt not much the wiser as to the cause of it all. He might have been inclined to suspect some sort of elaborate play-acting on her part, a game of mischief in which she had embroiled her sisters. But observing Mr Murray, who did not look at all the sort to spare the rod, Felix wondered how any of them would have dared to do such a thing. The fear of retribution would have been too great, and by all accounts these were well-ordered, dutiful girls. What benefit to them could there be in deliberately causing such chaos?

Janet herself was tearful and anxious. Her recovery seemed to bring her no mental relief. She was afraid of lapsing again – of being caught, as she put it. She was convinced that the Devil had her in his grip. He tried every argument he could to show her that this could not be so, but it was a wasted labour. She was adamant.

He left the house feeling frustrated and angry. That such wretched superstitions could so readily persist was lamentable.

He made his way down the hill, and stopped to rest and smoke the cheroot that had been denied to him earlier in the Rectory garden. This old, bad habit had lately become a renewed comfort to him, although he despised himself for it. Eleanor detested it as much as Major Vernon, and he was certain they were right, yet it did not stop him.

Now, lying back on a mossy slope, looking up at the sharp and transient blue of an April sky, he remembered how he had been as a boy, with the Glen and the Forest as his playground. It was now over ten years since he had left for Edinburgh and his formal education, and his life had changed out of all recognition.

The Felix Carswell of fifteen would have been most contemptuous of the gentleman lolling there in his fine clothes. The only thing that would have impressed him would have been his bag of expensive instruments. He would have been unable to countenance the muddy situation at Westerlochan Farm where there was no clear diagnosis, no brilliantly devised cure and certainly no glory for a devoted servant of science. He had earnestly believed that medicine was a calling to a priesthood, and he had been enchanted by the idea of performing heroic medical endeavours that would change the world for the better. He had been convinced that the pursuit of science would answer all the great questions of life. Now he was forced to reflect that it had only led him to more uncertainty. He felt he knew less than ever.

He sat up, lit another cheroot and considered the girls at Westerlochan Farm. They were convinced Effie Haynes had cursed them. Perhaps she had. Perhaps there was something in curses that was not yet understood. The power of words on the mental state of others could not be disputed. If a man was told he was a wretch, then he might believe it, if it was said with conviction and authority. If an angry woman told a man who loved her that he was a brute, he would feel her words like blows. Might a curse not be akin to that?

He pushed this idea away and staggered to his feet. It felt too outlandish. He determined he would look again for some physical cause.

Chapter Nine

Giles arrived at the Factor's offices the following morning to find that Carswell had just finished his examination of Mrs Gowans' remains.

"You must have been up before the lark," he said.

"I couldn't sleep," Carswell said. "It's just as well."

"What have you discovered?" said Giles. There was something about Carswell's manner that suggested he was unsettled.

"Death was caused by asphyxiation, as we suspected, but there is indication of a prolonged assault." He turned back the sheet covering her face. "It is easier to see this now. Observe those marks about her neck – those were made by the ligature, which was the silk scarf, as we suspected. But there is not just one ring of bruising. No, the ligature has been applied, tightened, then loosened again, at least four times."

"Because she struggled?" Giles said.

"I am sure she did," said Carswell, "but my feeling is that this is deliberate. It is possible to bring someone to the point of near death with asphyxiation, and then release them. If the trachea is compressed sufficiently the subject will be paralysed but will not die at once. The subject will be conscious but powerless. There was a case in France when a man subjected a series of women to such tortures and one of them managed to get away and describe what he did to her. It is in Orfila's book, which, of course, I do not have to hand. However, the gist of it is that I consider we may be looking at the murderer playing with the victim: tightening and loosening the ligature until she finally expired."

"Dear Lord," murmured Giles.

"Not pleasant," Carswell said. "And her underclothes show signs of assault. Her petticoats have been slashed and there are some signs of staining, but I cannot be at all sure about that. Especially as I have no microscope here."

Giles did not answer. He could not. These conclusions were too strange and shocking for hasty speech. He crouched down and looked carefully at the bruising on her neck, and then examined the torn underclothes: her sturdy petticoats had been deliberately ripped with a knife. Finally he turned to the jaunty silk scarf that Carswell had spread out on a side table, presumably to examine it for any further evidence.

"Do you think that is her scarf?" he asked. "She was soberly dressed otherwise."

"I did wonder about that," Carswell said. "Her husband will know. How did you find him? Would you put him in the field?"

"At first glance I would not say he was capable of this," said Giles. "But I only spoke to him in a superficial manner. We do not know his movements."

"In his favour, this does not at all fit any observable pattern for a wife murder," Carswell said. "The stones alone remove it from that."

"Yes," said Giles, taking them from the side table where they still lay wrapped up in his handkerchief. "Do you have your sketch to hand? I should like to lay them out again."

This they did, on a deep window sill, but it did not seem to make anything clearer.

"What good does this serve our murderer? Why has he done this?" Giles said. "It is such a strange finale to an act of sustained brutality. Five stones – not four, not one, but five."

"The pentagram?" said Carswell. "Perhaps the Devil likes things in fives."

Giles traced a line from one stone to the other. "One might read it as that," he said. "As a five-pointed star, I mean, not as an offering to the Devil. Surely this would be protection against him. That is how I have always heard it spoken of by country people. Like those little shapes made from straw at the end of the harvest. Is that the custom here? It was in my village."

"So this may be symbolic in some fashion?" Carswell said. "Protection or invocation?" He rubbed his face and yawned. "Excuse me. Those girls up at Westerlochan are utterly convinced Satan himself is possessing them. Perhaps they are right. This looks like the work of a devil to me. She must have suffered terribly – and for what? What on earth could the motive be?"

There was a knock at the door and Carswell quickly covered the body. It was Mr McDonald.

"I have Angus Lowndie here, Major Vernon," he said. "I believe you wanted to speak to him."

~

Angus Lowndie was a giant, rough-featured Highlander who sat down awkwardly. He was clearly not used to being allowed to sit in Mr McDonald's office, and Giles wondered if it would put him more at his ease to take him out of the building altogether. He would be happier, he was sure, with the sky for his roof.

"Perhaps you could show me something on the map here, Mr Lowndie," he said, getting up and going to the estate map which hung on the wall. "Where is the bothy that you have allowed Mrs Haynes the use of? I am a stranger to the area."

Lowndie got up, nearly upsetting his chair, and went to the map.

"Up here, yonder, sir," he said, pointing.

"I understand you and she are friends," Giles said.

"Aye, sir, of sorts," Lowndie said.

"And what about her sister?" Giles asked.

There was a slight pause, and Lowndie said, "What about her?"

"You have heard what has happened to her?"

"Aye," he said, and tugged at his beard.

"She was found about here," Giles said, pointing to the area where the body had been discovered. "Sam McPherson found her on his way to fix these sheep cots here."

"So I'd heard, sir," said Lowndie.

"It's not very far from the bothy," Giles said, glancing at him.

"No," said Lowndie.

"When did you last see Mrs Haynes?"

"I couldnae say, sir."

"All right, let me ask you another thing. What were you doing the night before last after you had finished your work?"

"I was at The Brodie Arms," he said.

"All night?"

"Aye, I had a bit to eat and the usual. And then I went to my bed."

"Which is where?"

"I lodge with the widow Gill. Here." Lowndie punched the map with a dirty finger.

"You did not go up to the Forest that night?"

"In that rain? Nay, sir."

"Very sensible. But the rain did not come on until after dark. Now, Mr McDonald has told me you were part of a working party, roughly here, all day."

"Aye, that's true."

"So, you might easily have gone to see Mrs Haynes on your way down, while the weather was still fair. Perhaps she gave you some tea, and possibly something else as well?" There was silence and Lowndie tugged his beard again.

"Maybe I was there a little while," he said at length.

"And perhaps you were interrupted?" Giles said. "Did

Mrs Gowans come calling?" There was another long silence. "Come now, Lowndie, you know that it will go better for you if you tell the truth."

"I didnae lay a finger on her!" he burst out. "I swear to God, sir!"

"But you did see her that afternoon at the bothy?"

There was a pause and he said, "Aye, she came preaching."

"Tell me exactly what happened, Lowndie," Giles said. "You were with Effie, and her sister came in?"

"Aye," said Lowndie, "and Bel was on her high horse, telling Effie she was nocht but a whore, and such, and that she'd be damned forever unless she mended her ways."

"That must have been irritating," said Giles, watching Lowndie carefully.

"Aye. And Effie gave as good as she got. They were always at each other like that. And so I took myself off. I wanted a drink."

"And do you know what time this was?"

"No, sir, except it wasn't dark when I went out and the rain was off. But Jamie at the Arms, he'll know when I got there. He has a big clock in the hall."

"Thank you, I shall certainly ask him about it," Giles said. "So, when you left the two women, Mrs Gowans was alive?"

"Oh aye, she was that, and screaming her damn heid off!" Lowndie said, putting his hands over his ears and wincing. "They both were!"

"You did not attempt to intervene?"

Lowndie shook his head.

"More trouble than it was worth," he said. "And I wanted a drink by then, so I left them at it. Women! Banshees, more like!"

"What was Mrs Gowans wearing?" Giles asked.

"What?"

"What was she wearing?"

"An old brown cloak and a black dress."

"Was she wearing a scarf?"

"A shawl maybe," said Lowndie. "A plaid."

"Nothing colourful?"

"I don't know. Why, sir?"

"Mrs Gowans was strangled with a brightly coloured silk scarf. Red and yellow, with a fringe, with flossy bits on it."

"Oh," said Lowndie. "That sounds more like the sort of thing..."

He broke off.

"Yes?" Giles said.

"The sort of thing that Effie wears. She has a scarf like that. Got it in Glasgow, she told me." He sighed. "If you are looking for who killed her, sir, you should talk to Effie. She hated her that much, I wouldnae put it past her. She's given me a few fair cracks in her time when the drink was in her. She's like a devil when the mood's on her, and that's the truth!"

Chapter Ten

Later that morning, Felix and Major Vernon went in search of Effie Haynes. Mr McDonald supplied them with a brace of sturdy Highland ponies, and as they made their way upwards in the direction of the old bothy and the Forest, Felix was aware of Major Vernon scrutinizing his seat.

"If you don't mind me saying," Major Vernon said, "for a man who professes to dislike horses, you seem very at ease."

"I don't dislike them. It is, I think, that they dislike me," said Felix. "But you are right. These are old friends whom one can trust entirely, and there is nothing like them on these tracks."

"Did you have one as a boy?"

"No," said Felix, "although Lord Rothborough had one put by for me. But my parents – well, you might imagine. And I have to admit I was a little aggrieved at it." He leant forward and caressed the neck of his pony, with its characteristic woolly coat.

"You should bring some of these down to Hawksby," Major Vernon said.

"I have thought of it, but Mrs Carswell, who as you know has charge of our stables, does not like them so much. She likes her Gelderlanders."

"Ah yes, they are beautiful, certainly," said Major Vernon. "But a touch temperamental. I can see a great deal of merit in these. Are they all so good-natured, or is it just that the Castle establishment has schooled them nicely?"

"No, they are all fairly placid. But they will give you a good canter if that's what you like. Ah, now, that is where she was found, if you remember."

Major Vernon drew up his pony and looked across the landscape of rugged moorland, the track rising steeply ahead of them.

"I am getting a better idea of the lie of the land now, especially now I am not expecting to see trees when it is called the Forest," he said. "But I did not get all the details of this place. Perhaps we should stop and have a better look."

He dismounted, and having secured his pony, went up the steeper slope to the little hollow where the body was found. Felix followed him, and they stood for a moment looking down.

"It was lucky that she was found so promptly," said the Major. "I wonder what caught Sam's eye? She might have remained hidden if he had not strayed from the track."

Felix went to the spot where the body had lain. He had left a few stones to mark the place.

"Is it your opinion that she was killed here?" Major Vernon said.

"There was mud on her clothing, her hands and her face and the ground here is unusually muddy. But that does not mean anything." He squinted, and tried to imagine what had been done. "I suppose she may have been face down during the attack. It makes sense with the ligature marks."

"It is easier to attack from behind, to overpower, especially if you are matched in weight."

"You mean if it was a woman?" Felix said. "Do you think there is something in what Lowndie says?"

"We cannot rule her out."

"No, I suppose not. But the ripping of her petticoats, and the staining –"

"About which you are uncertain. And if it is an emission of that sort, then it might belong to her husband, after all, and pre-date the ripping of the petticoats. Is that not possible, if they had relations earlier that day?"

"Yes, it is possible. The properties of that particular substance are not well studied. They ought to be."

"Another one for your list," said Major Vernon.

"I might leave that honour to some other man," Felix said.

Even a superficial consideration of how such a study might be conducted was enough to make him give pause. Although he entirely dismissed current medical opinion that self-stimulation was dangerous – he would cite Hunter on the matter – it was still a highly private act, which somehow precluded the collection of good samples. It was not at all like taking blood or collecting a urine sample.

"So, how do we reach the bothy from here?" Major Vernon said, going back to his pony.

"About half a mile further," said Felix, "and then a little beyond, across the hill, as far as I remember."

They made their way higher up the hill, and soon caught sight of the low, turf-roofed bothy. There were a couple of goats grazing nearby and some chickens scratching among a mess of broken-down furniture, split meal-barrels and burst cartwheels that fronted the cottage.

"Did she bring all that rubbish up here?" Felix said. "Lord Rothborough will not be amused. She should not be here by rights. McDonald ought not to have allowed her to stay. This is supposed to be a shelter for the men working on the hills."

"Perhaps she has other lovers than Lowndie," said Major Vernon, "who bring her strange gifts." There was smoke coming from the stunted chimney. "And she is at home." He went towards the doorway, shooing a chicken away as he did. "Mrs Haynes?" he called out, and rapped on the door.

There was a long silence, and then the door was opened to them a chink.

"Mrs Haynes?" Major Vernon said.

"Aye," she said.

"May we talk to you?" he said.

The door opened a crack and Effie Haynes, striking in her similarity to her dead sister, looked out at them. Seeing her, Felix remembered how handsome in life Bel Gowans had been. They both had lustrous dark hair and large hazel eyes.

"About what?" she said.

"About your sister," said Major Vernon. "I take it you have heard?"

Felix saw her straighten and stiffen as she nodded her assent.

"You'd best come in." She squinted a little. "Is that Mr Carswell yonder?"

"Yes," said Felix, moving a little so she could see him better. He was surprised to be recognised.

"I'd heard you were coming to the Glen," she said, as if reading his thoughts. "Your mother came up and bought one of my kids. She wanted a good milker for her cheese."

She pulled open the door and turned back into the dark interior of the bothy.

The low-ceilinged space was sweet with the smell of burning peat, and full of the same clutter as outside. In one corner a bedstead could be distinguished, heaped with old plaids and blankets. Two wary cats occupied low stools by the fire, and a huge iron pot hung above the fire. Mrs Haynes stood barefoot on the earth floor, a bright scarlet cloak wrapped about her, her uncovered, unpinned and crinkled hair falling down her back. She had silver rings in her ears and her appearance was so self-consciously picturesque that Felix wondered if she had worked as an artist's model on her travels.

"I'm sorry about Mrs Gowans," Felix said. "This is Major Vernon."

She said nothing but went and gathered up one of the cats into her arms and sat down.

"It will be a great loss to you, I suppose," said Major Vernon. She gave a shrug and gazed into the fire, her chin resting on the cat's head. "When did you last see her?"

"She was here the day before last," she said, after a while.

"At what time of day?" said Major Vernon.

"It was before that rain. Late in the afternoon."

"Had you asked her to visit you?"

"No," she said. "She came to bother me."

"I have heard things were sometimes difficult between you," Major Vernon said.

"She –" She broke off and shook her head. "Yes, we quarrelled from time to time." Then she sniffed, and having evicted the cat, reached for a stoneware jar at her feet. She poured herself out a measure into a teacup with a broken handle, and sipped it. "Will you take some, sir?"

"What is it?" Major Vernon said.

"Usquebah," she said.

"And not legal, I suppose?" Felix said.

"It's from Donnie Anderson," she said.

"You should not tell me that," said Felix. "The Sheriff –"

"Oh, the Sheriff himself knows all about Donnie and his still," said Effie, getting up and taking two more cups from a shelf above the hearth. "It is said to be the best in the country," she went on, pouring them each a measure. "Even your father would say so, sir," she added, handing the cup to Felix.

Felix was torn between the impropriety of the act and a genuine interest in tasting Donald Anderson's notorious whisky. He glanced at Major Vernon, expecting him to decline. However, he had obviously decided that this was a case of 'when in Rome' and had already taken a sip. Since he was not a great man for spirits, his expression registered some surprise.

"That is not for the faint-hearted," he managed to say. "Thank you, Mrs Haynes!" He gestured with the cup as if to toast her, and then set it down. Felix tasted his own and followed the Major's example. He did not at all dislike it, but it was not the moment for enjoying it. It needed the ease of an evening by one's own fire, after a good dinner, not halfway through a spring morning when one needed to keep one's wits sharp.

"May I?" Major Vernon said, gesturing to an empty bench.

"As you like," she said, and resumed her contemplation of the fire, this time cradling her cup of whisky.

"It's never pleasant to quarrel with one's brothers and sisters," Major Vernon said.

"We made it up," she said. "We made it up."

"Was that after Mr Lowndie left?" Major Vernon said.

"You know about that?" she said, glancing at him.

"Yes," said Major Vernon.

"He has a wooden heid," said Mrs Haynes.

"But he lets you stay here," said Major Vernon, "when I understand you should not be here."

"I will be where I will be," she said, with defiance. "And what does it matter to anyone?"

"Lord Rothborough might –" Felix began.

"He has all the rooms he needs," she said. "And if he's a Christian, he will not begrudge me this, will he?"

Felix had no answer for such directness and found himself glancing away from her gaze, at the indiscriminate clutter of the room. His eye came to rest on a shallow basket full of flat stones, of exactly the sort that had been lying on Mrs Gowans' back.

"Tell me, if you will, exactly what happened when your sister arrived, Mrs Haynes," Major Vernon said.

"I was sitting by the fire just as I am now, with Lowndie."

"And your sister came in?"

"Yes, and she was full of her talk. She'd been talking to the Rector again, and he'd filled her head with talk of Heaven and angels and sins and all that. Angus hadn't the stomach for it, and he saw he wasn't going to get what he came for so he went away."

"So he and you –?" Major Vernon said.

"Aye," she said. "He wants to marry me," she added with

a laugh. "But I cannae do that, can I?"

"Because you still have a husband living?" Major Vernon said. She nodded. "Where might he be?"

"If I knew that then I wouldn't be here," she said. "But we quarrelled and he was restless, even more restless than I am, so I let him go, like the fool I am, for I would have him back if he showed himself again. If he'd have me back –" She shrugged and sipped her whisky.

"So Lowndie was angry when he left? Angry with your sister?" Major Vernon said.

"He may have been," she said.

"Is he a violent man?"

"No," she said. "Not like some who take pleasure in hitting a woman. No, not that sort."

"So he left," Major Vernon went, "and you and Mrs Gowans had words?"

"But we made it up. I gave her my scarf. I know she'd liked it."

"So she left here quite happily?"

"Yes."

"What was the quarrel about?"

"Oh, I was sore because she wouldn't stop wi' her preaching and telling me what I should and shouldn't do. But we got through it and she left here happy enough."

"And that was the last time you saw her that night?"

"Aye," she said.

"And you have no thoughts as to who might have attacked her?"

"No."

"Were things quite straight between her and her husband, would you say?"

"They were happy enough."

"He wasn't rough with her?"

"Not that she ever said."

"And that night, when she left, you went with her how

far?"

"I didn't cross the threshold. She went and that was it." There was a pause and she added, "God rest her soul."

"There's nothing else you want to tell me, Mrs Haynes?" Major Vernon said.

"No."

"May I ask why you have that basket of stones?" he said. Evidently Major Vernon had noticed them too.

"They're just stones," she said.

"What are they for?"

"Nothing," she said. "I pick them up and bring them back here if I see one I like. Why, should I not? Do they all belong to his Lordship?" she added with a sharp glance at Felix. "It's no' against the law, is it?"

"No," said Major Vernon. "It's just that a number of similar stones were placed on your sister's body. You cannot tell me why they might be there, can you?" She shook her head. "It's very strange, is it not?" Major Vernon went on. "Is it a local custom?"

"I couldn't tell you, sir," she said, looking away.

"If something does occur to you, Mrs Haynes, you will tell me? I am sure you are anxious to know who did this to your sister. Thank you for your time – and the whisky."

Felix was aware of her watching them as they walked away from the bothy back to their ponies.

"So?" he said, when they were certainly out of earshot.

"A puzzle," Major Vernon said. "Like the stones. What do you think?"

"There would be no physical difficulty in her doing it, and she has the terrain on her side. She could easily have followed her down the track, attacked her from behind, strangled her and then retreated. In addition, the presence of that basket of stones, and the fact that she admitted that the scarf was her own gift, make the case against her quite strong."

"And the fact they had been prone to quarrelling," added

the Major. "But why slit her petticoats?"

"To make it look like a man attacked her? I suspect she is not a fool."

"No, she is certainly not that," said Major Vernon. "But the stones – that collection is a curious habit. Of course, collecting things is not unusual, but flat grey stones? If they had been coloured or pretty shapes or unusual in some way, it would seem less odd, but that stone is commonplace. It is everywhere here about. She was vague about her reasons for collecting them, and defensive, as if there were something about it that made her feel guilty. They must mean something, but what?"

"I cannot think of anything," Felix said.

"I suppose other people will have noticed that basket of stones. I don't imagine Lowndie was her only visitor. She had plenty of teacups ready for Donald Anderson's illegal usquebaugh, after all. I suspect she will have an appalling reputation down in the village. But your mother bought a goat from her."

"That was probably to stop her selling herself," Felix said. "I imagine the money is now in Donnie's pocket."

"No doubt," said Major Vernon.

"He is known to charge shockingly high prices," said Felix.

They mounted their ponies and began the descent into the Glen, leaving the Forest behind them.

They had just turned into the avenue leading to the Castle, intent on returning to the Factor's offices, when they saw two riders coming towards them. One was a groom in the Rothborough livery, and the other a lady.

"Is that not –?" Major Vernon began, drawing up his pony.

"Lady Charlotte," said Felix.

The recognition was mutual. She raised her hand in salute and cantered towards them.

"Good day!" she said, "Except it is not, is it? I have heard the news. Poor, poor woman!"

"Did you know her, Lady Charlotte?" asked Major Vernon.

"No, unfortunately. For I have not spent nearly as much time here as I would like, and she was only a name to me. But I understand she has a little girl –?"

"She would be well worth your attention," said Major Vernon.

"I shall make a point of it. Do you have any idea yet who might be behind this? From what Mrs Maxwell said it was quite a brutal attack. Everyone at the Castle is most disturbed, and yet at the same time, immensely relieved that you are here. I do hope you will go and see my mother as soon as you can, for she is naturally..." She gave a sigh. "I am sure you can guess!"

"Of course," said Major Vernon, glancing at Felix.

"And you must go as well, Carswell," Lady Charlotte said. "She is in no state to be silly about such petty things, and I want you to look at Augusta. She is not at all well and even my mother has noticed it. Augusta will not admit it, of course, and I am worried about her. These last few years of being so devoted to my mother have done nothing good for her. Will you go and see her?"

"Of course, but are you sure your mother –?" Felix began.

"She can be managed. It is exhausting, but it is possible. In fact, even the Prince – you have heard about him?" Felix nodded. "He will help us in this. He is most curious about you both, and since she is so besotted with him..." She gave a sigh.

"I'm afraid I did not catch this gentleman's full title," Major Vernon said.

"I'm not surprised. It is ridiculously long and absolutely impossible to pronounce. If I had not read his entry for myself in the Almanac de Gotha I would not have believed it to be true! Until I did, I thought he was a charlatan." She laughed and said, "Oh dear. I ought not to be so suspicious. That is Florence for you. It is full of people one cannot quite place, uprooted, so to speak. It is such a relief to be home!" She gestured about her. "It is quite beautiful here. I cannot believe I have never been here in the spring before. It seems more lovely than ever. I would live here all year, if I could. Perhaps I may yet," she finished. Then gathering up her reins, she resumed, "I'd better let you get back to your business – and please, please, do come up to the Castle as soon as you can! I would be extremely grateful."

"Of course," said Major Vernon.

She touched her brim, smiled, and cantered off again.

Major Vernon turned slightly in his saddle to watch her departure.

"I had better go and see Augusta," Felix said.

Chapter Eleven

"Should I stay, Major Vernon?" said Lady Rothborough. "Is it safe for me to stay?"

"I think so, ma'am," said Giles.

"You only think so?" she said. "Oh, I do not like that note in your voice. It would be no trouble to leave. We are not half-unpacked, if that much, for you know what servants are like after a long journey – they always go to work very slowly, I find."

Lady Rothborough was sitting as close to the fire as it was possible to get, with her feet on a footstool, and wrapped in a large cashmere shawl. Some of the fringe was trailing on the hearth, dangerously close to the flames, and Giles bent forward and pulled it back to safety.

"I don't know about that, ma'am," Giles said, "but let me be more definite about your safety. It is possible there is some danger here. The situation is not clear as yet, but if you take reasonable precautions and do not go out alone, you will be quite safe."

"But I never go out alone!" Lady Rothborough said, with some astonishment. "Why would I?"

"Then you will be perfectly safe."

She peered at him for a moment, considering his words, and then laid her hand on her breast, and nodded, as if accepting his pronouncement. "And the same applies for your daughters, of course," he added.

"I always think it looks extremely ill when an unmarried girl goes out alone," she said, "and not much better for a married woman. I'm sure your wife never goes about alone, Major Vernon."

As Emma did so habitually and would have considered it an affront to practicality rather than propriety to be told to do otherwise, he decided to change the subject rather than introduce further controversy. He had a suspicion that Lady Rothborough was the sort of person who thoroughly enjoyed being shocked.

So he asked: "Are you intending to stay here long, ma'am?"

"That I cannot say. I'm a little surprised at finding myself here, as I'm sure all my acquaintances are. I dare say my husband or my daughters have told you on many occasions that I do not like Scotland, which is true enough. It is those little insects I fear particularly – the little biting wretches. I cannot remember the name."

"Midges, ma'am?"

"Ah yes, of course."

"I don't think they are much of a problem at this time of year."

"If there is any sign of them, I shall leave. No matter what his Highness says. Tell me, have you met the Prince yet? He should be here," she added with a frown. "And as for my daughters..."

"Lady Charlotte mentioned that Lady Augusta was not well."

"Oh, she is always complaining of something," said Lady Rothborough. "It really doesn't signify."

"Mr Carswell has gone to see her. Lady Charlotte particularly requested it."

Lady Rothborough flapped her handkerchief and said, "He is a useful person, all in all, I suppose. Given there is no other medical man in the district one might trust if something were amiss, which I don't imagine it is with Augusta. But she and Charlotte do as they wish these days; they consider themselves quite beyond any sanction! And as for Maria – I have you to thank for that unhappy business, but I'm too generous to hold it against you, Major Vernon – I hope you appreciate that!"

"I do, ma'am," Giles said, working hard not to take offence. "I know Sir Mark is an unconventional choice, but he is a sound fellow and he will do everything he can to make her happy."

"You shall not talk me into it," she said. "I will not have it."

Mercifully the door opened and Mr Blair, the Castle steward, came in. He was a most impressive figure: tall and snowy-haired, and wearing the kilt.

"My lady, I have Mr and Mrs Wallace for you."

"And who are they?"

"The Minister of the parish and his wife, my lady. They wish to pay their respects."

"I suppose I had better see them, then," said Lady Rothborough. "Where is his Highness?"

"I cannot say, my lady."

"Send someone to find him," said Lady Rothborough.

"Yes, of course, my lady," Blair said, and retreated.

Mr and Mrs Wallace came in. Mrs Wallace was plump, pregnant and cheerful-looking, wrapped in a colourful plaid with a bright rosy complexion to match. She looked older than her husband, and was perhaps more comfortable in the world than him. She made her curtsey to the great lady with elegance, but no particular deference.

"Such a great honour, my lady, to know you at last, and to be able to thank you in person for all your kindness," Mrs Wallace said, when the introductions had been made. "The manse, ma'am, is perfect, in every last detail! I cannot go into the pantries in the kitchen without thinking of your kindness."

"The pantries, Mrs Wallace?" said Lady Rothborough, looking puzzled.

"Only a woman could have arranged everything so well," Mrs Wallace went on. "And the bookshelves in the study:

nothing could be nicer or more convenient. When I saw them I was sure it must be you behind it all, my lady."

"Hush, my dear," said Mr Wallace. "Can you not see that you are embarrassing her Ladyship? My lady, please excuse my wife."

"Oh, I do not think there is anything to excuse. I'm glad Mrs Wallace likes her pantries. I dare say I must have given some hints on the matter to my husband."

"I'm sure it was more than a hint. Thank you so much," Mrs Wallace said.

"It was no trouble at all," said Lady Rothborough, flapping her handkerchief again. "Let me look at you properly, Mrs Wallace – come and sit down here."

"Of course, my lady."

"You must be glad to sit down. When is the child expected?" she said.

"Oh, not till late this summer. I know, I'm rather large already," said Mrs Wallace.

"Will you go to Edinburgh for your confinement? I would advise it. There are some quite competent men there. Not as good as you would find in London, of course."

"It would be too great an expense," Mr Wallace said. "My wife is quite healthy and apparently there are several women in the village who have a reputation –"

"Women in the village? Oh, no, no! I cannot advise that," said Lady Rothborough. "You must get a proper accoucheur. There is no end to the evil that such women do. I have heard terrible stories. Some of them are little better than witches!" She shook her head and said, "I can scarcely believe I am saying this, but you must let Carswell look at her."

"That is the Rector's son?" said Mrs Wallace.

"Adopted son," said Lady Rothborough. "Felix Carswell is the result of my husband's immorality. He is, however, a proficient medical man, and I have heard from an acquaintance of mine in Florence, Mrs Yardley, that he is an outstanding accoucheur. It seems he saved her life and that of her child."

"That's true," Giles said. "And Mr Carswell does have a great deal of experience in that area."

"Mrs Carswell did say something of that to me," said Mrs Wallace. She smiled at the recollection. "She is a delightful person. I have never lived in the country before and she has been a fount of all wisdom, and, of course, so has Mrs McCroy. I never expected to find such friends here! Really, it is delightful!"

"Mrs McCroy – who is she?" said Lady Rothborough.

"She is the widow of one of the previous ministers here, my lady," said Mrs Wallace. "And I have learnt so many useful recipes and goodness knows what else. I do not think I ever knew proper housekeeping until I moved here, truly I do not."

Lady Rothborough's expression had no trace of encouragement in it. She clearly had no interest in discussing housekeeping.

"Major Vernon has been saying we must not go out alone, Mrs Wallace, because of what has happened to that unfortunate woman," said Lady Rothborough.

"Oh yes, Mrs Gowans," said Mrs Wallace with a shake of her head. "That is a terrible, wicked thing. She was such a good creature – such an example to us all."

"In what way, Mrs Wallace?" said Giles.

"She was properly charitable," said Mrs Wallace, "even at some cost to herself. That shop could hardly have turned a profit. I have often seen her put down her prices to a ridiculous degree so that some of the poorest folk could get what they needed and pay what they could for it, without it offending their dignity by making them take her charity. And she was loved for it, and rightly so! Who could have done such a thing? That is what I have been asking."

"It is certainly a large question," said Giles.

"It is rather worrying," said Lady Rothborough. "I suppose she was one of your flock, Mr Wallace?"

"No. She was on the verge of going over to the Episcopalian Church – that is, Mr Carswell's church."

"Oh dear, I'm sorry to hear that," said Lady Rothborough. "Really, it would be better for everyone if there were only one church for all the people on an estate such as this. I can imagine that some will say they have been to the other one when they have not been at all."

"Regrettably, that is sometimes the case, yes, my lady," said Mr Wallace.

"I find on my estates in Sussex that backsliding of that sort is far too common. They pretend they have been to the Baptists or the Methodists when they have been lying in their beds on Sunday mornings." She shook her head. "It is not as it used to be, not at all."

At this moment the door opened, and an immensely tall, broad-shouldered young man entered the room. He had the bearing and style of an officer in a crack regiment. His shock of pale hair had been most fastidiously curled and arranged, while his clothes were perfectly judged and impeccable tailored.

"Forgive me, forgive me, my dear lady," he said, going straight up to Lady Rothborough and kissing her hand. He spoke with a pronounced German accent. "I lost track of the time. I was so captivated by the view from my room! This place is enchanting, quite enchanting!"

"I am glad you think so," said Lady Rothborough. "I find it is all rather ugly and very bleak. The house is so plain and I do not think it will be comfortable."

"Yes, yes, that is true," he said, looking around the room, which was a model of the restrained elegance of the previous century. "It could certainly be a little more – how does one say it – romantisch? Perhaps that could be rectified, in time," he said, and then turned his blue-eyed gaze on Giles and the Wallaces.

"Prince, may I present Mr and Mrs Wallace and Major Vernon," said Lady Rothborough. "This is the Prince of Schwarzenburg-Meckleninghen."

When it came to Giles' turn to shake hands, the Prince set to vigorously pumping his arm.

"Ah, Major Vernon, it is a pleasure. I hear of all your exploits from dear Lady Charlotte. She follows your career most particularly."

Giles was not sure what he found more alarming: that 'dear' tacked in front of the lady's name, or the revelation of her avid interest in his work.

"You will be able to see him at work first hand, Prince," said Lady Rothborough. "With this sad business –"

"Oh yes, that poor dead woman!" said the Prince. "It is shocking. But I imagine you will have it all dusted and done soon, Major?"

"The phrase is 'done and dusted,' Prince," said Lady Rothborough.

"But how can that be?" he said. "Surely one must dust before one can be done?"

"I don't know. You must ask one of the maids. They often seem to have done before they have dusted!" Lady Rothborough said, and then looking pleased with herself, began to laugh. "Oh, dear me!"

"Now, I shall never get that right!" said the Prince. "You have spoiled it forever with your wit, my lady!"

"The Prince is working hard to improve his English, and my daughter is working on her German," Lady Rothborough said, in a tone that suggested the banns were about to be read.

"Lady Charlotte is an excellent student," said the Prince, with the air of a man in love. "So diligent."

Lady Rothborough beamed and looked for all the world as if she expected to be congratulated for arranging the match.

Chapter Twelve

Lady Augusta was lying on her bed with two spaniels slumbering beside her. She dismissed her maid, although Felix would rather she had not done so. It struck him at once that she looked most unwell, and the room smelt stuffy, with a distinct tang of vomit in the air.

"I didn't ask you to call," she said.

"I know, but your sister was worried about you. May I help you with anything?" There was a bowl and a cloth lying on the table nearby.

"I'm sure it will pass," she said.

"Your maid told me you have been –"

He did not get a chance to answer, as she suddenly reached for the basin and began to retch into it. He went to assist her but she attempted to push him away, only to accept his help a moment later. She then began to cry, and when he handed her a clean towel she pressed it to her face to hide her distress from him.

"It is the change in the water," she attempted to say, when she was more settled again. "What else can it be?"

"Let us see," he said, and drawing up a chair, began to enquire about what other symptoms she had been suffering. She answered each question with a certain wariness, and he began to realise that she knew perfectly well what was wrong with her. So he asked, as carefully as he could, "Are you feeling any unusual tenderness in your breasts?" She said nothing. "Have you perhaps had to lace less tightly than usual?" Again there was no answer. "Forgive me for asking this, but when were you last unwell?"

"I'm surprised you did not ask Williams about that as

well!" she said, biting her lips. "Oh, you know very well what is wrong, don't you?" He nodded and she began to cry again, bitterly this time, as well she might given her circumstances.

Felix let her cry, a little confounded at finding himself party to such a revelation. He could only imagine how Lord Rothborough would feel when he learnt of it, and then the question of how Lord Rothborough should be told loomed large with him, and all the other questions of what was to be done. That she had got herself in such a condition struck him as astonishing, and he even began to doubt his own diagnosis.

When she was a little calmer, he said: "You might let me examine you a little more carefully? It may be that you are mistaken. Fear can sometimes produce strange effects in these circumstances."

She nodded her permission, and as delicately as he could, he examined her. To his intense regret and no doubt to hers as well, there was everything to suggest that she was with child, and nothing much to suggest otherwise. She admitted to having missed her usual monthly flow twice.

After which, she grabbed at his hand and said, "For God's sake, Carswell, I know what you must be thinking, and you are quite correct, but I will not have you judge me! I am married. Do not think I should have allowed myself –"

She broke off, presumably silenced by his own failure to conceal his astonishment.

"You are?" he said.

She straightened and stiffened at that.

"Yes, of course!"

"To whom?"

"That is none of your concern," she said.

"If you cannot say who it is, then –"

"He is entirely my equal in rank. No one will object to it when it is known."

"Then why is it not known? Why on earth have you concealed such a thing when you know what pain it will cause your parents and your sisters? Who is he to insist on such a thing and leave you in this wretched state?"

"We have our reasons."

"They had better be excellent ones," Felix said. "If he is a perfectly respectable candidate for your hand, then why could you not do things normally? To marry someone in secret strikes me as only necessary if there is something dubious."

"You have no idea what I have been through. You have no idea how it has been with her."

"You mean your mother?"

"You do not know what she is like. I am sure you have heard from Maria how she has been with Sir Mark, and that business has hardened her. It struck me that she would never allow me to marry, and therefore we decided that this was the only way."

"I don't know how you can keep it from her, let alone from Lord Rothborough."

"She is not your mother," said Augusta. "You do not know her. She has disliked us our entire lives for not being male. And of course that is why she despises you, because you are a man! How different everything would have been if matters had been the other way about. You would not be able to lecture me then."

Felix was spared from having to respond to this unsettling remark by the maid coming in with the tea he had ordered for her, and they sat in silence while it was poured. Augusta then took some tentative sips, ate a little dry toast, and seemed to gather her courage a little.

"Indeed, how would I begin to tell her?" she said. One of her dogs woke up, jumped from the bed and went to sniff Felix's boots. "Goodness, how she likes you!" she added, as the dog rolled onto her back and allowed Felix to rub her belly. "She is usually so fussy. But I suppose you are one of us," she added with a sigh. "Whether one likes it or not."

"You must at least talk to Charlotte," said Felix. "I really cannot believe your husband has allowed this to happen. He ought to be here."

"He will be here shortly," said Augusta. "And I shall not tell anyone any more than I need to until he does arrives, and we can make a clean breast of it together. But unfortunately he has business to see to."

"And you will not tell me who he is?"

"That is no business of yours," she said.

"He has used you very badly."

"Oh, please, please, do be quiet!" she exclaimed, putting up her hands. "You know nothing about us and nothing about me. It is not your place to judge me. You are here as my doctor, not as anything else. I do not feel for you as my father or my sisters do, Carswell. This is a horrible necessity for me. That is all. I thank God that you are bound by your profession to discretion! Thank you for coming this morning, but that will be all! Do not come again. I will be perfectly well!"

~

Having taken his leave of Lady Rothborough, Giles asked Mr Blair to direct him to the library where he had agreed to meet Carswell. There was no sign of him, so Giles began to scour the shelves, wondering if, among so many books, he might find the answer to the curious business of the flat stones on Mrs Gowans' back. Was it perhaps the sort of information that never reached the pages of books, but was the preserve of country people who kept such ideas and their meanings to themselves?

He wished Mr Pope, Lord Rothborough's librarian at Holbroke, was there to guide him. It struck him that although this library was not on the same scale as the one at Holbroke, it was certainly extensive, and no doubt contained its own measure of rare and ancient books. He knew that the Rector was a frequent reader there, and he supposed that the young minister had the same privilege extended to him. He wondered if he should have asked Wallace to assist him, but on reflection he decided it had been better not to involve him.

There was something about the young man that made him feel uncomfortable. It was strange, for how could someone so inoffensive be in any way unsettling? Perhaps it was the sense of excessive and carefully cultivated virtue about him. It was a pose of goodness that Giles never found appealing, for there was in that always an implicit judgement of the failures of others.

The door opened and he glanced up, expecting Carswell. However, it was Lady Charlotte, still in her riding habit, looking fresh-cheeked and elegantly dishevelled after her ride.

"Blair told me you were here," she said. "And you look, if you do not mind my saying, a little lost."

"You are quite right. I can't work out your system here."

"That is because there is none, as far as I know. Yes, shocking, isn't it! There has been a plan for many years to send Mr Pope up to deal with it, but he will not be moved from Holbroke, and my father has not the heart to insist on it."

"Perhaps he is afraid of the midges, like your mother."

"He is afraid of anything beyond the library at Holbroke. Even another library cannot tempt him. He is one of the great fixtures of the house. I suspect he was born in that library. I cannot remember a time when he was not there." She gazed about her. "We must find a young man and lure him up here to set it straight. There really ought to be a catalogue. But failing that, you have myself, Major. What are you looking for?"

"Old Scottish customs," Giles said.

"Goodness," said Lady Charlotte. "Most antiquarian."

"What I'm after is what the ordinary people in this district did when someone died. The lighting of wake candles and that sort of thing. Where I grew up there were many odd little customs relating to death, peculiar to our neighbourhood. We may have stumbled on something in that line here."

"With this poor woman's death?"

"She was found face down with five flat stones lying on her back."

"That is strange."

"Indeed, but it may only be strange to us. It may be a commonplace. I need to know if it has any significance to the person who killed her."

"Papa did suggest a book on that subject to me, so there may be a copy of it here. It is called something like 'Ancient Lore and Customs of Scotland.'"

"That sounds promising. Is it a recent book?"

"I think so. He saw a review of it and sent for it."

"Then perhaps this section – the bindings look fresher."

They fell into silence as they scanned the spines. He found a couple of vaguely promising titles, and then Lady Charlotte exclaimed, "Ballencrieff! This is the very one!"

"Excellent," he said, taking the book from her. "Thank you."

"Now, what else can I do for you?"

"This will be sufficient for now. I'm a slow reader. And, will not your mother –?"

"Oh, I only irritate her," she said. "And to be frank she irritates me. We are not friends at present." She gave a sigh. "Oh dear, I can never hold my tongue, but you are an old friend and –" She gave a shrug and walked away with her habit skirt trailing behind her, rather self-consciously displaying her athletic figure, he thought. "I suppose you met his Highness?" she said.

"I did," said Giles. "He said you were studying German."

"It is useful to have a native speaker about if one wishes to make progress," she said.

"Like a French nurse?" said Giles. "But I don't think he sees it quite that way."

"He is a tiresome fellow," said Lady Charlotte.

"Your mother –" Giles began, but she put up her hand to silence him.

"I understand your wife is fluent in German?" she said.

"She is," said Giles.

"It is the sine qua non of an educated woman these days," she said. "My father is always telling me so."

"You might be advised to find a different tutor, then," Giles said.

"No," she said. "I shall use him as I like. After all, he only intends to use me. I am a mere object to be attained."

"Surely not?"

"Surely! You know as well as I that men are mercenary when it comes to a fat rent roll," said Lady Charlotte. "They may be good at couching it in sentimental terms but I have learnt to see through such disguises. Though perhaps you don't know, because you are not like other men. You married for nothing, I understand!"

She said it lightly, but he felt the sting in it. That she resented him for marrying at all was clear. Did that mean that her feelings towards him had not changed, or rather that they had festered into bitterness?

"The Prince may not be sharp," he said, "but he may be very kind and perfectly sincere."

"And therefore worthy of my consideration? Oh, Major, please do not disappoint me! You of all people –"

She would have gone on, but the door opened and Carswell came in.

"How is my sister?" Lady Charlotte said.

"She is –" He broke off and put down his medical bag on the nearest table, with some force so that the instruments and bottles inside it rattled. "You should go and talk to her at once."

"At once?"

"Yes, if you would. I have insisted she confide in you. I

hope to goodness she will!"

"About what?"

"I'm not at liberty to say. If she will talk to you, then we can talk about it."

"How mysterious."

"I would rather not be," said Carswell. "You can be assured of that. Please go and talk to her. She is somewhat unhappy, and –" He pushed his hands through his hair. "The sooner this is dealt with, the better."

"As you wish," Lady Charlotte said, and gathering up her habit train, she departed.

When she had gone, Carswell threw himself into an armchair and leaning back, exclaimed, "Dear God! I hope she manages to talk some sense into her!"

"Something serious, then?"

"Yes, and I wish I hadn't promised not to talk about the details, for I would value your opinion on this! It is a wretched tangle and Lord Rothborough will not be happy, I can tell you that much!" He got up again and went to study the clock. "I should get up to Westerlochan. I want to see those girls again, but first –" He went to the mantelpiece and took down a small box. He opened it and took out a key, which he held up to Giles. "Lord Rothborough does not generally lock books away, as you know, but there are some extremely rare and fragile items here that need a little extra protection." He went to a large press and unlocked it. He pulled open the doors and a smell of dust and old leather filled the air. "I remember him showing me this once, and of course it was all antiquarian and of no interest to me whatsoever! He was not amused at my indifference. But we may find something to help us. The papers relating to the witch trials are likely to be in here – they will not, of course, be objective in any way, but there may be something in them."

"You are still puzzled that the Murray girls should accuse Mrs Haynes of witchcraft?"

"Are you not?"

"I don't know," Giles said, picking up the volume of Ballencrieff. "There are ideas which we, with all our modernity, push away, but which persist despite everything. Like the corn dolls I mentioned. To those girls, witches may seem perfectly sensible. They do not have the benefit of lectures on gravity and microscopes."

"My father thinks that witchcraft still exists."

"I would agree, and I think that people practise it in all sincerity. But it is only whether it works or not that is in question, surely? I will come with you to the Murrays, if I may. I want to talk to them."

"That would do a great deal of good. They will not dare peddle you any falsehoods." Carswell was now on his hands and knees, pulling out a large box. "This looks likely." He opened it and began to leaf through the pile of documents. "Yes, this is it," he added, holding out a small leather-bound book.

Giles took it from him. It was stiff with age and creaked when he turned back the cover. It was printed, in Old Blackletter:

> Being a TRUE and FAIR account of the arrest and trial of the Witches of PITFELDRY in the year of Our Lord, 1672.

Then below in red was printed:

> Thou shall not suffer a witch to live.

Carswell was on his legs again and ringing the bell.

"I'll have them all sent over to you at Mrs McCroy's," he said, and going to another bookcase, climbed on a stool and took down a pair of volumes. "This will have to do for me – after all, Lord Rothborough cannot be expected to have all of a practising medical man's specialities, can he?"

Chapter Thirteen

At Westerlochan Farm everyone was out except Janet Murray, whom they discovered sitting on the settle in the kitchen, listlessly mending a shirt.

"Mother's gone to see the baby, Father's in the fields and Jessie and Agnes are at school," she said.

"How are you feeling now, Janet?" Carswell asked, pulling up a stool to her side.

"Tired," she said. "I'm really tired."

"But you have been able to walk about?"

She nodded, and glanced up at Giles.

"Who are you, sir?"

"This is Major Vernon, Janet," said Carswell. "He wants to talk to you about Mrs Haynes."

"Oh." She dropped her gaze to her lap.

Giles took another stool and sat down where she must look at him.

"Is that a difficult subject for you, Miss Murray? I hear you had a quarrel with her."

"Who told you so?" she said.

"Jessie told me," Carswell said.

"She shouldn't have said anything about it."

"She seemed to think it was important," said Giles.

"She's a wicked woman," Janet said after a moment.

"In what way?"

"You know –"

"I'm afraid I don't. Bad in what way?"

There was a long silence, and then Janet said, almost inaudibly, "She's a witch."

"I see," said Giles. "What does she do that makes her

so?"

"She makes love charms, and she says she can see the future. Said if I gave her money she would tell me the name of the man I'll marry. And she... she makes wee men out of wax and sticks them with pins. I saw her roast one on the fire once," she added with a shudder. "And that was just before Mrs Black fell down in the pass, and died!"

She gasped out this last revelation and cringed, leaning away into the corner of the settle to protect herself, as if she expected to be slapped for speaking so plainly. "Oh, I should never have gone there, I should never have spoken to her, and now she's turned on me, and if she hears I have said this to you, then –" She pressed her hands to her face.

"There's nothing to be afraid of, Janet," Carswell said.

"What do you know?" she exclaimed. "She's no' put the Devil on your back, or made your sisters dance round the room when we're trying to pray. She hasn't put a curse on you, sir, though she might, if she hears you've been asking me this. She can, you know, she can do anything she likes because she has the Devil in her bed. She told me so herself!"

"That she sleeps with the Devil?" said Carswell. "Surely not?"

"Surely she does! She told me so, and told me I should let him sleep with me too, and then I could have all the world and more!"

"It sounds to me," Giles said, after a moment, "that you have seen quite a lot of Mrs Haynes. Is that the case?"

"A bit," said Janet.

"And you liked her at first?"

"Aye, I suppose. And I didn't think there was any harm in it. But – but my mother told me she was wicked and I shouldn't have anything to do wi' her."

"Where did you first get to know her?"

"At Kirsty Macdonald's, down in the village. She's lookin' after Willy."

"That's your little brother, isn't it? Is Kirsty Macdonald nursing him?" Carswell said.

"Aye, my mother couldn't, so she has him, and Effie works there sometimes, cleaning and such, but not any more. But she did, and I used to go down to help with Willy who is the sweetest wee bairn, and sometimes we'd mind him and the other bairns – Kirsty's, that is – if she wanted to rest or go out, or such like."

"And that's when you got talking? She'd be full of interesting tales, I imagine," said Giles.

"Aye," said Janet. "I'd never heard anything like it. And she listened, really listened to me, and it was good to have someone I could speak my mind to, sometimes, for there's no one here, not like that. But I can see now, she was tempting me. When I wouldn't do what she wanted, she turned on me."

"What did she want you to do?"

"She wanted me to help summon the Devil. To take off all my clothes and dance round the fire and call him down to us, to do I don't know what, and I don't want to know! But wicked stuff, that's all I know. So I told her I would never do that, and she laid her curse on me, and on Aggie and Jessie, though what they did to be cursed, I don't know, and now her own sister is dead! That was her. She hated her. Told me she would be happy the day she was buried."

"These are very serious accusations, Miss Murray," said Giles.

"Aye, sir, I know, and I should not dare speak them if I didn't know them to be true. She is a witch, and as wicked as they come."

She spoke with what seemed to be perfect sincerity, looking straight at him with wide, blue eyes.

"But you feel guilty about dabbling in these matters," he said after a moment. "She may have tempted you with her talk of charms and tricks, but you allowed yourself to be tempted, didn't you?"

"I suppose so," she said.

"And perhaps that is what is making you so unwell? That you are ashamed of yourself?"

"But why should my little sisters feel all the prickling and itching?" she said. "They did nothing wrong."

~

When they had left the farm, Felix said, "We shall have to be careful, or they will be throwing Effie Haynes in the pool to test if she is a witch."

"I trust it will not come to that," said Major Vernon.

"What is going on? This is not the Pitfeldry I know!"

Major Vernon had no answer to this, and they rode on in silence, down the hill towards Pitfeldry. It was dusk now, and raining quite heavily, and the atmosphere was not conducive to conversation. At the turning to the lane to the Rectory, they parted, agreeing to meet again the following morning.

As Felix approached the Rectory, he was glad to see the friendly sign of lighted lamps and the sound of a fiddle drifting through an open window. He guessed the player would be Allan Dodd. On their last visit, Eleanor had been lavish with her shillings and her praise for his playing, and he had no doubt come back for more. It was deserved, for he was a fine player and Felix smiled to hear it. Witchcraft and inconvenient secrets were happily banished, at least for the space of an old measure.

He found them all in the drawing room, the furniture moved to the sides. Eleanor and Miss King were attempting a strathspey while his parents sat together, looking on, with Amadeus spread out at their feet. Felix signalled that no one was to stop and went and stood by the fire, while the dance went on.

Eleanor and Miss King might have wanted a room full of

other couples to stand up with, for they seemed to be dancing with ghosts, but Felix could not imagine a more charming sight. Eleanor in her white muslin had cheeks as flushed as the scarlet of Miss King's silk sash.

The piece ended and Miss King went and sat down, saying, "You have a better partner now," she said, indicating Felix to Eleanor.

"Shall we?" said Eleanor, stretching her hand out to him. It was impossible to resist such an invitation, and he took her hand and kissed it. Her skin felt delightfully warm.

"Do you know any waltzes, Dodd?" Felix said, and seeing his father frown said, "She's my wife, for heaven's sake!"

"Felix is right," Mrs Carswell said. "There can be no harm in it, and it is a charming measure."

"You should learn it, Mr Carswell," said Eleanor. "I think your wife would like to dance it."

"I don't dance, Eleanor," said Mr Carswell.

"But you have been tapping your foot, sir," said Eleanor. "That is halfway to dancing."

"Mr Carswell used to dance," said Mrs Carswell.

"Before I was ordained," he said.

"We used to dance at the assemblies in Perth," said Mrs Carswell.

"Mr Carswell, at a public assembly room!" said Eleanor. "I am shocked!"

This remark would not have been easily forgiven if anyone else had said it, but Mr Carswell only offered a smile and a wag of his finger at Eleanor. She smiled back, as if testing him, and then to everyone's surprise, he got up from his seat, and said, "Show me the steps, then, my dear, and I can judge for myself the harm in it."

"With pleasure," said Eleanor. "Now, you must put your hand here –"

It was quite a comical sight to see the Rector being delicately directed by Eleanor as to where he should place his hands and then how he should make the steps. Felix was forced to check his amusement by turning to his mother and offering his hand to her.

"I have lost my partner. Will you?" he said.

"I might manage it," she said. "I was watching the girls earlier. They have been whirling about all afternoon."

Allan Dodd did indeed have a waltz in his repertoire – fortunately a slow one – and for a few minutes they proceeded to dance, until Mr Carswell, having deemed it not scandalous in the least, decided to hand Eleanor back to Felix and waltz with his own wife, a gesture that seemed to please her greatly. Felix, for his part, could not remember ever before having witnessed his father doing anything so obviously for her pleasure. It was akin to that extraordinary choice of wallpaper. Was this some curious symptom of old age, this softening of ancient principles?

Eleanor tugged at his sleeve, and reminded him he must dance with her, which he did. As he turned her, he caught sight of Miss King. She was, he noticed, dabbing her eyes with a handkerchief, and then in a moment she had left the room.

"Is she –?" Felix began.

"Oh dear," said Eleanor, noticing her departure. She broke from Felix's arms and without another word left the room as well, leaving Felix to absorb the spectacle of his parents waltzing.

~

Giles had to pass The Brodie Arms on his way to Mrs McCroy's house, and although he was anxious to be back by his own fire, he decided to pay a brief visit in order to gather a little more information about Lowndie's comings and goings.

The inn, presumably part of the Castle estate, looked as if

it had been rebuilt in recent years to accommodate the increasing number of travellers who wished to tour Scotland and revel in the picturesque scenery. There was a handsome coffee room, into which the servant who greeted him was anxious to show him, but Giles explained his business and asked to be taken into the pot room.

It was busy, as might be expected in the hour after work on a rainy day. There was a large peat fire, and a good stink of ale, pipe tobacco and wet wool. An elderly sheep dog came up to greet him, gazing up with rheumy eyes. Giles made a noisy business of greeting the dog in return, while looking about the room. Some of the faces he now recognised as Lord Rothborough's foresters. They eyed him warily, perhaps worried he was about to trespass on their leisure. However, Lowndie was not with them. Had he gone back to his lodgings already, Giles wondered, or gone up to see Effie at the bothy?

A middle-aged woman – the only woman there, and clearly the landlady judging by her neat clothing and her command of the room – approached and enquired what he would take.

"Would you not prefer the coffee room, sir?" she added.

"Another time perhaps, Mrs –?"

"McNeill, sir," she said.

"Major Vernon," he said. She recognised the name and nodded. "I was hoping to speak to Angus Lowndie, but he is not here. I understand he often is."

"Aye, often enough," she said. "But not so much lately."

"Is that since he has taken up with Mrs Haynes?"

"You might say that," she said.

"Does Mrs Haynes ever come in here?"

"No!" said Mrs McNeill, "and I should not let her in if she did! This is a respectable establishment, and I take care to keep it so."

"I suppose you knew her sister, ma'am?"

"Aye," said Mrs McNeill, with a slight shudder. "God rest

her dear soul. She will be much missed. She was as good-hearted a creature as I've ever known." She gave another shudder. "And to die like that. Like poor Mrs Black in February. They never found her, though. This is better, at least – that they found her."

"Ah, yes, I have heard about Mrs Black," said Giles. "What happened?"

"She was coming through the Pass of Vorlich – I don't know if you have walked it, sir, it takes you from Pitfeldry to Dunkeld – but she was not coming from Dunkeld, of course, but Meigle, where she stayed. She was coming to see her daughter who is married to one of the gardeners at the Castle, and she walked that way once a week or more, because she came to mind the grandchildren. So she knew the path and knew the parts where you have to take care, for the path is awful narrow and worn in places, and it may have been icy, but she was as steady on her feet as I am. But all the same, she slipped and fell, and they never found her. Poor, poor soul."

"I take it there was a search?"

"Oh aye, Mr Wallace and Mr Macdonald organised it, and they searched, and searched, but they never found a trace of her. But there is a spot where they think she may have fallen, and Mr Macdonald had the path made over so it should not happen again. It's dreadful to think of. A wee step the wrong way and a stumble and –" She wrapped her arms around her. "And now poor Mrs Gowans. But that is no accident, they are saying – is that the truth?"

"I'm afraid so. It is not an accident," said Giles. "And, for the time being, you might take care not to go out alone, and tell that to your women friends as well." She gave a little gasp and a sharp nod. "This is only a precaution, but until we are certain what is going on here, it is better to be safe than sorry."

"Yes, sir, of course," said Mrs McNeill. She glanced about the room, and with a sigh, pointed to Gowans, who was sitting in a dim corner nursing a bottle. "And I should make yon widower go home. He's had quite enough."

"Does he often come here?"

"He does like a drop, yes," said Mrs McNeill.

"And do you know what Mrs Gowans thought of that?"

"She let him be. After all, he's no' a roaring drunk. More of a weeping one."

"You've not heard of him being violent?"

"To his wife? No, sir, never. I can tell you who is like that about here, and it's no' Gowans. But he should go home to his bed. I'll get one of the boys to see him back."

At this moment a servant came in and spoke to Mrs McNeill.

"If you please, ma'am, his Lordship in the coffee room is greetin' about the claret. He says it's spoilt."

"Spoilt! Why, it is not. I tasted it myself before it went out."

"He says to take it back and he will not pay for it. Will you speak to him, ma'am?"

Mrs McNeill adjusted her cap strings and then fixing her gaze on Giles said, "Perhaps you would taste the wine for him, sir? He would not dispute it if you were to do so. Because it is not spoilt, and he is playing an old trick to get another better bottle out of me. I have seen it before, but I should not have expected it of him."

"Who is this gentleman?"

"The Earl of Dunbar," said Mrs McNeill. "At least that's who he says he is! For I know the name, of course I do. I have heard it in connection with –" She thought better of speaking the lady's name, and said instead, "Let us go into the hall, sir. This is not the place for this conversation."

Giles, entirely in agreement, went into the hall with her. She led him to a corner under the stairs, and in a confidential tone began: "It's just as well you came in, Major Vernon, for this man has been worrying me. Mr Macdonald said you were a friend of Lord Rothborough. I heard it from Mrs Maxwell at the Castle, that this Lord Dunbar was the young man that was to marry Lady Charlotte. I don't know the ins and the outs of it, of course – and I should not like the family to think it is a topic of common talk about here – but a wedding is a wedding, and she is the eldest girl, and that will be talked of. And he was talked of. Then we heard it was all over, and that was that. So I was very surprised when he arrived here three nights ago – he did not write and ask for a room either. Of course, I couldn't ask him what his business was, but it has made me wonder – if I am not speaking out of turn, sir," she added.

"No, it's interesting, certainly."

"And now he's pulling a trick over the claret," she said. "Will you speak to him? I dare say his Lordship would want you to, sir, if you do not mind me saying so."

Giles had gleaned some fragments about this troubled affair from Lord Rothborough's letters to himself, and from Lady Maria's letters to Emma. That Lord Rothborough would be anxious to know Dunbar's reasons for coming to Pitfeldry was undeniable.

"Is that the wine?" Giles said. A decanter and a glass were sitting on a side table. "Let me taste it first, before I speak to him, though I'm sure you would never send out spoilt wine, Mrs McNeill."

"I will get you a fresh glass, sir," Mrs McNeill said, and went away to fetch one.

Giles took the stopper from the decanter and sniffed the wine. It did not smell spoilt.

He now considered what he knew of Dunbar. According to his various correspondents, he had an unblemished supply of blue blood, but meagre resources. There was no family estate, beyond a ruined castle. He was reckoned a brilliant man, and regarded as a compelling voice for the forces of reform. He was also known to be possessed of insatiable political ambition, and was often spoken of as a future Prime Minister. A marriage to Lord Rothborough's eldest daughter would, no doubt, have helped him greatly in his ambitions. It was likely he had not taken the ending of the engagement well, for what man could be easily resigned to losing such a woman as Lady Charlotte? Had he come here now to attempt to mend things between them?

Mrs McNeill returned with a glass, and poured him some claret.

He sipped it.

"I'm no great judge of wine, but I can't taste anything amiss with that. In fact, it's very good."

"Of course it is! It was recommended by his Lordship himself. He sent me to his own merchant in Leith for it, for he said there was no point serving bad claret with good food. I was a cook formerly, you see, sir, with the Earl of Anstruther, which is how I came to know his Lordship. So you'll have a word with him, sir?"

"Unfortunately, it seems I must," he said, putting down the glass.

"It's a low, low trick," she said, shaking her head. "I shall send him away tomorrow."

"Let me see what he has to say for himself first," said Giles.

Rather reluctantly, Giles went into the coffee room. There, sitting at a table by the fire, a book propped in front of him, was the man that Lady Maria had described as "shockingly ugly." She was exaggerating, perhaps, but the firelight and the frown he wore did make his unusual features look harsh and unpleasant.

"You're not the landlady," he said.

"No, my lord," said Giles. "Allow me to introduce myself – Major Giles Vernon."

"Excuse me, sir," the young man said, stumbling to his feet. He held out his hand. "Very glad to know you, sir. Dunbar at your service." They shook hands, and Dunbar offered him a chair at the table. "Will you join me?"

"Yes, thank you," he said.

"Well, well, the celebrated Major Vernon," Dunbar said. "I have wondered if I might ever meet you, but it is quite extraordinary to find you here."

"I'm on holiday," said Giles.

"You're staying at the Castle, I suppose?"

"No, my family and I are lodging just a little way from here."

"I hope you are comfortable. I cannot say the same for this establishment."

"Yes, I hear you had some difficulty with the wine."

"It was spoilt."

"I'm sure that this is the sort of place where great care would be taken that a gentlemen is not served spoilt wine. The landlady has a reputation to maintain, and she works hard to do so. You may be mistaken."

"Mistaken?"

"Perhaps you had burnt your tongue on the soup and it spoiled your palate. I have heard of that. That is the charitable explanation, I should say."

"What exactly are you implying, Major Vernon?"

"In my line of work, my lord," Giles said, "I come across a great many petty tricks, committed for the most part by petty minds, determined to cheat more honest fellows. In fact, one of my inspectors is determined to compile an index of such ruses in order to educate young constables. It's disappointing to find that such habits might have become fashionable among those who ought to be setting an example in their conduct."

"You tasted the wine?" Dunbar said after a moment.

"I did, and I regret to say I could not find fault with it. Nor could Mrs McNeill before she sent it out, and she knows better than me about such things, I should think. It is a pettyfogging trick, my lord, and you know it. Were you hoping she would send in a better bottle to mollify you? One for which you would not be charged? I suppose that a title often permits such self-indulgence."

Dunbar crossed his arms and leant back in his chair with a deeper frown.

"What I suggest is that you drink that wine and enjoy it," Giles went on, "and keep her good favour. She is quite prepared to send you packing and I'm not sure there is anywhere in the neighbourhood that would put you up so comfortably. As a former soldier, my advice would be not to give up a comfortable billet, if you intend to go on campaign."

"What do you mean, Major Vernon?"

"Why are you here, my lord, at this particular moment in time? I'm sure it is not to paint watercolours."

"I understand you are acquainted with the lady?" Dunbar said.

"Yes, and I am lucky to count her father as a friend."

Dunbar looked at him with calculating eyes. Was he wondering how much influence he had with Lord Rothborough? Then he said, "For a man so well known, I have noticed that Lord Rothborough does not have many close friends. You are indeed honoured, Major." He got up from his seat. "I shall go and tell them to bring back the wine. Perhaps you will join me?"

"No, thank you. I must get back to my wife and family. I have been out all day."

"Ah yes," Dunbar said, as he went to the door. "I have heard there has been some business in your line."

"A woman has been murdered."

"All very unfortunate," Dunbar said, and left the room.

~

Giles was glad of the old-fashioned comforts of Mrs McCroy's best bedroom. There had been sherry and bread and meat to welcome him home, as well as Emma, who looked better than he had seen her for some time – in fact so much so that he had hesitated to tell her of the day's events. Instead he let her tell him her news: the children had been marvellously entertained, had eaten vast amounts and gone to bed without a murmur when they should, utterly exhausted by the Highland air.

But then she had enquired with a glance and he could not resist the temptation to unburden himself.

"A purported witch," Emma said. "Oh dear. They seem to have quite a taste for that sort of thing here. I did glance over some of those old papers that came from the Castle. I hope you do not mind. My curiosity got the better of me."

"I hoped it might," he said, smiling. "It was not too taxing, I hope?"

"Not at all. I have nothing to do here anyway, which is a novelty in itself! And the story is fascinating, in an entirely repellent sort of way."

"So what happened?"

"I feel I should blow out another candle, and draw you closer to the fire," she said.

"That would not be such a bad idea," said Giles. "Or we could get into bed and you could tell me there."

So they got into the commodious, high bed and Emma lay in his arms and began: "There was an old woman, a widow called Bessie McPherson, who lived with her daughter and son-in-law, and she had the bad habit of quarrelling with her neighbours – you know the sort of person, I'm sure. She was charged with cursing a cow belonging to the woman in the next cottage. The cow had strayed onto her patch of kale – I think it was kale, or was it turnips? Whatever, the cow ruined it, and as a result she cursed the cow."

"Do they know exactly what she said?"

"No, there is only the testimony of the neighbour saying things like: 'I heard her evoke the name of Satan as she drove the cow off the patch.'"

"So one might interpret that as Bessie calling the cow an agent of Satan for eating her kale, rather than cursing the cow?" Giles said.

"Yes, but it seems to have been seen as a curse, and of course when the cow would not give any more milk, it was proof of it. In fact, it says that the cow's udders withered up in the sight of another woman, who then had plenty of other unkind things to say about Bessie, and her daughter."

"Such as?"

"That they were children of the Devil, and practised witchcraft. She said that Bessie and her daughter rode brooms to meetings of other witches in the next town, and that she had made a cake which, if you ate it, let you see the future."

"Were these statements taken under oath?"

"Oh yes, it seems to have been done with great seriousness. With a great deal of that Scots legal language which makes English lawyers seem plain spoken. I had to ask Mrs McCroy the meaning of some of it. Her father was a solicitor in Perth. She is extremely well read, by the way."

"She will be glad of your company, then."

"It must be said we did find a great deal to talk about," said Emma with a smile. "It was most stimulating, all in all."

"I shall have to ask her opinion about all this," said Giles. "She strikes me as the sort of person who does not let a great deal slip her notice."

"Oh yes, she is exactly that," Emma said. "She will know all the village quarrels and troubles. I understand that people come to her for advice."

"So, to return to the witches of 1678 – what happened after the withered cow's udder?"

"This is where it gets most strange. There were two sisters, girls of fourteen and fifteen – the nieces of the minister, Mr Browne – who fell down sick with convulsions, and the medical man they sent for – I cannot recall where he came from – could not explain it."

"His testimony is there?"

"Yes."

"Carswell will want to see that. And due to a lack of medical explanation they decided that witchcraft was the cause of it?"

"Yes, because one of the girls admitted that Bessie McPherson had baked a special cake for them which would let them dream of their future husbands."

"And that was thought witchcraft? Surely that is common enough. I remember my sisters doing strange things with apple peels on All Souls in an attempt to see who they would marry. That was not considered witchcraft."

"I have done that myself," said Emma. "But this cake seemed to have been made the source of the girls' woes. They were in a wretched state. And one of them attempted to put herself out of the window."

"Just like Janet Murray," said Giles. "Do you think she might have heard of all this somehow?"

"It was printed in a pamphlet, so there may be other copies in the village."

"Perhaps Janet may have read exactly what you have read," Giles said.

"And may be using it as a sort of script? Is she feigning in some way?"

"I don't know," Giles said. "What does she gain by doing so?"

"Attention?" said Emma. "It makes things less monotonous. A clever girl in a dull place will make trouble for entertainment."

"She seems too timid for that, but who am I to say? I have only spoken to her once, and the circumstances were not ordinary ones. We must ask Mrs McCroy about her."

"Yes, certainly," she said, and pressed a little closer to him, yawning. "Oh dear, I'm so sleepy. This bed is too comfortable."

"Can a bed be too comfortable?" Giles said, adjusting his embrace about her, so that there was scarcely a chink between them. Emma sighed at this and he wondered if this was the moment when they might resume their marital relations.

Having both been beset by illness over the last few months, that field had fallen fallow. They had not spoken of it directly and there had been no shortage of affection between them. It was only that he had not pressed her further and, even now, in this most ideal circumstance, he hesitated to suggest it. It was not that he did not desire her, but doubted if he was ready to pursue it. Neither did he wish to trouble her. She was calm and still in his arms, her breathing steady and suggestive of imminent sleep. So he kissed her head and closed his own eyes.

Chapter Fourteen

"What is wrong with Augusta that she needs such an early call?" Eleanor said.

"I'm not quite sure yet. That's why I want to see her again," Felix said, pulling on his shirt.

Eleanor climbed out of bed and went to the window. She pulled back the curtains and stood looking out.

"I do not think I shall ever tire of that view," she said. "And the weather looks much more promising today. We could go to the Falls of Iolair."

She looked back at him with an appealing smile, which – combined with her flimsy nightdress and unleashed hair – made Felix wonder if Augusta ought to be postponed and that marital harmony ought to be pursued. This was how he had always imagined marriage might be: delicious episodes of snatched but permitted intimacy. Yet he did not feel much inclined, which made him wonder at himself.

"Perhaps," said Felix, "if I can get back before lunch."

"Surely you will not be with Augusta all morning?"

"No, but I have a few other matters to attend to."

"Oh well," said Eleanor after a moment. It struck him that she did not sound too disappointed at this, and he felt relieved. "Perhaps tomorrow?"

"Yes, I hope so," said Felix. "In fact, God willing, both the Major and I will be at liberty tomorrow, so we can make a proper excursion of it. The children are eager to see the Falls."

Eleanor had wrapped herself in a shawl while Jacob came in with his coat and boots.

"Jacob, will you find Stevens for me?" Eleanor said, and then added, "No, no, do not disturb her. Miss King and I will manage for ourselves this morning. I simply cannot stay inside when it is so glorious." With which she ran out of the room.

"I hope Miss King doesn't mind being woken up," said Jacob, helping Felix into his coat. "She was up late. I think she doesn't sleep well. She was pacing about her room last night. I could hear her through the wall." Jacob was housed in the sliver of a room next to Miss King's. "Mrs Stevens will be glad to be left to sleep, I'm sure. She says this air fairly knocks her sideways."

Having finished dressing to Jacob's satisfaction, Felix crossed the hall to Miss King's room.

Eleanor had left the door half open and he could see Eleanor sitting on Miss King's bed, with her back to him. Her nightgown and her shawl had now slipped, leaving one shoulder bare, and her hair was glowing in the curtained light, making a red-gold torrent down her back. She was leaning over Miss King and murmuring something, and Miss King could just be glimpsed stirring under her coverlet.

Felix wondered again at his reluctance to suggest relations with her a few minutes ago. There was everything that he liked to see here, further spiced as it was by her going into another woman's bedroom. At one time the thought of one young woman waking another, languid with sleep, would have excited him greatly. Yet he found himself curiously objective. Yes, there was great deal of intimate charm to be observed through that half-cracked door, but at the same time it was like looking at a print. He did not believe that those two pretty creatures could be anything to do with him.

"You are such a belle dormeuse, Jenny, but you must get up," Eleanor was saying, bending even further over her friend. "I'd better kiss you awake."

Felix moved quickly away from the door and clattered downstairs with noisy haste, as if he were a boy late for school. He knew only that it was not his place to linger. His precipitate arrival in the hall brought Amadeus running out of his father's study, and he was glad to distract himself by fussing over the dog.

~

An hour later found him in Augusta's bedroom. Although he was extremely reluctant to be there after his visit the previous day and all it had revealed, he was glad he had taken the trouble. It was impossible not to feel for her. She was in some mental distress, as might be expected given the gravity of the situation in which she had found herself. She had all the ordinary symptoms of a woman in her condition, but her anxiety was making what might be trivial, if uncomfortable, into a grand malady. She had been retching since the small hours, according to her maid, and she had a headache and a great deal of bodily discomfort. He did what he could to reassure her and to make her comfortable, and managed to restrain himself from chiding her, for which she seemed grateful, in a grudging fashion.

Having left her, he had barely turned the corner in the passageway when he met Charlotte.

"So, what is wrong with her?" she demanded at once. "She would not tell me."

"I cannot," he said. "I am bound not to tell you."

"Does that mean that she is – ?" said Charlotte, after a moment. "It is that, is it not? What else could be so serious that she would conceal it from us – from me? She is with –" She broke off and stared at him. "Please, I beg you, tell me that is not the case."

Felix said nothing – it seemed all he could do. Charlotte closed her eyes for a moment, as if offering a prayer, and then went on, "I did try and talk to her, just as you suggested, but she would not give me any quarter. I knew it was something serious. I have not slept over this. Oh, how could she be such a fool! I suppose it was that Danish artist fellow who was hanging about. He painted my mother's portrait – it was most unflattering, although quite good in some respects – but she, of course, refused to pay for it. He will be the one responsible, I am sure of it. He and Gussie were always chattering together." She grimaced. "Oh poor, silly, silly Gussie! How could she be so –"

At this moment Felix was obliged to touch her on the arm to silence her, for a tall, fair-haired gentleman was coming up behind her.

"Good morning, my lady," he said, taking her hand, and bowing over it while clicking his heels. From his appearance and his accent, Felix guessed this must be the Prince. Charlotte made the introductions and explained that she had fetched Felix to see her maid, who had been ill in the night.

"How extremely considerate you always are, Lady Charlotte," said the Prince.

"It is rather that it is a great inconvenience to me if she is not well," said Lady Charlotte. "There is no one else to do my hair as I like it."

"That I do not believe, Lady Charlotte. You are a tender creature, that is the short and the long of it." He turned to Felix and said, "I trust the young woman is not seriously indisposed."

"No, it is just a question of rest."

The Prince nodded earnestly and then turned back to Lady Charlotte.

"I see you are dressed for riding," he said. "Will you do me the honour of riding with me this morning?"

"That's very kind, sir, but I'm afraid I cannot. Mr Carswell and I have other business. The child of that poor murdered woman –"

"Of course, of course," said the Prince. "I quite understand. And is there any progress on that, Mr Carswell? Has the famous Major Vernon identified the culprit? It does seem strange to me that anyone in this beautiful place could commit such a despicable act."

"No, we are still at the beginning of our enquiry."

"It will be her husband, I suppose," said the Prince. "Ach well, tomorrow, perhaps, Lady Charlotte?"

"Perhaps," said Lady Charlotte. "Now, if you will please excuse us?"

She fairly bustled Felix along the passageway and through a door into what appeared to be an unoccupied bedroom with the furniture still covered in dust sheets.

"That man!" she exclaimed. "It is a blessing you were with me. What is to be done about him? He is a torment. Mama thinks the world of him, and he thinks the world of himself! And he is only waiting for a chance to propose, I can feel it!"

"There is no obligation for you to accept him, though, surely?" Felix said.

"No, of course not, but I fear I shall be utterly worn down and marry him by mistake."

"You are the last person to be worn down."

"That's very kind," she said. "But my powers of endurance are not unlimited. If I were to marry him, it would please everyone immensely, would it not? And I am vain enough to like the thought of that."

"Except it would not please you, and I don't think Lord Rothborough would want you to marry anyone that you did not properly care for."

"That is true." She gave a sigh. "So, how do you find wedded life? You look very well for it. I shall call on Eleanor this afternoon, if I may? We have not set eyes on each other since we were children. I remember I was mortally envious of her red hair."

"She'd be glad to see you," Felix said.

"And, of course, I must also call on Mrs Vernon," Charlotte said. "I shall be interested to meet her. She is a lucky woman."

~

"I have news from the Sheriff," said Major Vernon, holding up a letter as Felix approached. They had arranged to meet outside The Brodie Arms. "His Substitute – is that the correct term? – will be here tomorrow, and some officers from the Perth constabulary."

"Do you think they will be able to untangle this?" Felix said.

"We have to allow them to attempt it. And of course, we shall give them all the information we have gathered so far."

"I'm not sure they will manage it without you," said Felix.

"It may not be at all complicated," said Major Vernon. "I learnt last night that Mr Gowans is a habitual drinker, not reputed violent, but if the circumstances are provoking enough, then – well, such cases are not unknown."

"But you don't really think he did it, do you?" said Felix.

"I cannot fully eliminate him. I haven't talked to him properly," Major Vernon said.

"Which I suppose you intend to do today – before the Sheriff-Substitute gets here?"

"Yes," said Major Vernon. "It would only seem prudent."

"Even Prince what's-his-name has his money on the husband," Felix said. "I had the pleasure of being presented to him this morning."

"What did you make of him?"

"A gilded horsefly intent on stinging poor Lady Charlotte. She is somewhat exasperated."

"Not easy to swot him away, I imagine," said Major Vernon. "You went to see Lady Augusta, I suppose?"

"I did," said Felix, frowning. "God help her!"

"Is she very unwell?" the Major asked.

"No," said Felix. "All I can say is that there will be a lot of bad weather to be got through in that area."

"That sounds unpleasant."

"It will be," said Felix, and noticed a gentleman coming out of the inn.

"Good morning, my lord!" called out Major Vernon, touching his hat brim.

"Major Vernon," said the gentleman, with a nod of his head.

"May I present my colleague, Mr Carswell," Major Vernon said, indicating Felix. "Mr Carswell, may I introduce the Earl of Dunbar."

They shook hands. Felix felt himself scrutinized with a mixture of contempt and wariness.

"On your way to the Castle?" Major Vernon said.

"Yes, I must pay my respects," he said. "Please excuse me. Good day." He went striding away.

"Lady Charlotte will have two horseflies to deal with," said Major Vernon.

As Lord Dunbar departed, he passed by a woman walking briskly towards them. She signalled to them.

"Maggie Shairp, is that you?" Felix said, as she approached. She had been a servant at the Rectory in his youth.

"Aye, Master Felix, it is!" she said, and went on breathlessly, "What a blessing to find you here. I was just on my way to the Rectory to get you. I need you to come to Kirsty. You remember her?"

"Of course," said Felix, feeling himself colour a little. It was not possible that he could have forgotten her. They were the same age and had played together as children, and then somewhat less innocently when they had grown a little older. She had permitted his kisses and other more dangerous liberties with an eagerness that had surprised him.

"Will you come and look at her?"

"At once," said Felix, with a glance at Major Vernon. "Perhaps you had better come too, sir. She is nursing Mrs Murray's child."

Mrs Shairp looked enquiringly at Major Vernon. Felix explained who he was.

"You are staying at Mistress McCroy's, sir?" she said.

"Yes."

"A fine woman. I work for her sometimes. She asks me up to bake for her."

"Mrs Shairp makes the best oatcakes in the Glen," said Felix.

"That's very kind of you to say so, Mr Felix," said Mrs Shairp. "Now come and look at Kirsty, will you? She'll be glad to see you."

It would be a curious reunion, Felix could not help thinking, as they walked to Kirsty's house. She was now Mrs Macdonald and lived in a neat cottage at the edge of the village. Mrs Shairp opened the door, saying, "Come in, will you?"

Felix followed Mrs Shairp into the only bedroom, while Major Vernon remained in the other room. Here he found Kirsty sitting on the bed attempting to feed a screaming baby.

"I've nae milk all of a sudden!" she said. "I can't understand it."

Mrs Shairp took the child from her and attempted to soothe him.

"Is that the Murrays' child?" said Felix, taking him from Mrs Shairp. "How old is he?"

"Six months," said Kirsty.

Felix put the child down on the bed beside Kirsty and examined him, as best he could, for the child was in a fighting spirit. "Has he been sick? How are his bowels? Has there been any fitting?"

"No, nothing like that," said Kirsty. "It is just I cannae feed him. I fed my Tam, just as usual, and then I took this one up and put him to suck as usual and suddenly, there's nothing!"

"He's not feverish. It may just be he is extremely hungry and the breast milk is not to his taste. You might try him on some goat's milk," Felix said.

"That is what I've been saying," said Mrs Shairp. "But she is thrawn."

"But where's my milk gone?" said Kirsty. "I have fed four children and my husband says I'm a wee cow, I give so much milk, but –" She began to cry.

Mrs Shairp sensibly carried the baby from the room, leaving Felix alone with Kirsty.

"When did this begin?" he said.

"This morning," she said with a sob.

"And your own child fed well?"

"Aye, I told you he did!"

Felix took her hand and felt her pulse. It was racing.

"May I?" He reached out and touched her forehead. She was slightly feverish. "Are your breasts sore at all?"

"Aye," she said, and looked away from him. "Oh Lord, that you should be here just now and asking me about all this! When Ma said she was going to get you from the Rectory, I nearly told her not to. I was thinking about that time down by the –"

"Yes, yes, I know," said Felix. "But that was years ago."

"You were such a dirty wee devil," she said.

"You didn't seem to mind."

"More fool me," she said.

"We are all stupid when we are young," said Felix. "Have you ever suffered from this soreness before, when you were feeding?"

"No."

"May I have a look?"

"I suppose so," she said, and pulled down her shift to let him examine her. Her breasts were red and swollen and she flinched at his touch.

"Have you seen those girls up at Westerlochan?" she said. "I heard you went up there."

"Yes. What of it?"

"Effie was here, you know," Kirsty said, "and I sent her away. And now this."

"What are you talking about?"

"If I hadn't given him to Effie Haynes to mind, then maybe he'd be taking his milk as he should –"

"Presumably you gave your own baby to her as well?"

"Yes."

"And he's as right as rain, is he not?" said Felix. "This is nothing to do with Mrs Haynes."

"You didn't see her and Janet Murray. Fighting like two cats, they were. And now Janet's sick and her sisters too. Effie Haynes is a bad woman, and everyone here will tell you so!"

"She has nothing to do with it!" said Felix, exasperated with her. "The problem is only that you have too much milk. Nothing more sinister than that. You need to let it down by hand. A warm compress will help."

"That never works with me. I can never get it to come with my hand," she said. "My Jamie, if he were here, he'd have a wee suck, but he's not," she added.

"When will he be home?" Felix said.

"Not till this evening," she said, and then after a moment said, "maybe you could do it?"

"I don't think that's appropriate."

"But I'm fit to burst," she said. "What's the harm in it? That bairn will be screaming all day. He won't take the goat's milk, I know that much!" And then she added, "After all, it's no' like you've never done it before, is it?"

This, regrettably, he could not argue with. In the course of their youthful embraces, she had permitted him to kiss her breasts.

"Very well," said Felix, but he was extremely reluctant to

proceed. Her suggestion was not an entirely foolish one, and endorsed by many authorities on the subject. But this was a situation he had not met with before in practice, and it did not help him that he was stirred by Kirsty Macdonald's gentle, peasant beauty and the memories of that dangerous encounter all those years ago.

"Well?" she prompted, lying back on her pillows, and pulling down her shift a little further.

He bent over and put his mouth to her nipple, feeling himself colouring as he did so. She moved a little, and lifted her breast up for him. He began to suck, horrified with himself even as he did, the seconds passing painfully slowly before the release of a sweet, hot gush of liquid. He felt profoundly disconcerted, if not ashamed, and his discomfort was not lessened by her soft sigh of relief. Their eyes met for a moment as he straightened up again.

"And the other," she said.

"There," he said, having obeyed her. He hastened out of the room to fetch back the baby. In a few minutes the child was contentedly feeding, and Kirsty now displayed all the innocent serenity of a Raphael Madonna, only lacking a blue veil and an Italian landscape behind her.

~

"I had an interesting conversation with Mrs Shairp," said Giles, as they walked away from the cottage.

"No doubt she believes Mrs Haynes is a witch as well!" said Carswell. He seemed agitated. "Dear God, what is going on here? This is Pitfeldry. I would not have thought people here were susceptible to such nonsense."

"I don't think the belief is universal. Mrs Shairp was not inclined to it."

"Thank God! It is to be hoped that she will talk some sense into Kirsty. She said that Janet Murray and Effie were fighting like cats, by the way."

"Yes, so I gather. According to Mrs Shairp, Janet provoked her by pulling rank. Her opinion was that Janet is too clever for her own good and full of daft ideas about her importance. Apparently she was away at school for a while and has only just come back to live with the family. Mrs Shairp said that she thought the school turned her out for making trouble."

"So, is she making trouble again?" Carswell said.

"It is hard to say. She has a great command of herself. Her confession the other night, if one might call it that, was certainly fearless, if it is a confabulation."

"We shall have to go up there again, I suppose," said Carswell, with a sigh.

"Certainly, it will be worth seeing if her account can be unpicked. It was interesting what she said about Mrs Black, though."

"Mrs Black?"

"Of Meigle. The woman who apparently fell from the path into the gorge – I forget the name. Janet alleged that Mrs Haynes roasted her image before the fire, did she not?"

"Oh, the Pass of Vorlich. Yes. Janet ascribed that to witchcraft, but that path is notorious! I remember someone dying there when I was a child, I am sure of it. You must ask my father to look through his journals. He has every death recorded in the parish, whether he buried them or not."

"That I shall do. Now, let us go and talk to Mr Gowans," said Giles. "With luck he will have sobered up. It may be an apposite moment, if he has anything of interest to say to us."

"You are hoping for a confession," Carswell said.

"I always hope for a simple explanation," said Giles, "but, as you know, I am usually disappointed."

The little shop was closed, but there was a liveried groom

standing outside, holding his own mount and a horse that Giles recognised as Lady Charlotte's roan mare.

They went in and found Lady Charlotte sitting with Mary Gowans in the kitchen, which made a touching sight. Lady Charlotte had clearly got the child's confidence, and as she rose to greet them, Giles saw her wipe away a tear.

"I was hoping to see your father, Mary," Giles said.

"He's no' here, sir," said Mary.

"He sent all the neighbours away who came to offer help yesterday," Lady Charlotte said, "and then left himself. Poor Mary has been alone here all night and all morning. Perhaps she should go to the Rectory?"

"Yes, that sounds like an excellent plan," Giles said. "So your father did not come home from The Brodie Arms last night, Mary?"

"No, sir."

"Has that happened before?" he said. "That he stayed away all night?"

"Aye, sometimes."

"And that made your mother unhappy, perhaps?"

"Very, sir, for he wouldn't come back until afternoon, and he was always ill."

"Did you know where he went?"

"I heard my mother ask if he'd been to Donnie Anderson's," said Mary.

"That would make sense," said Carswell.

"Where does he live?"

"He does not have a fixed address," Carswell said. "The last time I saw him, which was some years ago, was up in the Forest, the other side of Ben Liath. He moves his still about to avoid the excise men."

"Naturally," said Giles. He turned to Lady Charlotte. "Perhaps you'd better take Mary down to the Rectory."

"Certainly," said Lady Charlotte. "Shall we go and see if Mr Carswell has that book he promised your mother?" The child nodded. "Let us go and find your bonnet, then. And perhaps take a few things with you – Mrs Carswell may ask you to stay and help her."

They left the kitchen, and Giles said, "I wonder if Effie Haynes might tell us where Anderson is. She obviously saw him recently."

"To be honest," Carswell said, "it is unlikely that anyone will be able to tell us where Anderson is at present. He is as wily as they come. He has avoided arrest for years."

Chapter Fifteen

By the time they arrived at the Rectory, the sun had come out, and the wet weather of the last few days seemed a distant memory.

"Will it stay settled, do you think?" Giles said to the Rector, whom they found in the Rectory vegetable garden, a hoe in his hand. He was scanning the sky.

"For the sake of the young ladies, I hope so," he said. "My daughter-in-law does not like to be confined to the house. So you have brought Mary Gowans back with you," he added, glancing at the ladies, who were in the more decorative part of the garden receiving Lady Charlotte and Mary Gowans.

"We suspect Gowans has gone drinking chez Donnie Anderson," Carswell said. "Had you heard of that before?"

"Mrs Gowans did mention to me that he was inclined to tipple. She was forbearing on the subject, though I could tell it pained her. She wanted to bring him to a better place, but could not." He shook his head. "What a pretty child she is," he said, indicating Mary.

"Gowans sent the neighbours away and left her all alone. It was as well Lady Charlotte called on her," Giles said.

"A weak man," said the Rector. "Wasted on such a wife, and wasted, it seems, as a father."

"Would you say he was violent?" Giles said. "Or capable of violence?"

The Rector leant on his hoe and thought for a long moment.

"That I cannot say. Do you think he may have killed her, Major?"

"It's possible, but I would like to talk to him properly. Do you have any notion where we might find this Donnie Anderson?"

"I last saw him a se'night ago," said the Rector. "And he was anxious I should not see him. He melted away like a patch of ice in the first sun of the spring. It was down in the village, of course. I have no notion where his still might be set up at present. You may search long and hard before you find him 'in flagrante', as I think one might term it."

"Then we shall have to wait until Gowans crawls home, for crawl home he must at some point," Giles said. "I have a few other questions for you, sir, if you don't mind? I understand you have kept a journal for some years."

"Since I was a student. It was a habit my father had, and which I continued in his honour. It is a shame that the next generation did not take to the discipline –"

"That is unfair, Papa – a medical man's case notes are, in effect, a journal," said Carswell.

"But you do not make meteorological notes," said the Rector. "You were only asking the other day if I had a record of storms, were you not?"

"Yes, but –"

"Ten minutes," the Rector went on. "Ten minutes each day is all it takes. What man cannot spare that? And look at the value of it! Here is Major Vernon asking me to consult them, which of course I shall do with pleasure. Let us go in!"

They went into the Rector's study, where the journals lived in a cupboard set in the wall. They were contained in small notebooks, and inscribed in a tiny hand that was a struggle to read. But at the back of each volume was a list of deaths in the Parish.

"It was Mrs Black I wanted to ask about," Giles said. "From Meigle."

"Oh yes," said the Rector, searching through them. "She fell, we believe, into the gorge on the Pass of Vorlich, in February of this year."

"And there have been deaths there before?"

"Yes, yes," said the Rector. "But not for many years. For Lord Rothborough had the path made safe the last time it happened. It was properly reconstructed with a railing and so forth."

"But it was still dangerous," said Carswell, "especially in the winter months?"

"Yes, but Mrs Black was not taking an undue risk. Perhaps she may have been taken ill, and that was what caused her to fall," the Rector said.

"Her body was never recovered?"

"No. It is a great misery for the family, but they are staunch believers and consider her one of the Elect. But I have prayed for her and that her remains may be found so she may be laid properly to rest." He shook his head. "Why do you ask? What has this to do with Mrs Gowans?"

"Probably nothing at all," said Giles. "It is simply that if there is an unexplained death, all others within a certain period also need to be examined. It is a matter of routine."

"But there can be no connection, surely?" said the Rector.

Giles did not answer but continued to study the list of deaths for the year.

"No, I do not think so. Miss Henderson in January? What was the cause of that?"

"Old age," said the Rector. He gave a smile. "She was a fine old body! I miss our conversations. She was a very rigorous theologian. It was always stimulating."

"But she was not one of your congregation, Papa."

"By no means. But she was always glad to see me."

"She was not that old," said Carswell.

"Seventy-seven!" said the Rector. "That is a fine age."

"Yes, but there must have been some cause given. She cannot simply have lain down and expired. Did not Hamilton attend her?" Carswell said.

"Yes. But it was an untroubled death. Mr Wallace will tell

you so. He was there at the end. She fell asleep as he read to her from the Psalms. What better death could a good Christian woman ask for?"

"Certainly better than poor Mrs Gowans," Giles said. "Or Mrs Black for that matter."

"Indeed, Major," said the Rector. "Those, in their different ways, are troubling, especially here where usually very little goes amiss with anything. This business with the Murray girls –" He gave a sigh.

"Maggie Shairp has told Major Vernon that Janet Murray had been sent away from school for being a troublemaker," Carswell said. "Did you know that, Papa?"

"No, I did not," the Rector said. "I find it surprising. I do not read her as that type. She is uncommonly intelligent, of course, and that can lead to mischief, but she strikes me as a better sort of soul than that. But perhaps I have misread her. There are forces at work here that I fear are muddying the waters."

"There is certainly a lot of wild talk going about," Carswell said, "which the Major wishes particularly to discourage."

"You do not like when I speak of Satan being among us, do you, Felix?" said the Rector, after a moment.

"I do not like such superstition, no," said Carswell stoutly. "Evil is usually caused by defects in human character, not a horned beast, at least as far as I have observed."

The Rector shook his head at that.

"You do not like what you cannot see," he said, laying his hand on Carswell's shoulder. "It frightens you."

"That is why a microscope is more use to mankind than –" Carswell broke off.

"Yes?" said the Rector. "What would you say? More use than prayers or faith? Yes?"

"Yes, if you insist, sir!" said Carswell. "I cannot see the effects of those upon anything. Whereas, what can be measured, and observed – yes, that is where the truth can be found, and the help mankind so desperately needs. Things that seemed magical once can now be perfectly explained, and so it will be with all things. It is simply a question of time!"

The Rector, his hand still laid on his son's shoulder, shook his head and smiled, and said, "I think not, Felix, I think not." Then he turned back to Giles. "People are afraid, and rightly so."

"What is your opinion of Mrs Haynes?" said Giles. "Some very specific accusations have been made."

There was a silence while the Rector considered the point.

"She is certainly a witch," he said.

"Are we honestly going to speak in such terms?" said Carswell.

"What other terms should I use?" said the Rector. "She is engaged in the practice of witchcraft. I have been told so on several occasions."

"Told?" said Carswell. "You have not witnessed it for yourself, Papa, then?"

"I have no reason to doubt their accounts," he said. "People do not generally peddle untruths to me."

"No, sir, they would not dare, I imagine. But with the greatest respect," Giles said, "there may be embellishment for effect, especially in such a matter. It is very hard to speak of such a subject in a plain manner. It is too controversial."

"You are right, of course, Major Vernon," said the Rector. "What I have been told has been coloured by fear – and with good reason. In a small place such as this, anything out of the ordinary is liable to cause upset. These are honest, God-fearing people, and they are profoundly unsettled."

"By Mrs Haynes?" Giles said.

"Yes. I regret to say she seems to be at the root of it."

"And what have they told you she has been doing?"

"She has been selling spells, love potions, charms and so forth."

"Stupid but harmless," Carswell said.

"That is a matter of opinion," the Rector said.

"No, it is not," said Carswell. "Nothing of that sort can have any efficacy, and anyone who thinks it might deserves to be fleeced of their shillings."

"That is not all of it," the Rector went on. "It is the matter of curses that have disturbed people so. She has been known to suggest the laying of curses in order to settle scores. There was an outbreak of mange in John Watson's flock, which was laid at her door."

"Oh, for goodness sake!" said Carswell. "You cannot seriously believe that she could have caused that? Papa, please, tell me you do not think she sat by her fire roasting little effigies of Watson's tups, and lo –" He broke off and then said, "She must be a very clever woman to get money from someone for that. For that surely was her intention, at the bottom of it? To get money? Then it is fraud, nothing more, nothing less."

"As I understand it," Giles said, "the law was changed at the beginning of the last century to prosecute practitioners of witchcraft on such grounds. It became a civil rather than a religious matter."

"Quite!" said Carswell. "It is a low deception practised on the gullible, but it is not a pact with Satan."

"I would imagine she sees it rather differently," said the Rector. "I think she is quite sincere in her beliefs. And the change in the law is regrettable."

"What!" exclaimed Carswell. "Papa, you are not in earnest, surely?"

"I do not mean we should revert to the barbaric practices of the past," said Mr Carswell. "It is that meddling in this area represents considerable danger and the law should not make light of it. To reduce it to a civil matter –" He shook his head.

Carswell looked as if he were struggling not to speak. Then he threw up his hands, and said, "Please excuse me," and left the room swiftly, but shutting the door behind him with such care it was clear he was attempting not to slam it. The Rector sighed and said, "There is great evil brewing here, Major Vernon, mark my words, and that foolish woman may be at the root of it."

"Mrs Haynes?" Giles said.

The Rector did not reply, for the door opened and Mrs Carswell came in to ask if he would stay for luncheon.

"Lady Charlotte is joining us," she added.

"Thank you, but no, I really must go home," Giles said, feeling that Carswell would be relieved to have her bright conversation to carry them over what might be an awkward meal.

He encountered him just as he was leaving, standing in the lane beyond the Rectory gate, smoking a cheroot. Carswell was about to throw it away on seeing him, a gesture which Giles appreciated.

"Please, not on my account," Giles said.

"Thank you," said Carswell, and turning away, proceeded to take a drag on the cheroot as if his life depended on it. "Excuse me. I could not go on in there without –"

"It is never easy coming home," Giles said. "You should see me with my brother."

"You are only saying that to excuse me. I ought to be able to keep my temper with him. Why anything he says should surprise me, I don't know!"

"It is the familiarity which makes it difficult. To accept that there is a difference of opinion on something so profound when someone is a dear friend or relative is far harder than with a stranger. We want those we love to think always as we do, but unfortunately –"

"They never do!" said Carswell, throwing the cheroot on the ground and extinguishing it with his boot. "I will go and make peace. But what is to be done with all this? Should we go and try to find Donnie Anderson?"

Giles gazed up at the now cloudless blue sky and felt the warmth of the sun on his face.

"Would it be remiss to put the matter aside for the rest of the day?" he said. "Given that the Sheriff-Substitute is coming tomorrow and we are supposed to be on leave? The children have been baying for my attention. Perhaps things will come a little clearer if we take a small step back."

"Not at all remiss," said Carswell. "An excellent plan, in fact!"

So they parted, and Giles made his way back to Mrs McCroy's in the now surprisingly intense sunshine that made the yellow of the final show of daffodils glow fiercely, and seemed to be urging on the hawthorn to burst out in white and pink. There was already the faint hint of the sweetness to come and the buds looked swollen and plump on the branch.

He found Emma in the garden reclining on a rug, supported by a heap of cushions, a parasol carefully placed to keep the sun from her eyes. She was holding a book, but it seemed to be receiving very little attention, and she laid it aside at the sight of him.

"This can't be Scotland in April," he said, pulling off his coat and lying down beside her. "You look like a princess of Persia," he added, reaching for her hand and kissing it. Then he leant a little closer and kissed her on the lips.

"Isn't it wonderful?" she said. "As if May is determined to begin early."

"My favourite month," Giles said.

"April or May?" she said, and smiled. "How do I not know that?"

"May. And why should you?" he said, and kissed her again. "I don't know your favourite month."

"I'm not sure I have one. October, perhaps."

He affected a frown and said, "We shall have to agree to disagree on that."

"Or I could bow to your will, and agree that May is perfect?"

"No, please, please, do not," he said, and kissed her again.

"By all that is sweet and lovely, do not. Oppose me. It is the only way I will ever attain virtue."

She laughed and gently pushed him away.

"We have an observer," she said in a whisper.

Giles turned and saw it was Hamish, his shirt tail hanging out of his breeches and his hair standing up in greasy tufts.

"Have you been in a fight, Hamish?" Giles said, meaning it as joke. A look of misery crossing his face, Hamish turned on his heel and ran away.

"Oh dear," said Emma.

Giles struggled to his feet and went after him. To Hamish's credit he did not persist in his flight and surrendered by the gate.

"It wasn't really a fight and I didn't start it. It was just that they said things and I couldn't –"

"They being?"

"I don't know who they were. There were two of them, and we got talking and they said I was staying at the witch's house, wasn't I? And I said, no because Mrs McCroy isn't a witch, but they said she is, and the worst of all of them. So I said, they shouldn't talk of a lady in such a fashion and they just laughed at me, and said, she wasn't a lady, but she sucked Satan's – I don't like to say it – so I, well –" Giles nodded. "I know I shouldn't but it seemed so wrong that they should say such things about her. I know I should have walked away..." He grimaced and rubbed his arm. "I tried to hit him but he got me by the arm and gave me a burn. But then I managed to get away."

"Nasty," said Giles. "But otherwise no damage done?"

"No, I just got a bit of a kick. I'm sorry, Uncle Giles, I really am. I know that a gentleman ought to keep hold of his temper."

"Yes, quite true, but that was an unpleasant provocation," said Giles. "But you will have a nasty bruise to remind you to keep your counsel in future. Perhaps you should go and get cleaned up – Mrs Patton will have some arnica for your arm."

He went back to the house looking rather miserable, and Giles went back to Emma who had got up from her cushions.

"Is he all right?"

"Just a few bruises."

"Was it the village boys?"

"Yes, they were being vulgar."

"So he started a fight?"

"He was provoked. They insulted Mrs McCroy, in rather graphic terms."

"What a little gallant!" said Emma. "But oh dear, it is not good that he should use his fists."

"That is the least of our worries," said Giles. "He is thoroughly repentant. I do not think we should mention it again. No, it was what was said that is disturbing. Given how universally well regarded she is."

"What did they say?"

"That she was a witch, and worse."

"It sounds like the Murray girls have been exciting the imagination of their schoolmates," Emma said. "And, of course, any woman who has a position of independence will be labelled in such a fashion."

"A minister's widow?" said Giles.

"She is far more than that," said Emma. "Of course foolish, nasty little boys will call her names. How can they see a woman of intelligence and spirit as anything else, when they have been told that women ought to bow their heads and stay silent? They cannot: so they call her a witch."

Chapter Sixteen

"We are asked to drink tea at the Castle after dinner," the Rector said, holding up a letter as he came into the dining room. "In Lord Rothborough's own hand! He has just arrived, I understand." He gave the letter to Felix. "You must convey our apologies."

"Perhaps, dear," Mrs Carswell said, "we might all go. After all, how often does one get the opportunity to see a German prince?"

"You would like to go?" the Rector said.

"Yes," she said. "If you do not object?"

"As you wish, but I will remain here, if you do not mind. I am not made for small talk, as well you know, my dear. Now, let us pray."

After they had eaten dinner, the ladies left them, not to a decanter of port – for the Rector never allowed that – but to finish what wine there was. Eleanor had bolted from the room: in order, Felix suspected, to change her dress.

"What is it about women and royals?" said the Rector.

"It is like going to look at an exotic animal, perhaps," Felix said.

"No, no, it is not that," said the Rector. "Your mother, the most sensible of women, reserves in her heart a place for crowns and diadems that I cannot comprehend. She has at least two biographies of Marie-Antoinette and one of Maria Theresa."

"Then it is her Jacobite ancestry."

"I fear it must be," said the Rector with a sigh. "Make sure she does not stay too late, Felix," he said, getting up from the table. "Late nights always give her headaches."

"Of course," said Felix.

In the circumstances, Felix would happily have stayed at home, but there was no avoiding the excursion. The Rector's reputation was such that he could excuse himself with impunity, but Felix knew he had no such power of veto.

He went upstairs and found Eleanor, Miss King, his mother and Stevens earnestly debating what should be worn. Even his mother had changed her own dress for a festive-looking item in bronze silk. She looked at him and said, "You should change your waistcoat."

"Yes!" exclaimed Eleanor.

It was easier to obey than argue against such forces, and he did as he was told, before going downstairs to wait for them to finish preparing.

In due course, an open landau from the Castle arrived, and then the ladies came downstairs, looking – it had to be conceded – exceedingly fine. Even the Rector, who had come into the hall to see the party off, was moved to say that they had the appearance of angels, and insisted on handing them into the carriage, like a practised gallant. As they drove the mile and a half to the Castle doors, Felix wished he might share their innocent excitement. It would have been unkind to tell them he had already met the Prince and that he considered there to be nothing at all dazzling about him.

However, the Castle did present an adequately festive appearance, with torches set in the drive and forecourt, and a piper playing, as if for some far grander event than drinking tea after dinner.

"A proper show of Highland hospitality," said Mrs Carswell, as they drew up at the door.

In the octagonal entrance hall, where the walls bristled with broadswords and pikestaffs, they found the Vernons, as well as Mr Wallace and his wife. The latter fell upon Mrs Carswell in an excited flutter, and was equally enthusiastic on being presented to everyone else. But then Lord Rothborough appeared, wearing his Highland evening costume, a kilt and a matching jacket, and she was struck dumb, especially when he offered her his arm.

They went into the large drawing room upstairs, where hung the famous Gainsborough portrait of his grandmother. Such was the quality and size of the painting that she seemed, by some effect of the candlelight, to be there with them. She appeared to gaze particularly at Felix, and made him wonder again what she might think of him.

Charlotte was standing to one side of the portrait while the Prince stood on the other, as if they were armorial animals bearing a shield; he the lion, she the unicorn. Of Lady Rothborough and her other daughters there was no sign, and Felix wondered if this meant that some crisis was unfolding off-stage. Lord Rothborough betrayed no distress, but he was of course a practised public dissembler, and in those first few minutes was entirely focussed on the comfort of his guests. Mrs Wallace was carefully installed on a sofa next to Mrs Vernon and Mrs Carswell.

Eleanor and Miss King, their pale silk dresses glowing in the candlelight, walked about the room arm in arm, admiring the large capriccio landscapes that decorated the walls. They then came to rest in front of the sixth Lady Rothborough and gazed up at her with some awe.

"I feel I should curtsey," said Miss King.

"Oh indeed, I do, quite frequently!" said Charlotte, and did so now. "Dear Grandmama! How I wish I could have known her! We have her by Reynolds at Holbroke, of course, but that portrait is nothing to this one."

Felix felt a tug on his sleeve. He looked around to see Maria, who put her finger to her lips and indicated the door before quickly turning and leaving the room. Felix followed and found her waiting across the passageway for him.

"Is this about –?" he began.

"Augusta, yes!" said Maria, taking his arm and leading him

to a more secluded corner. "She is with child, is she not?"

"Have you talked to Charlotte?"

"No, not yet, but it's perfectly obvious! Her maid confirmed it, as much as she dared. She is afraid of losing her place, of course, and is in agony over it. It is wicked of Augusta to make people keep her sordid secrets. And you as well, it seems!"

"She probably regards me in the same light as her maid," Felix said.

"She should not! To get herself in such a condition and then to lie about it."

"In her defence –" Felix began.

"Can anything be said?" said Maria.

Felix hesitated.

"The man is more to blame. He ought not to have allowed such subterfuge."

"I cannot agree. In fact, I thoroughly pity him!" exclaimed Maria. "I imagine all this secrecy is her idea, not his. He must, of course, be in a state of romantic delusion! And as to who he might be – she did not give you any hints?"

"I cannot betray her confidence."

"Did she ask for your confidence as a doctor or as a gentleman?" Maria said.

"Both."

"Perhaps, given the gravity of the situation, you ought wilfully to misinterpret that. As a doctor, of course, you cannot pass on medical details, but who he might be, surely that is nothing to do with it?"

"Yes, I could, ordinarily, but –" He broke off. He could find no way to express the matter without implying she was married. Her husband, as the father of the unborn child, had his rights in the matter. "This business really is intolerable."

"Indeed! How dare she!" said Maria. "Perhaps if we were all to speak to her – Charlotte, you and I – then she would come to her senses."

"Perhaps, but I am not sure what good I can do."

"Later tonight. She will not come down now. She says she is too unwell. You may use that as a pretext to see her. Papa will be glad for you to go and see her, and my mother too, although she is pretending nothing is wrong."

"Do you think she has guessed?"

"I can't say. I've scarcely spoken to her since I got here. She is in a peculiar mood, so perhaps –"

"We should go back in," Felix said.

"Yes, but I can scarcely bear it. Poor Papa. I wish I could tell him at once. I cannot abide keeping this from him." She gave a shudder. "And for Augusta to have put you in this position!"

"It may not be quite as bad as you fear," Felix said, wishing to comfort her. Augusta's right to confidence now seemed to have worn as thin as the silk gauze that trimmed Maria's dress.

She looked at him intently.

"Do you mean she is married?" she said. "Oh, Felix, truly? But who is he?"

"That I don't know," Felix said. He could see from Maria's expression that she was running through various candidates in her mind.

"Charlotte will," she said, and went into the drawing room.

Chapter Seventeen

The Prince demanded music, and as princes were not to be denied anything, Maria went obediently to the piano. Giles suspected this was no chore for her, for she fairly skipped across the room. Neither would it be a chore for the rest of them to have to listen to her playing.

"That air you sang the other day, Lady Charlotte – what was it, now?" said the Prince. "That charming Scottish air."

"Oh, I don't know," said Lady Charlotte.

"But it was delightful! So melancholy. I really insist on a repeat performance. What was it called? Oh, yes: 'There will be no peace till Jamie comes home.'"

"This one?" Lady Maria said, picking out a tune.

"Yes, yes!" said the Prince. "Most spine-tickling."

"Oh, please, Lady Charlotte," said Mrs Carswell senior. "That is one of my favourites."

"Then of course," Lady Charlotte said with a smile, and crossed the room, while Lady Maria made much of the introduction.

Giles had never heard Lady Charlotte sing, and was intrigued to hear what sort of voice she had, compared with that of her sister. She proved to have a sweet, gentle mezzo, not extremely practised, but eminently suitable for such a song. Maria accompanied her with quiet but full chords to show it off to best effect, and Giles had to concede that the Prince had excellent taste in requesting it.

She had just begun the second verse, putting the audience in a pleasant state of anticipation, when Mr Wallace, who was standing near to Giles, side-stepped up to him and said, "I'm not sure I would let my daughter sing such a song, Major Vernon."

Giles tried to form his features into an expression which suggested that he would not engage – indeed, he even turned away a little – but Wallace, clearly the sort of person who thought that music was to be talked through, continued: "Burns cannot be suitable in such company."

Lord Rothborough now turned round and frowned, which ought to have been enough to silence any sensible man, but clearly Wallace was not sensible. Instead he persisted: "Do you not think?"

Giles was obliged to turn to pantomime: he shook his head, held up his hands and moved a few steps away. He sat down, as quietly as he could, so that he could give Lady Charlotte his attention, which in truth was not difficult, for she was now giving full vent to the drama of the song. In fact, she seemed to focus all her attention on him, quite as if he were the only person in the room, which both thrilled and disconcerted him.

She ended on the devastating line: "There will be no peace, till Jamie comes home," and appeared to be on the verge of tears.

There was a silence before the applause, in which Giles felt his pleasure and discomfort grow in equal measure. It obliged him to remember a painful scene that had passed between them: Lady Charlotte stifling her tears and yet speaking her heart. She had offered him a tempting salve when he had been a wounded man. Did she feel such things still, or was he only imagining it out of deep-rooted vanity? For what man would not like to think that he was still the object of such a woman's silent adoration. It was something of a relief when everyone began to clap, and the Prince went up, bowed and took her hand and kissed it.

"Exquisite," he said.

Lady Charlotte pulled her hand away as fast as was decently possibly, and retreated behind her sister and the piano stool.

"Mrs Carswell, Miss King," she said. "You must have a duet for us? There is something about you that makes me think of two warbling birds."

This was an observation with some truth in it. Both ladies were wearing pale feathers and ribbons in their hair, set in the same style and matching their pale dresses. Whether this was by choice or accident, it was impossible to say.

"We might sing the Mountain Bugle," said Mrs Carswell. "Do you have a copy?"

"I'm not sure we do," said Maria, looking through the music.

At this moment, Lady Rothborough made her entrance, accompanied by Lady Augusta. This lady, although she was as handsome and as well-dressed as her sisters, did not look so happy nor so in command of herself. She stood in her mother's wake, listlessly flapping a huge feather fan, and she managed only to return greetings with wan smiles and feeble nods.

"Goodness me," Lady Rothborough said, looking at the assembled company. "Quite the crush, it seems, Rothborough."

"Just our neighbours," said Lord Rothborough. "Now, Mrs Carswell, I think you remember my wife? It was many years ago."

"Yes, of course," said Mrs Carswell senior. "And I am very glad to see you among us looking so well, ma'am – I have heard such distressing reports on the subject of your health."

"Thank you – I am somewhat improved. Not entirely, of course, but that burden I must bear as well as I may. Now, is that your daughter-in-law?"

Mrs Felix Carswell came forward and made a pretty curtsey.

"Let me look at you, child," said Lady Rothborough. "You are the spit of your mother, you know."

"Yes, people often say that," said the younger Mrs Carswell.

"And she is well? I hear she went abroad."

"Yes, she is in France."

"France – why France?" said Lady Rothborough. "Italy, I might understand, but France – well, I for one cannot tolerate it."

"I don't know, my lady," said the younger Mrs Carswell. "I have never been to the Continent. But she is staying with an old friend in Paris."

"And who is this?" Lady Rothborough said, indicating Miss King.

"This is my friend, Miss King. Jenny, may I present Lady Rothborough."

"A great honour, my lady," said Miss King.

"King – now, you must be one of the Wiltshire Kings? You have quite a look of Lady Westercombe about you."

"No, my lady, I'm from Staffordshire. My father was a parson there."

"But who was his father?"

"A clergyman, my lady, in Staffordshire, and his father before him. And before that, tenant farmers I think."

"Tenant farmers?" said Lady Rothborough.

"Oh yes, quite small ones," said Miss King, "and I have some distant cousins who have the same farm still."

"Goodness," said Lady Rothborough. "Then you are lucky in your friendships, Miss King."

"No, I am lucky to have Miss King as my friend," said Mrs Carswell, taking her friend's hand in a rather touching fashion. Naturally, Miss King blushed a little and turned away.

"And this, Mama, is Mrs Vernon," said Maria. "Emma, my mother."

"Very pleased to know you at last, ma'am," Emma said.

Lady Rothborough nodded graciously in response but then began to look around her.

"Where is the card table?" she exclaimed. "Blair, why is the table not set up? See to it at once. It is always to be set up after dinner. Was I not clear on the point?"

"Of course, my lady, it will be seen to at once. In the meantime, I have a gentleman downstairs asking for you, my lady: Lord Dunbar."

"Ah yes! Show him up at once!" said Lady Rothborough. "Augusta, you will partner me. And Dunbar can partner with you, your Highness, yes?"

As Lord Dunbar was announced, Lady Augusta rose from her chair looking pale, and then staggered alarmingly. Emma, who was closest to her, managed to rise and catch her in her arms, but only just, and was struggling for some moments, before Carswell and Giles were able to relieve her of her burden.

"Let's take her out of here," said Carswell, and so they carried her into an adjacent room, where Carswell brought her back to consciousness by means of smelling salts. She stared wildly at them as she came round, and then burst into tears. Lord Rothborough and Emma had come with them, and Carswell yielded his place to Lord Rothborough in order that he might comfort her, but this seemed only to increase her misery.

"Might I?" Emma said, drawing a chair up to the sofa and taking her hand. "Perhaps if you were to leave us for a moment, gentlemen?"

"Of course," said Rothborough, and they left the room. "What is going on, Felix?" he said. "What is wrong with her?"

Carswell was about to answer when they were joined by Maria.

"So?" she said. "Mama says –"

"Go back to our guests, Maria," said Lord Rothborough, "and tell them that Augusta is quite comfortable, and that there is no cause for alarm."

"But –" she began, but he put his finger to his lips, and then waved to dismiss her.

"I'll go with you," Carswell said, but Lord Rothborough caught his sleeve.

"Not yet," he said.

Giles instead went back to the drawing room with Maria. Lady Rothborough received Maria's news with a placid indifference that was painful to observe. Now the card table was set up, she demanded that Lady Charlotte replace Augusta as her partner.

"I'd rather not," said Charlotte. "You know how badly I play."

"I will partner you, Mama," said Maria. Giles knew that Maria hated cards, and that this was a sacrifice made to save her sister from her unwanted suitors.

With typical industriousness, Mrs Carswell had opened her work bag and begun giving her daughter-in-law, Miss King and Mrs Wallace an impromptu lesson in covering tiny pieces of paper with scraps of silk.

"Won't you join us, Lady Charlotte?" said Mrs Carswell.

"Yes, do," said the younger Mrs Carswell, busily threading her needle. "It is utterly enslaving. Once one begins, one cannot stop. These little hexagons are so delightful to make."

"Yes, indeed they are," Mrs Wallace said. "It makes such a change from ordinary needlework. And such beautiful scraps! I never have such lovely scraps. Where do you find them, ma'am?"

"I have many kind friends who send them to me," said Mrs Carswell.

"My eyes are too weak for that, I'm afraid," said Lady Charlotte. "I must get eye-glasses."

"Most sensible," said Mrs Carswell, who had her own glasses perched on her nose. "You will find they make life a great deal easier. Mr Scott in Perth made these for me. His son was at the university with Felix and apparently he is set to be the great man for eyes in the coming years. He is practising in Glasgow now."

"Yes, and getting married," said the younger Mrs Carswell. "Felix has asked me to choose a present for them. It is a difficult thing finding wedding presents for people one has never met, I must say."

"A silver tray," said Mrs Carswell. "One can never go wrong with a silver tray."

Lady Charlotte smiled at that and came to sit by Giles.

"I imagine," she said, "one might acquire quite a few silver trays if one was to attempt matrimony."

"Curiously," said Giles, "we did not. Not a single one. I am sorry about Dunbar," he added, speaking more quietly. "I knew he was here. I should have warned you."

"It does not matter. I knew it anyway – Mama made a point of telling me," said Lady Charlotte. She sighed. "Is there anyone she has not insulted tonight? Is it a sport with her? I fear for her mind sometimes. There is a tendency in her that grows worse and worse..."

"Oh, partner!" Lady Rothborough exclaimed. "Is that the best you can do?"

"I'm sorry, Mama, but –" responded Maria.

"You threw away that queen at your last turn. You should have kept it back."

"I know, I'm sorry, but –"

"Please excuse my partner, gentlemen!" said Lady Rothborough. "She is quite the dunce!"

"Q.E.D.," murmured Lady Charlotte. She got up and went to Mr Wallace. "Perhaps, sir, you might take my sister's place for the next game? All the clergymen I know have the skill of the Devil at whist! It would make my mother very happy to have a good partner."

"I could not possibly, my lady," Wallace said. "I'm surprised to find a card table here, to be frank. And as for other clergymen playing whist – I'm not sure, my lady, what manner of men it is you are acquainted with, but I can assure you no ordained servant of the Kirk would stoop to cards."

"I have never understood what is considered so objectionable about cards," said Giles. "Yes, gambling, that is obviously an evil not to be encouraged, but a game of cards in itself? Why is chess morally acceptable and cards not, for example?"

"Quite," said Lady Charlotte.

"There are wicked associations with playing cards that no true Christian can ever be comfortable with," said Mr Wallace.

"That is most severe, Mr Wallace," said Lady Charlotte.

"Severe or not, it is the truth I strive to live by," he said.

"Perhaps then, Major Vernon, you will rescue her?" Lady Charlotte said.

"Certainly."

Maria looked pleased to find him standing at her place.

"Perhaps you might play for us again?" he said, as she yielded her seat to him.

"I don't care for music while at cards," said Lady Rothborough, shuffling and then dealing the cards. "I hope you like brisk play, Major Vernon."

"Oh dear, my lord," said the Prince to Lord Dunbar. "We shall be in trouble now."

"We shall see," said Dunbar.

"We had better take care, I think!" the Prince said.

Giles looked at his cards, aware of Lady Rothborough's eyes upon him. It was clearly a matter of great importance that she should win. He had no great interest in the game and he was, in fact, struggling to remember the rules. The only card games he played with any pleasure were childish ones with Sophy and Hamish, where their object was merely amusement. If this was amusement for Lady Rothborough, it was of a grave and urgent kind. He feared that she would declare him to be a dunce, and even as they played their first cards, he observed a frown forming on her features. The Prince and Lord Dunbar soon won a trick from them, which provoked a scowl. How strange it was, that this mattered so much to her, he thought, and to be so transparently disagreeable about it! A woman in her position, who could not manage to be gracious in such a trivial defeat, was to be pitied. However, he suspected that would be the last emotion she would have wished to evoke in him.

He had heard more than he wanted about the state of the Rothborough marriage, although Lord Rothborough did not talk a great deal about it. But he had hinted at the misery of it, and Giles now felt it for himself. Unhappiness seemed to seep from her, as surely as her diamonds glittered.

"I hope Lady Maria will play for us later," ventured the Prince, having won another trick. "She has quite the touch. It made me think of a performance by Chopin, when I heard her playing earlier."

"You have heard Chopin play, Your Highness?" Maria said.

"Yes, on several occasions."

"What was he like?" Maria said with enthusiasm. "I should love to hear him play. And that was an utterly outrageous compliment, sir, but I cannot say I do not like it. He is my idol."

The Prince got up from the card table and made her a bow.

"He is worthy of idolatry," he said, laying his hand on his chest. "I feel that myself."

"What did he play?" Maria said.

"On the first occasion –"

"Prince, the cards have been dealt," Lady Rothborough said. "We are waiting."

He turned back to Lady Rothborough, bowed again and said, "Might you indulge us a moment, honoured lady? Chopin is a subject that cannot be put aside, when two devotees come together."

"My understanding of that person," Lady Rothborough said, "is that he is a little Polish nobody who is living openly with a Frenchwoman who writes novels and wears trousers. Hardly a subject for idolatry, I should say."

"They are most entertaining novels," said Lady Charlotte.

"Are we speaking of George Sand?" asked Mr Wallace. "I have heard those books are immoral, and certainly should not be in the hands of any woman, married or unmarried."

"Chopin is not a nobody, Mama," said Lady Maria. "He is a genius, and although his life may be irregular, it cannot diminish the beauty and importance of his work."

"Please, sir," said Lady Rothborough. "The cards are growing cold."

"Of course, madame," said the Prince, and with a comic shrug sat down again. Another round went by, with the Prince and Dunbar once again winning. At this Lady Rothborough grew openly angry, threw down her cards and said, "I think you are all conspiring against me!"

She got up from the table, walked over to Mrs Carswell's sewing party, and stared at it as if it were some exotic exhibit.

"Won't you take a hand, Mrs Wallace?" she said. "The Prince is bored of cards. Come and partner Lord Dunbar."

Having issued this command and obviously not expecting to be refused, she turned away even before Mrs Wallace had begun to speak.

"I'm afraid I may not, Lady Rothborough," said Mrs Wallace. "As my husband says..."

"How extremely tiresome!" said Lady Rothborough. "I never before heard anyone make such a fuss about an innocent game of cards."

"The point is that cards are not innocent," said Mr Wallace.

"Oh, what nonsense!" said Lady Rothborough. "You had better take your wife home, Mr Wallace, if you do not like our habits."

"Indeed, my lady, I shall," Wallace said. "I cannot condone such an example being set to the people of this parish, by those who should know better!"

"Really, sir!" said Lady Rothborough.

"I had heard such excellent reports of your character, my lady, and yet it seems the reality is far short of the reputation!"

"Please excuse us, my lady," said Mrs Wallace. "It is only that my husband has a very strong opinion on this. It makes him quite uncivil. Mr Wallace, perhaps you ought to apologise. It is only cards, after all."

"Quite, ma'am," said Lady Rothborough.

"Only cards?" said Wallace, turning to his wife. "Do I need to tell you what they represent? They are a tool of the Devil and all those who indulge in them are inviting his presence. We cannot safely remain here."

"Then be so good as to leave!" said Lady Rothborough.

They departed, with Mrs Wallace looking mortified.

"What a very irritating young man!" said Lady Rothborough.

"We might play piquet, my lady," said Dunbar, picking up the cards and shuffling them with efficiency. This made her smile, and she sat down at the table again.

"Not a typical evening party in Scotland, I hope?" said the Prince to Giles in a low voice.

Giles shook his head. "It is Mrs Wallace I feel sorry for," he said. "I fear she will get the brunt of his ill humour. Poor woman!"

Chapter Eighteen

It was something of a relief when the evening broke up.

Giles had just seen Emma into their carriage when Dunbar appeared at his side with an enquiring look.

"I think you are going my way, sir, if I might impose?"

Such a request was impossible to refuse, though he would have much preferred to drive back alone with Emma.

"Yes, of course," he said, getting in and sitting down beside Emma. He expected the Earl to follow at once, but he did not. Giles glanced out through the still-open door and saw that one of the maids had detained him. She handed him a note and then ran away. This letter went straight into Dunbar's pocket.

Giles sat back and got an enquiring glance from Emma but was not able to answer, because now Dunbar climbed in.

"Very kind of you, ma'am, sir," he said, nodding to each.

A conversation of a bland and inconsequential kind was then attempted as the carriage made its way down the avenue towards Pitfeldry. Dunbar was put down at The Brodie Arms and they were alone again.

"The woman who gave him that note," Emma said, "was Lady Augusta's maid."

"You saw that?"

"Yes. Curious, isn't it?"

"Very," said Giles.

Emma went on: "If Augusta is in an interesting condition, as they say, and which I strongly suspect she is, one must look around for the rogue responsible."

"She did not admit that to you directly?" said Giles.

"No, but she knew what I was thinking. Nothing needed

to be said. I take it that Mr Carswell has formed a more professional opinion on the matter?"

"He has not said so directly, but yes, I suspect it was the conclusion he made."

"The sooner it all comes out the better," said Emma. "Goodness, I was biting my tongue just then! I'm surprised it is not bleeding."

"Why on earth would he play such a risky game? I would have thought he had more sense. But then, that business with the wine at the inn – he obviously takes some pleasure in risk."

"It's entirely consistent with what I have heard of him. Maria has always said that money was a great difficulty with him. One of the difficulties, that is. Apparently he has a reasonable competence, but he is unpleasantly greedy – and I understand he has a nest of younger siblings who need to be provided for. So if he could not get Charlotte, I suppose he turned to Augusta. She is worth at least ten thousand a year, is she not? I believe that most of Lady Rothborough's properties will be hers, in time."

"Only if Lady Rothborough chooses it," said Giles. "Rothborough has told me that her settlements were drawn up in such a way that she has that discretion."

"How unusual," said Emma.

"It is. But there is some justice in it, you'd agree?"

"Yes," said Emma. "It ought be the general state of affairs. But it gives her a great deal of responsibility – perhaps too much, given her character. She has made Maria's life a misery with her threats. And this business will not curry favour, will it? Yes, you are right, it is royally foolish of them. Is it too much to hope that it is genuine affection between them that has brought this to pass? A moment of folly, born out of better feelings?"

"One must hope so, for both their sakes. If he is responsible, he will have to marry her," Giles said.

The carriage drew to an unexpected halt. Giles had just

put down the window when Jock, the coachman, appeared.

"We thought we heard screaming, sir," Jock said, and then Giles heard it as well: a miserable, low howl, pitiful and full of pain. "That."

"Where is it coming from?" Giles said, climbing out of the carriage.

"That way –" said Emma, pointing through the open door.

She gave a shudder as the howl began again, and Giles found himself thinking of the marks on Bel Gowans' neck, and Carswell's interpretation of them.

"Shall we go and see?" she said.

"You wait here," he said. "Jock, do you have a lantern?"

"Aye, sir, I'll just get one."

"Call me at once, if you need me," Emma said.

So Giles set off with Jock down a tree-lined lane, until they reached the gates of the churchyard, which were standing open.

At the far end of the churchyard, at the entrance to the church, Giles could just see a woman standing, her back pressed to the wall of the church, with her hands raised. Seeing them she howled again.

"Help!"

Giles now ran down the path. The woman was Effie Haynes, and he realised that she was chained to the church wall by means of a massive iron neck ring and a pair of manacles on long chains.

"Help me!" she screamed again.

"The jougs," said Jock, coming up behind Giles. "She's in the blessed jougs –"

"Now, hold still, Mrs Haynes, and I will see what can be done. Hold your lantern up there, will you, Jock?" Giles said, getting close to her so he could examine the locks. She stank of vomit and whisky, and her hair was falling down all over the collar. He pushed her hair aside as gently as he could, and saw that her neck was raw and bloody from the chafing of the ancient, rusty metal. The collar was fastened with a crude bolt that in turn had been fixed with a more modern padlock, which was a relief, as the lock appeared to be a simple one and easily loosened. He did not have his lock-picking tools with him, but Mrs Haynes had a sturdy brooch fixed to her bodice, the pin of which might suffice. "May I?" he said, unfixing it. She flinched as he did so, clearly afraid even of her rescuers.

He set to work and after some struggles managed to open the padlock and draw back the bolt in order to release her from the collar. She gave a cry of relief and fell forward into his arms, helpless still because of the irons on her wrists. These were a greater labour to release. He was obliged to get Jock to support her as he worked on each in turn, and in releasing the final one, he snapped the brooch pin.

She was scarcely conscious by the time they got her back to the carriage.

"Shall we take her back with us?" said Emma, as she helped him get safely into the carriage.

"Carswell should look at her. Drive to the Rectory, will you, Jock?"

~

"The jougs are an old Scottish version of the stocks," said Felix. "Utterly barbaric, and why they were still hanging on the kirk wall, I don't know. I have always wondered why they were there. Why preserve an instrument of torture?"

"As a warning," said Major Vernon. "Jock said that his father used to threaten him with them if he misbehaved."

"Oh, wondrous!" said Felix. "A handy means of threatening innocent children, and now –" He sighed. "There has always been a rough edge to people here, that's true enough, but now it seems to have grown entirely out of hand."

"Fear and illicit whisky will be at the root of this," said Major Vernon. "The desire to find a scapegoat for the inexplicable. At least she is safe and comfortable now."

This conversation was taking place outside one of the servants' bedrooms at the Rectory, where Effie Haynes was now asleep. She had vomited several times on the kitchen floor and then passed out again, which had at least allowed Felix to clean and dress her wounds.

"As much as anyone who has taken that much liquor can be," said Felix. "I'm not sure when we will be able to get a lucid account from her, if ever."

"With luck someone will have seen something," Major Vernon said, "and be anxious to tell me about it. But I think it can wait until tomorrow. I don't know about you, but I should like to go to bed. It has been quite an interesting evening, all in all."

"That's an understatement," said Felix, as they went downstairs. "I take it Mrs Vernon has guessed what is wrong with Lady Augusta?"

"She has a theory, yes."

"She has put us all in a wretched position," said Felix. "Lady Augusta, I mean."

"It will all come out, soon enough," said Major Vernon.

"I hope so. How will you get home?" Felix asked, for Mrs Vernon had gone back in the carriage earlier.

"I'll walk," he said. "Who knows what I may find."

"Nothing, I hope," said Felix.

He saw him to the gate and then went back into the house. His father was still in his study, but the women had all gone to bed. He exchanged a few words with the Rector and then went upstairs himself.

He stood in the doorway a moment, his attention caught by the scene that met his eyes. On the sofa at the foot of the bed, Miss King was lying with her head in Eleanor's lap, having her hair combed out. There was something so intimate about this scene that he felt he must announce himself.

"Excuse me!" he said.

Miss King started up, blushing furiously.

"No, no, excuse me," she said, and hurried out of the room.

"It is the wind here, it tangles her hair," Eleanor said, getting up and putting the comb on the dressing table.

Her own hair was down, and from its glossy smoothness, had the look of also having been carefully combed. She stood in front of the glass, looking at herself, and Felix came up behind her and could not resist placing his hands on her bare shoulders. She shuddered a little at his touch and then turned around to look at him, with a smile.

"She's lucky to have such a friend," Felix said, pulling her against him now. "Perhaps you'd comb my hair one day?"

"If you are good," she said, breaking away from him. She went and climbed into bed. "How is that woman? Will she be all right?"

"I think so," said Felix, and began to undress.

He felt decidedly stirred up now and wondered what sort of reception his overtures might receive. There was something about her flushed complexion and the way she was sitting in bed waiting for him that reminded him of the early days of their marriage.

"Was it done because people think she is a witch?" she asked.

"She seems to have that reputation."

"If she is a witch," Eleanor said, "can she be put in prison for it?"

"Yes, because she would be selling false claims. It would be a sort of fraud."

He put on his nightshirt and got into bed.

"No, but if she really was a witch," Eleanor said. "If she could really do magic, for example?"

"But she cannot. Nobody can."

"You don't know that. You are always saying, after all, that there are still so many things to be discovered. Perhaps magic might be one of those things – perhaps it might be found to be real. I think I should like it to be real. A witch – it is such a powerful notion!"

"Yes, that's true enough," he said, thinking of Janet Murray and her convictions. "It seems to seduce people."

"I think," said Eleanor, lying down in rather a provocative pose, "I should like to fly across the glen on a broom handle."

"And dance about the meadows in your shift?"

"You would like to see that?" she said, in such a fashion that the only answer he could give was to kiss her. "I can imagine you stealing up to watch us all dancing in our cutty sarks."

She giggled with pleasure as he pushed up her shift and stroked her thighs.

"There's a regular coven, is there?" he said.

"I couldn't possibly say," she said, but the titillating image was now lodged in his mind, of Eleanor and perhaps Miss King, and quite a few other young ladies, "*queans, A' plump and strapping in their teens, Their sarks, instead o' creeshie flannen, Been snaw-white seventeen hunder linnen!*" – all dancing reels with abandon. Unlike the poet, however, Felix had no need to dispose of his breeks, being already in bed and wearing his nightshirt, so matters rapidly progressed to an energetic and enjoyable conclusion.

Felix lay back, a little astonished at what had happened. Eleanor lay in his arms, having wilted with pleasure. It was delicious to have her pressed against him in that state, feeling himself that extraordinary languor. It scarcely crossed his mind to worry about the consequences. Perhaps there was something to be said for witchcraft, after all.

Chapter Nineteen

Arriving at the Rectory early the next morning, Giles found Miss King in the garden. She was pacing the terrace, wrapped in several shawls, for it was still cool and damp. She appeared to be in a state of agitation, and started at the sight of him.

"Is everything all right, Miss King?" he said.

"It's nothing, Major, really," she said, hurrying towards the door. "I'm just a restless soul. Mr Carswell is with Mrs Haynes. Poor creature. Do you have any idea who did that to her?"

"I have a few ideas," Giles said, "but I feel at a disadvantage without local knowledge."

"It is beyond belief," she went on. "When Mr Wallace showed us that awful thing the other day, I could not have thought it would be used by someone in earnest."

"The other day?" Giles said. "When was this exactly, if you don't mind me asking?"

"It was on Tuesday," she said. "He gave us quite an extensive tour of the church."

"You don't remember how they were fastened? Or indeed if they were fastened?"

"They were locked shut. There was a padlock. Mr Wallace said he had put it there to stop children meddling with it."

"Thank you," he said. "That's useful to know."

"Then I suppose it is a question of who had a key," she said.

"Exactly. I shall have to see if Mr Wallace still has it."

Carswell met them in the hall and took him into the Rector's study. Here, Effie Haynes, her throat swathed in bandages, was sitting on a low chair by the fire. Amadeus was leaning against her and allowing her to caress him, which she did extravagantly, murmuring to him. She glanced up warily as Giles came in.

"How are you feeling, Mrs Haynes?" Giles asked, taking the chair opposite. He suspected that this hard, upright article was the favoured perch of the Rector when advising a parishioner. It made him feel like an interloper.

"Well enough," she said. Her voice was painfully hoarse.

"Can you tell me who did this to you?" he said, thinking it was best to get to the point.

She shook her head.

"Can you remember nothing about them?"

"I ken fine who it was," she said, "but there's no point telling you."

"There is every reason," he said. "They should be charged with assault. Do you not want them punished?" She shook her head. "Even if you will not tell us," said Giles, "it will be easy enough to find them. I suspect Mr Murray had a hand in this."

As he spoke, he snapped his fingers at Amadeus, who obligingly came to him.

"I wouldn't know."

"An angry father looking for someone to blame for his daughter's troubles?" She did not answer, but looked into the fire. "There is no justification in what has been done to you, Effie," Giles said. "This is not something to be suffered in silence. Please tell me who was responsible so that they can be punished for it."

She shuffled in her chair and pressed one of her bandaged wrists to her mouth, as if she meant to gnaw at the dressing. Then after a long silence she said, almost imperceptibly, "They did what they had to do."

"Who did?"

"Murray, and –"

"Yes?"

"And Gowans, and Angus Lowndie." She choked out the

names. "Oh, God help me! My own flesh and blood. My own sister..."

"Mrs Haynes, what you are saying?" Giles said.

She composed herself and said, "It was because... because I killed her. That was why they did it."

"Because you killed her?" Giles said. "Who did you kill?"

"Bel," she said. "I killed Bel."

"Let us start at the beginning," said Giles, reaching for his notebook. "You said to us that she left you on good terms, that you had settled your differences."

"Aye, but when she had gone, I fell to thinking and it was too much for me. I was still angry wi' her, I made up the fire and went to work."

"Went to work? What do you mean?"

"I asked him to do her harm," she said.

"Him?" Giles frowned.

"Lord Satan," she said.

"Do you mean to say you summoned the Devil to do her harm?"

"Yes. I put a wee doll with a scrap of silk about its neck and called it by her name. Then I set it on a pan over the fire and told him to hurt her."

She said this with a bald sincerity that was astonishing. Carswell, who had been standing by the door, came and sat down.

"And then what happened?" Giles said.

"I felt something. I felt in my bones that she was in pain. And then I knew that I'd gone too far. So I drew the pan off the fire and ran out. Then I found her in the ditch by the path, lying dead!" She howled: "I didn't mean to kill her, I swear it. I didn't mean her to die of it!"

"Tell me how you found her."

"She was lying on her back, staring up to heaven! So I turned her and put the stones on her back. At least then the beasts wouldn't eat her."

Giles glanced at Carswell to gauge his reaction. He was shaking his head in disbelief. Then the door opened and the Rector came in with Mr Finlay, the Sheriff-Substitute, who had just arrived.

~

After some discussion they decided that Effie Haynes should be removed to the Infirmary at Perth Gaol, pending further investigations and for her own safety. When asked if she wished to repeat what she had just confessed to the Sheriff-Substitute, she agreed to do so, and told him exactly what she had told them earlier.

"Is it possible," Mr Finlay said, when they were alone, "that this is a partial truth she is telling us? That she had some actual as opposed to supernatural hand in Mrs Gowans' murder? Is that consistent with what you have observed so far, gentlemen?"

"It is certainly physically possible that she could have done it," Felix said. "She has the strength, and she was in the right place at the right time."

"Her admission that she turned the body and put the stones in place suggests she was present, very close to the time of death," said Major Vernon. "But as to her being directly responsible – I am not convinced. There is the matter of the slashed petticoats."

"I think I may have missed that detail," said the Mr Finlay, consulting his notes.

"It is in my post-mortem report," said Felix, finding the passage for him. Mr Finlay read it and frowned.

"That is certainly curious," he said. "In the meantime, I had better see to the arrangements for her removal. I think that would be the best for all concerned. I suspect, after further questioning, Sergeant Gibson and his constables will discover who was responsible for last night's atrocity. Such cases are usually cleared up easily. There is always a boastful individual only too happy to tell all the evil he has done, wouldn't you agree, Major Vernon?"

"That is certainly a common enough type," Major Vernon said.

"Yes, indeed! And now, you gentlemen ought to be allowed to enjoy your holiday. Your assistance has been invaluable," he said, indicating the reports that they had submitted to him. "I cannot thank you enough! But I'm afraid that I must assume my responsibility and absolve you of yours."

"With pleasure," said Major Vernon.

"Truly?" said Felix when they had left Mr Finlay and gone into the hall. "You are happy to relinquish this to him?"

"What else can we do," said the Major, "other than let things unravel as they may? We have done what we could, and perhaps in this case that is quite enough."

"I can scarcely believe you said that," said Felix, opening the door to the drawing room.

They found Eleanor and Miss King sitting together on a sofa. Miss King had a book in her hand, and was reading aloud.

> At first, an azure sheet, it rushes broad;
> Then whitening by degrees, as prone it falls,
> And from the loud-resounding rocks below,
> Dash'd in a cloud of foam, it sends aloft
> A hoary mist, and forms a ceaseless shower.
> Nor can the tortured wave here find repose...

"That's rather fine. What is that?" the Major said.

"James Thomson," said Miss King.

"And marvellously appropriate, given what I am about to propose: an expedition to the Falls of Iolair-bhu..." He stumbled over the Gaelic, and said, "No, I cannot say it. An expedition to the Spouts?"

"Iolair-bhuidhe," said Felix.

"Oh yes, yes, I'm longing to see them again," said Eleanor. "When shall we go?"

"How long does it take to get there?" said Major Vernon.

"Oh, it's no distance," said Eleanor. "At least it did not feel that way. If one goes on horseback, an hour at most, yes, Felix?"

"Yes," Felix said, not entirely sure what to make of the Major's determination to relinquish the case and pursue his own pleasure. "An hour and a half, really."

"Then tomorrow, perhaps?" said the Major. "If we leave after breakfast that should give us sufficient time. Now, should we find a guide, Carswell, or do you know the way well enough?"

"I could guide us," said Eleanor. "I have only been that way once, but I swear I remember every step. It was exquisite!"

"Then we will be in good hands," said Major Vernon, smiling.

The arrangements for the expedition perfected, Major Vernon took his leave. Felix escorted him to the garden gate.

"Are you sure that we ought to be leaving matters as they are?" Felix said. "There is so much that is unsatisfactory. And after what happened last night –"

"Sometimes, we have to be seen to remove ourselves from the fray," said Major Vernon.

"What is your theory, then?" Felix said. "You have a theory?"

"No," said Major Vernon. "Not yet. But I do know that we ought to take a step back, if only for a while. I want to take a breath and watch from the sides. This is not my country and I feel as if I scarcely understand anything. There is something dark and dangerous here, and it needs to be approached with caution."

"You do have a theory," Felix said.

"No," the Major said again. "Emphatically not. At least not about Mrs Gowans. But there is another matter I wanted to talk to you about: Dunbar."

"What about him?"

"Do you know if he visited Lady Rothborough in Florence?"

"Yes, he came to see Lady Charlotte, although of course she did not wish to see him. Why do you ask?"

"Just as we were leaving last night, Mrs Vernon and I saw him take a letter from Lady Augusta's maid. I'm in several minds as to what to do with this information."

"You are assuming she was acting as a postman rather than communicating on her own behalf?" Felix said.

"Yes," said Major Vernon. "That would put a few minds at rest, but I think not, given Lady Augusta's predicament."

"She told me she was married," said Felix. "But why on earth would she marry him? Especially after all that happened with Charlotte."

"Perhaps she took advantage of the rejection, and he saw the advantages of transferring his affections to the second sister. She stands to inherit her mother's fortune, does she not?"

"I don't know," said Felix. "We must tell Lord Rothborough. If she will not, then –"

"This is all speculation, of course," said Major Vernon.

"It sounds entirely plausible to me," said Felix, "from what I have heard of Dunbar. This must be why Charlotte would not have him. She found him out, but presumably Augusta is too stupid..." He sighed. "I should not say that of her, but she is quite impossible! And I ought, by rights, to go and see her again today."

"Surely you do not have to go unless she calls for you?" said Major Vernon. "Given she was well enough when you left her?"

"I don't know. If this is Lord Rothborough's first grandchild, then –" He gave a nervous laugh. "It's a pity no medical man could be persuaded to set up a practice here, then I would not be obliged to see to her. The elders should sack the minister and install a doctor in that manse, if they had any sense! Yes, that would be an excellent thing, if every Church of Scotland minister were to be replaced with a medical man."

"You exempt your father's denomination from this revolution?"

"Yes, certainly. I may not see the world quite as he does," Felix said, "but I know the good he does. It is real, practical good. He calmed that girl Janet Murray when I could not, and I have seen him with people who have suffered great loss, and it has been quite extraordinary to see how he helped them. Your brother-in-law has that gift too. If a priesthood is to mean anything, surely it must be that – to be of real use to ordinary people! Not to preach at them but to comfort them. That Wallace fellow! I hear he was quite objectionable last night."

"Shall we say, he seems to lack social resources. Which reminds me: Miss King said an interesting thing to me earlier," the Major said, "about the jougs. Wallace gave them a tour of the church and explained their purpose to them. He told them he had put the padlock on them to stop the local children meddling with them. So he must have the key. I wonder whether it is still in his possession, or is that even the question we should be asking? After all, it would only require it to be left unlocked for it to be put into use. You do not need the key to lock it."

"Are you suggesting that he might have left it open deliberately in order to encourage their use? I do not like the man, but I can't quite imagine that of him. And how is this stepping back from the fray?"

Major Vernon would have answered, but at this moment a figure on horseback loomed into view on the far side of the garden wall. It was the Prince. After the usual greetings had been exchanged, Major Vernon took his leave, and watching him set off, Felix wondered if he would make a detour by way of the Manse to discuss the matter of the padlock with Mr Wallace. It did seem scarcely credible that the Major intended to leave matters as they were. His terrier instincts were too strong for that.

"I have come in search of gamboge!" the Prince announced, with a flourish of his feathered hat. "Oh, and to pay my respects to your delightful ladies, Mr Carswell."

"Do you mean the paint colour, sir?" said Felix.

"Yes, I have none left, and the Rothborough ladies have none, and I wondered if I might discover some here."

"I have some," said Felix.

"You paint, Mr Carswell?" said the Prince.

"I draw for my work, and sometimes it helps to colour an illustration, when preparing reports and so forth."

"Then, I am in the luck! May I beg some from you, sir? I am anxious to take advantage of this glorious weather. I understand it never lasts long."

"That's true enough," said Felix. "Yes, of course. And if I have none left, I know my wife has a watercolour box that she never touches. Please come in."

He felt that keeping the Prince away from Lady Charlotte was a useful service he could render her.

Eleanor, Miss King and his mother were delighted by the Prince's appearance in the drawing room, and Felix left them in order to attend to Effie Haynes' departure. He wrote some instructions for her care, and entrusting her to the constable, could only hope that the nurses at Perth Goal had some pity and understanding. He was still puzzled about her motives, indeed by her entire system of belief. He was inclined to suggest she should be committed to an asylum for the insane. But then most of the world would have to follow her, for if such sincere belief in the impossible meant insanity, then most of the world was deranged. This conclusion depressed him, as it always did, for he often felt he was the aberrant one for being unable to see beyond the material world. He was never able to lift the veil into that other realm where gods, angels, demons and other strange entities lived – beings which were, it seemed to most people, as real as their dining tables and the joints of mutton set upon them.

Mr Finlay and the constables having departed, along with their prisoner, the Rector withdrew into his study, demanding no more interruptions for the day, as he had his sermon to write. Felix went back to the drawing room and found his mother sewing. She informed him that the Prince and Eleanor had gone into the garden for a watercolour lesson.

"How on earth did he persuade her to do that?" Felix said. "She has absolutely no interest in it."

"He said he had some tricks to show her," said Mrs Carswell. "It was slightly surprising. Not to speak ill of Eleanor, but I would have thought Miss King might be a more receptive pupil. She has a definite talent with her pencil. She showed me the portrait she has painted of Eleanor. It is a lovely thing, don't you think?"

"I don't know," Felix said. "She has not shown it to me."

"I suppose she is worried that a husband's eye might be too critical. But she ought not to be afraid of that, as it is charming and I know you will like it. It captures her character so well."

"Where is Miss King?"

"She went upstairs to write her letters."

Felix went to the window to observe the painting lesson. Eleanor was standing at an easel, well placed to observe the view of the Glen, while the Prince was making up colours for her.

"I suppose no one ever dares say no to a prince," he said.

"You don't mind it?" said Mrs Carswell. "I did wonder for a moment if I ought – I thought Miss King would stay with them, you see."

"I wish him joy," said Felix. "He might make a painter of her yet."

"Ah, there is the post," said Mrs Carswell, hearing the door.

"I'll fetch it," said Felix.

There was a clutch of letters to be distributed: two for his father, four for his mother, who kept up a most extensive correspondence, one for Eleanor and two for himself. Miss King also had two, so he went upstairs and tapped on her door.

"Miss King, I have your letters."

She came to the door after a moment, handkerchief in hand.

"Thank you," she said, taking them. She looked as if she had been crying.

"Are you all right?" Felix said.

"Oh, it's nothing," she said, with a forced smile. "Thank you for these," she added.

"Are you sure? Shall I get my mother?" he said.

"It is nothing," she said, laying her hand on his arm for a moment. "You are really too kind, Mr Carswell."

"I hope those are good letters," he said.

"I doubt it," she said, and then glanced away. "Oh dear. One ought to be grateful for letters of whatever sort."

"Even bills?" he said.

"Perhaps not bills," she said. "Thank you. If you will excuse me."

"Of course."

She shut the door gently, and Felix, his own letters in his pocket – one of which he suspected was a bill he had overlooked – went down the passageway to his old bedroom. He had been using it as a dressing room and study and it remained shabby and familiar, as yet untouched by Mr and Mrs Carswell's surprising fever for decorating. He found a paper knife and went to the window to raise the blind so he could read his letters. From the window he had a good view of the painting lesson in the garden below. Eleanor was laughing and waving her paintbrush about wildly, while the Prince was wagging his finger at her, playing the stern schoolmaster. There were abandoned sketches thrown on the grass, and the Prince was laughing now, as if he could not keep up the scolding, especially when Eleanor grabbed one of the papers from the grass and began to rip it up.

He watched and tried to gauge his feelings in respect of this little pantomime. His mother had wondered if he minded it, and he found he did not. Eleanor was only being Eleanor – a bright flower, sweet with nectar. Just as the bees were now hunting out the pale blossoms in the apple trees, so men would be drawn to her. It was a fact of nature, but he knew that she reserved her ultimate ardour for him. Last night had proved that amply enough.

Chapter Twenty

Giles walked back towards Mrs McCroy's, wondering if he had made the right decision. He was concerned about Emma and the children. He was painfully aware he was neglecting them for the case. It was not fair to abandon them out of self-love, for that was all it was, in essence: an arrogant belief that he, of all of them, could solve the matter of Mrs Gowans' death. He was not indispensable to the forces of justice, nor was he irreplaceable. Another competent man could take on the task, and, with local knowledge, he might get to the heart of the matter far quicker. It was ridiculous in operational terms to imagine he could not replaced. After all, he had made a point of encouraging his subordinates to learn the craft.

On this occasion it was better to walk away. His duty was with his wife and children. But the chase was so tempting, and he felt it keenly as he walked past the gates to the churchyard, and glanced in and saw the jougs hanging there. The Manse was only a little way off. It would only be a moment's work to call and ask about that padlock. However, he managed to keep to the path, and continued back to Mrs McCroy's.

He was rewarded by the sight of one of the Rothborough carriages drawn up outside the house, with Hamish perched on the driver's seat next to Jock. They were deep in conversation of an equine kind and Hamish was being shown how to hold the reins and the whip.

Seeing Giles, Hamish said, "May I take them out, Uncle Giles? Lord Rothborough said I might, but only if you agreed to it."

"I shan't let him go far or fast, sir," said Jock. "And this is a very placid team."

"Your aunt does not object?"

"No, sir," said Hamish. "So may I?"

"Then yes. You won't get a better teacher, so mind you do exactly what you are told. It's a fine opportunity for you. Thank you, Jock."

The coachman nodded in response and the lesson began, with Hamish looking as if he were on the verge of driving to Heaven itself.

Giles went into the house and found the owner of the horses, Lord Rothborough, along with ladies Charlotte and Maria in the drawing room with Emma.

"You let him go, then?" said Emma.

"I can't think of a safer pair of hands," said Giles. "I was tempted to go myself. I might have learnt a trick or two."

"Jock taught us all to drive," said Lady Charlotte. "He will have to take Miss Sophy out."

"Certainly," said Emma. "It is an indispensable skill for a woman, but I think we will wait until Hamish has got into his stride. He will not like a younger sibling getting such a privilege before him. Children are extremely – now, what is the word, litigious? – about such things, and I do not want him resenting her."

"Oh, quite," said Maria. "Sir Mark's nephews are just the same. It is so vexing! I suppose we were as bad, Papa?"

"Somewhat," said Lord Rothborough. "When I gave you that pearl necklace before your appointed time, Augusta was not pleased. Oh dear," he went on, frowning at the memory. "Poor creature. How wretched she was about such a trifle! She was always so unsettled, so unhappy, and now this –"

"Have we all drawn the same conclusion about this matter?" Giles said.

Lord Rothborough nodded.

"I have told him about Dunbar and that letter," said Emma.

"I shall have to go and see what he has to say for himself," said Lord Rothborough.

"You should horsewhip him, Papa," said Lady Charlotte. "That is the least he deserves. I'd be happy to do it myself."

"Tempting though that may be – especially for you, my dear – I fear that it would not do us any good," Rothborough said.

"No, because he is a wily devil and will make us look the wicked party in this," Lady Charlotte said. "That is how he has been all along! I told mama that I did not want him in the house in Florence, but she would not listen. And what has he done? He has gone like a snake after the weakest of us! For her fortune, I am sure. He cannot love her. He is incapable of affection of any sort. And now he has got himself into this family with this appalling behaviour, and we will have to accept it, as if it were intended! And Augusta is no better – to allow herself to be persuaded into a secret marriage – how feeble minded! How utterly shameful! We will be a laughing stock!"

"Only if the facts become known," said Lord Rothborough. "It needs to be put about that Lady Rothborough and I have known all along and that the match was approved before it was made. We shall say it has not been publicised for some other entirely innocent reason."

"Then we may as well lie down and allow him to rule us all, Papa. Why should his wickedness be rewarded? You must take the strongest of lines with him. You do not know him as I do! Oh dear God, my poor sister. To be married to him! She will never be happy. Cannot it be annulled?"

"Not with a child on the way," said Rothborough.

"I wonder if their marriage is even legal," Lady Charlotte went on.

"I have been wondering how they contrived it," said Maria. "There are plenty of impoverished clergymen in Florence who would no doubt do the deed for ready money."

"That might not be enough to make it legal," Giles said. "I am not entirely au fait with marriage law, but –"

"A fake secret marriage," said Rothborough. "Dear Lord. Yes, you are right, Vernon, that end of it may be extremely slippery."

"I'm sorry to point it out," said Giles.

"If it is fake, then we will have to get them married again, and as soon as possible," Lord Rothborough said. "And then send them to the country for a twelve month. Perhaps to Montrose."

"Oh, Papa, that would be very cruel," said Maria. "That is a miserable house. Augusta hates it! There is not a warm corner in it."

"It would be as much as they deserve," Charlotte said. "Yes, keep him out of town and make Lord Standish dismiss him from his post, Papa, that is what you should do. That will really hurt him."

"That would hurt me too," said Lord Rothborough. "I'm in no position to ask Standish for favours, unfortunately. Nor would Standish do it, I fear. He is too lazy to do without Dunbar these days. Yes, Dunbar may be a scoundrel, but he will have to be made into a useful scoundrel." He got up from his chair. "Now, I shall go and see what he has to say for himself. We are dealing with too many suppositions and accusations here. He needs to be allowed to say his part before we go any further with this. It may be that we have the facts entirely wrong."

"I doubt that very much," said Lady Charlotte. "I shall come with you, Papa."

"No, no," said Lord Rothborough. "You are still too hot by half."

Giles showed him to the door.

"Whether I can be cool, of course," Rothborough said when they were in the hall together, "remains to be seen. Have you any hints for me? I feel a direct attack will do no good."

"No, certainly," Giles said. "And I am not sure I can tell you anything that you do not already know. All I can say is, it's a matter of showing you are armed and at the same time concealing your weapon. And of course, the last thing you want to do in this situation is make a false accusation. I suspect you do have your man in Dunbar, but there is always the risk you may be wrong."

"I'm tempted to be a coward and ask you to sound him out, but this is a duty I cannot shirk. My poor girl and her foolish heart! I blame myself entirely for this. I have been a poor father to her and I do not know how I shall begin to mend this."

When Lord Rothborough had gone, Giles was about to return to the ladies, when Sandro came toddling down the hall loudly demanding his attention.

"I'm sorry, sir," said Greene, coming after him. "He would not stay in the room a minute longer, hearing your voice."

"That's all right," said Giles, lifting him into his arms and enjoying the warmth of his small, sturdy form pressed against him. "How now, Sandro? How goes the day?"

"Soldiers!" said Sandro. "Play me!"

"I'm not sure I may, just now," Giles said. "Let us ask the ladies first."

Giles carried him back into the drawing room. Lady Charlotte was standing in the window, while Emma and Maria were on the sofa.

"I don't think you have met this one, Lady Charlotte," Emma said. "This is Alexander."

"Sandro to his friends," said Giles.

"How do you do, Sandro? What a handsome young fellow you are," said Lady Charlotte, shaking his hand.

"Play me?" said Sandro, ever the opportunist, and wriggling in Giles' arms.

"May I?" said Lady Charlotte, gesturing to take him. Giles hesitated to consent, fearful that Sandro might explode with displeasure, but to his surprise Lady Charlotte had the measure of him, and he submitted with smiles.

"What shall we play, then?" she said.

"Are you sure, Lady Charlotte?" Emma said.

"Of course," said Lady Charlotte.

"I think we had better go into the dining room," said Giles, knowing that Emma and Maria would be happy to be left to talk in private.

"Soldiers!" said Sandro, as they left.

The soldiers were nothing but a battered set of ninepins that had come from the Ffordes. Sandro had turned them into his regiment when Sophy had painted faces on them. Sandro liked them neatly lined up for inspection, and then he would topple them each in turn as if they did not meet his exacting standards.

"He is a general in miniature," said Lady Charlotte, who was happy to get down on the floor and assist him.

"Where is Sophy, Greene?" Giles asked.

"She went out with Mrs McCroy," said Greene. "They are so fond of each other, sir, it's quite a thing to see. Mrs Patton and I were wondering if she had had a little girl of her own and lost her."

"I hope not," said Giles.

"If you are quite happy with Master Sandro, sir, I will go and have a cup of tea, if I may?"

He dismissed her and got down on the floor with Lady Charlotte and Sandro.

"They need names. Do they have names?" she said.

"This one has a name," said Giles. "This is Sergeant Magpie."

"That is an excellent name," said Lady Charlotte, picking up the ninepin and offering it to Sandro. "Sergeant Magpie, at your service, sir!"

Sandro took it and hugged it.

"Magpie," he said. "Magpie go to bed." Then he wandered off and began to arrange a bed for the Sergeant on a cushion.

"He is most beautiful," said Lady Charlotte.

"He is mostly a little wretch," Giles said, "but yes."

"He must think you are his papa."

"I don't think so. Hamish and Sophy will not let him think that. They miss their father a great deal and it is not my place to supplant him."

"I think you have every right to, given what has been done to them. Is it true that the grandparents have not answered your letters?"

"They seem remarkably uninterested," said Giles. "That is their loss and our gain."

"It seems," said Lady Charlotte, picking up another of the ninepins and turning it in her hands, "that our fortunes have changed a great deal since we last met. That summer... Mrs Vernon is –" She broke off with a sigh and carefully replaced the ninepin in the line. He remembered how she had looked at him during her song in the drawing room last night, and he felt most uncomfortable.

"I'm really very happy for you," she went on. "It seems quite a miracle to me that anyone can ever find another person with whom they can truly be themselves – and that the person is suitable in all other respects."

"Considering that you have all the advantages of youth and charm, I should think that the odds of such a miracle happening are strongly in your favour. There will be someone who will read you right and be in a position to –"

"Oh, I wish I had your faith. I might as well marry one of these ninepins!"

"Dunbar has hurt you. But he is not all men. I am sure –"

"Of course, if that is what I want," she said. "Marriage. Perhaps it would be better not to hazard it. After all, my parents have not been happy, have they? And I know many similar disasters. Disappointment seems to be the rule, in fact."

"Do not grow cynical, I beg you."

"You beg me?" she said, and turned away towards Sandro. "Oh, Sandro, do you hear what your uncle says to me? He begs me not to be cynical, and yet how can I be anything but?" She pulled him into his arms and kissed the top of his head, and surprisingly he did not resist. He giggled with pleasure so she kissed him again.

"Because you know better," he said, getting to his feet, feeling this conversation was better ended. He offered her his hand to help her up. She released Sandro, took his hand, and allowed him to assist her, and then, when she was on her feet again, clapped her other hand over his and held it so hard it was as if she meant to hurt him. She looked as if she was about to speak, but suddenly she pulled her hands away, and briskly left the room.

Chapter Twenty-one

The expedition to the Spouts was to be made on those sturdy Highland ponies that did not seem to mind if they had to carry a man or a child, or even picnic hampers and painting equipment. The animals and their grooms were supplied with Lord Rothborough's compliments from the Castle stables, but the immediate family declined to join the party. Felix supposed that meant that Augusta had finally made a clean breast of it and that a sort of council of war had begun.

As their departure approached, with the weather very favourable and no summons to the Castle arriving, Felix felt he was actually on holiday. His mood was further sweetened by another careless, pleasant night with Eleanor. She had been eager and he had thoroughly indulged himself. Now she was skipping about with excitement, her plaid shawl wrapped about her and her velvet hat quivering with feathers, and he did not think he had ever seen her look so beautiful.

"We must not forget Ossian," she said.

"I have it," said Miss King.

"Of course you have!" said Eleanor. "You never forget anything. It is marvellous. But will you be warm enough with that old shawl? I told you to take my Kashmir."

"This one is quite warm enough, and that one is too precious to take out to the hills."

"When it was made from goats who live in the mountains of Hindustan?" Eleanor retorted. "I shall go and get it."

"Eleanor, there is no need –" Miss King began, but Eleanor had already gone back into the house. She sighed and said to Felix, "I'm sorry. I did not think it quite right that I should borrow it, since I understand it was a gift from you."

This was true enough, but it had not been a gift of great significance, even though it was rare and shockingly expensive. It had only been a heavy hint from Lord Rothborough that had made him buy it. He would not have thought of it otherwise. Eleanor had been pleased with it, but she had not worn it nearly so much as the plaid his parents had given her.

"I don't mind, and it is better you keep warm," he said, and then, seeing a rider at the bend of the road, "is that the Prince?"

"He is going to join us," said Miss King. "Eleanor asked him yesterday."

Why she had omitted to tell him this was puzzling. He supposed the atmosphere at the Castle could not be comfortable and the man could hardly be blamed for wishing to escape it. The Prince presented himself with unexpected humility, as well as the usual heel-clicking and hand-kissing. "I'm really so very, very grateful, sir," he said, making a low bow.

The Vernons arrived soon after, complete with Sandro riding in a basket saddle, his pony led by Major Vernon.

"You've gone native," said Felix, amused to see that the Major had draped a plaid about his shoulders.

"It's a sensible precaution," said the Major. "The shepherds in Northumberland wear them on the hills."

"That looks splendid, sir!" said the Prince. "You might have stepped out of the pages of Sir Walter."

"But you must get one of those soft blue bonnets to go with it, Major Vernon," said Eleanor. "I have often said to Felix that he should wear the clothes of his country, just as Lord Rothborough does when he is here. He looked so distinguished last night."

"It would be utterly ridiculous for me to wear the kilt," Felix said.

"I must agree with your wife, Mr Carswell," said Mrs Vernon. "I think you would all look most picturesque in the kilt. Lord Rothborough's tartan ensemble last night was very becoming, and it does make a pleasant change from all that black broadcloth and white satin. If we ladies may dress in every colour of the rainbow, why should not you gentlemen? It was always the fashion, until this century at least. I love how the gentlemen dress in old pictures."

"You do not love the wigs, though," said Major Vernon.

"No, I cannot love the wigs," she said, laughing. "That is a custom that is well buried."

The ladies were soon mounted up, and Felix, who had been appointed principal guide – although he was sure the two grooms from the Castle knew the way better – took his place, leading the first pony, which was Mrs Vernon's. As she had no need of any assistance, being an accomplished horsewoman, he took Sophy's bridle instead, and was pleased to observe how well Mrs Vernon was looking.

The route was a familiar one to Felix, but none the less beautiful for that. Neither did the weather betray them. It was as if all the difficulties of the last few days were cast off, as they wound through the narrow paths that led up through a dense grove of huge trees, a noble mixture of pines and oaks, while beneath – where the sun still reached – drifts of pale blue harebells and bright yellow aconites could be glimpsed. Then the roar of the falling waters began to steal over them.

"Is that really the Falls?" Mrs Vernon asked.

"Yes," said Felix.

A few minutes later they emerged into the clearing of the great basin with the towering cliffs above, over which the water hurled itself to such effect, tumbling some thirty feet into the pool below, creating a white and crystal torrent.

"Oh, my goodness," murmured Mrs Vernon. "I can feel it on my face."

Sophy gazed at it all in wonder.

"Mrs McCroy said there is an entrance to the Kingdom of the Fae through the water," she said. "In the cliff there."

"That's the story, yes," said Felix.

"I wish it could be true," she said. "I wonder if you can see it. May I get down?"

Felix helped her from the pony, and she ran forward to the water's edge.

"Should I go after her?" Felix said.

"No, she's very sensible," said Mrs Vernon, and indeed Sophy stopped herself where she could come to no harm. "Unlike Hamish," she added, for the boy had also dismounted and was already negotiating the broad, flat stones that formed a sort of promontory into the waters. Fortunately the Prince was as eager, and had gone with him.

"He is not quite how one imagines a prince," said Mrs Vernon, as she dismounted from her own pony. "Maria was saying that he is really quite intelligent and sensitive, at least where music is concerned."

"That isn't how Charlotte sees him," Felix said.

"I don't think he is serious about that," said Mrs Vernon. "Maria thinks he is not and that Charlotte has nothing to worry about. Who knows – perhaps he is only going through the motions to please his parents? I would imagine they want him suitably married. Or is he kicking up his heels and vexing them by pretending to pursue an Englishwoman instead of the young lady they have picked out for him?"

"You have gone into this very thoroughly," Felix said.

"It is impossible not to speculate about royals. Their titles almost seem to invite it. We forget they are real people, perhaps."

"You didn't consider him as a possibility for Augusta's admirer?"

"No. He was only recently with them in Florence. Dunbar, however – oh, how will all that work out, I wonder? I feel terribly for them all. It seems wrong to be making a charming excursion when one's friends are suffering such horrible weather, so to speak."

The ponies all tethered, the rugs spread and a fire laid and lit, the picnic was now properly under way. Major Vernon and Hamish went to collect water for the kettle from the Spout itself, while the Prince cut the bread and the meat and proved himself surprisingly useful to the ladies. With nothing to do, Felix stretched out on the ground and gazed up at the sky, thoroughly enjoying his present idleness and the prospect of lunch.

Sophy came and sat beside him.

"May I ask you something, Mr Carswell?" she said.

"Of course," he said, sitting up.

"Did you not say you had bathed in the pool here?"

"Yes, but some time ago."

"I was just wondering if there is a door behind the water. If you could see it when you were in the pool."

"There is a sort of gap, yes. Not wide enough for a man to get through, though. If it had been big enough, I think I would have tried to go in."

"To see if it led to the Kingdom of the Fae?"

"No, just to see what was there. A rock chamber would be wonder enough, don't you think?"

"I suppose so," said Sophy.

"There might be stone pillars carved out by the water," Felix said. "I have read about some extraordinary caves – I cannot remember where, but they had crystals on the wall, formed by the minerals in the water reacting with the minerals in the stone. Perhaps that is the sort of cave people saw and imagined might lead to a fairy kingdom, because they did not know how it was formed."

Sophy nodded and sighed.

"Why does everything have to have a sensible explanation?" she said.

"You mean rational, I think," said Felix. "And just because it is rational does not mean it cannot be interesting or beautiful. Many times in chemistry, several dull things can be put together and will make something beautiful. Like crystals.

Take common salt. Have you ever seen that under the microscope? When we are back in Northminster I will show you. And Celia has a fine collection of crystals – she will be glad to show you them, I'm sure."

"But we can still have stories?" Sophy said. "To pretend to explain things, as well as all the proper explanations? Stories are so lovely."

That she had a point he could not deny.

"Yes, I think we must," he said, at which she smiled. "Oh, look, I think lunch is ready!"

~

"No, I'm quite happy to stay here with Sandro," said Emma. "I have no head for heights, as you know." The proposition was that they should climb to the head of the Falls. "Even if you say the path is quite safe. Do not mind about us."

So leaving Sandro sleeping in a nest of blankets, and Emma reading Mrs Carswell's copy of Ossian, the others began the climb. It was not arduous, but it was steep and twisting in places, and some attention was required so as not to lose one's footing, but there were wonderful glimpses of the cascade through the trees. Finally they emerged into a small clearing which placed them on the very brink of the waterfall.

"Lord Rothborough has talked of building a bridge across here," said Carswell.

"I wish he would," said Hamish, creeping alarmingly towards the edge.

"Come back from there, Hamish, please," said Giles.

"Yes, indeed," said the Prince, catching Hamish by the shoulders. "Please, we do not want you plunging over."

"I do hope he does not build one," said Mrs Carswell. "It would spoil it."

"It might be useful," said Miss King.

"Nothing should be allowed to intrude on such a scene. It is perfect as it is – wild, raw nature!" said Mrs Carswell.

"Is this the spot where the soldier leapt to his death?" said the Prince.

"No, that is at Vorlich," said Carswell.

"Someone must have tried to jump it," said Hamish. "I reckon you could. If you got a good run up." He took a few steps back and stood poised as if he meant to attempt it.

"It's at least eight foot," said Carswell. "You'd kill yourself for certain if you did try."

"I can jump eight foot," said Hamish. "Remember when we were playing with Tom, Sophy? I jumped eight foot then."

"You did not," said Sophy.

"I did!" said Hamish. "And I bet I could jump that. Don't you think, Uncle Giles?" Giles shook his head and Hamish made a face. "But –"

"I wouldn't put money on that," said Giles. "Besides, it is utterly daft. The only certain outcome would be you breaking your neck."

"Quite," said the Prince. "I understand the temptation, Master Hamish, but it is a temptation that must be resisted. I do agree with you, however, that a bridge would be an excellent thing, and we must persuade Lord Rothborough to see to it."

"Then I will persuade him otherwise," said Mrs Carswell.

"I am tempted to design one," said the Prince. "I have designed a few buildings for my own estates."

"It's a pity Tom is not here," said Hamish. "He would know exactly how to do it."

"And who is Tom?" said the Prince, taking out his sketchbook.

"Tom is my nephew," said Giles. "He is set to be an engineer."

"Ah, a useful profession," said the Prince. "Now, what

style should it be?"

"We should do a few different styles," said Hamish, "so we can give Lord Rothborough a choice."

"Yes, he would like that," said the Prince. "You have your sketchbook there? And Miss Sophy, will you design one, too?"

The children settled down with the Prince to draw imaginary bridges.

"I should ask him to stay as a tutor," said Giles to Carswell. They had found a natural rock seat with an impressive view of the waters. "Though I don't suppose I could afford him."

"I'm going to show Jenny the little pool," said Mrs Carswell. "We might be able to find some purple orchids," she added. "No, no, don't disturb yourselves."

"You remember the way?" said Carswell.

"Of course," she said, and the ladies disappeared into the woods. Giles supposed they had also gone to answer the call of nature that a gushing set of waterfalls and several cups of tea would be liable to provoke, and wondered if he should send Sophy with them. But she was utterly absorbed in her drawing, as was Hamish and their royal tutor. He wished he had the talent himself to record the scene for Emma. There was something delightful about the row of seated figures, one tall and two small, against the background of such startling beauty.

Carswell had taken out his own sketchbook, but seemed to hesitate to begin. He was instead looking at his sketch of Mrs Gowans' body.

He handed it to Giles, saying, "Do you have a theory yet?"

Giles looked at the sketch.

"I wish I could say I had," he said, "that some wonderful inspiration had struck me, but it has not, at least not so far." He looked out over the waterfall. "But her petticoats. That is a curious detail. Presumably," he added, dropping his voice so that the children should not hear, "that was part of the torture. If it was as you described."

"I'm confident that was what was done," said Carswell. "Though why –?"

"Quite," said Giles. "And with all Effie Haynes' talk of the Devil, one must wonder who she was really talking about. That is the key to this."

"Do you think she knows who it was and was masking it with that nonsense?" Carswell said. "That she was too afraid to say who it was?"

"It is possible," Giles said. "Perhaps in Perth she will be persuaded to say more."

"I can't imagine there will be anyone there who will have your talent for coaxing the truth out of people."

"It is not a talent, it is only a question of practice," said Giles.

"I don't have any great faith in the authorities here," Carswell said.

"You think we should not have stepped back," Giles said.

Carswell closed his sketchbook and considered the point.

"It hasn't been unpleasant to take care of other matters," he said, "if you catch my meaning." Giles smiled, and Carswell went on, "My parents bought a new mattress for our bed. It was quite striking."

"They must be wanting grandchildren," Giles said, laughing.

"That must be it!" said Carswell. "And perhaps –" He broke off and pushed his hands through his hair. "We should not disappoint them? That business does not alarm me quite as it did. Eleanor is – well, steadier is not the word for it, for she is not really, and neither am I, to be frank, but I think we are both a trifle less idiotic these days. Does that sound right to you?"

"I wouldn't have described either of you in such terms," Giles said. "But I think there is a moment for such things."

Carswell went down to see how the drawings were coming on, and Giles felt his own need to excuse himself and disappear into the woods. That task accomplished, he could not resist continuing the ramble a little further in search of flowers for Emma, spurred perhaps by the thought of what might be accomplished that evening, after such a pleasant day.

However, he found nothing that he liked enough to pick, and he was about to turn back, when he came into the clearing and discovered the small pool that Mrs Carswell had mentioned. Indeed, the two women were there, as they had said, but he immediately sensed he should not alert them to his presence.

They were standing face to face, holding hands, their heads bowed, the distance between them a matter of inches. There was obviously a deep and significant conversation under way. Then Mrs Carswell moved a little closer, and pressed her hand to her friend's cheek, before leaning forward to kiss her.

He turned away quickly, and retreated as quietly as he could.

Chapter Twenty-two

In making this retreat, Giles discovered he had lost his way. He found himself on an unfamiliar path, one that went up steeply, and it was not long before he had broken through the trees and was gazing out at the open country that the locals called the shealings and used for their summer pasture. Even though he was no stranger to wild scenery, it struck him as exceptionally bleak and rough, though the sun was bright on it. Pulling his plaid about his shoulders, he decided that the animals and their keepers were hardy breeds.

A little way off he spotted a makeshift habitation sheltering in a rocky cleft. There was a plume of smoke rising from its haphazard roof. Someone was clearly in residence, but there was no flock of sheep to accompany it. Hoping to ask for directions, he approached it, and as he did so he noted how the entrance to the hut had been carefully screened by branches. In fact the entire structure had a clandestine air about it. Somebody had clearly gone to considerable trouble, and the name and reputation of Donnie Anderson came to mind.

He stopped and considered what he ought to do. If this was Donnie Anderson's infamous establishment, he had no wish to send him further into the hills with a show of authority. He decided it would be best to play the ignorant tourist and blunder in to gather what intelligence he might for the constables.

As it was, his approach had not gone unnoticed. There was, no doubt, a lookout chink in that leafy screen. A small man, grizzled and wiry with age and weather, emerged with two large, rough-coated dogs at his heels. He was dressed in the ancient costume of the Highlander, but there was nothing picturesque about it. Similarly, the dogs were of a type not bred for beauty but for a show of power in their owner. One of them came lurching forward towards Giles, barking and snarling.

"Dinnae mind him, sir," said the man. "He will not harm ye."

Unless you decide otherwise, Giles thought, and put his hand out to the dog.

"What a fine fellow you are!" he said, and managed by means of fussing to subdue him. Having thus established his credentials with the dogs, he enquired, "I have lost my way, sir. Can you direct me back to the head of the falls?"

"Staying with his Lordship, are you?" said the man.

"No," said Giles.

"I heard there were strangers about," said the man. "There are more of them each year, since that McNeill woman took over the inn."

"It is not surprising," said Giles. "Such beautiful country. And the whisky – well, in fact I had heard that the best whisky is to be found in the most unexpected places."

The man frowned.

"So, you are no' lost?" he said.

"Oh, I am," said Giles. "But I think I have stumbled on something I meant to look for. An acquaintance of mine in Perth told me that Mr Anderson makes the best whisky in this district. I wonder if I may be speaking to him now?"

"You are," said Anderson. "And you are?"

"Colonel Long," said Giles. "Might it be possible to sample a glass?" He reached into his pocket. "It has been a thirsty climb, all in all."

"I don't see why not," Anderson said, and went back into the hut.

Giles followed him to the low entrance and looked in. There at the back was the glowing fire, with the gleaming, fat-bellied double copper set on it, and stretched out on the hearth, in a profound slumber, was the large, distinctive form of Angus Lowndie. As his eyes grew accustomed to the dark, Giles saw there were two others there: Gowans snoring in a corner, and another man whom he did not recognise. This latter fellow, dressed as a country farmer, began to struggle to his feet, but he was so intoxicated he failed and sank down onto the floor again, his head in his hands. Giles wondered if this could be Mr Murray.

Anderson unconcernedly busied himself pouring out a dram into a pewter cup.

"Interesting company," said Giles.

The third man groaned, causing Lowndie to stir and roll over. Giles saw he was clutching a bright fringed scarf against him, like a child holding a favourite toy.

"Wh... who the devil are you?" Murray managed to say, again attempting to stand up. This time he succeeded, and gazed at Giles, his expression registering some pain.

"Mr Murray, I presume?" Giles said.

Anderson whipped about and said, "How do you know him?"

"I think we must deal plainly, Mr Anderson," said Giles. "My name is not Long, but Vernon. The Sheriff-Substitute would like to talk to your guests in connection with an incident two nights ago in the churchyard, involving Mrs Euphemia Haynes."

Murray groaned again and turned away.

"She deserved it," he said. "The bitch was asking for it."

"But your conscience doesn't like what you did, I dare say, Mr Murray?" Giles said.

Murray lumbered past him, anxious to leave the hut, knocking Giles as he did. He then fell on his knees on the turf outside and began to throw up.

Giles turned back to Anderson.

"Naturally the Excise Officer would be glad to know what is going on here. You look well bedded in. It can't be an easy business moving your equipment about."

"What are you driving at?"

"I want to take hold of these three men. Even in their deplorable condition, I cannot manage that alone. I shall have to go and get help. If you give me your word you will not assist them in escaping, in the next few hours, I will not alert the Excise at once. It would give you a chance to make arrangements."

Giles did not like making this offer, but he did not want to lose his chances with Gowans, Murray and Lowndie.

Anderson scowled.

"Give you my word?" he said. "When yours disnae seem to be worth much, Colonel whoever you are."

"Who is the Excise man?"

"That would be Crichton."

"And where is he based? In Pitfeldry?"

"Dunkeld."

"Then how likely am I to see him? My business in this case is not your business. I would not go out of my way to mention it."

Anderson looked over the two slumbering men and then at Murray, who was now lying on his side in the sun, exhausted from the violence of his vomiting.

"To tell you the truth," he said, after a moment, "I dinnae think they'll be going far. But I can see it would be better for you that they were kept tethered, so to speak. And as I've not had my money from them yet..."

"Was Effie Haynes here with you the night before last?" Giles asked.

"Aye, she was, for a while. She came with Angus. She was singing all the old songs. She has a pretty voice."

"Then what happened?"

"Murray and Gowans turned up."

"Looking for Effie?"

"Gowans said that Effie had been turning tricks, and of

course that sent Angus out of his mind. And yon man, Murray, he was half-cut already. And they had a few drinks and then they took her off."

"And you didn't think to stop them?"

"Who was I to stop them?" said Anderson. "She's no saint. If she needed a lesson, then –" He shrugged.

As he walked away, Giles decided that he would definitely inform the Excise man of Anderson's whereabouts.

~

As there was no official lockup in Pitfeldry, it was decided to confine Murray, Gowans and Lowndie in some of the store rooms attached to the Factor's offices. Sergeant Gibson, a sharp young man in whom Giles saw a great deal of potential, had already determined that Murray was the ringleader, having made a thorough set of enquiries. He had deduced that Anderson's illicit still might have some bearing on the case, having heard of Effie's propensity for his wares, and he had already sent for the Excise officer.

"It's a stroke of luck you hit on Anderson, sir," Gibson said, as they stood in the courtyard. "He's always a hard man to find, and we are always wanting to find him."

"Luck has a great deal to do with this job," Giles said. "But we should not let that be generally known, for the sake of our reputations."

At this point Lord Rothborough arrived on foot from the Castle.

"I hear your excursion was interrupted in a good cause," he said.

Giles presented Gibson to him and explained what had happened.

"I think Sergeant Gibson will be able to get the full story

out of them, my lord," Giles said. "He has done some excellent groundwork in a short time."

"That is praise indeed, Sergeant," said Lord Rothborough. "You probably know something of the Major's reputation?"

"I do, my lord," said Gibson, "and to tell you the truth, I was hoping that I'd get to see him set those fellows straight."

"I promised Mr Finlay I would not," Giles said. "If there is any difficulty, I will be happy to assist, but I do not think you will have any."

They left him and his colleagues to their work, and went into the stable court. Here they met Carswell, mounted on his pony. He had taken in hand the business of returning the picnic party to their various lodgings, while Giles and the Castle grooms dealt with Murray, Gowans and Lowndie. Hamish, naturally, had wanted to assist with the latter operation, but the Prince managed to persuade him, with a great deal of flattery, that they could not manage without him.

"All safely home," Carswell said, dismounting. "The Prince and Mrs Vernon are drinking tea and talking German, Sandro is reunited with Greene and is extremely sleepy, and Mrs McCroy has sent the children to hunt for eggs."

"Excellent," said Giles. "I hope Mrs Carswell was not too disappointed that we had to cut things short."

"No, I don't think so," said Carswell. "How is Augusta? Does she need to see me?"

"I think it might be wise," said Lord Rothborough. "When she did allow me to speak to her today, she was not comfortable, poor child. It is obvious what is wrong with her, but will she admit that to my face? No! I understand how wretched she must be, but why is she so afraid of me? I told her plainly that I would not shout or scold her."

"How did it go with Dunbar?" Giles asked.

"He admitted nothing. It was breathtaking," said Lord Rothborough. "I shall set you on him, Vernon, and you must show him no mercy! In the meantime, just to add to this delightful situation, my wife declares that we must have everyone to dinner on Monday night, and dancing afterwards! She is anxious that she offended Mr Wallace and wishes to make amends."

"Will she make amends with him with dancing?" said Giles, rather astonished. "He was so strong against cards."

"Apparently he has declared dancing acceptable! I would rather not have him in the house, but she can never resist a clergyman scolding her. He was here all this morning, can you credit it? She is going to give up cards for him, she informs me. She was burning all packs of cards she could lay her hands on."

"Goodness," said Giles.

"She will never manage it!" Rothborough went on. "She has been a slave to them since she was a girl. It is her only amusement. She does not read or care for music. It is only by some miracle she was not a gambler as well. There has been a lot of that in her family, unfortunately." He gazed up at the sky and the looming clouds. "We can only hope that we have a spell of appalling weather and she will be driven back to Italy! Frankly, her presence here is insupportable!"

Chapter Twenty-three

Augusta agreed to see Felix. As Lord Rothborough had said, she was not comfortable. She was lying on her bed, her complexion pasty and her eyes red. Her little dogs were careering about the room restlessly, and began yapping at Felix's heels.

"I think they need to go for a walk," Felix said. "And some fresh air would help you, I think?"

"I can't go out, I really can't."

"Have you eaten?"

She shook her head.

"You should try. Some broth and dry toast, perhaps."

She made a face at that, and then sank back on her heap of pillows, gazing up at the bed canopy.

"You have a responsibility to your child, you know," he said.

"Do you think I don't know that?" she exclaimed, sitting up. "I would not let you in here if I did not know it."

"Then you should at least attempt to take my advice," he said.

"I might manage some toast," she said.

"That would be wise," he said. He fetched the tray from the table and set it on the bed beside her. She took a glass of barley water and some toast.

"There," she said, when she had finished.

"You might go down to dinner. It's often the case that pregnant women cannot eat all day, and then find that in the evening they can."

She wiped her hands on her napkin and said, "Perhaps I shall attempt it. We shall see."

"I think it would reassure everyone, if you did. Lord

Rothborough is –"

She put up her hand to silence him.

"Yes, yes, I know how he is!" she said. "Really, you are impossible. I think I should be glad that you are not my proper brother. That would be intolerable!" Felix could not help smiling at that. "A second Papa, indeed, that would be something like it." This train of thought seemed to revive her. "How very odd it must be for you: to be thinking always what might have been."

"I don't think of it much," Felix said.

"But how can you not?" she said.

"Because it is only speculation. Besides, if things had been different, I would have been a different man."

"But does it not irk you?" she said.

"It has been better for my character to have to make something of myself. I should not have been allowed to study medicine."

"No, certainly you would not."

"You sound as if you would not allow your son to do the same," he ventured.

"No, and I have often wished you had not, you know, Carswell – at least until this week, when it has, I must concede, been useful. But I still think it is too servant-like a profession for a gentleman."

"Given the burden of confidentiality," Felix said, "would you not prefer we were all gentlemen? Or gentlewomen, perhaps? I've sometimes thought that I have no place in this branch of the profession. It would be better if women were allowed to train as well."

"That is a horrible notion," said Augusta. "That is the sort of thing Charlotte talks about."

"I'm glad to hear it," said Felix.

"What do you think of the Prince?" Augusta said.

"In what respect?"

"For Charlotte."

"She does not like him," said Felix.

Augusta nodded and sighed. "It's a great pity she does not."

"Is that your guilty conscience speaking?" said Felix.

"What do you mean?"

"Because your husband was engaged to her." She flinched as he said it. "Did you expect me not to try to identify him?"

"How did you guess?"

"Mrs Vernon saw him taking a note from your maid. Now, unless she is involved with him in some way, one might assume it was from you. Naturally, I have not told her you are married, since you told me not to, so no doubt she is thinking far worse things. I can't imagine why you have allowed this situation to run on; it is doing you no good. Why will you not come clean?"

"I promised him I would not. Not until all is ready."

"Isn't that taking wifely obedience a little too far? And it is wretched of him to make you lie to everyone like this."

"I'm not lying!" she exclaimed. "It is not lying. How dare you speak to me as if I were one of your horrible criminals! It is simply that we are not quite ready to announce it."

"And you are quite happy for everyone to think the worst of you?"

"No, of course not!" she said. "But unfortunately it is necessary. There are certain questions that need to be settled."

"For example: was your marriage legal?" Felix said.

There was silence, and then she scrabbled off the bed, exclaiming: "Oh, I knew I should not have spoken to you! Dear Lord, you are just like Papa, only worse! Far worse!" She stood before him for a moment with clenched hands, as if she meant to beat his chest, but her misery overcame her, and she threw herself against him and began to sob. "Do you think this is easy? It is torture, utter torture!"

She clung to him fiercely and he comforted her as best she could. Then, when she was a little calmer, she detached herself and walked across the room, saying, "But I promised him, and he is my husband – in the eyes of God, certainly he is – and so I must."

"Are you uncertain about the legality of it?" he said.

She shook her head, and taking the handkerchief he offered, dried her eyes.

"After the event, I thought it prudent that we should check," she said. "Would you not have done so?"

"Yes."

"He was rather dismissive to begin with," she said. "In fact he scolded me for having such doubts. It was unpleasant, but I persuaded him. Especially after I had contrived that we could be man and wife properly, if you understand me."

Felix nodded and wondered how often men were persuaded to do things they did not like, by the promise of congress. "You will think me manipulative, I dare say," she went on. "And immodest. But we were married in the eyes of God, if perhaps not in the eyes of the law." She sighed. "I asked him to make enquiries, and we decided we would keep our secret until those enquiries were certain. But I had not anticipated that I would be –" She rubbed her stomach, and sighed again. "I suppose this is God punishing me for my wickedness. But it makes me ridiculously happy at the same time, despite everything!"

"Then you must talk to Papa," said Felix. Her emotion and candour had made him forget himself. "Lord Rothborough, I mean. Excuse me. He will set everything right."

"How strange to hear you call him that," she said.

"I try not to," said Felix. "I do not like to offend my parents or you and your sisters."

"But he is your Papa as much as mine," she said. "Who can deny that? I have always been jealous of you," she went on, "from the moment we knew of your existence. I felt he loved you much more than the rest of us, but perhaps this is not true."

"It is certainly not," said Felix.

"It must have been difficult for him," she said. "I never really understood it before I found myself in this condition. How the world turns over in your perception when there is a child to be considered. I love it already and I suspect Dunbar feels the same, although he does not like to say so. But I have high hopes of him being a doting father. He is a tender creature, although you would not guess it until you know him properly."

"So will you talk to Lord Rothborough?" he said.

"Might you talk to him first?" she said, and then added, with a sweet, petitioning smile, when he attempted to protest, "Oh, please, Felix, would you?"

~

Lord Rothborough was alone in the library. He was sitting at his desk writing, surrounded by papers.

"If you wanted Major Vernon, he has gone home," he said to Felix. "Or at least so he said. I can't believe he will be able to resist interviewing those rogues. I had Murray down as a thoroughly respectable man when he took over at Westerlochan. His references were impeccable, at least."

"May I speak to you?"

"Of course," said Lord Rothborough, laying down his pen and getting up. "I was hoping you might wish to. So?"

"Perhaps you should sit down again," said Felix, suddenly feeling weary. "I think I should like to."

So Lord Rothborough resumed his seat, and Felix pulled a chair up to the desk and related what Augusta had confided in him.

"My poor child," Lord Rothborough said. "At least she has come to her senses. Well done, Felix – you have succeeded where I could not. I'm pleased she has put her trust in you – it shows she is not lost to all good judgement. She will need her family when she has such a path ahead of her, and I shall not be here forever, shall I?"

"Don't speak of that, please," said Felix.

"A sensible man anticipates his mortality," said Lord Rothborough.

"Yes, I know, but –" Felix did not like to linger on this topic. A world without Lord Rothborough seemed as difficult to imagine as the oceans drained of water. "So what will you do next? Talk to Dunbar again?"

"I'm inclined to send for them both and bang their heads together! However, that would not do anyone any good." He leant back in his chair and rubbed his face. "It is not the match I would have made for her. I was never easy when Charlotte was engaged to him, and she has said things about him that I do not like. However, I must have faith in Augusta's ability to manage him, and in his own sense of her worth. It's perhaps too much to expect him to be a devoted husband, but he may yet be a dutiful one. He will have the resources to be virtuous now, after all, since he has managed to snare her without a settlement."

"Which is decidedly unvirtuous," said Felix. "Can anything be put in place to protect her?"

"I shall have to consult Sir Robert," said Lord Rothborough, alluding to the solicitor who had drawn up Felix and Eleanor's marriage settlement. "It may be too late. But if the marriage is shaky, then we have a chance to scrabble something together on her behalf. But it is hardly ideal. As the Prince said at dinner last night, it will be making a pig's purse out of a silk ear!"

At this moment the door was flung open and Lady Rothborough entered at some speed, as if with the force of a gust of wind behind her.

"Aha!" she said. "Here you are!"

"Yes, indeed, ma'am, here we are," said Lord Rothborough. "Is there something –?"

She did not answer but went straight to the writing table where she began, in a rather frenzied manner, to turn over and examine the papers.

"Are you looking for something in particular?" Lord Rothborough said, going to her side. "I would rather you did not disarrange those –" he added, only for Lady Rothborough to snatch up the pile, and step away from him. She glanced at each sheet in turn before throwing it on the floor. "Ma'am!" Lord Rothborough said. "What are you doing?"

She stopped for a moment and threw the remaining sheets she had not examined onto a chair and went back to the desk. This time she began on the drawers.

"Where are they?" she demanded.

"Where are what?"

"Her letters! Why is this drawer locked, Rothborough? Are they in here?"

"It is locked because there is cash in there," said Lord Rothborough.

"Open it."

"Ma'am, really –"

"Open it!"

Lord Rothborough took a bunch of keys from his pocket, and began to look for the key. As he did, Lady Rothborough stared at Felix and said, "What is he doing here?"

"Mr Carswell has been to see Augusta."

"Why?" she said.

"Why?" echoed Lord Rothborough. "Because – why, ma'am, when you would call a physician for a cut on your finger –"

"I would not!" she said. "And Augusta is well enough. She told me her so herself this morning. So thank you, sir, you may go!"

"Well enough?" said Lord Rothborough. "She is our

daughter, not a servant, Frances. She has been in a miserable state for goodness knows how long –"

"It is the change of water from Italy, that is all," said Lady Rothborough.

"That does not mean you ought not show her a little compassion."

"Oh, you are a fine one to talk of compassion, Rothborough!" said Lady Rothborough. "Fine indeed!"

Lord Rothborough unlocked the drawer and pulled it open.

"There you are," he said.

She examined the contents of the drawer, and being unsatisfied by what she saw, she slammed it shut.

"Where are they?" she said again.

"What are you talking about?" said Lord Rothborough.

"I think you know very well," she said.

"Believe me, I don't!" said Rothborough.

"Carswell will help me," said Lady Rothborough, turning to Felix. "He will know her hand."

"Whose hand, ma'am?" Felix said.

"Do not play the innocent with me," she said, wagging her finger at him. "You know quite well – as do you, my lord!" she added.

"You might be speaking of her Majesty for all I know," said Lord Rothborough, with a careless, calm air. Felix realised then who this mysterious and contentious correspondent must be.

"No, of course not," said Lady Rothborough. "As if he would be receiving personal letters from her!"

"Given Mr Carswell has a growing reputation as an accoucheur, it would not surprise me in the least," said Lord Rothborough. "Did you not hear from the Duchess of Bridgefield, Felix?"

"Oh, be quiet!" exclaimed Lady Rothborough, putting her hands over her ears. "Be quiet! I will not be treated like this. I will not be mocked! You know perfectly well who I mean, Rothborough! That woman – his mother! I demand to see them."

"Then I fear you will have to be disappointed," he said. "I don't have any letters from that lady."

"And you expect me to believe that?" Lady Rothborough said. "When I know for certain that you correspond with her." She went back to the desk and began again to scrabble through the disarranged papers. "I know you are guilty, Rothborough, I know it!"

"Look all you like," said Lord Rothborough, going to the door. "You will not find anything."

"Where are you going?"

"To talk to our daughter. She is in need of her mother's care, but that is probably too much to expect from you."

Felix followed him from the room. When the door had shut behind him, Lord Rothborough reached into his coat and took out a letter. He pressed it into Felix's hand.

"Perhaps you would post this in the village for me?" he said.

It was addressed to Mrs Martinez at Greywalls, by Stanegate, Northminstershire.

Chapter Twenty-four

Giles experienced a moment's temptation as he walked past the Factor's offices, but reminded himself that Gibson had proved himself a sound worker and also that those men would probably not be much good for interviewing until the drink had worn off. As he made his way towards Mrs McCroy's house, he also wondered if they would really be able to shed any light on Mrs Gowans' murder.

He turned to unpicking Effie Haynes' confession. She had told them she had been sitting by her fire, putting the doll with the scrap of silk about its neck in a pan over the flames and then calling on the Devil to harm her sister. That she had done this he did not doubt.

Her certainty that something ill had come to her sister had been born from her intention to hurt her. She had presumably gone out of the bothy to see if her incantation had worked, and found herself to be more successful than she might have imagined. Yet perhaps she had not expected such a fast result, and had gone out because she had heard something. Had she heard her sister scream? Might she have seen or heard something else that could be of more use to them than her strange ramblings, induced, he suspected, by her painful experience of the jougs? The best way to get a false confession was to use violence upon a suspect. Had that been the intention of her captors? If so, it could not be considered a well thought out plan.

Lowndie, Murray and Gowans made for a strange alliance, that was certain. Giles stopped for a moment, wondering again if he should go back. Gowans may well have killed his wife. It was a dreadful commonplace that female victims often met their fates at the hands of their husbands or lovers. Was it possible that Gowans enlisted Lowndie, who was clearly angry with Effie, and then Murray – also disaffected with her – in order to shame and discredit her publicly, and by such means misdirect the investigation? A risky strategy, certainly, but he might be feeling desperate. The signs of torture on her neck, her torn petticoats with the possible traces of semen – were these the marks of an angry husband, unable to deal with a wife who was, it seemed, his superior in many respects? It was an easy matter for him to have followed her to the bothy and taken out his frustration on her, for once and for all. If that were the depressing truth, then Giles supposed that Gowans would not be able to bear his guilt very long and would soon confess all to Gibson.

As he turned down the lane towards Mrs McCroy's, in the fading light of the day, a sharp spring breeze nipped at his heels and he thought of the child Mary Gowans with her listless sweeping. She faced a bleak future. For Gowans would hang if he confessed. It was as well Lady Charlotte had taken such a prompt interest in her, although her alacrity in doing so was slightly alarming. He did not feel comfortable with her heeding his words.

He went back to thinking of Gowans and wondered if the man really had it in him to cross the line. He had observed enough murderers now to notice that there was often a mysterious mental flaw, which gave them an abnormal appetite for violence. His hand on the gate, he concluded that if he were the culprit, then Gibson would find it out soon enough, and it was good that he was in custody. That was quite sufficient for now, and he should apply his duty to Emma and the children instead, which was not duty at all, but a pleasure.

It was a little before seven, the lamps had been lit and the house felt calm as he crossed the threshold. He expected to be greeted by Hamish or Sophy, but there was no sign of anyone about, not even any of the cats. He went into the sitting room and saw Emma lying on the sofa, sleeping, with one of the cats nearby. She looked so tranquil that he decided not to disturb her, and went straight upstairs to change his coat.

Crossing the landing, he heard Sophy say, "Flora, Flora, stay here!"

He went to see what she was about and found her sitting on the bottom step of a staircase that was concealed behind a door. Flora, the other cat of the household, was wriggling in her arms.

"She wants to go up," said Sophy.

"Is she not supposed to?" Giles said. He had not realised there was a staircase there. It led, he imagined, to the servants' bedrooms.

"Oh no, she may go up. It's just that she will not come down if she does, and Greene wanted me to find her because she is missing Widdershins."

"I think we all are," said Giles, reaching out and stroking Flora's magnificent striped head. "What is up there that is so irresistible?"

"Come and see," said Sophy, dropping Flora, who at once turned tail and galloped up the steep staircase. Sophy got up and followed.

"Are you sure we ought to?" Giles said. "Has Mrs Mc-Croy said you may?"

"Oh yes, it's all right," said Sophy.

So he followed her up, and as the stair turned he became aware of the mingled scents of dried herbs, flowers and spices. It was a smell that took him back to the fragrant mysteries of his mother's carefully tended still room. He found he was smiling as he emerged onto the top step and saw before him the bunches of lavender, bay and rosemary hanging from the ceiling. But it soon struck him that this room was far more than a still room. Yes, there was plenty of evidence of a high cultivation of the domestic arts: the carefully folded linens on the shelves, the work basket on the chair by the window, placed to catch the best light, but it also had the aspect of a library. There were rows of old books neatly ranged in glazed cabinets, and curious prints in heavy oak frames decorated the walls.

One of these particularly drew his eye: it showed a group of women dancing naked, in the manner of the famous Three Graces. However, these were the not young, impossible beauties so common in classical scenes, but rather a group of individual women, varied in age, whose faces and flesh showed marks of real life. If the artist had intended to ridicule them for not being young and comely, he had failed, because there was a great deal of beauty in such honesty – at least so it struck Giles. Those were the hips that had supported children, the breasts that had given milk, and the hands that had comforted and healed, and sewed and cooked, indeed that had done all the interminable and difficult labour of womankind. Even their feet, on the black and white tiles of the floor on which they stood, had an enchanting solidity about them. He could almost sense how many miles had been walked. In fact, so real was it to him, that he expected any moment that one of them would turn and ask him how he dared to stare so shamelessly at them in their nakedness.

"Are you sure we should be here?" he said. He felt like a trespasser.

"Yes, it's all right," Sophy said. "I've been making lavender bags up here. Actually, it isn't just lavender, it's Mrs McCroy's special mixture."

She took the cork stopper from a large stone jar on the table and inhaled. Giles joined her. It was a heady mixture, far more potent than his mother's carefully cultivated pot pourri. It was heavy with the scent of crimson roses and cloves. "Do you like it?"

"Yes," said Giles.

"It's lovely," said Sophy, inhaling again. "And inside the bag you put a little message. That's what really does it."

"Does what?"

"Makes the person have happy dreams."

"I see," said Giles.

He glanced back at the print. Above the women's heads hung a glass sphere, similar to one hanging in the window here. He went back to the picture. What were those curious lines drawn on the black and white tiled floor?

Sophy had restoppered the jar and was crouching down, coaxing Flora to come to her.

"I think we should go downstairs," said Giles, scooping up the cat. Sophy's innocent description had an irresistible charm about it, but something was making him uneasy. It was harmless, surely, to put such a message in a lavender bag, and yet it might almost be described as a spell. The village boys had told Hamish exactly what they considered Mrs McCroy to be. Perhaps there was some truth in it.

~

"So what did you find to talk to the Prince about?" Giles asked Emma, when they sat down to dinner together. They were alone. The children had eaten earlier and gone to bed.

"Hexen," said Emma.

"Hexen?" Giles said. "Oh, witches. I suppose that is to be expected."

"Not just that," said Emma. "We covered a great deal of ground. It was very stimulating, if a little exhausting. I was quite glad when Hamish dragged him out to look at the three-legged dog."

"That is one of the wonders of Pitfeldry," said Giles, who had seen this fabulous animal loitering in front of The Brodie Arms. "But it was very good natured of him to go with him."

"He could see I was tired," said Emma.

"Even better. I should be alarmed that such a handsome

young man is being so considerate towards my wife. A prince, no less."

"I don't have the energy to flirt. That is the most exhausting thing of all. You are quite safe."

"But I suppose you discussed his romantic endeavours?"

"It was touched on," she said. "Perhaps a little more than that. Poor soul, he is slightly desperate. There is a young third cousin allotted to him, of whom he is fond, but that is as far as it goes. He went to Italy to try and fall in love with someone his mother might approve of, hence his attentions to the Rothborough ladies."

"And has he fallen in love?" said Giles.

She shook her head and laughed.

"Lady Charlotte is quite safe," she said. "So I told him to make it clear to her. He agreed it should be said." She laughed again. "No, the worst of it is that of all of them, it is Maria he finds the most agreeable, but of course she is the least available."

"That may have something to do with it."

"Oh, he is not so perverse."

"It's common enough that we want what we cannot have."

"That is too cynical, Giles," Emma said, and returned her attention to her soup.

"So you are sure he has not been involved with Augusta?" Giles said after a moment.

"The idea danced across my mind, but I honestly think he is incapable of concealing anything like that. He is so frank and open. I like him. He reminds me of Charles a little."

"Yes, I can see it. By the bye, was there a letter from him today?"

"No, and I don't expect one until the examinations are over. Speaking of universities, Franz-Friedrich knew Professor Holznecht. He studied under him for a term, in fact, at Heidelberg."

"Franz-Friedrich?" said Giles, smiling.

"Hamish was calling him that."

"With his permission, I trust?"

"Of course, and he said to me he would consider it a token of my esteem if I were to use it too."

"Are you sure you were not flirting?" said Giles, laughing now.

"It was so sweet, I could not refuse him," Emma said.

"I think we should be grateful to the three-legged dog. Otherwise your honour might have been severely in danger."

"That is outrageous," said Emma, smiling.

Jean came in to clear the soup places and leave a dish of collops in their place. When she had gone, Giles said, "So, how did you get talking of witches?"

"He saw all those books you had sent down from the Castle. He told me how the witch-hunts in parts of Germany had been a kind of madness, with hundreds of people imprisoned and executed for working magic. And all in such cruel circumstances and on no evidence at all. It strikes me that the Devil was working in the hearts of those who were trying to stamp it out. Whatever the witches were supposed to have done, it was nothing compared with the wickedness of the witch-hunters!"

~

Later that evening, when he was about to get into bed, Giles found – on adjusting the pillows – a little bag made from scraps of chintz hiding in the bedclothes. He stood and sniffed it for a moment, wondering if it was Sophy's work, but the scent struck him as different from that in the jar. This was equally rich, but there was something else subtle in there that he could not place, except that it pleased him. He tucked it back under the covers and waited for Emma to finish her prayers and join him.

She rose from her knees and pulled off her nightcap, shaking loose her hair as she did so. She smiled as she climbed in beside him and Giles wondered if she had been praying at all.

Having blown out the candle, he pulled her into his arms. He slipped his hand under the low neckline of her nightdress, burying his face in her hair as he did. Her hair smelt of roses, and he found himself thinking of the image of those dancing women, hanging in the attic above them. Were those women witches? he thought, as he kissed Emma's neck. Was Mrs McCroy a witch? Were all clever women gifted in the arts of enchantment that men could never learn, let alone understand?

"Shall we?" she murmured.

He answered with his actions, kneeling over her, kissing her forehead and cheeks. His longing for her was fierce now, at least in his mind, for in the moments that followed, he began to realise he was in no position to satisfy her, let alone himself.

He sank back down beside her, after some futile attempts. He felt thoroughly wretched.

"Excuse me. I must be tired. Perhaps tomorrow morning –?"

"Yes, of course," Emma said, putting her arms about him, as if he were a child to be comforted. "It doesn't matter."

But all he could feel was restlessness and her own carefully unspoken disappointment.

~

Giles was on horseback, galloping across a bleak moor, following an elegant woman on a white horse. He tried to catch up with her, but the gap between them got longer. Was this Emma? Afraid that he would lose her, he shouted out, but his voice seemed tiny and inconsequential.

Then, just as she seemed to disappear over the horizon, she was on his horse in front of him, their bodies touching, her loose dress flapping in the wind. He wrapped his arms around her, and as the horse rose and sank, he seemed to be intimately entwined and unable to stop a wave of pleasure that accompanied this rhythmic movement. She leant forward to put her arms around the horse's neck, her body braced against his, and the tide inside him became unstoppable. His horse was now running through a stream, and he could feel the sun-warmed water splashing on his leg. Then the woman he was embracing turned around – it was Charlotte, flushed and triumphant. "You're mine now, Giles!"

The scene crumbled into blackness. Giles started, and struggled to understand where he was and what was real. The waves of pleasure were still pulsating uncontrollably, and wakefulness revealed the truth of the stream's splashes – they were the shameful product of his disturbing dream.

Chapter Twenty-five

The Rector was not a self-indulgent preacher. It was rare for him to exceed a quarter-hour, a fact much appreciated by his small congregation. That Sunday morning the congregation was increased and the sermon shortened, a typical measure of his humility. He stuck faithfully to the text in hand and did not mention witches, nor murder. Yet prayers were offered for the repose of Isabella Gowans' soul, and the presence of Mary Gowans at Matins made it impossible to imagine this was an ordinary Sunday in Pitfeldry.

There had been a debate in the house that morning about whether she ought to be spared church. Felix's mother had thought it might be too painful for her, but Mary had apparently told Stevens she wanted to go. Stevens, who seemed ready to take the child as her own and had declared she had the making of a first-rate lady's maid, sat with her now, sheltering her from the curious stares of the congregation. Felix supposed this attention was because she was counted one of the Kirk folk by the Episcopalians, and not expected to be seen at Matins.

In fact there was plenty for the regular members of the congregation to stare at that morning, with the Castle pew occupied by Lord Rothborough and two of his daughters, as well as the Prince. Eleanor and Miss King, as well as Felix, were in the Rectory pew.

During the course of the service it began to rain, which curtailed the usual socializing in the churchyard – no doubt this was very disappointing to most, but Felix was glad of it. He exchanged only a brief word with Lord Rothborough, who asked him to come up to the Castle after lunch.

Such a summons could not be ignored, although he would rather have stayed in the drawing room by a good fire, with Amadeus lying on his feet. But it was just as well he had to go, if only because of Amadeus' perversity in apparently preferring him to the Rector. He sent the dog off to his proper master and climbed into the carriage, which he was glad of since the rain had not lifted.

It was entirely appropriate that the weather had turned so foul as he entered the drawing room at the Castle. The room, which looked magnificent at night, was less appealing in the dreich light, and was empty except for Maria who was sitting on a low stool by the fire, wrapped in several shawls.

"I have a cold," she said, with a loud sniff.

"Then you should go to bed."

"I cannot. Papa needs me," she said, and then putting out her hand to him said, "he needs us. Oh, Felix, I'm so glad you are here."

"You should go to bed," he said, touching her forehead. "You are running a temperature."

She shivered. "Oh dear," she said. "That may be so. But I'm never ill."

"This might be as good a moment to be ill as any," said Felix.

"It would be shirking to go to bed," said Maria. "Papa has asked Dunbar to come."

At this moment, Lord Rothborough came into the drawing room, and frowned at the sight of Maria huddled under her shawls.

"She ought to go to bed," Felix said.

"There," said Lord Rothborough. "You cannot argue with that."

"But do you not –?"

Lord Rothborough shook his head and said, "Bed, my sweet. It is the best thing for you. I cannot have you getting really ill."

"True," Felix said, and stretched out his hand to assist her.

Maria hesitated a moment, and then allowed him to help her up. "I do feel rather weak," she said.

"Go up with her, Felix," Lord Rothborough said, "and you can look in on Augusta while you are there."

"It is just as well he does not charge us, Papa," Maria said, managing a smile. "Are you terribly expensive, Felix? I'm sure you ought to be."

"It depends on the patient," Felix said.

Felix was only too glad to be dismissed upstairs with Maria, but as they were leaving, Lord Rothborough said, "I shall send for you when Dunbar gets here, Felix. I shall need all the reinforcements I can get."

Felix was tempted to say: "Then why not send for Major Vernon?" for he seemed better suited to such a situation, but as the wilting Maria pressed on his arm, with tender sisterly affection, he realised that Lord Rothborough, in his own way, was expressing his familial need, and that he could not ignore. Whatever the public ambiguity of his position, the private truth was that he was the eldest son, with all the honour and responsibility that implied. Lord Rothborough wanted him there at this moment of acute crisis and it made Felix understand how gravely wounded he must be by Augusta's behaviour. He might appear calm and resigned to it, already seeking the best salves for everyone's reputation, but that could not take away the pain. As an act of deceit, it was breathtaking.

Having got Maria to bed, he went to see Augusta. She was sitting at the dressing table, having her hair arranged by her maid. She dismissed the girl and, still facing the looking glass and tweaking her ringlets, said, "Thank you for speaking to Papa."

"You look much better," said Felix.

"I feel so," she said, rising from her stool and facing him. She was now wearing a wedding ring and an elaborate and matronly lace cap.

"Have you talked to him?" he said.

"A little," she said.

"And your mother?"

She twisted her wedding ring and said, "I shall later. When Papa and my husband have talked."

"He will be here quite soon," Felix said.

She nodded and said, "You were right. It is better all laid out."

"He should never have made you do it," Felix said.

"I take full responsibility for my part," Augusta said. "But sometimes what must be done, must be done."

"You have hurt him, you know," said Felix.

"And you have never done so?" she responded coolly, and turned back to her dressing table and her open jewel box. She picked up a bracelet and examined it, as though nothing in the world was wrong. In fact, she seemed quite pleased with herself, as if the enterprise had been wholly successful. Felix wondered how much the scheme was Dunbar's creation, and how much was hers. Had she used her feminine wiles to manipulate him into the scheme? Even a man such as Dunbar, a reputedly brilliant, hard-headed man of affairs, might be outmanoeuvred by a daughter of Lord Rothborough, offering a heady combination of money, position and physical charm. She had politics in her blood, after all.

A footman came in with a message saying that Lord Rothborough wished to see Mr Carswell in the library.

"You will send for me soon, I think," she said, just as he left, leaving him in no doubt that she was the prime mover in the whole disreputable scheme. She was like a chrysalis who had just hatched into a butterfly. She was now every inch the Countess of Dunbar, and showed every sign of becoming formidable with it.

He found Lord Rothborough alone in the library. He had put Dunbar to wait elsewhere. Felix reported the change in

Augusta's demeanour.

"I don't think Dunbar stood a chance against her," he said. "Or I suppose he recognised how useful she would be to him and it was all worth the risk. I suspect they are well matched in that."

"God help us, yes!" said Lord Rothborough. "I've been thinking that myself. We shall have to see what they do with themselves. A Prime Minister is always well served by a consort who has a mind as agile as his, and who has the same political instincts. Take Lord and Lady Breferton – it was hard to say sometimes who was the guiding hand. I should never have thought that Augusta was so minded, but it seems she is. I'm ashamed to say I may have underestimated her."

There was something in his manner that suggested he was torn between paternal pride and intense shame at having allowed the situation to arise in the first place. He had been outmanoeuvred by someone he had imagined harmless and under his control. It was as if he had picked up what he thought to be a blunt knife, and found himself bleeding.

"So, let us go and see what my Lord Dunbar has to say for himself," Lord Rothborough said.

Dunbar had been made to wait in an odd sort of room, a large hall that had the aspect of a broad corridor. It was hung with badly painted family portraits and drab tapestries, and furnished with uncomfortable-looking chairs that clung to the walls as if they could not stand up of their own accord. There was a fireplace at each end, but they were not lit, and the dull light of the afternoon storm and the slapping of rain on the casements added a great deal to the lugubrious atmosphere. It was a palpable insult to have put him there, as Felix knew quite well. He had been made to wait there himself more than a few times when a boy, on such occasions when Lord Rothborough had cause to be particularly annoyed with him. The one merit of the room was its great length. It had been a comfort to pace up and down, in an attempt to soothe his nerves.

However, Dunbar had apparently made himself quite at home, and was sitting at the far end, on one of the less ridiculous chairs, reading. He got up as they came in, and made a supercilious sort of bow, the pamphlet he had been reading still in his hand.

"For you, my lord," he said, offering it to Lord Rothborough. "It is Grendon's latest memorandum on monetary regulation. He mentioned to me that you were an advocate of reform in this area and we thought you might like a copy. He touches on the matter of universal income."

"Six shillings a week and a cottage for everyone?" Lord Rothborough said, taking it. "A pretty notion, and one that young men get hold of in every generation, only to realise when they turn thirty it is nonsense. I found it most seductive when I was an undergraduate."

"Grendon has a novel turn of mind on the subject. I think you will find his arguments convincing."

"Yes, convincing as a recipe for disaster. If you remove the motivation to work, my lord, you destroy society. Mr Grendon is a talented man, though, and you are lucky to have him as an acquaintance," said Lord Rothborough. "Here, Felix, you might amuse yourself with this. Or make spills for the fire with it – after all, we are not here to talk about political economy, are we? I rather wish we were, but alas, no. The game is up, my lord. I have talked to my daughter."

There was silence for a moment, and Lord Dunbar said, "Then my wife will no doubt have explained why we took this particular course of action. My lady Rothborough's implacable opposition to any candidates for her daughters was so well demonstrated, we decided –"

"You will not use my wife as an excuse for your behaviour, Dunbar," said Lord Rothborough. "That is not acceptable."

Lord Dunbar went on, quite undeterred: "My wife and I, having formed a profound attachment, and wishing to become man and wife, but with no hope of having it sanctioned in the usual way, decided that we would marry in Italy, before forces were contrived to separate us."

"Do you mean by the other lady in my family that you disappointed?"

"She, my lord, disappointed me," said Dunbar. "I will remind you that it was Lady Charlotte who ended our engagement."

"She was disappointed in your character, and now I can see why," said Lord Rothborough. "So you went after Augusta."

"Augusta and I formed a genuine attachment, but Lady Rothborough would not allow it. She did not regard me as a suitable candidate and therefore we took action."

"And you did not think that my consent was necessary? No, you did not ask it, because you knew that I would not have given it either. After all I have heard of you from my eldest daughter, sir, I would not have let you in the house!"

"Lady Charlotte can scarcely be said to be an impartial witness," said Lord Dunbar. "Our difficulties were as much her doing as mine."

"Saying that does you no credit," said Rothborough.

"I am not interested in your opinion of me, my lord," said Dunbar.

"Clearly not," said Rothborough. "You are interested in Augusta's fortune. But I think you have found your match in Augusta, who seems to have cooked up this ridiculous plot, and had you behaving like the silly hero in an opera buffa. You will be laughed at, Dunbar when all this comes out."

"Those of us in public life, my lord, are well used to that. One would not have lasted five minutes if one cared about such things. I think you, of all people, standing here with your bastard, must know that laughter and ridicule mean nothing to sensible people. It is just the buzzing of flies in another room."

"And it means nothing that your wife will be laughed at?"

"Augusta feels as I do," said Dunbar. "Now, perhaps we should talk business. I am anxious to see my wife."

"No, we shall not talk business! You can manage on her pin money for now," said Lord Rothborough. "I need to consult my lawyers and I need to see hard evidence that this wedding was legal."

"I have the marriage lines here," said Dunbar, reaching into his coat and taking out a packet of papers. "I think you will find everything is in order. I took the liberty of asking Mr Houldsworth, of Houldsworth and Ibbotson, to look the matter over. Everything is in perfect order, in his opinion, which I have appended for your convenience." Lord Rothborough sat down and began to study the papers. Dunbar now addressed Felix.

"Perhaps you could recommend an accoucheur in London? I should like to express my thanks for your care of my wife over the last few days."

"Send him a bill, Felix!" exclaimed Lord Rothborough. "And do not think you will be living in town, my lord. I have a house overlooking the Basin of Montrose which will do nicely for you to set up housekeeping in. It is a decent property and there are even three or four families in the neighbourhood who might ask you to dinner, although they will not like your radical opinions."

The door opened, and Lady Rothborough came in with Augusta on her arm. They had a look of conspiracy about them and it was evident that Augusta had decided to speak to her mother after all.

"Aha," Lady Rothborough said, smiling at what she saw. She led Augusta across the room to Dunbar, took his hand and laid it over her daughter's. Then after a moment of almost sacramental silence, she said, "I have had your things sent up from the inn, Dunbar – it is ridiculous you should be staying there. Now, the matter of your house in town –"

"Madam, what are you talking about?" said Lord Rothborough.

"Where they shall live," said Lady Rothborough. "You will need to be near the House, of course. There is nothing worse than having a dinner ruined by a division, but if one is nearby the evil is considerably reduced."

"Excuse me?" said Lord Rothborough.

"Will you not consider your daughter's comfort, Rothborough," said Lady Rothborough, "or are you going to be awkward? I, for my part, can only be pleased. It occurred to me in Italy that it might be a good thing when I saw how downcast poor Dunbar was by Charlotte, and how pleasantly they went on together. I dare say I even hoped it might happen. Of course, I would much prefer to have been consulted, but in the circumstances I will overlook it. There is no lasting harm done. Dunbar, come and kiss your mother-in-law." The gentleman dutifully did so and then kissed his wife. "And an interesting event already expected!" Lady Rothborough went on, clapping her hands. "I know it will be a boy. I feel it, and all that sickness, Augusta – that very often means a boy. I was never sick, more is the pity."

"There is no proof in that either way," Felix said.

"We will seek your opinion when we want it, Carswell," said Lady Rothborough. "In fact, perhaps you should go back home to your little wife. I do hope you are happy with her. The Blanchforts always were a most rackety family, and as for your wife's mother's people, well! I don't suppose you have been told much about them. There was a habit of looseness amongst them – such stories going about. The sort of stories I would have hesitated to tell you, Augusta, before you were married."

"Married or not, they are all scurrilous trash," said Lord Rothborough. "Perhaps you will excuse me, ma'am – I've had quite enough of this silly conversation. And Augusta, do not think you will have your house in Town. You have made a scandal and you both must suffer for it. You can stay here a few days, and then you can take yourselves off to Montrose. The house is in good order – you can learn housekeeping until your child comes into the world."

"Papa, you are not serious. Dunbar would have to resign his post with Lord Standish."

"What a shame. There will be others in time, sir, I'm sure of it."

"But we must be in London!"

"No, that is my final word on the matter."

"Oh, what a wicked, unreasonable man you are!" exclaimed Lady Rothborough. "How wretched to see you treating our darling child in such a terrible fashion!"

"They will not starve," said Lord Rothborough, heading towards the door. "Felix, come with me and see how your sister is, will you? Maria is not at all well, ma'am, in case you had not realised."

At this moment Blair entered.

"Mr Wallace is here, my lord."

"Ah yes," said Lady Rothborough. "He has promised to read me his sermon from this morning, and I should very much value his counsel at such a time. Show him into my sitting room, Blair." When the butler had gone, she went and kissed Dunbar and Augusta ostentatiously. "I am sure your papa will see I am right, soon enough," she added. "I think Carlton House Terrace might be suitable. Such nice walks in the park."

This was enough to make Lord Rothborough leave the room, and Felix followed him. The door having closed behind them, Rothborough said, "Tell Maria I shall be up in due course. I need a space to steady myself and find my manners. It will not do to go to her and berate her mother! It would be too cruel."

~

Felix found Maria tucked up in bed, with Charlotte sitting on the counterpane beside her. They were engaged in cutting out birds and flowers from some printed stuff, and the bed was covered in a shower of snipped corners and threads.

"We are distracting ourselves," said Charlotte, getting off the bed and brushing the debris from her skirts.

"Very wise," said Felix.

"There was a scene, I take it?" said Charlotte.

Felix related what had happened, and the sisters gazed at him.

"What a turnabout!" said Charlotte. "Oh, really – Mama should be ashamed of herself. How utterly inconsistent. But she cannot object to you and Sir Mark getting married now, Maria."

Maria blew her nose and said, "I think she might. She always finds a way to obstruct it. And Dunbar is not Mark, is he? She does not like Mark at all."

"She did not like Dunbar very much," said Charlotte.

"Yes, but she thinks she can control him. Mark will not be controlled."

"I do not think she will control him," Charlotte said. "He is too wily for that."

Maria started to sneeze, and Charlotte began clearing away their flower cuttings into a basket.

"I shall take these down to Mrs Wallace's girls' Bible class," Charlotte said. "The girls might like to do something with them. I promised I would go and inspect it this evening. It will be a good excuse to get out of the house." Maria sneezed again, and Charlotte said, "I hope I get your cold – then I shall not have to go into dinner with them all. Must he really come here? Can they not be packed off to Montrose at once?"

"I don't think they will be here long," said Felix.

"Thank goodness!" exclaimed Charlotte. "It is just like Lydia and Wickham in Pride and Prejudice, is it not? To have a man of such doubtful character forced into the family, and we all have to tolerate it! How will we bear it? I always wondered how on earth Mr Darcy could stand to have such a man as his brother-in-law!"

"That is why Miss Austen is such an excellent author," Maria said. "Any other novelist would have killed them off in a convenient carriage crash as a punishment for their morals and to make it easier for everyone else. But she shows that we have to live with these things, whether we like them or not."

"You are beginning to sound like a wise old woman, Maria," said Charlotte, kissing her. "And not at all like my little sister."

Chapter Twenty-six

Giles had no strong opinions about Sabbath observance, and neither did Emma, but since they were in the house of a clergyman's widow, it seemed right that the children should be kept quiet and a little curtailed. This was not an easy matter by any means, but the indifferent weather helped.

Giles found himself in charge of Hamish, with only Bible stories to sustain them. Fortunately they hit on the subject of military strategy in the battle of Jericho, and passed an agreeable hour or so laying out fortifications in wooden blocks on the dining room carpet. The only awkwardness was Hamish's questioning of what it actually meant by Rahab being a harlot, and Giles rather struggling for a definition, and then eventually settling on language that was perhaps too plain for a ten-year-old. Hamish looked disgusted, for he did not like to see a man kiss a woman.

"But the point of the story is that she was exceptionally brave in hiding Joshua's spies, and that as a result her family were all safe," Giles went on, feeling – not for the first time – that hiding enemy spies in a brothel was a clever tactic.

The conversation soon turned to other matters, namely the business of the three-legged dog, whom Hamish was convinced was homeless.

"It's stopped raining," he said, going to the window. "Could we go and look for him? It would be a Sunday-ish sort of thing to do, if he doesn't have anywhere to go."

"You think we should bring him back here? I'm not sure how Mrs McCroy or her cats would feel about that."

"He's very nice," said Hamish. "And it isn't fair that he doesn't have a master."

"We don't know that. I'm sure he belongs to someone."

"Well, they don't take very good care of him. They shouldn't be allowed to have him if they don't look after him properly. He always looks so hungry."

Giles was forced to agree with him.

"Go and find Sophy," Giles said. "Let us go and see how he is."

It was an excuse for a walk, and he was restless and in need of one.

Emma was in the drawing room reading a book that the Prince had given her after church. It was printed in intimidating German Gothic script.

"I hope that is suitable for a Sunday, Mrs Vernon," he said.

"Not at all," she said, smiling.

"I thought I would take the children for a small walk. Will you come with us? More wholesome than foreign novels."

"It's not a novel," said Emma. "I'm not that bad."

"So? It looks quite nice out now."

He put out his hands to her and pulled her up from the sofa, in which action she laughingly participated. Having her in his arms, he kissed her, and so enjoyable was this, he realised it was a different sort of exercise his body was craving. That, he was sure, was the cause of that ridiculous, shameful dream. After last night's peculiar turn of events, he was anxious that he might fail again and he experienced a nagging fear of leaving Emma unsatisfied once more. Had there been no children waiting to find three-legged dogs he would have suggested they slip upstairs and attempt to remedy matters. Stealing a Sunday afternoon to have relations struck him as stimulatingly sinful. He could only hope that the effect would last into the evening, because Hamish had now come in with Emma's bonnet and shawl.

~

The three-legged dog was not to be found, and Hamish was melancholy. He suggested that they look round the church-yard, because he had seen it there several times.

"Perhaps he belongs at the Manse," said Sophy.

"No, he would not live there," said Hamish. "He is too nice for Mr Wallace."

"Hamish!" exclaimed Emma.

"Dogs do not like him, Aunt Emma. Amadeus growled at him, and why would he do that if there was not something wrong with him? Dogs know."

"It's true," Sophy said. "He did growl at him."

"It must be the smell of his boots," said Emma, "or some such."

"So shall we look in the churchyard?" said Hamish.

"You may, if you do not go about calling loudly," Emma said. "For my part, I am going home. It is too cold out here now. Sophy, will you come with me, or would you rather stay with your uncle and Hamish?"

Sophy answered by taking her aunt's hand and pressing herself affectionately against her.

"We shan't be long," said Giles, feeling the bite of the cold himself.

They departed, leaving Hamish and Giles at the open gates to the churchyard. Hamish rushed in eagerly, while Giles strolled after. Ahead of him lay the main door to the church, the jougs hanging to the right. Giles reflected that if he were the minister here, he would have had them removed or at least covered up until such time as they could be taken away for good. If they had once seemed a harmless relic, they could hardly be considered so now. He wondered why Wallace had not done anything about them. Perhaps it was not entirely in his power to do so, for the elders might overrule him. They had a veto over a minister's appointment, after all. The local proprietor might propose the minister, but the elders could reject his choice if they did not find him to their taste. No doubt their power extended to a hundred small matters in the parish, and that was perhaps why the jougs remained.

While Hamish hunted under the table graves, Giles tried to imagine being called to such a life as that of the minister at Pitfeldry. What would he have made of such an opportunity if it had fallen to his lot? He supposed he would have managed to make himself comfortable. Managing the elders might be a challenge, but the place was beautiful, after all, and he liked country living. However, for a man like Wallace, conspicuously town-bred, with unfortunate manners that seemed to set him against people of all degree, it could not be easy to adapt himself to it. It was no doubt easier for his wife, who was a much more personable creature. Perhaps the sense of vocation made it all seem easier, or at least bearable. To be called to work by the Almighty was, no doubt, a great bolster to the self-love of a particular sort of man, and Wallace was, Giles suspected, that sort of man.

Hamish returned to him, looking even more miserable.

"I hope he's all right," he said. "I've seen him every day, except today."

"I'm sure he is stretched out in front of a good fire and dreaming of herding sheep," said Giles. "Let's go home, shall we?"

As they turned back they saw Lady Charlotte and Carswell coming into the churchyard. They had the look of having had a long walk through a brisk wind, provoking that high colour in their faces that was a family characteristic, along with the ravens-wing hair. Lady Charlotte wore a sensible but handsome country dress and was wrapped in a bright tartan plaid. She waved on seeing them, her face washed over with a smile of careless pleasure, not unlike the expression she had worn in his wretched dream of the previous evening. She quickened her step down the path towards him, with an eagerness it was impossible not to find both alluring and flattering.

"How fortunate," she said. "I am going to inspect Mrs Wallace's Sunday School," she added.

"Perhaps the dog is there," Hamish said.

"Which dog is this, Master Hamish?" asked Lady Charlotte.

"The three-legged dog, Lady Charlotte. Have you seen him?"

"Oh, you mean Sandy Donaldson's dog," said Carswell. "No, I have not seen her today."

"Ah, so she does have an owner, Hamish," Giles said.

"She does, or rather did, for Sandy died some years ago," Carswell said. "I think her name is Star."

"Star," repeated Hamish, with pleasure. "So who does she belong to?"

"That is a very good question and one I cannot settle for you. She lives where she chooses."

"But that isn't right," said Hamish. "She ought to have an owner. If I lived here, I would make her mine."

"Do you not have a dog of your own?" Lady Charlotte asked.

"No," said Hamish, as if it were a great injustice. "I do not. Do you have a dog, my lady?"

"I have a spaniel called Otto," said Lady Charlotte. "I am not like my sisters. I prefer to have only one dog at a time."

"I should be quite happy with one dog as well, Uncle Giles."

"Yes, yes," said Giles, "I'm very aware of your views on the subject, and believe me, I quite understand your sentiments."

"Then why cannot I have one?" Hamish said.

"This is neither the time nor the place for these petitions," Giles said. "And you know the matter is under consideration. It is a question of when, rather than –"

"So does that mean, yes?"

"At some point, I think so. But when, I cannot say."

"Ah, how wonderful!" exclaimed Lady Charlotte, almost as pleased as Hamish. "What a beneficent uncle! Now, let me persuade you of the merits of our particular breed of spaniel: they are the best of companions – they are even acceptable to cats, if the introduction is made properly. I believe there is a cat at Rooke Court?"

"Widdershins, yes," said Hamish.

This conversation got no further as Mr Wallace was now coming through the gate towards them. He looked a little puzzled to see them there.

"Mrs Wallace has invited me to inspect her class," said Lady Charlotte.

"I am going there myself, my lady," said Mr Wallace. "I think you will find it instructive."

"I hope so."

"I should be interested to see it myself," said Giles.

"You are very welcome, of course," said Mr Wallace, "and your nephew would certainly profit by it."

Hamish looked most uncomfortable at that, and looked at Giles imploringly for some form of release.

"Perhaps not, Mr Wallace. I think he will distract the girls," said Lady Charlotte. "He would be too much of a novelty for them and he would be better off studying his catechism at home."

"Yes, quite," said Giles, grateful for Lady Charlotte's quick wits. "Run along home, will you, Hamish, and mind what Lady Charlotte tells you!"

"Oh, of course, Uncle Giles, yes, yes, I will – my lady..." Hamish added, then snatched her hand and kissed it before running off.

"I think you may have another suitor," murmured Carswell.

"This way, my lady," said Mr Wallace, offering her his

arm. They went ahead, and Carswell said, "There's no chance I can go home and study my catechism, I suppose?"

"I wanted to see if the Murray girls were there," said Giles.

"Ah, yes," said Carswell. "It might be instructive in that respect."

They followed Lady Charlotte and Mr Wallace into the schoolroom which was attached to the Church by a little covered passageway. There were about twenty girls present, sitting on long forms, while Mrs Wallace was sitting at the front reading to them. The girls got to their feet when they came in. He noticed that the Murray sisters were present, scattered amongst their peers. Janet Murray, at the back with the older girls, looked pale and thin in comparison with her more robust companions. Giles wondered why her mother had not kept her at home.

"Now, my children," Mr Wallace began. "You heard my sermon this morning and I trust you paid attention. Firstly, what was the text from the Old Testament?"

All of the hands went up.

"You," said Wallace, selecting a girl.

The girl rose and said, "Deuteronomy eighteen, verses nine to twelve."

"Very good, my child. Now, who can repeat any of the verses?"

This time rather fewer hands went up.

"You," said Wallace, choosing a red-haired girl of about Sophy's age.

"When thou art come into the land which the Lord thy God giveth thee, thou shalt not learn to do after the abominations of those nations," the girl began. This was not the text that Mr Carswell had preached from that morning. The girl went on with impressive confidence but in a flat delivery quite devoid of expression: "There shall not be found among you anyone that maketh his son or his daughter to pass through the fire, or that useth divination, or an observer of times, or an enchanter, or a witch, or a charmer, or a consulter with familiar spirits, or a wizard, or a necromancer. For all that do these things are an abomination unto the Lord: and because of these abominations the Lord thy God doth drive them out from before thee."

"Very good, Margaret," said Wallace. "Very good indeed."

Giles glanced at Carswell, irritated that Wallace had chosen such a text. It was presumably not the one prescribed for the day. What had he meant by choosing it, if not to whip up fear and gossip?

Wallace went on: "Now, we have our text – what was my exposition? Janet Murray, will you answer that? Stand up, Janet Murray, and answer me!"

"I do not think I can, sir," she said, in a whisper.

"Come, my child," said Wallace, and gestured at her to stand up.

"I can't, sir," she said.

"Janet Murray, I command you to stand and answer me!"

"No, sir, I cannae!" she burst out, and began shrieking, as if in great pain. She was rocking on the form on which she sat, and the girls on either side of her jumped up and away from her as if repulsed by something. Carswell went rushing to the back of the room, and crouched down by her, taking her hands, trying to see what was wrong with her. This action she forcibly resisted, kicking him away, and then finding her legs, she jumped up and rushed through the classroom to the front, where she fell on her knees in front of Wallace and screamed: "Thou shalt not suffer a witch... a witch to live!" at the top of her voice, after which she collapsed onto the floor, and lay there writhing.

The room had already erupted in screaming as Carswell ran to attend to her.

"Silence!" Giles shouted. "Silence here, at once!" This had

some effect and the noise died down. "This class is dismissed. Go straight to your homes, and do not chatter about what you have seen. Your friend has been taken ill, that is all!"

"Come, girls," said Mrs Wallace, beginning to shepherd them towards the coat pegs. "Put on your cloaks and bonnets, now."

Lady Charlotte went to assist her, crouching down and helping the younger ones with their ribbons. Janet's sisters, however, stood as if frozen, unsure what to do.

"Go home, both of you," Giles said, "and get your mother. We are going to take Janet to the Manse. Yes, Mr Carswell?"

"Yes," said Carswell, who was on his knees with Janet on the floor. She seemed to be having a convulsive fit. He had taken off his overcoat to make a pillow for her head as she flailed about, and he was now inserting a folded handkerchief into her mouth, presumably to stop her biting her tongue. At length she seemed to grow calmer, and lay there only shivering, her gaze flitting about in terror. Carswell removed the gag from her mouth and helped her sit up a little.

"I'm going to..." she managed to say, before leaning over and vomiting profusely at the feet of Wallace himself, who stepped back with an expression of extreme distaste on his face.

"Oh, you poor wee thing," said Mrs Wallace, offering her own handkerchief and some salts. "Let us get you back to the Manse, and see if we cannot make you feel a little better there."

"Can you walk, do you think?" Carswell said.

"I don't know," said Janet.

"We will carry you if necessary," said Giles.

"Wallace, go and see that the fire is made up," said Mrs Wallace. "We cannot bring her back to a cold room, can we?"

Wallace looked as if he were about to reproach his wife for her tone of command, but it seemed that the smell of vomit was too much for him and he covered his mouth, stepped over the debris and stalked out of the room.

"There is a pail of sawdust in the corner there," said Mrs Wallace, who, with Carswell, was helping Janet to her feet. "One never knows with children, does one?"

Pleased by Mrs Wallace's firm and sensible direction of affairs, Giles went to fetch the pail, only to find that Lady Charlotte had already laid hold of it.

"I'm better used to dirty work than you," he said, putting out his hand to take it from her.

"One must start somewhere, surely?" she said, and went to scatter sawdust.

Janet now seemed to be reasonably steady, supported as she was by Carswell and Mrs Wallace. Indeed, the woman's motherly embrace was probably the greatest benefit to her, and together they left the schoolroom.

"Mr Wallace has forgotten his Bible," Lady Charlotte said. It was lying on the table, and Giles picked it up.

"That was an unwise text for him to choose this morning," he remarked, opening it at the marker, which then slipped onto the floor. It was a thin, plaited affair, grey and dull brown in colour. "Is this made of hair?" he said, stooping to retrieve it.

"Yes," said Lady Charlotte, coming to look at it. "His mama's, I suppose."

"A custom I have never understood," Giles said, replacing it and closing the Bible, glad not to have to look at it.

"You are not sentimental, of course," Lady Charlotte said, putting the pail back in its corner.

"Yes, I am," said Giles. "You saw me give in to Hamish. That was pure sentiment."

"Yes, I suppose so. I do hope you gratify his desire sooner rather than later," she said, as they left the schoolroom.

"I'd rather thought of drawing it out as long as possible to keep him in check."

"No? You are not serious, I hope."

"No, Mrs Vernon and I are agreed on it. She is a great lover of dogs as well. It is just that we have not settled on a breed we both like. She likes pointers while I am not so enthusiastic. I would like another greyhound, but they are known to destroy cats, and Widdershins is the mistress of us all now, of course."

They had arrived at the Manse, where they followed the others into the drawing room. Here Mr Wallace was obediently raking up a fine inferno. Janet collapsed on the sofa, and Mrs Wallace went out in search of brandy and hot water. Carswell made a cursory examination of the girl.

"When did you last eat, Janet?" Carswell asked.

"I don't know. I couldn't eat my dinner. I can't eat these days. It makes me sick to put anything in my mouth."

"Have you lost weight?"

"Aye, I suppose so."

"And have you begun bleeding at times? I think you told me so, before."

"You mean the curse, sir?"

"If that is what you call it, yes."

"Yes, but not since we came away from Ayr. Not since I was away at school."

"Is that when you lost your appetite?" said Carswell. "When you moved up here?"

She nodded.

"My mother says I'm being too dainty and I should be grateful for what the Lord puts on my plate."

"You mother is right," said Mr Wallace.

"I quite understand, Miss Murray," said Lady Charlotte. "I knew a girl who suffered exactly this way when she was about your age. Everything was disgusting to her. It did pass, however."

"No, my lady, I know you mean to be kind, but that has nothing to do with this. What happened back there, it was like the other day, sir, as I told you, it was... him."

"Him?" said Carswell. "You mean you think again that Satan had hold of you?"

"I don't think it, sir," she said. "I know it! That is why I couldn't stand up. That is why I was screaming – he was choking me from the inside. It was just the same."

"You need rest and better food," said Carswell. "Have you no friends in Ayr you could go back and stay with? I think that would do you enormous good."

"No," she said, "and he will not let me go. She will not let me go either, for she must do as he bids."

"She?" said Wallace. "Who do you mean, child?"

"You will not accuse that poor Mrs Haynes again, I hope, Janet," said Carswell.

"No, not her. No, she is nothing compared to his other creature here."

"Who are you speaking of, Janet?" said Wallace.

"Mistress McCroy," Janet said. "She is a witch, and no mistake."

Chapter Twenty-seven

The men left Lady Charlotte and Mrs Wallace attempting to feed Janet some broth, and went into Wallace's study. This was a spartan, ugly and excessively tidy apartment. It was heavy with books, as would be expected, but there was no sense of a lively scholar's mind at work. Neither was there much comfort offered for the visitor. There was a single chair set at the writing table. His parishioners, Giles supposed, had to stand while confiding their troubles to him, if they felt moved to do so. It was a wonder that more of the villagers had not drifted towards Mr Carswell's church, and his more sympathetic nature. Yet, if you had been raised in that grim theology, and sincerely believed that everything was predestined – including your place in Heaven or otherwise – then to look elsewhere would have been incomprehensible. What would be the point of it? It could make no difference.

"She is bordering on the malnourished and nothing she says can be taken very seriously," Carswell said. "She has picked up a lot of silly notions somewhere. I must say, sir," he added to Mr Wallace, "I do not think it was wise of you to preach from that text this morning! You are only encouraging this by doing so."

"I must concur with Mr Carswell," said Giles. "I certainly think her last accusation should go no further. The girl is not in her right mind."

"It was not an accusation," said Wallace. "It was a denunciation. The powers of good and evil are at war in that child, and we dismiss what she says at our peril. I cannot ignore it. She is a member of my congregation and I must investigate it. I am obliged to root out evil in my flock. Mrs McCroy will have to answer to these charges in front of the Presbytery."

"I may be a stranger here," said Giles, "and enjoying her hospitality, but it strikes me that she is one of the most respected women in this place. Are you really intending to subject a woman like Mrs McCroy, the widow of one of your own profession, to what I am sure will be a thoroughly humiliating procedure that will only cause gossip and bad feeling in the town?"

"You are very strong for her, sir," said Wallace. "Janet Murray was clear. I cannot ignore what she says."

"In my profession an unsubstantiated accusation is always treated with great suspicion. What evidence do you have to take such a step against her?"

"Janet Murray's testimony is sufficient. You saw her, did you not? She was possessed and there must be a conduit for such evil. The Devil chooses his lightning rod, and I have had my suspicions about Mrs McCroy for some time. This only confirms it."

"I would think very carefully about taking this any further, Mr Wallace," Giles said. "You will do more harm than good, and that poor girl will suffer the most for it if you use her in this fashion. She does not know what she is doing."

The door opened and Mrs Wallace came in.

"Mrs Murray is here now, and with a gig," she said. "It is quite a blessing – she drove down to fetch the girls from the class. Agnes and Jessie met her on the road. I think she was worried about Janet."

"Excellent. I will go back with them to make sure she is settled," Carswell said, and left the room. Giles followed with Mrs Wallace, but Wallace remained in the room.

"Will you come and speak to her?" Mrs Wallace said.

Wallace said nothing, but rather abruptly closed the door in their faces.

"I think I have upset your husband," Giles said, wondering if he ought to go back and mitigate his words a little. He had perhaps been too strong, but he had never expected an educated man to be so unreasonable.

"Oh, never you mind about him, Major Vernon," said Mrs Wallace. "He is always shutting himself away like that. He has his little humours, that is all."

Carswell departed in the gig with Janet and Mrs Murray, and it remained for Giles to take Lady Charlotte back to the Castle. He felt reluctant to do so after that disturbing dream, feeling he should not expose himself too much to her company. But he could not allow her to walk back alone, not just for reasons of ordinary civility, but because whoever had murdered Mrs Gowans was still at large, and there was no evidence that he might not choose to attack another solitary female. Indeed, even as she was fastening her bonnet ribbons and they were about to set off, he found himself turning the facts of the case over in his mind again, thinking of the other deaths in the area. It was, at least, a useful distraction, and he was silent for a few minutes as they set out.

"What are you thinking so deeply about?" she said.

"That accident in the Pass of Vorlich when Mrs Black was killed in February. I was reminding myself to speak to your father about it, and to Mr Macdonald. The path was rebuilt. Did you hear anything about it?"

"No. How shocking – I had no idea that someone had actually fallen from it. It is a very treacherous path. I have walked along there with Papa and it was frightening, and he regretted taking me there. I am glad it was rebuilt. Who was Mrs Black?"

"She was from the next parish. I think her daughter lives here, which was why she was walking that way. It might be counted a short cut."

"A most dangerous one, but I suppose if she were familiar with it, and she had a stick to lean on... oh dear!"

"Her body has not been found."

"No? That is truly awful. Her poor family."

"It is odd, as well, for I am sure the search was thorough.

But in a deep, heavily wooded gorge, which I take it to be?" Lady Charlotte nodded. "Well, such a place may conceal many secrets, no matter how careful the search. But with the reconstruction of the path, one might have thought –"

"Do you think this may not be an accident?" Lady Charlotte said, interpreting his silence.

"If this investigation were my responsibility," Giles said, "which it is not, I would take pains to make sure there was no doubt about it."

"It would be a great kindness to that family if it could be settled. To not be able to bury her – oh, how they must always be hoping she returns by some means or other. As it is, it must seem she has vanished into thin air."

"I wonder why it was assumed she had fallen there. There must have been some evidence on the path. Your father will know the details, I am sure. Tell him I will call tomorrow – if I may?"

"Of course," she said. "We shall all be glad to see you, and that is most conscientious of you, given that you are not supposed to be engaged on this."

"Mr Carswell wondered if it was possible for me to restrain myself."

"I think he is right," said Lady Charlotte. "And he has, no doubt, caught the same disease from you."

"He is certainly the best of colleagues," Giles said.

They walked a little further in silence, and then Lady Charlotte said, "What a curious little man Mr Wallace is!"

"More than curious. Malicious, I fear," said Giles. "He wishes to accuse Mrs McCroy publicly and make a spectacle of her. I hope I haven't hardened his resolve."

"In what way?"

"I was perhaps a trifle direct with him. I told him that it was a foolish idea. Some people respond well to bluntness – it is just what they need – but I suspect Mr Wallace may be one of those men who need to have any good advice served up to them with gloved hands and on a silver salver."

"If he sincerely believes it, nothing you say, however carefully, will dissuade him. That is the nature of fanatics, surely? His face did light up when Janet said Mrs McCroy's name."

"That's interesting. What can have passed between them to make him dislike her so much?"

"I don't think he likes women at all," said Charlotte. "I do feel for his wife. She is a pleasant soul."

"Yes, better suited to be the minster here, I should say," said Giles.

"It is a pity that cannot be! Perhaps one day."

"What shall we have first, then, my lady – a female Prime Minister or a female Archbishop of Canterbury?"

"Either would be striking, and a great benefit to society," said Lady Charlotte. "But when, who can say? I do not like to practise divination."

"Not in this climate, certainly. You will have Mr Wallace hauling you up in front of the elders."

"What if Mrs McCroy has been practising witchcraft?" Lady Charlotte said. This was the question he had been asking himself, thinking of what he had seen in the attic. Were those old books perhaps volumes of spells, and were those three dancing women witches?

"So long as she has not been charging money for spells, she may do as she likes," he said. "That is where the law stands. But what the Kirk says about the matter, I don't know. I do not know what sanctions Mr Wallace has at his disposal."

"She might be excommunicated, I think," said Lady Charlotte.

"That would be wicked on his part," said Giles. "Do these people not understand forgiveness? This doctrine of predestination appalls me, I must confess."

"Yes, it is terrible," said Lady Charlotte. "I have never understood the appeal."

"That a man cannot drown because he is ordained to

hang, isn't that what they say?" Giles went on. "Which means a man can do as much evil as he likes. It makes no difference if he is good or not. He is damned or saved all the same. What a notion!"

"There is quite a frightening novel on the subject," Lady Charlotte said, "which Mr Wallace will not approve of me having read: Hogg's 'Memoir of a Justified Sinner'. Nor would my mother, for that matter," she added with a sigh, gesturing at the Castle which now lay within sight. "Oh dear, I must go back into all that. Dunbar will be at dinner. I wish I could catch Maria's cold and hide away. I cannot bear the sight of him, and now he is my brother-in-law!"

"I'm sorry. It will be a trial for you."

"He is a dreadful man! That is the long and the short of it. It took me some time to find out, and fortunately I did, but now we shall never be rid of him! Perhaps I should marry the Prince and run away to wherever it is he comes from. Though even that seems impossible. I don't think he is serious – in fact, Maria tells me he is not." She sighed. "I had better cultivate my spinsterly arts, had I not? What shall I learn? I could weave brooches out of hair, like Mr Wallace."

"What?"

"He has a little loom. I saw it in the drawing room. That explains the bookmark, does it not?"

"That's a strange pastime for a man. No, for anyone."

"Mrs Wallace said he is very skilled at it. He sends for hair from Glasgow." Giles began to laugh. "Truly, he does."

"Whose hair?"

"I think poor women sell it. There is even a trade in it. They make it into ringlets and wigs and so forth, and it seems you can buy it to make jewellery."

"That I did not know," said Giles, still laughing. "What a singular booby he is! He talked through your song the other night as well – another black mark against him."

"He did not? The rogue! That ought to be an indictable

offence, in my opinion. When one has worked up one's courage to perform at all, how galling to be ignored!"

"Does it frighten you all so much to do it?" Giles said. "Should I not demand to be entertained in future? I feel I have been torturing you all."

"No, of course not. Many women like to perform and take great pride in it," said Lady Charlotte. "Maria is never happier, but I do not care for it much. It is not my natural metier."

"You have a fine voice," Giles said. "And it was an affecting performance. You should not doubt your powers."

"Thank you, sir," she said with a smile and a half-curtsey. "I am encouraged."

"Good," he said. "I should be extremely sorry if I never heard you sing again. Once was not enough to satisfy me."

Even as he said this, he regretted it. It sounded too much like an expression of courtship rather than a simple compliment. He realised that this conversation, running on so pleasantly between them, was leading them into a dangerous place, and that he must check himself. It was too easy to be beguiled by her. He knew his mistake for certain when she laid her hand on his forearm and gazed at him.

"I will sing for you whenever you like," she said, and then even before he had begun to remove her hand, she pulled it away as if she had been burnt, no doubt realising that she had also said too much and with too much transparency. She stepped away briskly. "Really, it is too impossible," she said, in slightly choked tones. "I always forget myself with you. Please, please excuse me!"

She began to walk away towards the Castle, never once looking back at him.

He walked home feeling thoroughly ill at ease with himself, a sensation not at all mitigated by discovering Emma, Sophy and Hamish taking tea with Mrs McCroy in the dining room. It made for a cheerful, domestic scene of the sort he usually delighted in, but he could think only of Charlotte's wretchedness and how he was at the root of it. He had recklessly enjoyed the sunshine of her admiration and his own vanity had blinded him to the danger. She was wounded badly, and he had done nothing to help her.

"That was a long Bible class," said Emma, stretching out her hand to him. "It is as well you spared Hamish. What happened?"

"Janet Murray was taken ill again. I was at the Manse," he said, sitting down. "Where is Sandro?"

"Tucked up in bed. He was extremely tired and sore-tempered, and then he started sneezing. I think he has a cold coming on," said Emma.

"Should I get Carswell? Is it a fever?"

"He is warm, but I don't think it is serious," said Emma. "The worry is if we all catch it from him."

"I have some cordial that might help him," Mrs McCroy said. She was sitting opposite in charge of the teapot. "Would you prefer coffee, Major Vernon?" she said, about to pour a cup for him.

"No, no, tea will be more than sufficient, thank you," he said, taking the cup from her, wondering at the same time how and when he should tell her of Janet's accusations and Wallace's intentions. He hoped she was well versed in the law of the Kirk, or had friends who were, and that they would know how to nip the business in the bud. Surely Wallace did not really have the power to do such a thing to a member of his congregation?

"Will you not have something to eat, sir?" he heard her say.

"Giles?" Emma now prompted him.

"Excuse me – I'm rather preoccupied, aren't I? Yes, may I have the bread and butter, please?"

"I'm sorry to hear she was ill again," said Mrs McCroy.

"Mr Carswell was there, fortunately," said Giles. "Hamish, did you have any luck in the end?"

"No," said Hamish. "But I ran straight back just as you told me to, so there was no time for looking. Do you think Lady Charlotte will let me see her spaniel? Perhaps he might have puppies for us. Lord Rothborough does breed puppies, doesn't he?"

"Puppies?" said Emma. "One puppy at most, at present, that is the agreement."

"If Sophy and I had a puppy each we would not fight over it."

"And one for Sandro too," said Sophy.

"That is not helpful," said Emma. "Now, have you both finished? If so, you may get down – and Sophy, I do not advise you to wipe your hands on your dress. That is what a napkin is for. Or better still, go and wash them. You too, Hamish."

When the children had left, Emma said, "I think if we get half a dozen puppies it will not be enough. He had better be a Master of Foxhounds. That is the only thing for it."

"There are worse ways to make a living," Giles said, and drained his cup. He got up from his place. "I think I will go and look at Sandro."

"Let me find that cordial," said Mrs McCroy, also getting up. "It is only a syrup made from rose hips. But children like such things when they are ill. My own little girl used to like it sometimes, and so I make it still, out of habit, I suppose. I don't really know why – excuse me," she said, and hurried from the room.

"Oh dear," Emma said. "So there was a little girl. How terrible that must have been for her."

Giles sat down again.

"I have some wretched news for her," he said.

"What?"

"When I said Janet Murray was taken ill, it was not as simple as that. She had a sort of fit, and began talking all manner of nonsense, and ended it all by accusing Mrs McCroy of witchcraft."

"Goodness."

"The worst of it was that Wallace seized on it and is now determined to bring her in front of some disciplinary court. Carswell and I tried to reason with him, but he is not inclined to be reasonable!"

"I am sure you will find a way to stop it," said Emma.

"I hope so," said Giles. "Perhaps Lord Rothborough will have some effect on him. Do these people not have the equivalent of bishops to keep them in line? Perhaps Mr Carswell will know to whom we should speak. But I shall have to tell her now, so she may gather her defences. She may have friends who can help her. You said she was a lawyer's daughter, didn't you?"

Emma nodded.

"What sort of witchcraft?" she said.

"A conduit for evil – that was Wallace's phrase. What a slander!" said Giles. "And he preached a highly inflammatory text this morning, so the whole of Pitfeldry is now nicely primed for a witch-hunt. I cannot imagine what possesses a man in his position to act so irresponsibly to those in his charge. I have no evidence, but I'm quite sure that he will be behind that business with the jougs."

"You are running as warm as Sandro, my dear," said Emma, getting up and pressing her hand to his forehead. He took it and kissed it.

"This has not proved much of a holiday, has it?" he said. "Forgive me."

"What is there to forgive?" she said, kissing his forehead. "It is hardly your fault, my love."

He kissed her hand again and was tempted to open his heart to her, but he had no wish to pain her merely to have the comfort of her freely-given mercy and understanding, which he was sure on this occasion he did not deserve.

He went upstairs to Sandro's temporary nursery where he found both Greene and Patton in attendance, as if he were a small royal personage. The fire, the comfortable chairs and the chance for a pleasant gossip may have had as much to do with their presence as concern for Sandro's plight, but Giles felt reassured nonetheless. Sandro was asleep, lying on his back, his arms flung wide; he looked flushed, but not inordinately so. He stirred and opened his eyes when Giles took his hand and bent over the bed, and looked pleased to see him.

"Magpie," he said. "Want him."

Giles obliged, retrieving the toy from the covers. The ninepin sergeant had acquired a nightshirt made out of a handkerchief, and, rolling onto his side, Sandro embraced him and fell back to sleep.

Having dismissed Sandro's loyal attendants to go and drink tea in the kitchen, Giles sat down by the fire and listened to the breathy, snuffling sounds of Sandro's sleep. One of Mrs McCroy's large striped cats had slipped into the room when Greene and Patton were leaving, and had taken up a post on a chair by the door, eyeing the scene in such a knowing way that Giles found himself thinking of witches' familiars.

A little while later he heard the sound of footsteps coming down the attic staircase, which he realised must lie adjacent to this room. The door opened again, and Mrs McCroy came in carrying the bottle of cordial and a little ticking pillow with a ribbon attached to it which she proceeded to tie to the bed post.

"Just a few herbs to help him breathe," she said, pressing her hand to Sandro's forehead. "He is so bonny. What a gift you have in him, Major."

"Certainly," said Giles.

"Mrs Vernon told me how the children came to you," she said. "And that you lost a little one of your own."

"I did," Giles said. "And you, I think?"

She nodded.

"It's a grief that never leaves you," she said, gently smoothing Sandro's pillow. "May I sit with him a while?"

"Of course," said Giles, sitting down again, and indicating the chair opposite. "In fact, there was something I needed to speak to you about."

"Oh yes?" she said. "There is nothing wrong here, I trust?"

"No, we could not be more comfortable. No, I wanted to talk to you about Janet Murray."

"Yes?"

"When she was taken ill this afternoon, it was a sort of hysterical fit that overtook her, at least as far as Mr Carswell can ascertain. She has suffered from this sort of thing before, and it seems to give her delusions, which take the form of saying foolish things about witchcraft and so forth."

"I see," said Mrs McCroy. She snapped her fingers, and the cat came straight to her and jumped onto her lap.

"Tonight she accused you of it," Giles said, impressed by the show of obedience from the cat. "Which perhaps would not have been such a serious thing – given that she is not well – had not Mr Wallace decided that her words were to be taken at face value. He has decided that you should be publicly accused of it. I am unsure of the procedure – it is some church committee?"

"The Kirk Session court of discipline," she said.

"And that's a serious thing, I take it?"

"Yes."

"I tried to dissuade him, naturally, but he was adamant."

She considered for a moment and said, "Mr Wallace must believe what he must believe. I have nothing to fear from public censure. Let him do what he will."

She got up and went to the bedside, where she stood looking at the sleeping Sandro like a pilgrim contemplating some holy statue.

"With respect," Giles said, "surely it is better that it

should not happen at all? I intend to speak to Lord Rothborough about it. He will perhaps be in a better position to talk some sense into Mr Wallace."

"As you wish," she said. "I thank you for your concern on my behalf, Major Vernon, but what you have told me does not alarm me."

She bent over to kiss Sandro on the forehead, and left the room.

He sat by the fire for a while, contemplating what she had said, until Emma came in. She smiled at the sight of Sandro so peacefully asleep.

"He will be his usual self again soon enough, I hope," she said, taking the seat opposite Giles. "Though the quiet version is not disagreeable."

"I told Mrs McCroy about Janet Murray's accusations."

"And?"

"She didn't seem much perturbed. I would have thought she would be angry, at least. She struck me as resigned to it, almost as if she had expected such a thing for a while. It was rather strange."

"Think of those silly boys who Hamish was fighting," Emma said. "They called her a witch. It is a gross insult, and it is especially silly of a man of the cloth to take it up, but perhaps she has heard it all before. She does not care because she is a sensible woman. We women are adept at putting on armour, you know, and in time, the armour becomes part of who we are."

"It still must be stopped," he said. "Wallace is a troublemaker, that is clear enough. Hair looms and all!"

"What are you talking about?"

He explained what Lady Charlotte had discovered, and it made her laugh.

"That is why Mrs McCroy cannot be afraid of him," she said. "How could anyone be?"

Chapter Twenty-eight

"Mr Carswell, Mr Carswell, you have to get up at once!"

Felix felt a hand grasping his shoulder and heard Jacob's voice, blunt and raw.

"What?"

"There's a message from the Castle. You are wanted there at once."

Jacob had been trained to wake him as roughly as necessary, for Felix knew he was a heavy sleeper and emergencies demanded such graceless treatment, but in that sleep-laden moment he resented the intrusion extremely.

"I'll get your clothes ready," Jacob went on. He was now dragging back the curtains.

"Leave those, for pity's sake. You'll wake Mrs Carswell."

"I am awake," said Eleanor, sitting up. "What has happened, Jacob?"

"I don't know, ma'am," said Jacob. "Only that it's very urgent."

Felix flung himself out of bed, his heart pounding, a hundred lurid scenarios running through his mind: had Lord Rothborough fallen ill? He followed Jacob across the passageway to his old bedroom and there scrabbled into his clothes, gathered his thoughts and restocked his medical bag.

Not long after, he was booted, mounted and heading for the Castle, encouraging his horse to more celerity than he usually felt comfortable with. He was glad he had taken the risk. At the front door of the Castle, he was met on the steps by Lord Rothborough emerging to meet him. He came forward to catch his horse by the bridle, as if he were an ordinary stable hand, except that stable hands did not usually wear crimson damask dressing gowns. As he approached, Felix could see that Lord Rothborough was unshaven and pale.

"It's Lady Rothborough," he said, as Felix dismounted. "Something terrible has happened. She's dead."

~

When he had first gone into Lady Rothborough's bedroom, Felix assumed that there would be some simple explanation for her death. She had been under a physician's care for some time, and although he was not privy to the details of her ailments, he had gathered they were serious. However, Lord Rothborough had indicated that she was prone to exaggeration in these matters, and he had a suspicion of this himself. So he had approached it with all the calmness he could muster, knowing that despite his connection to everyone about him, that the coolest professional demeanour was what would help them all. The atmosphere was already becoming febrile.

He was obliged in the first instance to clear her rooms, including in this Lord Rothborough. Fortunately he realised that this was necessary and took her maid in hand. The poor woman was in a state of near collapse having discovered the death in the first place. He closed the door on them all, opened the curtains fully to get all the light he could, and set to work.

Ten minutes into his examination, he began to feel that something was amiss. Lady Rothborough had apparently choked to death on her own vomit and lay tangled up in the bedclothes in a tortured position, suggesting she had suffered a succession of violent convulsions. That in itself was enough to give him pause. The more he looked, the more he was overtaken by an uneasy sense of abnormality in both the physical evidence he observed before him and in the general circumstances, or at least what he had learnt of them so far. In the usual course of events, he suspected, she should not be dead. Had there been an accident, or was something more sinister to blame?

He looked about him once more, carefully scrutinizing her bedroom and the adjoining dressing room. The dressing room was reached from the bedroom through an odd little space, carved out of the ancient castle walls, and containing as might be expected in such a convenient location, a commode, concealed behind a tapestry screen. There was no door between the two rooms.

In the dressing room, which was elegantly furnished and more like a sitting room, he discovered a large travelling medicine chest on a side table, one of those extravagant and useless pieces of cabinet-making aimed at wealthy hypochondriacs. It was unlocked, and full of the usual phials and bottles, none of which alarmed or surprised him. Next to this was another, less showy, box which contained another selection of bottles and jars containing the medicines prescribed by her physicians, as well as letters from them with careful directions for their administration. Most of these were harmless nostrums, which may or may not have done her Ladyship good. They served mostly, he suspected, to line the pockets of those who prescribed them. However, there was a bottle of salts of baryta which could not be described as harmless. It was almost empty, and it was this that concerned him most of all. Vomiting and convulsions would be consistent with an overdose of salts of baryta.

He had noticed a small burn mark on the corner of her lips, suggesting she had taken a quantity of something liable to irritate. Had someone made a mistake in the dose? After all, such things happened with depressing regularity.

He returned to the bedroom. On the table by the bed was a tiny, thick edition of the Bible, with a long embroidered marker sticking out of it. Beneath was a leather-bound journal with a clasp. He hesitated to examine it, so personal did it seem, but the clasp was open and he knew Major Vernon would not have paused. Even as he picked it up, he realised that would have to be the next step – the Major would have to be fetched, and perhaps Mrs Vernon too, he thought, having glimpsed Maria's stricken expression. She would need her friend at such a moment.

Lady Rothborough's journal was written in pencil, in a tiny hand that was hard to decipher. He was forced to carry it to the window and squint at it. There was much written with a great deal of underlining, sometimes two or three times, not to mention copious scatterings of exclamation marks. At times, however, she resorted to capitals – this at least made for legibility, but Felix could not like what he read. They were, in the main, furious complaints.

> CHARLOTTE WILL NOT LISTEN TO ME. SHE LOOKS AT ME WITH CONTEMPT. MY OWN CHILD DESPISES ME!!!! WAS OBLIGED to receive THE FRENCH BASTARD by R, WHO HATES ME.

He turned quickly to the last page. It was dated for that Sunday, and he could just make out that she had noted two Bible passages, presumably those she had read that morning, and she had also written "read morning prayer."

Then the writing became almost impossible to decipher until he turned the page and saw written in capitals:

> MY HUSBAND. MY CRUEL HUSBAND WISHES ME DEAD. I SWEAR TO THE LORD THIS IS TRUE!!

He closed it after the most cursory examination, for those phrases alone were enough to make him feel most uncomfortable. He put it down again where he had found it, for Major Vernon would wish to see everything exactly as it had been discovered. Neither did he wish Lord Rothborough nor any of his daughters to see the journal until he had spoken to Major Vernon about it.

He covered Lady Rothborough with a sheet and left the room, locking the door behind him and pocketing the key. It was just as well, because there was a footman and a housemaid waiting in the passageway, the latter armed with the tools of her trade.

"Am I not to clean in there, sir?" she said. "Where is she to be laid out?"

"Not yet," Felix said, and turned to the footman. "Where is his Lordship, Tom?"

Tom showed him to the breakfast room, where he found Lord Rothborough, accompanied by ladies Charlotte, Augusta and Maria as well as Dunbar and the Prince. All were still in their dressing gowns and obviously waiting to see what he would say, but he had no wish to speak to anyone except Lord Rothborough.

"So?" Lord Rothborough said.

"May we have a word alone, sir?"

"Of course," Lord Rothborough said, and ushered him out of the room. They went into the empty dining room and Felix shut the door behind him.

"I do not like it," he said. "There is something wrong."

"What are you saying?"

"I cannot say it was a natural death. I need to speak to Major Vernon."

"Dear God," said Lord Rothborough, and sat down on one of the chairs ranged against the wall. "What are you suggesting?"

"It is possible there was an accident of some sort. That is the most likely thing, but –"

"Yes?"

"How did she seem last night? Was she unhappy?"

"She is" – Lord Rothborough paused to correct himself – "was always unhappy. But we were all wretched last night."

"When did you last speak to her?"

"Late last night in her bedroom."

"Was it a quarrel?"

Rothborough sighed.

"Yes," he said. "And I wish to God I had kept my temper, but she said things I could not allow to pass. Why did I not? After all this time, have I learnt nothing? I was very cruel to her." He broke off, and pressed his hands to his face. "God forgive me!"

Felix found he must sit down himself. The vast, chilly room seemed to entomb them. He felt a sick fear that he might learn something he could not bear to know. He had heard the confessions of murderers, and he had observed men and women crushed by the unbearable pressure of their guilt – now he searched his own father for those terrible symptoms.

Major Vernon had once remarked of interviewing a possibly guilty suspect: "If you sit long enough and in silence, they will tell you everything you need to know."

He pushed his hands through his hair and let that silence begin. It was a necessary torture for both of them. Felix knew that if Lord Rothborough had done such a thing, he would not be able to conceal it from him, and so he let the moments pass.

Then Lord Rothborough said, "Yes, we must get Vernon here. You and he will get to the bottom of this. One can only pray it was an accident and that she did not decide to destroy herself."

"Had she ever threatened that before?"

"Yes," said Lord Rothborough. "At one time, I made sure she did not have anything noxious to hand, but lately – oh dear heavens, what has she done to herself?" He got up and stood before Felix, his hands resting on Felix's shoulders. "Whatever you find out, Felix, I beg you to forgive me for whatever part I had in it. I am a wretched excuse for a man, and no example for you. You have surpassed me in everything that matters." He bent and kissed him on the forehead, and Felix, rising from his place, felt his father shaking with emotion. He put his arms about him and allowed him to give vent to his misery. "I cannot bear to have you think ill of me, my boy – that is what pains me most of all, that I have been such a poor father to you, in every way. Just as I have been such a monstrous husband to that poor, poor creature."

~

Lady Charlotte, in the plainest of black dresses, her hair arranged more severely than usual – presumably in her haste to be dressed in the wake of such a momentous occurrence – had the look of a penitent as she greeted Giles that morning.

"This is dreadful," she said. "That Carswell feels he must send for you – the way this has happened. But I cannot say I'm not very glad to see you. Oh, my poor mother! And I had been at war with her for so long, and made her so unhappy, I know it! How ever shall I bear this?"

She stretched out her hands to him, her red-rimmed eyes full of tears, and although it seemed ungenerous in the extreme not to comfort her as he guessed she wished, he knew he must not. Clasping his hands behind his back, he said, "It is terrible, but you are stronger than you know, my lady. You will find the necessary courage, I'm sure."

She nodded, pulling back her own hands, and clasping them together.

Lady Maria joined them then, and in her own typically impulsive way, insisted on flinging her arms about him, and saying, "Oh, my dear, dearest Major, how good it is to see you here!"

"Mrs Vernon will be here soon. She says if you do not want her, you are to send her away at once and not to mind about it."

"Send her away? Oh never, never!" said Maria, her arms still about him. In fact, Giles was obliged to gently detach her, before she soaked his waistcoat and made her sister even more wretched. This done, she took it in good part and dried her tears; remembering herself, she said, "You will want to go up. Shall I show you –?"

"I will find my own way," said Giles, wanting to get his own sense of the circumstances.

A strange death in a strange house, he thought, as he climbed up the turnpike stairs. It was as well to attempt to distance himself a little from its inhabitants, he decided, but that was no easy task.

He was not alone for long. A bend in the passageway revealed Carswell, striding about in his shirt sleeves.

"Thank God you are here," he murmured. "This way. I have locked the room."

Carswell turned the key in the lock and they went in. Carswell then fastened the door behind him. "I really think it better we should not be interrupted, at least in the short term."

Giles nodded and looked about him. Carswell's medical bag was lying open on a table, paper and ink nearby where he had started to take notes. His coat was thrown over a chair.

"Let us sit down and we can start from the beginning," Giles said, taking off his own coat – the room was warm, airless and did not smell pleasant. He set his own notebook and pencil on the table and said, "Who found her?"

"Her maid, Mary Parsons."

"Have you talked to her yet?" Giles said, noting the name.

"No. She was in something of a state. Also she is quite deaf, apparently, so it is not an easy matter at the best of times."

"So she finds her mistress will not wake, and speaks to whom?"

"James Bodley," said Carswell, "who woke Lord Rothborough. And after that I was sent for. I arrived here at just before nine and found the room full of folk, so I cleared them out, and what was left is what you see here, apart from my things. No one has been in since, except me."

Giles looked about him again.

"And that is the dressing room?"

"Yes," said Carswell. "And there is no way out through there."

"Cause of death?"

"Asphyxiation on her own vomit. I think she was poisoned by something, by some means as yet to be established, but we have a good candidate in salts of baryta."

"Which are?"

"It is a common prescription for digestive trouble. It is harmless if taken in small doses, but the jar is thoroughly cleared out, and the date on the bottle is the beginning of the month. If it had been taken sensibly by one person, a half teaspoon a day at most, there is no way the bottle could have been emptied. There were two ounces in there, according to the label."

"And a large dose is poisonous?"

"Fatal. It is the only thing I can find in here that could have done such mischief. But we have not searched elsewhere. Must we search everywhere?" he added, with a frown.

"If you can establish that that was the cause, then no," said Giles. "What other indications did you find that suggest it?"

Carswell got up, went to the bed and uncovered her. Giles went to the bedside and was shocked by what he saw. It was a miserable end to what did not seem to have been a happy life.

"She appears to have suffered convulsions, which are consistent with baryta poisoning, as is the violent vomiting. There is a burn here, at the corner of her mouth. Something has irritated it, and baryta in quantity would be liable to burn."

"Your presumption seems reasonable," said Giles. "But why can it not be an accident?"

"Because it tastes extremely bitter. It would not have been palatable in a large quantity. She would have realised at once that the dose was too high. Which leads me to think that she either took a large dose deliberately, or someone else forced her into it. That latter supposition is pure fancy. I think she destroyed herself."

"Because?"

"Look at this," said Carswell, going to the bedside and taking up a bound journal with a clasp. "Her diary. It is – well, read it for yourself and then tell me if she did not wish to end her life."

Having studied a few pages as best he could, Giles said, "It is possible. Goodness, her hand is hard to read. Perhaps one of her daughters will be able to read it?"

"I would rather they did not," said Carswell. "And as for Lord Rothborough! I wish I could throw it in the fire, to be frank!"

"We can't do that," said Giles, closing it and putting it in his pocket. He then covered Lady Rothborough again. "Perhaps, when the whole thing is legible, it will not seem so slanted towards that theory."

"But if you disregard that solution," Carswell said, "you are left with murder. I must rule out accident."

"Don't rule it out yet. As you know, accidents can cause curiously misleading effects. We must talk to her maid."

"You should speak to my father first," said Carswell. Giles realised he had never before heard Carswell refer to his relationship to Lord Rothborough so plainly.

"Yes, I should," said Giles. "But first I want us to make a proper examination of the rooms here, before anything is disturbed."

"What are we looking for?"

"Anomalies," said Giles.

Carswell nodded, and they set to work. Carswell made careful notes about the medicine chests and the various medications, while Giles looked through the cupboards and drawers. He was not sure what might present itself, but he knew from experience that there was an eloquence in tiny things.

"So what have you found?" said Carswell as he came into the dressing room.

"A lozenge on the floor by the commode," he said. "Have you a box of lozenges there?"

He held out his hand containing a small, pink, diamond-shaped lozenge.

"There is nothing here like that. Perhaps one of the servants dropped it. It looks like a cough drop or some such," said Carswell, taking it and sniffing it.

"It must have been dropped in the last twelve hours," said Giles. "The servants in this house would not have let it lie there long, not in their mistress' bedroom. The same with these," he said, showing Carswell the pair of little ivory-handled sewing scissors he had found.

"Where were those?"

"Under the bed."

"I suppose those belong to Lady Rothborough?" said Carswell.

"Perhaps not," said Giles. "There is a work box on the side table there, and the scissors are in place."

"It is curious," said Carswell.

There was a knock at the door.

"May I come in?"

It was Lord Rothborough. Carswell gave Giles an enquiring glance, and Giles nodded. He went and opened the window before he allowed Carswell to unlock the door.

Lord Rothborough came in and they shook hands.

"Felix is uneasy," he said to Giles. "Can he be right?"

"If you could just give us a little more time, my lord, we may be able to give you a clearer answer," said Giles, putting the lozenge and the scissors down on the table. "I appreciate that this is difficult."

"No, I perfectly understand." As he spoke, he went over to the bedside and stood looking down at Lady Rothborough. "You must do what must be done, and God knows, there is no one else I would trust with this. If she has destroyed herself –" He reached out and touched the linen that covered her forehead. "Then –" He was struggling with his emotions. "That will be a burden I shall carry for the rest of my life, and beyond the grave, no doubt."

Chapter Twenty-nine

"Miss Parsons – or is it Mrs?" Giles enquired.

"You'll have to speak louder than that, sir," said James Bodley. "She is very hard of hearing – aren't you, Mrs Parsons?" he added loudly. "Hard of hearing?"

"Oh, yes, sir," said Mrs Parsons. "I'm nearly deaf these days. My lord is going to send me to a man in Edinburgh that Mr Carswell says is quite a miracle worker. It was because my lady used to get so cross with me." She frowned as if she had said something improper. "I did my best, sir – it cannot have been easy for her, and I was very lucky to have a place, I know it."

"Nonsense, Mrs Parsons, my lady was lucky to have you!" Bodley said. "She ran through goodness knows how many maids before you came, and you are the only one who has stayed more than a year."

"How long have you been with the family, Mrs Parsons?" Giles asked, speaking as clearly and distinctly as he could without actually shouting.

"Nearly twelve years now, sir," said Mrs Parsons, who mercifully seemed to understand him. She sighed. "What an end to it, what an end! And I remember as if it were yesterday when I was helping Mrs Hope at Holbroke lay out your own dear wife. And now I must see my own lady to her grave. Will she be buried here?" she added, turning to Mr Bodley.

Mr Bodley made a gesture to express his ignorance on the point.

"Perhaps, Mrs Parsons, you could tell me what happened last night?" Giles said. "When was the last time you saw Lady Rothborough?"

"It was about eleven. That is usually when she lets me go. I gave her medicine to her as usual, helped her undress and so forth, and then arranged the bed. Then I left her to her prayers."

"And she did not call you in the night?"

"No, sir."

"What was her mood last night?"

"She was most unhappy, I have to say that, sir. She'd had words with the young ladies, and with my lord too. I was in the dressing room, you see, sorting out her things as I often do of an evening, doing a bit of mending. She likes – liked to have me within calling distance in the evening."

"So you could hear these conversations?" Giles said.

"Yes, but I could not make out what was being said – but they were all at odds, that I could tell, even with my poor ears."

"And was that unusual?" Giles said.

"Not lately, no," said Mrs Parsons. "And, Mr Bodley, you may look at me like that as much as you please, but that's the truth, isn't it? This is not a happy family, and it would be wrong to lie about it. My lord himself would agree with me. He told me I must tell the absolute truth, no matter how bad it seems."

"So she was in some distress when you attended her, last thing?"

"Yes. She'd been crying and she was looking through her Bible for comfort."

"Tell me what medicine Lady Rothborough takes."

"It's always the same," said Mrs Parsons, reaching into her pocket and taking out a piece of paper. "I have it all written out – Lady Augusta wrote it out for me, because Dr Parozzi's handwriting was so hard to read, being foreign. She made sure it was all straight. We didn't want to make any mistakes." She handed the paper to Giles.

"May I keep this?" said Giles, glancing down at the paper.

"I want Mr Carswell to see it."

~

Finding himself alone with the late Marchioness and wondering if a full post-mortem would be necessary, Felix had decided he would make a more thorough external examination while he could. He began by removing her elaborate nightcap, and was obliged to cut the strings of it with his knife, for the knot was pulled very tight and could not be unpicked by hand. This tightness stuck him as curious. It could not have been comfortable, although it was secure. He removed the nightcap and found himself faced with a sight that the lady would have been most distressed for anyone, let alone Felix Carswell, to see: a head of thinning, wispy hair touched with grey. On the left side, there was an area that had been roughly cut away. He wondered if she had done this to herself, and if it was a symptom of the agitation that her journal displayed. It was not unknown for patients in mental distress to inflict wounds on themselves. He supposed any such marks would add weight to a conclusion of self-murder.

However, his further investigations were curtailed by a knock on the door and a message from Major Vernon, carried by Tom, the footman. He was not sorry to leave.

Lord Rothborough – practical even in the most trying circumstances – had allocated them the library for their private use, and here Felix found Major Vernon sensibly eating a late breakfast. Discovering he had an appetite, despite everything, Felix sat down and joined him; not until the smoked salmon and poached eggs were done, and the coffee cups had been refilled, did they turn again to the business in hand.

Major Vernon began by handing him the copy of Dr Parozzi's directions.

"Does anything strike you as unusual?"

"No," said Felix, "and it confirms the view both Lord Rothborough and I have taken that there was nothing very much wrong with her, at least physically. Her mental state, however –"

"You are tending towards suicide?"

"It does seem the most likely explanation. Not that that is of any comfort to anyone, especially my poor father."

"I'm not sure about suicide."

"Why not?" Felix said. "Lord Rothborough has told me that in the past he considered her in danger from such a course. She may even have attempted such a thing before."

Major Vernon drained his coffee cup and got up from the table.

"In some respects," he said, beginning to pace the room, "it would be the easiest answer." He ceased his pacing and gazed out of the window, his figure caught in the intense shaft of morning sunlight streaming through the vast casement. "But the easiest answer may not be the right answer, and we owe her the truth, most of all."

Felix sat in silence for a moment and then said, "But you cannot be thinking this is murder. If it is murder, then we must consider everyone, and –"

"And you have not already done so?" said Major Vernon. "Given how often in such cases it is those nearest to the victim that are most likely to be the perpetrators – and given what you know of relations between them all and how things have broken down. It must be looked at, however painful, if only to eliminate them. And you also forget that we have strangers in the house, about whom we know very little: the Prince and Lord Dunbar. What is their true story, I wonder?"

Felix did not find much comfort in this and sat drinking the last of his coffee, various distressing scenarios flitting through his mind. Major Vernon now commandeered one of the writing tables and was laying out sheets of paper.

"And also," the Major went on, "we have any number of unknown persons to consider. The door to her room was not locked. In a large house like this there is always a great deal of coming and going." He began to scribble names on each of the papers and then glanced up at Felix. "The sooner this is done –"

"Yes, of course," said Felix, getting up. He looked down at the table. The first paper was headed "Lord R". Felix picked it up and said, "I did tell him earlier if there was anything that he had to say to me, he should say it there and then. I am certain that he would not be able to keep that from me."

"Well done," said Major Vernon. "And what was your conclusion?"

"He feels responsible, certainly, but I do not think he has any hand in this. It is not in his nature, no matter how frustrated he might be with her. Besides, what is the gain in it? That is the question you often ask."

"Yes, quite," said Major Vernon. "Even when the act is impulsive, as it often is, there is a gain. For example, that man Hocking from Market Craven who attacked his wife with the poker – remember what he said?"

"'I wanted her to shut up'," said Felix. He pushed his hands through his hair. "I suppose, if we are being entirely objective, one must then say that this is a gain for my lord. They have had years of misery and now it is ended."

"And why now?" Major Vernon said.

"Because of the provocation of her coming here unannounced. I was here the other day and she flew into one of her rages. It was something to see. She was angry because someone had told her he was writing to my mother, which indeed he is, which does not clear these waters, does it? That is why I asked him directly. I thought if there was any possibility of his having any part in this, he would break at once if I put the question to him. And he did not."

"Then put him to one side," said Major Vernon. "Let us

look now at the young women." Seeing him grimace, he added, "Family members are implicated in murder nearly as frequently as –"

"Spouses, yes!" exclaimed Felix. "Very well – if one must be frank, then Charlotte has been at loggerheads with her mother for months because she will not marry. Maria, ditto, because she cannot marry, and as for Augusta – well, Augusta had got the better of her, as far as I could see. Lady Rothborough had given them both their blessing – mostly, I think, to spite my lord."

"Mrs Parsons says that all three young ladies as well as Lord Rothborough visited her in her room last night, and there were heated exchanges," said Major Vernon.

"Even Maria?" said Felix. "She has been in bed with a cold."

"Mrs Parsons may be mistaken. Perhaps the ladies sound similar to her. She could not make out what was being said, only that there were quarrels."

"Yesterday Maria sounded as if she had a cold and could not stop sneezing. And of all of them, she is the least likely to have a hand in such a thing, surely? In fact, I ought to go and tell her to get back to her bed and rest."

"And then, perhaps, you should see to the Countess."

"Augusta? Yes, I suppose we must call her that now. He stayed here last night, by the by."

"So I gather."

"Now, if one wants to talk about gain," Felix said, "that's a most interesting question. Given there has been no marriage settlement, and Lady Rothborough's will was spoken of as favouring Augusta – well, surely if Dunbar wanted to control his wife's property, then that would be a most effective manoeuvre? Without a settlement, the money will go straight to him."

"Money is an issue with him, I have evidence of that," Major Vernon said. "He attempted to defraud the landlady at

The Brodie Arms by calling a bottle of good claret spoilt."

"It makes a great deal of sense," Felix said. "Once the news of the marriage was out he had to act promptly to get the money before any settlement could be made. What better way than killing Lady Rothborough?"

"It's an interesting theory," said Major Vernon. "And it has some merit; although it is extremely risky."

"He has already demonstrated a liking for risk with this ridiculous secret marriage caper. He is not to be trusted."

Major Vernon began to walk down the room.

"We ought to consider that whoever did this seems to have thought that the risk was mitigated by the strong possibility of it being suicide," he said. "That it was arranged to appear so. The person would also need to be aware of her medical regimen and the directions given by Dr Parozzi, written out by Lady Augusta for Mrs Parsons, and plainly stating the risks of an overdose."

"Augusta knew, and Dunbar was in Italy with them when Parozzi was attending her," said Felix.

"It may have been merely incidental information when he heard it – that his obstinate potential mother-in-law is taking a potentially lethal substance on a regular basis. But he is not the sort of man to forget such a detail. He is known for his command of detail in Parliament, after all."

"I try not to read about him," said Felix. "I never liked what I saw."

"Then we must be even more scrupulous than usual and not let such things influence our thinking. But I agree with you. When I met him first in the inn the other night, I was not impressed. But that does not make him a murderer."

"But you will speak to him?" Felix said.

"In time, yes. In the short term, we should keep our own counsel on this, and, obfuscate a little. I want whoever is behind this to feel quite secure for a while. It is painful to have to do this to our friends, but in the interests of justice it is necessary."

He began to gather up his papers.

Felix nodded and turned back to the coffee pot in search of consolation. Only the tepid dregs were left.

"In the meantime," Major Vernon went on, "there is also the matter of the pink lozenge and the scissors. They may signify nothing at all. But bear them in mind. Now, let us go and examine the substance of all those heated conversations."

Chapter Thirty

Giles and Carswell found ladies Charlotte and Maria in the breakfast room, along with Emma and – annoyingly – Mr Wallace. Of course, he could not be faulted in being there. It was his duty to comfort the bereaved, but it did not seem from the countenances of the ladies that he was providing much of it.

"A terrible business," he said. "I came as soon as I heard. And to think I was only with her yesterday afternoon, when she was so full of life and hope! God's light was truly in her heart. She had realised her faults and was determined to do better, and then –" He shook his head. "Very sad, very sad, but we must not question the Lord's plan. And the suddenness of this, it is a great lesson: we should always be prepared for our own demise. As it says in –" He extracted a Bible from his pocket, but Lady Charlotte interrupted him.

"Thank you so very much, Mr Wallace," said Lady Charlotte, "I shall endeavour to remember that. Your words have been a great balm, but perhaps you will excuse us? My sister is not at all well, and now that Mr Carswell is here, I should like him to examine her."

"She may well be infectious," said Carswell, opening his medical bag.

Giles went and opened the door.

"We had better leave them to it, Mr Wallace," he said, and they went out into the passageway.

"Why are you here, sir, may I ask?" Wallace said. "Mr Carswell is here, no doubt, because of his connection with the family. Is it, I wonder, the sudden nature of her death that concerns you?"

"I am here as Lord Rothborough's friend," said Giles.

"But you are investigating the nature of the lady's death, I understand? Mr Carswell sent for you for very promptly."

"An unexpected death will throw up questions – it is inevitable," Giles said. "But they are usually quickly settled, as I'm sure they will be in this case."

"But there are doubts? It was not the result of her illnesses? You must understand I am as concerned as anyone over this. I was with her for most of Sunday afternoon and she seemed very well to me. It is all most curious." He scratched his greasy-haired head. "I hope there has not been any foul play."

"Why would you think that, Mr Wallace?"

"She intimated to me that she was most unhappy about her relations with her daughters and her husband. Naturally, I advised her that she must do all in her power to put things right, and she agreed that she would make as many efforts as she could on her part, but that there was only so much that could be done with people who she felt bore her considerable ill will. It strikes me now, in the light of this unhappy event, that she may have perceived she was in some danger from them. I put that to you, sir, with some regret, given you are a friend of this family, but one must be plain in the face of such terrible occurrences as murder. She has been murdered, has she not? That I must conclude from your presence here."

"She did not say she felt directly threatened, though?"

"No, no, she was not so direct. But she did not feel safe, that is my reading of it. Poor, poor lady! But God be thanked, sir, that you are here! From all I have heard of you, I know you will not spare anyone, not even your friends, in the pursuit of justice. Now, I must go and speak to that unfortunate maidservant of hers, or rather I must shout at her!" he added.

Giles was glad to see him go, and went back into the breakfast room.

Lady Charlotte was standing at the window, while Maria was lying on the sofa, her head in Emma's lap.

"Mr Carswell, will you please tell Maria she must go back to bed?" said Lady Charlotte.

"I cannot be ill now," said Maria, attempting to straighten herself, as Carswell approached her. "What if Papa needs me?"

"You don't have any choice about it," said Carswell. "And the better care you take of yourself now, the more use you will be."

"Very well," she said.

"I'll help you," said Emma.

"Just before you go, may I ask you a couple of questions?" Giles said.

"Of course," Maria said.

"Last night, did you go to your mother's room?"

"Yes," she said.

"When was that?" said Charlotte, turning from the window.

"About nine. I would not have gone, but she sent me a note. Tom brought it. I sent him back to say I was unwell and could it wait until the morning, but she insisted I come. So I went."

"What did she want?" Giles said.

"Oh, it was thoroughly disagreeable," Maria said, reaching for her handkerchief and blowing her nose. "She wanted to tell me that I must not sulk about Augusta's marriage, and more importantly I was to get no notions of her consenting to mine. She said she still considered marriage to Sir Mark – 'that person' as she always calls him – an utterly degrading prospect that could not be countenanced. So I said I wished she would not speak of him like that. I told her how wretched it was for me to have to hear her say such things and that of course, I did not want to displease her, but –" She broke off, tears overcoming her. "Oh, I said some terrible things to her. If I had known – but she provoked me! I could not help myself." She began to cry in earnest.

"Let her go to bed, Giles," said Emma. "This can wait,

surely?"

"Yes, yes, of course. Just one last question for you," said Giles, reaching into his pocket and taking out the ivory-handled scissors. He laid them on the table. "Do either of you recognise these?"

"No," Maria said, having examined them.

"No, I have never seen them before," Charlotte said. "They are rather curious. The ivory has cracked. They must be quite old. Why do you ask?"

"I found them under the bed in your mother's room. Might they belong to Mrs Parsons?"

Charlotte shook her head.

"She keeps hers on a chain and she is never without them. They have handles shaped like a crane's head – they were a Christmas present from me and my sisters."

Maria and Emma got up to leave.

"I'll come with you," Carswell said.

They left the room, and Giles was alone with Lady Charlotte.

"I wasn't the only one who was summoned, then," she said, sitting down at the table. "I went in just before ten for my scolding. I left shortly afterwards because she was so outrageous I could not keep my temper. I did, however, tell her that she had lost all respect for herself in behaving as she did. A fine thing for a daughter to say to a mother on her deathbed."

"What did she say to you?"

"That I was cruel and unfeeling. That I had too much of my father's blood in me and that my obstinacy would be my ruin. That I was thoroughly immoral. It was nothing she had not said to me before, but I was tired after that business with Janet Murray and having to deal with Dunbar at dinner, and I could not bear it. I was there all of ten minutes. There is only so much screeching one can abide. Dear God!" she exclaimed, getting up and going back to her stance in the window, with her back to the room. "I know many of her difficulties were not of her own making, but she never, never could be reasonable, and what is the result? She is dead in these horrible circumstances, and all our tears are conflicted ones." She turned back to Giles. "And how must it look to you, I wonder? What on earth is going on behind those clear-sighted eyes of yours? These questions all mean something – they are leading to a conclusion, and it is not a comforting one."

"At this stage I am thinking only that my friends are in distress and I want to help them," Giles said.

"And what if it was one of us who killed her? What then?"

"That is hardly a fair question to ask," Giles said. "There is no answer to it. In fact, we have no definite evidence yet to say it was murder. It may be –"

"You do not know that we have not been in some great conspiracy, Maria and I," she said. "And Papa as well, for we shall all be much happier now she is gone, that is the simple truth! And Augusta as well. In fact –"

"Yes?" Giles said.

"My mother's will. Have you seen it?"

"No," said Giles.

"Augusta is the sole heir to all her unsettled property. It is a considerable amount. It was to have been divided with Maria, but she had it redrawn to cut her out when she became engaged to Sir Mark."

"You are certain of this?"

"Yes. I was there when it was done. Of course, I did everything I could to protect Maria's share, but she would not be persuaded. I think we have been given some old family portraits, but that is all. Augusta will inherit Limpersleigh and the associated estates and investments. Or rather her husband does, given the lack of settlement. Dear Lord, then all this is my fault," she went on. "I should never have let him into the family. I was blinded by him, and this is the result."

"This is all circumstantial," said Giles. "And it is certainly not your responsibility."

"But I knew quite soon that he was wrong, in some fashion. Oh, I cannot describe it, but I knew, even when he was first making love to me, that he was not someone it was safe to be unguarded with. Yet I let down my guard. I couldn't help myself. I have been aware all along how defective his character is, and still he has a habit of smoothing out the imperfections, of making one ignore them because of his stature and charm. But one takes the smallest step back and sees that it is all superficial glamour." She gave a shudder. "Poor Augusta. She is to be pitied."

She sat down again at the table, and went on: "There is something else I must tell you. The reason I finally broke off the engagement with Dunbar: I saw him strike a woman. I was not meant to see it, of course. It was at Lady Brancaster's at New Year. I was staying there, as was he, and the whole affair – I see it now – was to bring about some lasting conclusion between us. Lady Brancaster is a great admirer of his. She feels he will be Prime Minister for certain. She left us unchaperoned rather too often for my comfort and I found I was running about the house trying to avoid him, at the same time trying to tell myself I should marry him and be done with it. Anyway, I had taken myself off for a long walk about the park with Otto, and I quite lost my way. I came back through a hamlet at the edge of the park, and there I saw him being importuned by some poor unfortunate baggage of a woman. She was drunk and making a scene, and instead of giving her a shilling and walking briskly away, he struck her across the face and pushed her back, making her stumble. He did not see me do it, for I picked up Otto and ran away. I should have stopped and helped her, but I am not so good."

She looked across at Giles with an expression that wanted absolution.

"In the circumstances, I think you might forgive yourself

that," said Giles, "given what you had just witnessed."

"I should have helped her. It would have helped me," she said. "And I should have confronted him about it."

"I would imagine ending the engagement might have given him pause for thought," Giles said.

"Yes, it might, if he had been any ordinary, decent man, but he is not ordinary and I do not think him at all decent," Charlotte said. "He took it quite calmly. That was the worst of it. As if it did not matter, after all. It was most unpleasant. He has a cold heart. I should have seen that from the start, but I was foolishly desperate. We first met when I was – well, I think you know."

"That was a long time ago," Giles said, after a moment. "And things have changed a great deal."

"Yet I feel nothing has changed at all. Perhaps men are more mutable of heart, but a woman, her object once fixed –"

"No, please!" Giles said, getting up. "I told you then that there was nothing, and there is nothing now."

"I know, I know," she said, getting up and following him across the room. "But that does not stop my feelings. I wish I could prevent them, but –"

"Then do!" he exclaimed, putting up his hands to distance her from him. "For there is nothing so wasteful than throwing good after bad. Find your self-respect! I cannot supply it!"

He meant to give her pain, but even as he had spoken he knew that the distress in his voice and her own craven weakness was acting against it. Her expression was truly pitiable; she was like a whipped dog.

"For heaven's sake," he said. "What is to be done with you?"

"I wish I knew," she said, and threw herself against him. He struggled for a moment, and then let her cry in his arms.

The door opened and Emma came in. Charlotte broke away at once, but Giles saw the expression on Emma's face and he did not like it.

"I forgot my shawl," she said, swiftly retrieving it and leaving without another word.

Chapter Thirty-one

Felix and Major Vernon found the newly acknowledged Earl and Countess in one of the smaller sitting rooms at the Castle. Dunbar had made himself thoroughly comfortable there, expropriating the writing table for his books and papers, while his bride sat by the fire, engaged on a piece of Berlin work. If they were trying to dispel any note of scandal, then this was calculated to do it. Even the spaniels were lying obediently in their basket, although one of them jumped up at the sight of Felix, only to be shouted back into place by Dunbar.

Augusta laid down her tapestry and said, "There seems to be some question over the manner of my mother's death. Is that why you are here, Major Vernon?"

"Yes, it's not entirely clear exactly what has happened," said Major Vernon.

"But what was the immediate cause?" Dunbar said.

"She seems to have been poisoned by her own medicine," Felix said. "How or why is the question that we are trying to answer."

"Poisoned by something Dr Parozzi prescribed?" Augusta said.

"Yes – most probably the salts of baryta," Felix said. "She took them for her digestion, I understand?"

"Yes, she suffered a great deal from that," Augusta said. "But she suffered a from many other things. She often said to me that she was astonished she was still alive. Are you sure?"

"I cannot see any other obvious cause. There may have to be a post-mortem."

"No! Oh, no, please, that would be too dreadful. How can you even suggest such a thing? Major Vernon, you cannot agree with this?"

"It may be the only way. It is distressing, but –"

"It must not come to that," she said. "You must write to her doctors, Carswell. She was not well. To be honest, I have been expecting this day for many months now. I have been prepared for it: that she would be taken from us, and suddenly. She always said that was what she felt would happen: God would snatch her away and it would be a relief to her."

"She never talked to you about ending her own life?" Major Vernon said.

"No!" said Augusta. "She considered self-murder utterly abhorrent. You are not entertaining such an idea, I trust?"

"We must entertain all ideas, however unpleasant," said Major Vernon. "The situation is not straightforward."

"No, no, I will never believe that she could have done that," said Augusta. "And if my sisters make such a suggestion, let me tell you that they are mistaken."

"Why do you think they would?" Major Vernon said. "Was this something you discussed, perhaps? I have been told that she was subject to fits of melancholia."

"Yes, but not to that extent. She considered it a sin, as do I. It would not have occurred to her to do such a thing, even at the darkest of times, and last night she was perfectly contented. In fact, I have not seen her as happy for months! She was very pleased that she was to be a grandmother at last." Her voice broke and she turned away towards the fire. "Oh, please, please – must we talk of her like this?"

"Quite," said Dunbar. "My wife has enough of a burden with her grief, without all this pointless and painful speculation. This is clearly an accident; a horrible, tragic accident."

"I'm afraid it is not," said Felix. "There is no evidence that it was an accident. That overdose was either taken deliberately by Lady Rothborough or she was forced into it in some fashion."

"This strikes me as a fantasy," said Dunbar. "I have no

wish to disparage your professional knowledge in this area, gentlemen, but what on earth could there be in this house, of all houses, to support such speculation? This is not some filthy back-court in Northminster where people are murdered for their clothes. We are speaking of the Marchioness of Rothborough!"

"Unfortunately, my lord," said Major Vernon, "murder is no respecter of persons. And yes, you are right to speak of poor souls being killed for the clothes on their backs, because it points to a common cause of murder, and one which we must ask today: who gains from this person's death?"

"That is an impertinent question, considering the lady in question," said Dunbar.

"I agree," Major Vernon said. "In your situation it must look so. After all, you and your wife stand to gain a great deal from this tragedy."

"What do you know of that?" said Dunbar.

"I know that you have not signed a marriage settlement, which would protect your wife's money. It seems that your wife is heir to all her mother's estate. A double portion, I'm informed, since she had excised Lady Maria from the will."

"I told her not to do that!" Augusta burst out. "I did not want Maria to suffer, for she will need her money if she marries that scoundrel Hurrell. I begged Mama not to change it, Major Vernon, you must understand that!"

"Of course," said Major Vernon.

"It was so much money, and she was so stubborn about it," said Augusta, giving a sob. "Mama's money. I never thought of it until now. And as for my marriage settlement, that will be seen to at once! Oh, I know how it must seem, Major Vernon, and you are right to be suspicious, but goodness, no – Dunbar and I realise that it is a mere oversight. He understands how things are. Do you not, my dear?"

"Yes, of course," he said, taking his wife's hand and patting it. "And you should be very pleased, sir, that my wife is so tolerant of your intrusions."

"He must do what must be done," said Augusta.

"Might I ask when you last saw your mother?" Major Vernon said.

"I went up with her after dinner," said Augusta. "And as I said, she was very happy. We were talking about where we ought to take a house in Town, though of course my father would not hear of it – but she was certain he would come about. She gave me a bracelet from her jewel case – it is part of a set – the rest is in London, in a vault, but she wanted me to have the whole parure as a wedding present. It was not a Rothborough heirloom, of course. I should not have accepted that. Those are for Charlotte alone. It was one of her family pieces." She gave a great sigh. "No, we had the pleasantest conversation we have had for many months. It was such a mercy to be forgiven and understood. I could never have expected it to go so well. She told me that Mr Wallace had put her in a better frame of mind about things in general."

"When did she speak to him?"

"She was with him all afternoon, and for some time the day before. She had felt unhappy about her obsession with card-playing, and he had managed to make her see she was in error about it, and steer her mind to better things. She said she found him wonderfully comforting."

"And how long did this conversation with your mother last?"

"Until just before nine. I went to bed. I was rather tired, as you might imagine, and of course –" She smiled at her husband. "It was something of a special occasion."

"I quite understand," said Major Vernon. "So I take it, my lord, that you joined your wife at about the same hour? At nine or so?"

"I did," said Dunbar. "I am not quite sure of the hour –"

"No, but he did not keep me waiting," said Augusta. "And we were together for the rest of the night, naturally."

~

When they left them, Felix said, "She seemed keen to affirm that he was with him all evening, did she not? Had he told her to say that?"

"I can't help wondering," said Major Vernon. "And the whole story is so at odds with the others. Before nine, she was sweet as a lamb and handing out bracelets, and then poor Maria is made to get up from her sickbed for a scolding at nine, and then Lady Charlotte goes in at ten, for another tongue-lashing. We had better speak to Lord Rothborough now. Mrs Parsons said that he went to see her last night. It is possible he was the last person to see her alive."

A footman directed them to Lord Rothborough's dressing room, where they found him sitting by the fire with the prayer book open on his knees. He looked tired and anxious.

"Come sit down," he said. "You will have questions for me, I imagine."

"I'm afraid so," said Major Vernon, and took the diary from his pocket. "Were you aware that Lady Rothborough kept a journal?"

"No. Is that it?"

Major Vernon gave it to him. He flipped through a few pages, his frown deepening as he did. Then he closed it and laid it to one side. "Merciful Lord," he muttered.

"I'm sorry you had to see that in these circumstances," said Major Vernon.

Rothborough nodded.

"It had to be done," he said. "So?"

"Mrs Parsons said she overheard you talking with Lady Rothborough late last night."

"That is a tactful way of putting it."

"What time was this?" Major Vernon asked.

"It was after ten. I had not meant to go and see her, but I

was going along the passage, and Charlotte came out in such a wretched state that I could not forbear any longer. I was extremely angry with her, I can't deny it."

"What passed between you, may I ask?"

"She was crowing about Augusta and Dunbar and telling me that I was being utterly unreasonable and that it was a matter for rejoicing. I told her I could not rejoice, that I did not trust Dunbar. So then we turned to poor Mark Hurrell whom she said was a far worse candidate for a husband, with such bad blood in his family. I told her it was better that Maria risk being happy with him than miserable with someone else merely because of his unfortunate circumstances, and that they were deeply attached and liable to make a happy couple, if she would only allow it. For which I got a great deal of abuse for apparently favouring Maria over all the others and being as blind in regard to her faults as I am to yours, Felix. And that was when it got very unpleasant."

"That business with the letters, I suppose," Felix said.

"Yes, and I confess to you humbly now that I was in error when I lied about that. But you saw how impossible she was! I have tried to be patient, but sometimes I cannot manage it. When one is ashamed of one's conduct, it is easier to blame another person for it, and I admit I have always blamed her for my unhappiness, rather than taking responsibility for my own sins, of which there have been too many."

"The letters?" Major Vernon said.

"Someone had told her that I was writing to Mrs Martinez," Lord Rothborough said. "In fact she had been told a great deal more than that. That was the substance of our quarrel last night. She accused me of having made Mrs Martinez my mistress. Where she had learnt this, I am not sure. I suspect Dunbar may have stoked the fire for his own purposes, for I have been warned that a rumour to that effect has been going about. It is not true, for what it is worth. I have helped her, and we are friends, but she will not permit anything more between us."

"But Lady Rothborough did not believe you?" Major Vernon said.

"Of course not. And why should she? She knew what I was, after all. I have not been a good husband, nor a good man. That you both know." He reached out and took up the journal again, and turned it in his hands before laying it down again. "Even on our wedding night, it was not right between us. I was bored in her company. I remember sitting with her at dinner and thinking how little sensible conversation she seemed to have. I consoled myself that such arrangements often turn out very well, that a man and woman can grow to love each other, and that all my fears would be unfounded. I vowed I would try to do my best, and yet I never did. I always held myself apart from her. I judged her every day of our wretched association, and I always found her wanting. I have been nothing but a selfish, ungenerous wretch and she saw me for what I was. When she accused me last night of never loving her, she was quite right."

They were silent for a moment.

"I asked you this morning if you had anything to say to me," Felix said.

"Yes," said Lord Rothborough, "and what I will say is this: if intentions could have killed her, then I did. I left those rooms in a state of helpless rage and I wished her dead, truly I did. When she wrote that last line, she wrote the truth."

"But you left her alive?" Felix forced himself to ask after another long pause.

"God be thanked, I did," said Lord Rothborough. "And at about eleven, I spoke to Bodley briefly, but I did not go to bed at once. I spent most of the night in here, writing to your mother, Felix. I decided that I must give her up, for Frances' sake, for the sake of my own soul, for I felt so wretched. She had been in such a state that it seemed the only thing I could do. It was my intention to go to her first thing today and tell her that I had decided to end our friendship –" He knotted his hands together and pressed them to his lips, bowing his head.

"Thank you for your candour," said Major Vernon.

"What are you thinking now, then?" said Lord Rothborough. "I fear she must have destroyed herself. That is the only explanation which makes any sense to me. As I told Felix earlier, I have feared before that it would come to this. I know the temptation of it myself," he added. "When despair comes on, there seems no better remedy."

~

"I do not like that tone in him," said Felix to Major Vernon as they left Lord Rothborough. "I shall ask Bodley to keep a close watch on him. In fact, I think I should stay here tonight."

"That may be wise," said Major Vernon. "Now, let us go and talk to the Prince."

The Prince was in his room, supervising his manservant in packing.

"I am going to the inn," he said, dismissing the servant. "I do not like to stay when I am a stranger to the family. It is an imposition at such a time."

"I am sure Lord Rothborough does not mind," Felix said.

"I will not trouble him," said the Prince. "The inn is perfectly adequate for my needs. So, I suppose you must question me? I am hearing that her death was not natural. I had some words with Lady Charlotte." He shook his head. "How shocking. And it is not the only death since I have been here. Are they connected, is that not what you must ask?"

"What makes you say that, Your Highness?" said Major Vernon.

"Because it is so uncommon. Two respectable women, although of very different degrees, both dead in the same neighbourhood in a manner that cannot be explained. Of course, I do not understand your methods, sir, but I have a little knowledge of probability."

"That's interesting," said Major Vernon.

"But perhaps irrelevant," said Felix, "given that we are not yet in a position to say how Lady Rothborough died. There is a possibility she destroyed herself, you see."

"Oh, I am most sad to hear that. But Lady Charlotte seemed to imply that some other hand was at work here, and my own observation of the lady would be that she was not likely to do that. She was, as well, quite high-spirited at dinner last night. Delighted in the marriage revealed! Quite in contrast to my lord Rothborough, I think."

"You were with the family in Italy, I understand?"

"Not under the same roof. I have my own house in Firenze. My godfather left it to me. It is not far from Lady Rothborough's villa, however."

"How did you all become acquainted?"

"It was through the charming Mrs Yardley," said the Prince, "whom I understand you gentlemen know. She is to be married to Count von Bruggen, who is an old friend of mine. A nice match, I think."

"So Lady Rothborough invited you to join her in Scotland?" said Major Vernon.

"Yes, because I was eager to see the place for myself. I think I probably forced her hand a little, because she was not too fond of Scotland, but she saw me as a candidate for dear Lady Charlotte and was quite happy to ask me. And at first, I thought that Lady Charlotte and I – but you soon realise when a thing will not be. Her heart, I think, is not available to anyone." He shrugged.

"Perhaps you could tell me what happened after dinner?"

"I sat and had a little wine with my lords Rothborough and Dunbar. It was awkward, as you might imagine, and we were not there long. Then we had tea with the ladies, again not for very long, and then my lady Rothborough went upstairs with Lady Augusta, and Lady Charlotte, and I think Lord Rothborough was not long in leaving us either. And then Dunbar suggested a game of billiards, which I don't much care for but I obliged him. And it proves that he plays like the Devil himself! He is so intent on winning it gives me a headache. It was most peculiar. Why did he not want to go up to his wife, if they had been apart for so long? I could not understand that. No, all he wanted to do was play and play again, and smoke and smoke his filthy cigars, and it was past eleven before I managed to get to bed. I was most glad to get there after such an evening!"

"I can imagine," said Major Vernon. "And you remained in your room all night?"

"Yes. I took a little, oh, what do you call it here? – laudopium? – for my head, and after that I don't remember falling asleep until Heinrich woke me this morning with the news that poor Lady Rothborough was dead. At least she was happy last night, or at least it appeared to me."

"But no one else was," Felix said.

"No," said the Prince. "Not at all."

Chapter Thirty-two

"I suppose the question we must ask," said Major Vernon, "is whether Lady Rothborough's mental state could have deteriorated to the point that she decided to kill herself in the space of a few hours. Do you think it likely?"

"I don't know," said Felix. "And the means of it – it strikes me as more and more strange, if it is suicide. She must have known that baryta was a poison if taken in a large dose, but to choose that means is decidedly unusual. If her desperation was so great, that might explain it, but it is a peculiar sort of desperation that leads to suicide and I am not sure the evidence we have supports it. I may have thought that a few hours ago, but now – perhaps not."

"You are suspicious of Dunbar."

"And you are not? He lied to us about the billiards, or rather Augusta did. He did keep her waiting."

"She would not wish to admit that, for it is humiliating for her. She must convey a state of perfection between them."

"She will be struggling to do that. Do you think she might know something? I wonder if we should not talk to her again, and alone."

"It may have to come to that," said Major Vernon. "But perhaps later. I need to gather my thoughts. And you should go home and tell them what has happened. We should both go home."

Felix agreed, and they set out on their separate ways.

The day had decided to be generous – the signs of the previous day's storm had dried away, and by the time he turned through the Rectory gates on his pony, it was warm and sunny. The Rector was tending his vegetable patch in his shirt sleeves, assisted by Mary Gowans.

"I must go to them," said the Rector, once Felix had imparted the news. "Mary, my child, fetch my coat and hat, will you?"

The girl ran off into the house.

"She is remarkable," said the Rector. "So like her mother. So, I take it that you and Major Vernon feel there may be something untoward? You would not have been away so long if you did not think something was amiss."

"Unfortunately, yes. We thought at first it might have been suicide, but it is beginning to look as though that is not the case."

The Rector shook his head. Mary came out of the house with his things. She was too small to help the Rector into his coat, so Felix did the honours.

"Mary, you must tell Mr Carswell what you told my wife and me this morning," the Rector said.

"What about?" said Felix.

"Mary is anxious about her aunt," said the Rector.

"When they took her to Perth, everyone was saying she'd be hanged there," Mary said.

"We sent her to Perth so that she would be safe," Felix said.

"But everyone says it was because she killed my mother, that she said so herself."

"Your aunt was confused. I do not think she killed her."

"That is what I said, Mary," said the Rector.

He set off down the path, and Felix and the little girl went and sat on the bench beneath the window.

"But they had such a fight," Mary said. "I was there. I wasn't supposed to be. It was in the shop. I was hiding behind the counter."

"When was this?" said Felix.

"On Monday. The day my mother went to see her. But this was in the morning. Aunt Effie came in and gave her some money and Mother wouldn't take it, though I know she was owed it. That's what she said. She said she couldn't take that money because it was gotten in sin and that she'd sold herself for it. So they had a right old fight about it, and in the end Aunt Effie went storming out and banged the door behind her, and the money was still on the counter. Mother picked it up and put it away in her pocket. It was gold."

"Gold? Was it a sovereign?"

"I don't know, sir, I've never seen one."

"And then?"

"Mother went out of the door. She didn't even put her bonnet on. So, I came out and went to the door to see what she was about. She was going down the street, and I went out of the door a little and I saw some man was talking to Aunt Effie and Mother was going to speak to them, and that's all I could see – I had to go back in then, because father was calling me from the kitchen."

"Can you describe this person?"

"It was a gentleman, for he had nice clothes on, dark clothes, and all neat. He was tall, with dark hair and a tall hat, and he had a stick. He walked away when my mother came over – he went back towards the inn."

"This was on Monday morning?" he said.

"Yes, sir."

"Thank you, Mary. Major Vernon will want to hear about this, so if you can keep it clear in your mind for us?"

"I will try."

"Would you know this gentlemen again if you saw him?"

"Yes, I think so."

As she said this, Eleanor and Miss King came out of the house.

"Oh, has the Rector gone out?" Eleanor said. "We were about to have tea."

"Mary, Mrs Stevens is looking for you," said Miss King. "I think she needs to measure you." The girl ran off.

"He's gone to the Castle," said Felix. "Have you a spare cup for me?"

"Yes, of course," said Eleanor. "What has happened? You have been away so long."

"I'll tell you inside."

He followed them into the drawing room where his mother was sitting in front of the tea table. He sat down and told them all that had happened, and the room fell silent. He drank a hasty cup of tea and set out again, not feeling at all refreshed.

He had thought to go straight to the Major with the information Mary Gowans had given him, but as he passed The Brodie Arms, he decided to go in and pursue the matter for himself.

"Oh, Mr Carswell, is it true?" said Mrs McNeill, coming out to greet him. "That my lady is dead?"

He nodded.

"God rest her soul," said Mrs McNeill. "Can I do anything for you, sir?"

"I wanted to ask you about Lord Dunbar," he said, at which she frowned. "When did he arrive here?"

"Saturday last," she said. "And he left yesterday, as I dare say you know."

"Did he have any dealings with Effie Haynes?"

"Effie Haynes – oh yes, and not to my liking. I tried to stop it, for I have the good name of my business to consider, but she slipped in and into his – well, I think you can guess where and what I mean, sir."

"When was this?"

"That first Saturday night, and then on the Sabbath after! I should have booted him out, but we have had a lean winter, and I can't afford to be choosy." She gave a great sigh.

"Did you ever see him talking to Mrs Gowans?"

"Oh well, yes, that was quite the scene! I should have said this to your friend, yon English gentleman, when he was here, but I forgot. She came in and gave his precious lordship his money back – the money he gave to Effie. She had owed it to Mrs Gowans, it seems, but she said she would not take such dirty money. Brave soul, for she no doubt needed it."

"When was this?"

"Monday morning."

"How did he react?"

"He just pocketed it, as if he did not care. I suppose it meant he got what he liked for free. But it was a brave thing for Mrs Gowans to do, and perhaps it did her no good."

Felix pondered the implications of this as he went up to Mrs McCroy's house. Here, he found Major Vernon and the two older children about to embark on a walk. Mrs Vernon was tying Sophy's bonnet strings, but she was not dressed to join them.

"I think I have Sandro and Maria's cold," she said, turning back into the house. "I am going to rest. I have a sore throat."

Major Vernon stood watching her as the children ran on ahead.

"I wonder if I ought to stay with her," he said.

"Let her rest," said Felix. "The house will be quieter without the children."

"Well, Sandro is still there, so not entirely," said Major Vernon. "But it is better that these two are worn out a little."

"I'll come with you," said Felix.

They began their walk, and Felix told him of his conversation with Mary Gowans and then Mrs McNeill's account.

"That's unpleasant news," said Major Vernon. "Dunbar is doing himself no favours."

"He has a perfect motive for killing Mrs Gowans. That was a thorough humiliation. Perhaps they met again, near the bothy, and he lost his temper with her."

"Lady Charlotte did tell me he had a rough streak," Major Vernon said. "Then we shall go and speak to him this evening, and let us hope that will be an end to all this! Oh, for a straight and honest confession from a man with a conscience! How remarkable that would be."

"Yes, it would," said Felix.

They were interrupted by a dog barking with great enthusiasm. Hamish was on his knees, greeting the muddy, bramble-tangled three-legged collie known as Star.

"There is my girl!" he exclaimed. "My Star! I've been looking for you everywhere, girl."

"Look, look, Uncle Giles," Sophy said, "she came to find us!"

"She has found a bone," Hamish said, continuing with his extravagant embrace. "What a clever girl!"

Felix ran forward, and snatched up the bone that the dog had dropped on the ground. It was exactly as he guessed – its shape was too distinctive to mistake. He reached for his handkerchief and hastily wrapped it.

"What is it?" said Major Vernon.

Felix drew him aside and said quietly, so the children would not hear: "A human jawbone."

~

It was Star who took them to the body.

Insistent and noisy, she went hurtling down the bank, as if three legs instead of four were of no matter to her. Felix was forced to venture through a fresh and extremely sharp crop of brambles in pursuit, and was frequently in great danger of losing his footing entirely, for the precipitous surface was sodden and glassy from the recent rain.

It was a curious spot, where a branch of the River Pit met a burn descending from the higher, rough ground forming a deep, hidden cleft, which was easy to overlook. From the path along which they had been walking, the depth of the ravine was impossible to guess. As he made his cautious descent, he wondered how on earth there could be human remains in such a place. It was both puzzling and disturbing.

As he grew accustomed to the landscape, he saw the likely source of the jaw bone. A body, or at least the remains of one, lay cradled in a furious tangle of young birch and hawthorn, with the briars, woody and vicious, covering the whole in a shroud of new greenery. Some of the brambles had even begun to grow around the bare bones, quite as if they were innocent honeysuckles searching for support on a garden trellis, and as a result they had anchored them in place. Some heavily-decomposed flesh remained, the scent of which was what had no doubt attracted Star, but maggots and other animals had done a great deal of work on it. It was going to be a challenge to retrieve it.

Catching the now over-eager dog by the scruff of her neck, he examined what he could, but it was a struggle. How and when had the body arrived there? He found another piece of the skull and a few shredded ribbons nearby, and what looked like a fragment of a wool shawl.

He perched as best he could, the dog struggling to escape now. He did not want to release her and have her disturb any more of the evidence. Major Vernon had gone for help. He wondered how long it would be before it arrived, and speculated it might be easier to descend to the bottom of the gorge and then climb back up the burn to safety. How they were to remove the bones was another matter. Some of them, he knew, would never be recovered.

Then he turned to speculating. Was this unfortunate soul the late Mrs Black? She had vanished in February, assumed to have fallen from the path at Vorlich, walking to see her daughter. He remembered that her daughter lived at the Castle Cottages, not far from this very spot, and the path could be considered equally dangerous at that time of year. The state of decomposition was not inconsistent with a passage of three months, a lingering Scottish winter delaying the effects a little.

He examined the piece of skull he had managed to retrieve. Part of the parietal bone, it was odd the way it had broken up. Had it been broken by force? Had she received a blow to the back of the head and then been pushed down the bank? Looking at the evidence, this seemed unpleasantly possible.

Chapter Thirty-three

By eleven the following day, the evidence they were able to retrieve confirmed Felix's early theories.

Mr Macdonald and a party of foresters had worked until darkness to take up what remains they could, by means of ropes and baskets. They had been taken to the Factor's offices, and Felix had come in early the next day, having spent an imperfect night at the Castle. He had been joined soon afterwards by Major Vernon, who was a useful assistant and a willing student of human anatomy.

As they pieced together the fragments, it soon became clear that the body belonged to a woman and that she had met a violent death.

"What sort of weapon do you think?" Major Vernon said.

"To shatter the skull to this degree, you will need to have hit it several times and with some force. A fallen branch or a walking cane with a metal head? Remember that case last year, where the parietal bone had been pulverised with the stock of a fouling piece?"

"Wielded by his brother, yes," said Major Vernon, frowning. "So we have a defenceless woman walking alone, attacked from behind until unconscious or dead, and then disposed of down the bank. Whoever did this has been fortunate she was not discovered earlier."

"Perhaps the spot was chosen for concealment," Felix said. "I wonder if whoever it was did not go down the bank and push her further into that knot of saplings. He could easily have arranged the bramble canopy over it, and let nature take its course. When did Mrs Black go missing?"

"On February twenty-third," said Major Vernon, consulting his notebook. "The weather was constant rain, with ice still on the ground, according to the Rector's notes."

"Consider also that they all said she was missing at Vorlich," said Felix. "Where did that idea come from?"

"Yes, that is curious, and with hindsight it feels like a misdirection," said Major Vernon, staring down at the bones on the table. "We need to look at the Rector's weather diary again. If, for example, the weather took a turn for the better at the beginning of the month, she would be well buried with the first growth. Brambles are notoriously vigorous."

"They will grow even if the weather is dismal," said Carswell. He touched his cheek. "I was fairly lacerated yesterday."

"In a good cause," said Major Vernon. "We shall have to go and talk to her daughter. It must be her," he added, fingering the torn fragments of the woven shawl that they had managed to bring up as well. "Who else is unaccounted for hereabouts? But why? What possible motive could there be for killing an innocent woman in such a brutal fashion?" He frowned and massaged his temples.

"Do you have a headache?" said Felix. The Major had a history of migraines.

"Perhaps, but it doesn't matter."

"Or you have caught Lady Maria's cold. How was Mrs Vernon, by the way?"

"Still very tired. It is as if any progress she has made has evaporated, and I cannot help thinking I am to blame."

"How?"

The Major gestured at the table and then walked away to the window.

"This business of ours is always set to pull me away, when she is my first duty. It has to be attended to now, of course, but in the future – sometimes I think I have lost the stomach for it," he added, turning back to Carswell. "We hoped for some relief coming here, and what do we find?"

"Did you sleep at all last night?" said Felix.

"No. And neither did you, by the look of it."

"Too true," said Felix.

The Major went and sat down on the bench at the side of the room, again rubbing his temples.

"There is another matter," he said.

"Yes?"

"Charlotte," said the Major, after a pause. "She has an idea about me: she formed it that summer at Holbroke when Laura died, and she still feels it."

"Does she still think she is in love with you?" Felix said.

"She says so. I don't know how it can be anything real. I suspect she has embroidered the idea in her fancy all through her romantic misfortune with Dunbar, but she protests it to me so sincerely! And, of course, of course, I have tried to disregard it, because it is nothing but foolishness and nonsense – yet I feel helpless with pity, and flattered – so ridiculously flattered – that I forget everything I should. I let her cry in my arms yesterday, like a fool, and Emma saw it but has said nothing, because she is the soul of forbearance."

"And she will forgive you for it," said Felix. "Of that you can be sure."

"Yes, of course, but forgiveness – must I demand that from her? That is what I cannot bear. You can forgive those who harm you, but does that heal the offence? No. She will still be in pain when I am absolved from it. That is what I cannot contemplate. What have I done to her? Emma should be everything to me, and yet one foolish young woman sobs in front of me and my vanity is stoked to a degree that my mind conjures up the most –"

He broke off. "Excuse me."

"You have heard out all my idiocies," said Felix, "and given me the best of advice. I'm not sure I can equal any of that, but I can say that I know Mrs Vernon will forgive you and she will expect you to forgive yourself. You should take something for that head and get some decent rest. I can see you are straining your eyes. A dark room as soon as you can manage it. Besides, we ought not to go any further with this until we have seen the Sheriff."

"You are right," said Major Vernon, getting up. "Thank you. But we owe it to her family to tell them what has happened first. Let us go and talk to them."

~

Mrs Black's daughter lived in a neat square of white-harled cottages set on the fringe of the Castle Park that had been constructed by Lord Rothborough for estate workers and their families. She was married to one of the gardeners, by the name of Thompson, and the house showed evidence of his trade in the pots of scented spring flowers arranged on the kitchen window sill.

Major Vernon laid the fragments of shawl and ribbon on the kitchen table, and Mrs Thompson recognised them at once. A mixture of distress and relief seemed to take hold of her. She said she had been dreading such news but at least now she had an answer.

Major Vernon went and fetched her neighbour. In fact, a crowd of women soon came in, and took charge of Mrs Thompson and her children, all acting in a sober, good-hearted, practical way, quite at odds with the violence of the poor woman's end. The puzzle of that seemed even greater, as they drank the tea that was pressed on them and answered all their questions as best they could.

"She can go to her rest now," said Mrs Thompson. "That is all that matters. She can rest in peace."

"Soon enough, I hope," said Major Vernon. "I'm afraid you will have to wait until the Sheriff permits the burial."

"It worked then, Jeanie," one of the women said to Mrs Thompson. "I shouldn't have believed it would, but it did."

"Hush, Margaret," said another. "You should not speak of that."

"What worked?" said Major Vernon.

"Oh, it was nothing," said the same woman.

"It was Mistress McCroy," said Mrs Thompson. "She has a power to find things, and I asked her to find my mother. And now she is found."

They left her to her grief shortly afterwards and began to walk back to the village. They soon met Mr Wallace coming along the path towards them.

"Did I see you coming from Mrs Thompson's cottage, gentlemen?" he enquired.

"You did," said Major Vernon.

"Is that in connection with the recovery of what I have heard – and I fear I may have heard right – of human remains?" He shook his head. "Quite shocking. What poor lost soul could that be, I wondered. Perhaps you have discovered who it is?"

"We have reason to believe it is Mrs Black from Meigle."

"And you have just taken that sad news to her daughter, of course," said Mr Wallace. "It is as well that I am here. I shall go and speak to her at once. She has been tried sorely by her mother's disappearance, and I fear she may have fallen into dangerous beliefs, in her desperation. The Devil always comes to us when we are at our weakest."

"What do you mean, Mr Wallace?" said Major Vernon.

"She has been dabbling in the dark arts," said Mr Wallace, "or rather, asking for assistance from those who do. In her grief, she has been wicked and foolish and instead of listening to those who are called by God to lead the flock into safety, she has strayed far from where she ought. She has gone to feed at the teats of Satan."

"How can Satan have teats?" said Felix, repressing a smile

at the bizarre image his words had conjured. "Is he a woman now?"

"I have come to believe that it is the case," said Wallace. "Yes, sir, picture that if you will: Satan is a beautiful woman, with luscious tumbling locks –"

"And horns and a tail?" Felix said, laughing now. "I can't think that adds much to her beauty. Of course, some men might like that. I might myself if it were nicely done!"

"You may mock as much as you please, Mr Carswell, but let me warn you that when you feel temptation, it will have the feminine touch. Now I have pointed this out to you, you will see it, and you will learn to check yourself. When your pretty young wife pouts and makes some foolish demand and you cannot but resist giving in to it, then Satan has caught you. And," he went on, turning to Major Vernon, "when a woman pretends to virtue but in truth walks in the way of evil, and yet you cannot see it clearly –"

"Are you speaking of Mrs McCroy?" said Major Vernon.

"Yes," said Mr Wallace. "I am, and she is responsible for Mrs Thompson's lamentable behaviour. She has encouraged her to seek her mother by means of devilish formulas, when she should have been on her knees and praying to God for thanks that her mother had been delivered from the trials of this world."

"And was Mrs Black one of the elect, do you think, Mr Wallace?" said Felix.

"That is not my place to say," said Wallace.

"I suppose you believe yourself one of them," Felix could not resist saying. "How could you not?"

"You clearly have very little understanding of our theology, sir," he said.

"Only what I have seen all my life here: that it is a doctrine that gives the ordinary man no incentive to virtue," said Felix. "And is a positive encouragement to wickedness in some respects."

Major Vernon said, "What precisely are these devilish formulas of which you accuse Mrs McCroy?"

"I do not know exactly, but I do know that she has been consulted by half the women in this place, and has been the cause of much sin."

"And you still mean to accuse her publicly of this?"

"I do," said Mr Wallace, "and not before time!"

"But do you have any solid evidence against her?" Major Vernon said.

"Janet Murray. Look at her condition. Could you explain it, Mr Carswell?" Felix did not have a chance to answer. "She has been brought low by the power of Satan which that woman McCroy has drawn down."

"But why Janet Murray?" Major Vernon said.

"Because Mrs McCroy attempted to make an adept of Janet," Mr Wallace said. "But Janet struggled and resisted. She came to me with her fears. And now she is tormented! It is clearly the hand of Satan."

"It's more likely her age and all the foolish talk going about," said Felix. "She is highly suggestible."

"Quite," said Major Vernon. "I must repeat what I said to you on Sunday, Mr Wallace, I do not think it is in anyone's interest to pursue such an accusation. The atmosphere is already febrile. After what was done to Effie Haynes, we should be cautious about making accusations. By the way, why were the jougs left unlocked that night? It has been puzzling me. If they had not been left unlocked, then Murray and his friends could not have assaulted her in such a fashion."

"What do you mean, sir?" Wallace said.

"Miss King mentioned to me that when you gave her and Mrs Carswell a tour of the Kirk that the jougs were locked. I wonder why were they were unlocked, and by whom?"

"Are you accusing me of this carelessness?" said Wallace. "I assure you I do not keep the key on my watch chain – it has been lost for some time. I should like to know where it is, and

I was as shocked as anyone at what happened. However, the individual involved is another example of the corruption that is stealing through this place! If others are moved to such acts, then we cannot be surprised, surely?"

"No, but neither should we be complacent," Major Vernon said. "Any suggestion from those in authority that such acts are justified is extremely dangerous. This is why I must ask you again to desist from making a public spectacle of Mrs McCroy. No one can profit by it, and in the circumstances I think it would be a dangerous example to those people who you have been brought here to serve. You are their pastor. Lead them gently, I beg you!"

Wallace was silent for a moment and then said, "I find your stance very perturbing, Major Vernon. Your reputation has you as a seeker of truth and justice and yet you seem to dislike the utterance of the truth when you are faced by it. When we spoke that first afternoon about your niece and nephews, you wished me to hide the facts when there was a clear duty for me to remind them of their parents' reprehensible behaviour, and now you wish me not to discipline a member of my own congregation on a serious matter because – well, I don't quite know why, unless it is because you have succumbed to her wiles whilst staying at her house. In which case it is even more important that she is exposed for what she is! And as for gentleness, that is not what is required here. No, what is needed is the scourge of fire, that consumes all in its path!"

He made a sweeping gesture and then set off briskly towards the Castle Cottages.

"Poor Mrs Thompson," said Felix. "That is the last thing she needs."

Major Vernon grimaced and said, "That is the last thing my head needs, certainly. What an appalling little –" He broke off and rubbed his face. "I think I need to go home and deal with this."

~

Giles got back to the house, his head scarcely bearable now. Emma and the children were at lunch, but he could not face eating, so he made a hasty excuse and went upstairs in search of the flask of laudanum in his dressing case. He drew the curtains, perched on the edge of the bed and with shaking hands tried to open the little flask. There was a knock at the door. It was Mrs McCroy with a tray of green tea.

"I understand that this is your favoured remedy for a migraine," she said.

"Thank you. How is Mrs Vernon?" he said.

"She is quite well," she said, in her low, calming voice. "Now, you must rest."

"Yes, I must." He offered the flask to her. "A couple of drops in the tea usually suffices."

"Very well," she said, and went to pour the tea.

He pulled off his boots and said, "I have been to see Mrs Thompson. She confirmed it was her mother we found last night."

"She will be glad to have an answer at last. It has been a long torture for her."

"She was," Giles said. "You were mentioned. She said you had helped in the search. I was a little confused – how?"

"Oh, I am not sure about that."

"She said you have a power to find things."

She offered him the cup and saucer. "Two drops as you said, Major Vernon."

"Did you cast a finding charm?" he said, taking it from her. "I have heard of such things before. In the village where I grew up there was a woman who had such skills."

"Yes, there are indeed such people," she said.

"Are you one of them?"

"Does it matter? What matters is that she is found and

her family can grieve as they should."

"I do not wish to judge," he said. "I only wish to know. If you did help find her, then – well, I don't know what it means, but as you say, you have helped that family greatly."

"Then that is what it means," she said, going to adjust the curtains. "It is rather warm in here now. I shall put the sash up and close the shutters. That will be more comfortable for you."

"Mr Wallace is angry with you. I tried again to dissuade him, but he seems to be succumbing to the most ridiculous notions," he said. "He is determined, unfortunately. I thought I might talk to Janet. If she could be persuaded to withdraw her accusation –"

"Do not mind about that now," said Mrs McCroy.

"It will be seen to. The man is a – he is unfit for his position!"

"Hush, sir, and be calm. You must not concern yourself with this now, if you know what is good for you."

"You are right," he said, draining his cup and setting it down.

"My late husband used to suffer from migraine," she said. "I found that a gentle manipulation of the scalp was often helpful to him. I might, if you like, attempt it? If you can bear it?"

"I will try anything," said Giles. "Thank you."

"Come and sit here," she said, indicating a chair.

He did as he was bid and she stood behind him, and with cool finger tips she began by gently raking through his hair. He was a little startled at first by this, and part of him was inclined to resist – for there was surely pleasure in it that was illicit – but as she began to knead his scalp, he found the benefit of it overtook him. A cooling rush eclipsed the pain for a long moment, and he closed his eyes and allowed himself to breathe deeply.

"There," she said, after several minutes.

He felt heavy-limbed and calm, and wished she had not stopped. "Thank you," he managed to say.

She left him to his tea and rest. He stretched out on the bed, aware of the scent of lavender and roses rising from the pillows. His head was still wretched, but he felt less tormented. A hundred questions remained, along with the pain behind his eyes, but lying still, he felt able to dismiss them for the time being, and allowed himself to drift into a pleasant state of idle calm where nothing very much mattered.

Chapter Thirty-four

Felix was surprised to see Major Vernon come striding into the library with his usual energy.

"Has your migraine gone?"

"Not entirely. It will no doubt come back later with force, but in the meantime, we must get on. Dunbar, in the first instance."

"I saw him when I arrived. He came in here to consult Suetonius. He wanted to check a quotation for a paper he is writing. He was extremely calm. He even asked me who he should read on sanitary reform."

"Business as usual, then?"

"So it would seem."

"If he is feeling confident, this may be a good moment to speak to him. Unless it is the confidence of an innocent man, of course," added Major Vernon.

"Or the confidence of an utterly ruthless man," said Felix.

They found Dunbar in the same little sitting room as before, working at his writing table. However, his wife was absent this time, and he looked irked to be interrupted.

"I'm glad to find you alone, my lord," said Major Vernon, sitting down without being asked. "It's about time we had a frank conversation."

"It is? About what, may I ask?"

"You arrived in Pitfeldry last Saturday, I understand."

"Yes."

"And put up in The Brodie Arms?"

"You know quite well I was staying there. Perhaps we could get to the point? I do not think you like wasting time, Major Vernon. I certainly do not."

"Tell me about your dealings with Effie Haynes."

"I may have spoken to her at the inn," Dunbar said.

"I think it may have been a little more than conversation. According to the landlady, she was in your room."

"What of it?"

"I shall let the circumstance of a recently married man procuring the services of a village harlot pass," said Major Vernon. "That is not what concerns me. No, it is the aftermath of that transaction. On Monday morning, you gave Mrs Haynes what she was owed for her services – a nice gold sovereign, or perhaps only a half sovereign – the sum does not really matter. What matters is that she went to her sister's shop and tried to pay off her debts with it. Mrs Gowans would not accept the money. She did not like the way it had been earned, and she then returned the money to you. Is that true?"

"It is," said Dunbar.

"And later that afternoon – you have no doubt heard this – Mrs Gowans was strangled as she made her way home from the cottage where her sister lived."

"I had heard that," said Dunbar.

"In fact there was more to it than that. More than a simple strangulation. Mr Carswell?"

"The evidence suggests she was brought to the point of asphyxiation several times before she died," Felix said. "She would have been rendered paralysed but still conscious of what was happening to her. There were also indications that her attacker may have raped her. And then he slit her petticoats with a knife."

"A thorough violation of an entirely innocent woman," Major Vernon said. "A respectable, much-loved woman who was not afraid to stand up for what she believed was right. I never had the pleasure of meeting her in life. I think it would have taken some courage to come to you, my lord, and hand back that money. A rare sense of honour, wouldn't you agree?"

"What is it you wish me to say, Major Vernon?" said Dunbar. "Are you expecting me to break down and confess to something? I cannot oblige. I remember her, of course, and I was irritated by her, that I will admit, but I had no more dealings with her. Why would I? She gave me back my money. In a way it amused me to see such foolish pride. I would have had more respect for her had she kept the money. Her sister earned it honestly."

"You were not tempted to seek her sister out again?" Major Vernon said.

"No."

"She is a striking woman," said Major Vernon. "And inexpensive, I dare say, compared with the whores in London these days. I know you are interested in the value of things. I once read one of your papers, my lord, on the differences in the cost of living between cities in the north and the south. How a quart of milk is more expensive in Halifax than it is in Exeter, but snuff and sugar are cheaper. It would have been an interesting addendum to see the market rate of prostitutes compared."

"Indeed," said Dunbar, "it would. But our present climate does not allow for such plain speaking, does it?"

"I will be plain with you, sir," said Major Vernon. "I know exactly the temptations of such women. I was a slave to it myself at one time, so I find it hard to believe that you did not go and seek her out again. She is handsome for the type, a rare creature in such a place as this. Did you go back that afternoon?" Dunbar fiddled with his signet ring. "It will be easier if you tell me the truth, my lord."

There was a pause while Dunbar considered the point.

"Very well – I did," he said.

"When was this?"

"It was a little after one. I wanted a walk and the weather had cleared. She had told me where I might find her, and yes, I was willing to be amused. I had had a letter telling me that my wife would not be here when she said she would be, and that irritated me. So I went to clear my head, so to speak."

"Thank you."

"But I must emphasise that I did not see Mrs Gowans again. I did see that rough fellow – Lowndes – is that his name?"

"Lowndie?"

"Yes. We crossed paths when I was leaving. She mentioned she was expecting him and I should not linger there – not that I wanted to. It was obviously a regular assignation. I would talk to him, if I were you, Major Vernon."

"Noted," said Major Vernon. "And did you meet anyone else on your excursion?"

"Only that squat little woman who is married to the Minster. I ran into her just as I was coming back into the village."

"Mrs Wallace?"

"Yes, she. She asked me if I had seen her husband – rather as if he were a lost piece of livestock. Perhaps that is how she sees him."

"And this was at what time?"

"I can't be certain. It was still light and it was not raining. It had just begun to rain when I got back to the inn, however, for I remember being relieved at having missed it. There, will that satisfy you?"

Major Vernon did not answer but made a few notes in his book, and then laying it down, said, "Thank you for your frankness. Now, there is another matter which we must discuss. I am trying to establish what everyone's movements were on the night of Lady Rothborough's death. I have come across a discrepancy in your case."

"In what respect?" said Dunbar.

"The Prince said you were with him for most of the evening. Playing billiards."

"I did play a couple of frames."

"And when did you go up to your wife?"

"I'm not entirely sure."

"The Prince said you were together until after eleven."

"Did he say so? Was it that late? Again, I have no real recollection. Perhaps it was that late. My wife was not fretting when I did come in, so I cannot have been so tardy. I am sure she would have told me if I had disappointed her."

"I'm not so sure –" Felix put in, but Major Vernon put his hand up to silence him.

"So eleven, approximately?" Major Vernon said.

"If it matters to you, then yes," said Dunbar.

"It matters, I'm afraid," said Major Vernon. "We are of the opinion that Lady Rothborough did not commit suicide. Your wife was adamant on that point, and the other indications seem to support her view."

"It is distressing for her, whatever the case. She has lost her mother," said Dunbar.

"Yes, and she has gained a fortune prematurely. That must be of some comfort to you both."

"That is where you are wrong, Major Vernon," Dunbar said, getting up and going to the door. "It is most inconvenient. I should rather the lady were not dead and the lawyers were working away on my wife's behalf. I wanted her fortune protected. I have creditors, you see, sir, and they will want their pound of flesh – well, rather more than a pound of flesh, to be frank. As it stands now, they will take me for all I have. My late parents were profligates with money and I have been obliged to service their debts, as well as my own. What inheritance I had was heavily encumbered. That money will scarcely be of any use to me. It is a great misfortune to us both that Lady Rothborough is dead." He opened the door. "Perhaps I might get on with my work now? I have to earn my living."

When they had left the room, Major Vernon said, "I suppose that will be easily enough verified. He is an unpleasant man, but I do not think he is a murderer. And I have given him something he can use against me. That was unwise."

"We could easily tell Augusta about Effie Haynes," said Felix. "That ought to keep him quiet."

"He does not seem much ashamed of that," Major Vernon said. "And she may be perfectly aware of what sort of man he is."

"She will not be amused when she finds her fortune goes to pay for his father's debts."

"No, I suppose not."

"And Maria's portion as well!" said Felix. "That is a wretched twist."

They returned to the library.

"Perhaps this is nothing to do with money," Major Vernon said. "Perhaps we should look for connections between the women. As the Prince said, it is unusual that there should be three unnatural deaths in such a remote area. Geography counts for something. They all have a connection with Pitfeldry – Mrs Black's daughter lived here, Mrs Gowans kept the shop here, and Lady Rothborough was the wife of the local estate owner."

"They are all middle-aged women," Felix said. "Mrs Black was just fifty, Mrs Gowans thirty-nine, Lady Rothborough –"

"Forty-eight," said Major Vernon. "All married women. Mrs Black widowed."

"All mothers," said Felix.

"The greatest discrepancy is in social degree," said Major Vernon. "We have a marchioness, a shop-keeper's wife and a labourer's widow."

"And no pattern is discernible in the manner of death," said Felix. "Battered to death with an unknown weapon, strangulation, and then poison. There might as well be three different hands at work, with three entirely different motives. How can any of them be linked? We cannot make such an assumption, surely, at least not on the information we have at present. It feels to me like a horrible set of coincidences, if I'm honest. Such strange clusters have been known to occur before, as you know."

"Yes," said Major Vernon. "Yes, we still do not know enough. They are all shadows to me. We cannot know why they were killed until we truly know who they were. In the meantime I must go up to Westerlochan. I need to talk to Janet Murray. Will you come with me?"

~

Westerlochan Farm was bathed in a golden glow of late afternoon sunshine and they found Janet Murray and her sisters in the arched farm court. The younger girls were playing with some kid goats, whose antics were so delightful that it was impossible not to stop and watch them. The youngest went running up to Carswell with one of them in her arms, anxious to show him, and Giles wished that Sophy and Hamish were there to see them.

"I'm glad to see you up and about," he said to Janet, who was standing a little to the side. "Are you feeling better?"

"Yes, sir, I think so."

"Have you managed to eat today?" said Carswell, who now had a struggling animal in his arms. He was obliged to let it go free, and it went bounding away.

"She ate her breakfast," said the youngest girl. "But then she threw it all up again."

"Aggie!" said Janet. "That's not true –"

"Well, you did," said Aggie, "and you made yourself do it. Didn't she Jessie?"

Jessie nodded, and pointed with her fingers towards her mouth.

"Perhaps we should go inside?" Giles said to Janet.

Giles, Carswell and Janet went into the empty farmhouse kitchen where the fire was in danger of going out.

"Is your mother here?" said Giles.

"She's gone to see the baby," said Janet. "And there's a lot to do with Father away."

"Come and sit by the window, Janet," said Carswell. "I want to look at you properly."

Giles made up the fire while Carswell examined her, making her open her mouth and looking at her throat.

"So why did you make yourself sick?" Carswell asked when he was done.

"I would have been sick anyway," she said. "I felt it, so I –"

"Are you sure that's the case?" said Carswell. "You haven't done this before?"

"Maybe," she said, after a moment. "I don't mean to, it's just I don't want the stuff in me. It feels so... so vile." She shuddered. "I manage to eat a bit and then, I just have to get it out of me."

"And it's become a habit?" said Carswell. She nodded. "When did you start to find it so hard to eat? Was it when you came home from school, or before then?"

"At school," said Janet.

"Perhaps another girl was doing it?" Carswell said. "Was that it?"

Janet did not answer.

"Why did you leave school, Janet?" Giles said.

"Do I have to tell you?" she said, with a sudden flare of anger.

"I think it might help if you did," said Carswell.

Giles took a chair and sat down near her.

"I was nearly expelled from school," he said. Now he had her attention.

"What did you do?" she said.

"A friend and I introduced a sow into the headmaster's study."

"Good God," murmured Carswell.

"You did not!" said Janet. "Did you?"

"I did, and the consequences were not pleasant. But I was allowed to stay until the end of the year. I should not have liked to have gone home in disgrace. That would have been much worse, I think."

"It was only a bit of fun," Janet said. "We were only playing."

"Like my pig. What was the game?" said Giles.

"I don't want to say."

"I know, but I think you'd better," he said.

"It's all very well for you," she said. "Gentlemen can do things like that and get away with it. But if a girl does it..." That there was some truth in this Giles could not deny. "And what you did was just plain daft –"

"And what you did, wasn't?" said Giles.

"It wasn't meant to go the way it did," she said. "It was just we thought we'd give the others a good scare. Just to start with anyway," she added in a mutter, looking away. "But then –"

"Did this scare involve trying to summon Satan?" said Carswell.

She hung her head and murmured: "Yes. But we weren't going to do it, just pretend that we were taken over, just to scare the others. It worked with most of them, but there was one girl, Mary-Jane, who laughed at us, and then she said she'd tell on us, and so –"

"You did it again?" said Carswell.

"We wanted to make it real and then, I don't know how, it began to feel real, and it was so frightening, but I couldn't stop it, somehow, though I tried to, I really did, because we knew it was wrong, and it was making all the little girls so scared, and some of them were dancing about with like my sisters were, as if we'd set them doing it. Oh, I don't understand it!" She pressed her hands to her face. "It must have been the Devil himself. We did ask him to come and so he did! And now he won't go away! I can't get rid of him!"

"Let's go back to the food," said Felix. "Was this when you stopped eating properly?"

"It was the food at school. They got a new cook and it was always so greasy and smelly, and three or four of us there were... we just couldn't keep it down. It made us feel sick all the time so we got rid of it. We had to eat it at table or we'd be in trouble, so we'd go to the privy or there was a ditch in the yard, and, well, you know – it always felt better after."

"And now you can hardly eat," Carswell said. "You know you cannot carry on like this, Janet – it will kill you."

"Would that matter?" she said. "I would rather be dead, for no one really cares for me. Especially not here!"

"I know it will be hard, but you must try to overcome this," Carswell said. "If you start to eat better, then you will feel more in control. This is why you are so convinced about the Devil taking you over – your mind has become disordered because of your lack of proper nourishment."

"Do you mean I am mad?"

"No, of course not."

"I'm not mad. It is true. I feel him take me over," she said. "I am not mad. Don't say I am mad, please. I don't want to be sent away like Effie. She's gone to the madhouse, isn't that so?"

"Where did you hear that?" Giles said.

"Someone said so to me on Sunday at church."

"Mrs Haynes has been sent to the infirmary at Perth Gaol," said Carswell. "Not the asylum."

Giles glanced through his notebook.

"If this is the case, Janet, why did you tell me that it was with Mrs Haynes you began dabbling in witchcraft?" he said.

"I don't know, sir."

"You weren't ready to tell me the whole truth, I suppose," Giles said. "That you had begun with it at school. Perhaps you sought her out, knowing her reputation?"

"Maybe," she said.

"I see," he said. "So there was a sort of attraction there. You say you want to get rid of the Devil but you went to a reputed witch about it."

"I thought she could help me. Mrs McCroy couldn't, so –"

"You went to her about this?" said Giles.

"Not exactly. It was just when I first came back, she was kind to me, and she said she would help me, she seemed to understand, but then she cut me off. So I went to Effie."

"Cut you off?" said Giles. "In what way?"

"She told me she could not help me, that I could only help myself, which I couldn't! I thought she understood, but she didn't! I only asked her for help, and she turned her back on me."

"Is that why you denounced her to Mr Wallace?"

She was silent for a while, and then said, "Yes. But she is a witch. I'm not lying. Effie told me she was as well. Effie learnt everything from her. She said she is very powerful. So that's why I said it."

"And there is no chance that you might be mistaken about this?" Giles said gently. "What happened between you? She has obviously offended you. How did you come to turn to her in the first place?"

"It was when I was sent home. She said she'd give me lessons. Ordinary lessons, that is. That was why my mother sent me to school in the first place so I could be a teacher. And my stepfather doesn't like me, and I don't like him, so I was glad to go."

"So you went to her for lessons, and then?"

"She asked me what had happened at school. I didn't want to tell her, of course, but she got it out of me and said she could help me. Then she started talking about all these strange ideas, and how I might have a gift, and to be honest, it scared me even more. So I stayed away, and then she was angry with me for it, and said I wasn't what she thought I was but just a silly girl."

"Strange ideas?" Giles asked.

"She said that it wasn't the Devil taking me over, but that there are powers we can harness for good or evil, if we have the gift. A sort of witchcraft, I think, but she said I must never call it that."

"Mr Wallace has plans to accuse her publicly of witchcraft," Giles said.

"He can if he likes," said Janet.

"But your part in all this would have to come out if he does," said Giles. "Are you prepared for that? Would it not be better to say you were mistaken?"

"Why would I do that, if she is a witch? It says in the Bible that a witch is a bad thing. Mr Wallace preached his sermon on it."

"But Mrs McCroy told you it was not witchcraft," said Giles. "She was talking about something else, perhaps. There are many shades of belief about these things. There are Eastern religions that are quite different from our own. They all believe different things. That is true amongst Christians to some extent as well."

She stared at him as if he had said something blasphemous, and he felt he had little hope of making her retract her words.

"Will you consider taking it back?" he said. "No one would think the worse of you if you did."

She gave no answer.

"I'll come and see you again tomorrow, Janet," said Carswell.

Chapter Thirty-five

"Will you take a glass of wine, Major Vernon?" said Mrs McCroy, unstopping the decanter. He had found her in the dining room, adding some last touches to the table.

"Are you not joining us?" said Giles, seeing only two places laid.

"No, not tonight, if you will excuse me," she said. "So?"

"Just half a glass, thank you."

She handed him a glass.

"I was at Westerlochan," he said, having taken a sip, "talking to Janet. I tried to dissuade her, but I think she is still angry with you."

"She would be, yes," said Mrs McCroy.

"I think she might be persuadable yet, if she could come to realise she has no grounds for her anger."

"She has every ground," said Mrs McCroy. "I treated her poorly."

"I'm sure that cannot be the case –" Giles began but she held up her hand to silence him.

"I should have persisted. She is an intelligent child. Did she tell you what had happened between us?"

"Yes, and I found it interesting, I must confess. She talked of a sort of harnessing of powers. It made me think of the finding charm for Mrs Thompson. Janet said you told her it was not to be called witchcraft. I think I see why. It is something other than that, something more?"

She said nothing for some moments, and then asked, "Where were you raised, Major Vernon?"

"In Northumberland – in the north of the country, near Alnwick."

"That is a place like this, in some respects," she said, "where the old ways have never left. The old wisdom, that is. You feel drawn to it, perhaps, because of that. It may be that you have always had the sense there was a great deal more to it than the black letters of your prayer book."

Now it was his time for silence. Her manner did not allow him to be glib.

"Not everyone can see it," she said, and touching him gently on the arm, passed by him and went to the door. "I hope your dinner will be satisfactory."

Emma came in a little later to find him staring out of the window at the last remnants of the light.

"How is your head?"

"A great deal better," he said, turning to see her. "Is that your new dress?"

"Yes," she said.

"Extremely fetching. And flowers in your hair?"

"Sophy was being silly."

"I don't think it's silly at all. It's quite a crown, though."

"I'm rather worried she has devastated Mrs McCroy's garden making it. When I was kissing Hamish good night just now, he said I smelt of sage and onion."

"Let me see," he said, and went and kissed her. "Sage and rosemary, certainly."

"How is your head?"

"Quite gone, remarkably," he said, remembering Mrs McCroy's cool hands upon him.

They ate dinner, and then decided they would go straight up to bed. As they went upstairs, he was aware of a curious atmosphere. There was a sweet scent in the air, the source of which he could not place. Was it incense in some form or other? It was pungent and heady, like a bottle of old Malmsey.

He paused for a moment on the half-landing by the large, many-paned window that overlooked the garden and the country beyond, caught by the beauty of the crescent moon gleaming white and gold against the dark sky.

Emma opened their bedroom door.

"I'll just go and see the children," he said, and went down the passageway with his candle. He found them all asleep, except for Sophy who sat up at the sight of him, demanded an embrace and then settled down to sleep again without a single word being spoken. He left her, thinking – not for the first time – how extraordinarily fortunate it was to have such charming creatures in his life. He returned to their bedroom.

"Emma?" he ventured, and then found he could say no more.

She was standing motionless by the window looking out at the same landscape he had just admired. Here the light of the moon seemed brighter, illuminating her pale skin. For she was quite naked. Her chemise was lying on the floor forming a pool of white linen on the floor. She had let down her hair, and it was flowing down her bare back in an irresistible cascade of darkness. The window was slightly open, and it was clear that she was enjoying the caress of the breeze on her bare flesh.

He felt lost in admiration to see her like this, like a creature from a dream. Except she was his creature, or rather, his mistress, or perhaps even his goddess. He could not make sense of any of it, but something told him this was not meant to be defined. It was beyond rational observation. They had moved somewhere else entirely.

He set his candle on the fireplace and snuffed it out with his fingers, hardly noticing the heat. The dusk enfolded them as he pulled his clothes off and finally, naked himself, he went to her, as she still stood bathing in the soft breeze. He took her hands and kissed them. Then they wrapped their arms about the other and for a moment or two, they clung together.

Then they went to bed, and all was well, and as it had not been for many months.

He woke later with Emma asleep in his arms. She sighed

into wakefulness, and he got out of bed to light the candle and use the pot.

"What time is it?" she said.

"Nearly midnight," he said.

"Goodness."

"Goodness indeed," he said, bringing the candle to the bedside and climbing back into bed. "I saw a print upstairs, and there were naked hexen dancing in the moonlight. Just as you were."

"Hexen," she said. "Impressive. We shall make a Germanist of you yet, Major Vernon."

"Hexen. It is such a satisfying word. It seems to suggest both contempt and awe."

"And fear."

"Yes, that too," he said.

"But you do not disapprove?" she said.

"Of being brought to my senses? No," he said, "I'm glad of it. I have been in a foolish place – well, I think you may have guessed at it."

"Charlotte," she said after a moment. "Maria did tell me that she once... and of course she will persist with loving you, Giles – it is exactly what I did myself. I fixed my heart on you when I first knew you and so has she. How can I not understand that and forgive it?"

"Yes, forgive her, but I don't think my part in it is so –"

"She is young and passionate," said Emma. "Why would you not be flattered? How can one not enjoy such an onslaught? After all, I was flattered when the Prince told me that I have beautiful eyes and that my German accent is almost perfect, but it does not mean –"

"He said that to you?"

"Yes!" she said, laughing. "That afternoon after we had been to the Spouts. It was adorable. I almost burst into tears. For which I ask you to forgive me."

"He is right about your eyes," Giles said, pressing his

hands to her cheeks and kissing her. "And he has very good taste. Though I am not so sure I ought to take him as a tutor for the children now."

"What?" said Emma.

"It was just that he has the measure of Hamish. If he were penniless it would be an excellent opportunity for him."

"Tutor to a threadbare family like ours?" said Emma, smiling.

"I'm sure your Cousin Stephen would be willing to pay, oh, perhaps as much as thirty guineas a year for Hamish to learn German. He is keen for him to have a commercial education, after all. Shall I write to him and ask?"

"Stop being ridiculous. Thirty guineas would not pay for his waistcoats."

"Thirty guineas all found, mind. Patten will look after his linen, which is worth something. He would have his own room. He could have the back attic – the window stays shut if you wedge it with folded paper. Every other Sunday off. Is that not reasonable?"

"Stop it," said Emma, laughing helplessly now.

"I think he would be quite contented," Giles went on. "And he could write love poems to the lady of the house in a language the master cannot understand."

"You should write novels," said Emma. "You are wasted as a rat-catcher."

"Certainly it might be easier," said Giles. "This business –"

"Sleep on it," she said. "It may all be clearer tomorrow."

"I cannot sleep again, just yet," he said, slipping his hand inside her nightdress. "Meine liebe hexe, shall we...?"

Chapter Thirty-six

Felix found Lord Rothborough and Maria waiting for him the following morning, having arranged to breakfast with them. Maria appeared to have put the worst of her cold behind her, but she looked fragile and diminished in her mourning clothes. She was one of those women who did not suit black. Lord Rothborough, for his part, looked a little more composed than previously, but he too was subdued. It was left to Felix to do what he could to console them. Yet Lord Rothborough clapped his hand on his shoulder and told him that it was the greatest comfort in the world to have him there, while Maria nodded in agreement, gazing at him with her wide, red-rimmed eyes in a fashion that broke his heart.

It was painfully clear that their suffering had been increased by the ambiguous nature of Lady Rothborough's death and their disagreements with her. If she had faded away, surrounded by her family, after a long illness, and with peace made and blessings liberally dispensed to all, how different would this mourning be for them. As it was, they were caught in the vicious teeth of uncertainty, a state – he had begun to realise – that humankind found extremely difficult to deal with. It was liable to torment even such strong souls as Lord Rothborough and Maria.

"You've asked Sir Mark to come?" he said to Maria.

"Yes, I wrote to him as soon as we knew. With luck it will not take too long to reach him. I know he will come at once."

"I wrote to him as well, Maria, and I told him to bring a wedding ring," said Lord Rothborough, getting up from the table. "You may as well marry him as soon as you can."

"May we? Oh, Papa!" exclaimed Maria, jumping up and

running to him. "Are you sure? Will it not look scandalous?"

"Do we care how it will look?" Lord Rothborough said, embracing her. "You have been engaged long enough. Who knows what fate will throw at us all next? You must get what happiness you can, my love, and quickly. I am sure the Rector will marry you."

"Oh yes, I should like him to marry us, and I am sure Mark will like him very much too," said Maria, running to Felix, smiling through tears as she threw her arms about him. "Oh, goodness!"

"You should take a drive in the carriage," said Felix, taking her hands and kissing them. "That will blow the rest of your cold away and make you look your best for when he does get here. It's quite mild again today."

"Yes, the weather looks set fair," said Lord Rothborough, going to the window. "The weather never matches with our sentiments except in poetry."

~

Felix had arranged to meet Major Vernon at the Factor's offices. He was with Sergeant Gibson, freshly arrived from Dunkeld, and was showing him Mrs Black's remains.

"A crack on the back of the head, you say, sir?" Gibson said.

"Several cracks," Felix said. "Altogether a great deal of force."

Gibson frowned.

"I heard of a case in Edinburgh," he said, "in the autumn end of last year. There was a woman of the streets found with her head smashed open from behind. She was found in one of those closes off the Grassmarket – I can't remember the name of it."

"I remember reading about that," said Major Vernon. "And it was never established who was to blame?"

"No, sir – they thought it was her pimp, but he couldn't have been there at the time. It would have been one of her punters, I should think."

"And your point is, Sergeant?" said Felix.

"Just that he may have strayed northwards, sir. People move about a lot more these days, don't they?"

"Quite possibly," said Major Vernon.

"I've heard it said that a murderer can get a taste for it," Gibson added.

"That is certainly true in some cases," said Major Vernon, and began peering at the skull fragments.

"What news on Messrs Murray and company?" Felix said.

"They are all to be charged," said Gibson. "They all made a full admission. It will be a spot of hard labour in Perth Gaol for them."

"That is good news," said Major Vernon.

"I have a letter from the Sheriff for you, sir," said Gibson. "But he is a bit behind the times now, of course, with this, and of course that dreadful business with her Ladyship –"

"Yes, that will require some settling," said Major Vernon, glancing over the letter.

"I'm glad you are here, sir," said Gibson. "Both you gentlemen, in fact. This is not the normal run of things for me, I can tell you."

"I should be worried if it was," said Major Vernon. "And we will do everything we can to help you. You have already excelled yourself. I shall certainly be telling Sir Henry Mackie how well you have conducted affairs here. Have you been encouraged to study for an inspectorship?"

"No, sir, I had not really thought of it. There are no posts to make it worth my while, to be honest – though I might want to get on, it would be a hard study for no gain."

"You might transfer to a different force. There are plenty

of vacancies for men with talent and application."

"He wants you in Northminster," said Felix.

"Move to England?" said Gibson. "With respect, sir, I'm no' so sure about that."

"To one of the northern counties," Major Vernon said. "I'm not talking about Surrey or anywhere barbaric like that. I am a Northumbrian, Sergeant Gibson. We are more cousins than enemies."

"That's not what they say in Berwickshire or Lauderdale," said Felix.

"That is ancient history," said Major Vernon.

"Spoken like a true reiver!" said Felix.

"What's a few head of cattle amongst friends?" said Major Vernon. Gibson looked a little puzzled by this exchange. "Excuse us, Sergeant."

Leaving Gibson to make his notes, Felix said, "I think I will go up to Westerlochan while the weather holds," said Felix. "Will you come and talk to Janet?"

"I am not sure she will be pleased to see me. I might be better off trying to persuade Wallace again," said Major Vernon.

~

The maid who opened the door told him that the Minister was not at home.

"Do you know when he will be back?" Giles enquired.

"I don't know, sir. He did not tell me. Would you like to speak to the mistress?"

"Yes, certainly."

Mrs Wallace was frowning over her accounts in the drawing. She smiled at the sight of him, clearly glad of an interruption.

"I was hoping to speak to your husband," Major Vernon said.

"Have you tried the church?" she said. "He keeps a study of sorts there. I think he prefers it to his study here. But please, stay and drink a cup of tea, won't you, Major Vernon? You will get very wet if you go out again. It has turned most unpleasant."

"Thank you," said Giles.

"Or a glass of sherry? I know gentlemen sometimes prefer that to tea."

"No, tea would be very welcome."

"I'll go and see to it," she said.

Left alone, he looked about the room. There were a great many portraits crammed on the walls, not all well painted, but clearly of great significance to their owner, who by the look of the faces, was Mrs Wallace herself. There was also perhaps a little too much furniture for the room – the old, solid mahogany of a hundred years ago, too good ever to be dispensed with and very well taken care of. On a small table by the window was a contraption which he guessed must be Wallace's hair loom which Lady Charlotte had mentioned. He found himself staring at it. There was a braid in progress: dark, golden red hair. He wondered how Wallace had obtained it, and recalled a plait falling loose from under Mrs Gowans' crushed cap and bonnet.

There was a pasteboard box next to the loom. It contained, just as he feared, more hair, in varied colours. There was also a little tin box which rattled when he picked it up. It contained diamond-shaped pink lozenges, of exactly the same description as the one he had found in Lady Rothborough's room.

He was holding the open tin when Mrs Wallace came back into the room.

"Excuse me for prying," he said. "But what are these?"

"Mr Wallace's voice preservers," said Mrs Wallace, looking a little surprised to see him standing with the tin.

"And are they a common type?"

"Not at all. He has them made up in Edinburgh, and is very particular about them. I must write for some more. He is running short, and that will not do. Why do you ask?"

"Because –" he began and then broke off. "It is a little hard to explain why at this moment, and I have a few more strange questions for you. This hair – where does all this come from?"

"Oh, I don't know. Somewhere."

"He sends for it? Like the lozenges? Lady Charlotte told me there were women who sell their hair. I suppose he buys it?"

"No, I don't think so. I don't know where it comes from. I don't ask."

"Does it trouble you where it might come from?" he said.

She turned away, caressing her pregnant stomach. She murmured to her unborn, and then said, "Where is that girl with the tea? I am really very thirsty."

She went towards the door.

"Have you lost a pair of scissors, Mrs Wallace?" he asked.

She stopped.

"Scissors?" she said, turning back. "Yes, I have. My favourite pair: they were a present from my mother."

"With ivory handles?"

"Yes, although the ivory is all cracked. I would not change them. I was sad to have lost them. Why do you ask, sir?" she said.

Major Vernon took the scissors out of his pocket and laid them on the table.

"These ones, ma'am?"

"Oh, but where did you find them?" She reached out to take them, but Major Vernon laid his hand over them.

"I'm afraid I can't tell you just now. And I must keep them a while longer, but I cannot stay and drink tea. I have to find your husband. If you know where he is, you must tell me. It is very important."

"In the church, I suppose, as I said before."

~

The weather did not hold. By the time Felix reached Westerlochan a spring storm of some violence was whipping itself up, like a child about to have a tantrum. Felix was glad to hurry into the shelter of the farmhouse. Mrs Murray was in the kitchen in the midst of preparing a hogget's head for the pot. She did not seem pleased to be interrupted. She sent Jessie upstairs to fetch down Janet.

"She's been in her bed all morning. She can get up for you," she said. "How am I supposed to do everything myself? Sometimes I think she is only pretending to get out of her work! Now Murray is not here..." She gave a sigh and dumped the sheep's head into the pot. "Do you know anything about that? I cannot get anything out of that Sergeant from Dunkeld. He said they had all been taken to Dunkeld to answer to the Sheriff. It had better be sooner than later, for I can barely manage here alone, and now Jacky has taken himself off, what am I to do?"

"I don't know," said Felix. "Perhaps your neighbours –?"

"They are no friends to us!" she said. "We are not liked here, and I know that may be my husband's doing, for he is a proud man and hard to know, but he is a good man and God-fearing. But these people, these Highlanders, with all their queer fancies – no, we do not belong here. We ought never have come here. We were better off in Ayrshire, that's for sure!"

"I will speak to Jacky," Felix said. "He ought not to have quit."

"Thank you," she said. "That would be a help."

"And you are quite well, and the baby? Is he still at Kirsty Macdonald's?"

"Aye, he's doing well enough. If they would just let Murray come home, then all would be well. Why he must answer to the Sheriff, I don't know. That woman deserved all she got, and everyone knows it!"

"She's no' there," said Jessie.

"What do you mean?" said her mother.

"She's no' in her bed or in her room."

"Well, she must be about somewhere. Go and look in the attic. Aggie, you go as well."

"She won't find her," Aggie said. She was standing at the table, picking out stones from the dried peas. "She's gone out."

"What?"

"When was this?" Felix said.

"First thing. She told me not to say," Aggie said.

"And you listened to her?" said Mrs Murray, marching round the table, her hand raised.

"I've told you now," said Aggie, adeptly dodging her mother's blow.

"What am I to do with you all!" exclaimed Mrs Murray. "You are all wicked, wicked girls!"

"She put her Sunday bonnet on," said Aggie.

"Well, that's something. At least she has not gone roaming in her shift," said Felix, as the rain slapped the window. "Did she say where she was going?"

"No," said Aggie. "Down to the village, I suppose."

"Let us hope no harm comes to her. I will see if I can find her," said Felix, taking up his hat, not relishing the prospect of the ride back down to Pitfeldry.

By the time he reached the Rectory he was soaked. Mrs Vernon and the children had also taken shelter there from the storm and a cheerful atmosphere in the drawing room had taken over. Eleanor and Miss King had got Hamish and Sophy involved in a noisy game of cards, while his mother was utterly engrossed with Sandro.

"Will you stop for lunch, Felix?" she said.

He shook his head.

"I can only stay a minute. I have to find Janet Murray. She has gone off somewhere without telling her mother. You did not see her on your way here, Mrs Vernon?"

Mrs Vernon, who was installed by the fire, frowned and said, "No. That sounds worrying."

"Yes, it is. She is too frail to be out in this weather."

"Perhaps she went to see Mr Wallace," said Mrs Vernon, getting up. "I understand my husband was encouraging her to do so."

"Yes, he did, but she did not seem very taken with the idea."

"She may have found her courage." She went over to the window. "It looks as though this squall is passing through. I will come and help you find her, if you let me?"

"If you feel strong enough –"

"I feel perfectly well," she said.

They met again in the hall a few moments later. Mrs Vernon had wrapped herself in a sturdy-looking cloak. "The only thing that concerns me is that it looks extremely slippery underfoot," she said. "I wonder if the Rector would mind if I borrowed one of these?" She pointed to the hall stand, which contained several shepherd's crooks.

"No, not at all. My mother often uses this one," said Felix, handing one to her. "And in fact, I'll take one myself."

So armed, they set out to look for Janet.

Chapter Thirty-seven

There was no sign of Wallace at the church, but Giles spotted a shawl in mixed stripes of blue and white lying on the floor, which he recognised. He had seen it wrapped around Janet Murray's shoulders the previous day. Did that mean she had come into Pitfeldry to talk to Wallace after all, or perhaps her mother or sisters were about the place? Yet he could not quite imagine any of them tossing something so warm and useful so heedlessly onto the stone flags.

He looked about with more care.

There was a small door ahead of him which led to the back of the churchyard. Here, on the muddy turf ahead of him, were assorted footprints that formed an unmistakable track in a particular direction. He followed them through the graves and came to the churchyard wall, and a gate that had been left ajar. This led to a path descending into a steep wooded area – carved out, he imagined, by the river Pit which wound through the Glen of Pitfeldry.

As he got his bearings, he heard piteous screams rising up from the gorge, and at the same time he smelt smoke.

He hurried down the path, as best he could, for it was precipitous and formed from stones that were glassy from the recent rain. As he descended, the smoke became denser, obscuring his view. It was the choking, eye-stinging smoke that came from burning wet wood, and he felt his lungs protesting at it. He almost lost his footing entirely and was obliged to clasp onto a bending sapling in order to steady himself. He paused as long as he dared, for the screaming had not abated. He peered ahead, desperately trying to make out what was going on ahead of him, but the smoke was now so thick he could barely see anything, other than that the path opened out into a rocky basin with a pool in it.

"Janet Murray, is that you?" he called out, thinking he recognised her voice in that shout.

"Here! Oh, help! Here!" That was not Janet but Mrs McCroy.

"Here! Yes, it is!" screamed Janet.

He started off again at once, but managed only a few steps before Wallace sprang out of the fog into his path. He was brandishing a large knife. Behind him Giles could just make out Janet Murray and Mrs McCroy. They appeared to be tied to a tree, and Wallace was building a bonfire at their feet.

Giles knew he was in no position to disarm him by force. That was the quickest way to get stabbed.

"Put that down, Mr Wallace," he said. "Put it down now."

In some circumstances a man could be persuaded by words alone to lay down his weapon. Giles had witnessed it on occasion. He hoped he had the right words and that Wallace would realise that everything was lost, and desist. But at the same time he feared that Wallace would feel he had nothing to lose. There was no way he could escape the gallows. The evidence had spoken. Giles' one advantage was that Wallace did not know that.

"Think what you are doing," he said, inching forward. "You have a chance here to save yourself," he said. "If you lay a finger on me, you will be hanged, for certain. If you put down that knife and surrender yourself, then this will go better with the authorities for you."

"The authorities," said Wallace. "What do I care about that? This is God's work. Two witches, sir, do you see them there?"

"Wallace, you must stop this," Giles said, again risking another step. He was about to say that he would imperil his soul, but realised that would make no difference. Wallace no doubt believed that his place in Heaven was certain. Giles wondered what he could offer him, and then realised there was one gambit that might succeed, albeit an extremely dangerous one. He hesitated a moment longer, finding his courage, and then said, "Let them go," he said, "and you may have me."

"What do you mean?"

"You have never killed a man, as far as I can work out. Quite a few women, yes, but that is easy sport for you. Impressive though it is to have taken captive these two and subdued them, I must point out, Mr Wallace, that they are only women. But to kill a man: that is a different matter entirely."

As he spoke a sudden merciful breeze whipped along the river bed and cleared the smoke a little so that he could get a better grasp of his surroundings. He was still two steps above Wallace on the path, and to the left of him was a large pool, with a rocky cliff towering above it. He saw now that all the trees about were hung with rags, and remembered the old custom of women placing such tokens there in times of illness, in order to charm away sickness.

"You may kill me, Wallace," he went on, taking those last two steps down, his hands raised. "And you can see how you find it. Slowly, quickly, however you like it."

"Is this some trick?"

"No. Let them go and I will surrender myself to you. In fact..." he said, and got down on his knees in front of Wallace. That this was a sort of madness, he knew, but at the same time he felt the gesture might pique Wallace's interest. "There, sir."

Wallace smiled but it was also clear he was attempting to discern what his strategy might be. At the same time, Giles saw he was now in a far better position to lunge at Wallace and seize the knife.

"Dear lady of the moon, help us now!" It was Mrs McCroy. "I beg you, now, dear lady! Help us, noble Hecate!"

This was exactly the distraction he had needed. It made Wallace turn, and Giles had his chance.

He threw himself forward and managed to bring him

down onto the muddy ground, and the knife was knocked from his hand. Giles then attempted to get him in some position in order that he might get him under restraint, but Wallace was wild in his resistance, and stronger than his slight frame suggested. He soon recovered himself and hurled himself at Giles, sending them both sprawling at the water's edge. Giles fell into the water and before he could right himself, Wallace had his hands on him and was holding him under. He tried to push himself up and break free, but a terrible weariness came over him. He felt the air desert his lungs and then blackness reigned.

The black lifted and he was walking along a passageway which resembled one of the corridors in the new Infirmary Building in Northminster. He was walking towards Mr Harper's office, but then he felt Carswell's hand on his sleeve, and he turned back to speak to him, only to find himself lying on his back with Carswell looming over him, his expression grim with concentration. At the same time he was pumping with his flattened palms on Giles' chest. The pain was utterly excruciating and he cried out at it, before finding himself coughing. Then, Carswell had his arms about him, pulling him so that he could not choke on the stream of watery vomit that now propelled itself from him, like a devil being expelled.

~

Felix had read several accounts of the procedure to revive the drowned, but he had never witnessed it, let alone had the opportunity to put it into practice for himself. The moment he saw Major Vernon lying face down in the pool he knew that he would have to act, and quickly. At the same time, Wallace was staggering out of the water. Mrs Vernon – apparently oblivious to any danger – dashed forward, wielding her shepherd's crook, and cracked him across the forehead with it. He fell backwards and lay groaning on the shore. She hit him again and he passed out.

In the meantime, Felix had dragged Major Vernon from the water, desperately trying to remember all the stages of the procedure. The clarity of mind that came when dealing with strangers threatened to desert him entirely in that moment. His fear at losing him made his hands shake as he made a cursory examination. There were no signs of life and his skin was already turning blue. Felix knelt over him, checked that there were no obstructions in his mouth and then bent down to press his lips to his and attempted to blow the breath of life back into him. A first attempt did nothing, despite pounding rhythmically on his chest. He was afraid for the Major's ribs. It had not been so long since they had healed, and any violence was liable to break them again, but it had to be done. He crouched down and again blew into the Major's mouth, this time with all the force he could muster from his own lungs, making himself giddy. He turned swiftly to pounding on his chest and this time did not restrain himself. He felt a rib crack and at the same time a heartbeat returning, and with it the Major attempting to cry out in pain. A minute later, he was panting in Felix's arms, having vomited up the water from his lungs.

"Dear God..." he exclaimed. Mrs Vernon was with them now, but only for a moment. She had tears streaming down her face, but it did not stop her ransacking her husband's coat tails to discover a pair of hand cuffs. She then dashed away to secure her prisoner. At the same time, Mrs McCroy and Janet Murray, whom she had released from captivity, ran with their smouldering skirts into the pool in order to extinguish the flames.

"What is this place?" Major Vernon whispered hoarsely.

"The Witches' Pool," said Felix.

~

It was approaching evening by the time Felix got to speak to Janet Murray. He found her curled up in a nest of quilts in a small, warm bedroom at Mrs McCroy's house, and he took the opportunity to sit down, realising suddenly he was exhausted and extremely hungry. Mrs McCroy's maid had left a bowl of soup and some oatcakes and butter for Janet, but she had not touched them.

"May I?" he said, indicating the oatcakes.

"You are not going to nag me to eat?" she said.

"Not just now," he said, buttering an oatcake.

"How is Mrs McCroy?" she asked.

"She has some burns on her legs, like yours," he said. "But she is quite comfortable. She is resting with her cats on the bed. How are yours? Not too painful, I hope."

"They are a bit, but I can bear it. It doesn't seem much really, considering.... Is Major Vernon going to be all right?"

"I hope so," Felix said, with his mouth full.

"Do you know what he said?" Janet said. "He told Wallace he could kill him if he would let us go free. He knelt down on the ground and told him to kill him instead of us." She gave a shudder.

Felix put down his half-eaten oatcake.

"Dear Lord," he murmured. "Is that really what happened?"

Janet nodded.

"I thought we were all done for," she said. "And then Mrs McCroy started praying to the moon, and he turned round – Wallace, I mean – and the Major threw himself on him, and made him drop the knife. Then they had that awful fight and Major Vernon ended up in the water... and then you and Mrs Vernon came... How did you know we were there?"

"We didn't. We saw the smoke from the churchyard and

it seemed odd," Felix said. "But how did it all happen in the first place? How did he come to get you down there?"

"I think it was all my fault," said Janet. She reached out and picked up a corner of broken oatcake.

"Those are Mrs Shairp's," Felix said. "They're very good."

She took a tentative bite, carefully chewed it then swallowed.

"If I don't have to have meat," she said, "I think I could manage to eat more."

"That sounds reasonable," said Felix. "Now tell me what happened? Why do you think it was your fault?"

"I went to find Mr Wallace. It was because of what Major Vernon said about Mrs McCroy, and I couldn't sleep for thinking of it. So I thought I would tell him I was wrong about Mrs McCroy. So I was looking for him, and I'd just got to the church and I saw Mrs McCroy coming along, and it felt like a sign and that I could talk to her and explain things. I was already feeling faint from walking, and it started to rain, so we went into the church to talk. We were sitting there and I was feeling so ill, but I told her I was sorry and I was going to try and put it right, and she said she was sorry, and I wasn't to worry about anything, that she'd look after me, and we were both crying our hearts out and it was... oh, it was lovely, like everything might be all right. But then he came in."

"And then what happened?"

"Mrs McCroy asked him to get help because I was sick. She asked him to find you and he left, and then we heard him lock the church door behind him, and that's when we started to get afraid. And when he came back, he'd got a knife, and he grabbed me and had it on my neck and said that he'd slit my throat there and then, in the church, if we didn't do what we were told. So we did. He tied us up and made us go down to the pool and then tied us to that tree, and I felt so weak and afraid, and I kept thinking, if I'd done what I was told and not done any of that wicked stuff at school then this would not have happened and then if I had eaten properly, then I'd have some strength to fight him, I'd be able to stop him. But I hadn't any strength." She took another piece of oatcake from the plate. "So I'm going to try to eat," she added, holding up the piece.

"Good," said Felix, getting up and going to the door.

"Are you sure Mrs McCroy will be all right?" she said. "What can I do to help her?"

"You could eat something and rest," he said.

He returned to Major Vernon's bedside. He was asleep, resting on a pile of pillows, his chest encased with splints and bandages. Mrs Vernon was sitting with him.

"He has been a little agitated – perhaps a nightmare," she said. "But it seemed to pass. And no signs of fever, thank God!"

"He will need to be watched for the rest of the night," Felix said, feeling the Major's pulse. "I will stay here." He did not like the shallow, rattling quality of the Major's breathing, even though he looked outwardly peaceful.

"Your father was here," she said. "He has taken Greene back with him to the Rectory. We thought it better if the children stay there for a few nights. Sophy was very upset to hear about it all. She adores him so much," she added.

He looked down at the Major. "I wish I had not needed to crack that rib again."

"I am very glad you did," said Mrs Vernon. "And what else could you have done in the circumstances? When we are called to act, we must act."

"Well, no one could dispute your courage, ma'am," he said. "I don't think I could have managed that half so well."

"I am quite surprised at myself," she said, "but in the moment, I was so angry there was nothing else to be done."

Major Vernon stirred and opened his eyes. Mrs Vernon went to his side and took his hand.

"Go back to sleep, my love," she said softly. "You must

rest as much as you can."

He closed his eyes, and seemed to drift away again.

"I am going to get something to eat," said Felix, "and then I will come back and relieve you for a while."

"There is no need," Mrs Vernon said. "I shall not leave him."

Chapter Thirty-eight

"Is Wallace in a fit state to be questioned?" said Major Vernon.

"Yes, but you are not in a fit state to question him," said Felix, very alarmed to see Major Vernon coming into the Factor's office. It was only a day after the incident at the Witches' pool. "I told you to stay in bed for at least a week. Strictly, you should not even be moving about. You will wreck the strapping on your ribs. Sit down at once and let me check it."

Major Vernon dutifully obeyed and let Felix examine him.

"And how did you get here?" he added, relieved to find that he was in a better state than might have been imagined.

"I drove," he said. "And I will happily go back to bed, but I cannot rest until we have dealt with him properly. And I slept well last night and most of this morning."

"I cannot believe Mrs Vernon has allowed you out of the house," said Felix.

"She threatened me with a shepherd's crook, that's true," said Major Vernon. "But we agreed terms. And yes, I am extremely tired, and in some pain, but I must do this. I owe it to Mary Gowans, and Mrs Thompson – not to mention Lord Rothborough – to get a confession out of him. I cannot lie in my bed until it is done."

"Very well," said Felix, "but if you are in any difficulty, I will call a halt to it."

"Agreed," said Major Vernon.

~

Wallace was sitting handcuffed before the Factor's desk, with Major Vernon opposite in Macdonald's usual place. Felix, Sergeant Gibson and one of the constables were also in attendance. They had been there for fifteen minutes and Wallace had answered each and every question put to him with an insolent silence.

"Very well, Mr Wallace," said Major Vernon. "I'm beginning to understand you. You are seeking to exhaust us. Yes, I am exhausted, but I'm not remotely satisfied. You have, however, set me thinking about marriage." The Major got up from his seat and walked across the room. "Now what is it that the prayer book says? 'An honourable estate, ordained by God.' Is it the same in the Scottish prayer book? Such a lofty ideal, an honourable estate, and how often reality falls short of that. I'm sure you would agree with me, Mr Wallace. So many men are made wretched by their wives. Instead of being supported by them, they are tormented by them. Their lives made unbearable by their foolishness, their meddling and their inability to realise how a decent wife ought to behave. It is not surprising that so many men are driven to murder the silly creatures."

Major Vernon now grabbed a stool and sat down by Mr Wallace.

"So, how shall we describe Mrs Wallace?" he said. "What a trial she has been to you. That is quite plain. I was in your drawing room – all those second-rate, feeble portraits of her family. Her parents – I think I spotted them – both very stout parties. Gluttons, perhaps, like their daughter? What an odious situation she has put you in. Did she trap you into marriage, Mr Wallace? She struck me as the sort who would trap a man to get what she wanted."

It was chilling to hear Major Vernon talk with such sincerity in this style.

"I am not sure I could have borne it." Major Vernon now lowered his voice and drew his stool closer still to Wallace. "Do you know what I would have done, if I were you, Mr

Wallace, if I had been cursed with such a woman? I would have taken up the poker and smashed open her head. Or perhaps I would have strangled her with her own shawl. Or even – and this would have been amusing – I would have made up a dose of her medicine and made her drink it in front of me, knowing it would kill her. That would be most satisfying. Women are ridiculous about their health. They are always taking those foolish potions and claiming they are unwell, when they are strong as oxen. They just like to pretend they are weak to torment us. Yes?"

This was said so softly that it was scarcely audible but it made Wallace stir in his seat and snigger. Felix now understood why the Major had baulked at this task.

"That last lady – well, sir," Major Vernon went on, "she was a trying creature. I was there when she insulted you. I felt the offence on your behalf. To be spoken to like that in such a manner! A gross humiliation and quite unnecessary. I entirely understand why she had to be corrected. And what a delight to have her abase herself to you, to confess all her faults and beg you to help her be a better creature."

There was a long silence and then Wallace said, "She did deserve it."

"Of that I have no doubt," said Major Vernon. "She certainly did. She had forfeited any right to mercy. Tell me, now that we are being frank, how did you contrive it? It was very well done. You had us all quite puzzled."

"It was not so difficult," said Wallace. "It was a matter of biding my time."

"Yes, yes, very stealthy!" said Major Vernon. "And you went prepared. Your voice preservers! If you had not dropped one, I would never have guessed you were there! We should not have known we had you to thank for such clever work."

Wallace was beginning to look confused, which Felix supposed was the Major's intention.

"Speaking of clever work," Major Vernon went on, "what

will you make with your souvenir? A brooch, perhaps? Or a bracelet? Or a prayer-book marker? What an interesting recreation. Does it make you remember the pleasant moment, is that it?"

Wallace was now breathing hard and staring at Major Vernon.

"There is nothing so beautiful to a man as a woman's hair," Major Vernon said. "How ingenious to keep a museum of those pleasant moments, Mr Wallace. You must, as you comb it out and set it on your little loom, remember the delightful circumstances in which was acquired. I dare say you were quite excited, when Mrs Gowans – that wretched, outspoken bitch – fell silent, at last, and you could clip one of her black braids and add it to your collection."

At this point Major Vernon reached into his pocket and took out a braided bookmark, and laid it on the desk on front of Wallace. His cuffed hands jerked up to take it, but he was not close enough.

"You may have it," said Major Vernon, "if you tell me why you did it."

"As you said," Wallace said, straining now to reach the bookmark. Major Vernon pushed it out of reach.

"She spoke out of turn?"

"Yes," Wallace said, now out of his seat and considerably agitated.

Major Vernon whipped the bookmark off the table.

"What did she say?"

"That I was... that I was in error." He attempted to snatch the bookmark from Major Vernon. "A woman should not speak to a man like that, especially one who is her superior. A woman should certainly not speak to an ordained minister in such a fashion. It had to be done! She had to be silenced." He then attempted again to get the bookmark. "Give that to me! That is my private property! You said you would give it to me!"

"Sit down," said Major Vernon.

He laid the bookmark down on the table with some care, at a tantalising distance from Wallace, and then went and sat down opposite him. Wallace stood looking at it like a dog eyeing a tasty scrap, and eventually sat down again.

"Tell me what happened," said Major Vernon.

"I was provoked," Wallace said. "She spoke to me in such an insolent fashion that I could not allow it any more. So I... I..." He raised his cuffed hands and mimed the action of tightening a ligature about an invisible neck. "She shut up then." He gave a slight giggle in the pleasure of recollection.

"Then you took your pleasure over her," said Major Vernon. "And slashed her petticoats. Which reminds me of another death – a prostitute in Edinburgh last year was found with slashed petticoats and a smashed head, not five hundred yards from where you and your bride were living. Can you tell me anything about that? Is that why this is so precious? Is some of her hair in here?" Major Vernon picked it up now and examined it. "I can see at least three different shades."

Now he laid it down again within reach of Wallace, who snatched it up with his fettered hands and clutched it to him.

"What about the woman in Edinburgh?" Major Vernon went on. "Did you go to her as a customer? What happened?"

"She was unclean," said Wallace. "There are so many unclean women in that city. What does it matter if there is one less? In fact, she was better destroyed. It was necessary."

"I think I understand you now," said Major Vernon. "I know why you did not kill your wife. You can only kill her once, but if you find other women who annoy you or displease or offend you in some way, then you have the pleasure of destruction and your bed will still be warm at home. You feel a splendid mercy in that. She is spared because you can spare her, and for that reason alone. But every time you kill another woman you imagine killing her as well. It doubles the pleasure of it for you. That is why you love that little bookmark so much. That mixture of hair. Your wife's hair is mixed with all the others. Yes?"

He reached out and plucked the bookmark from Wallace, who howled in protest, and attempted again to retrieve it.

"Give that to me!"

Major Vernon shook his head.

"I would have liked to make another one," Wallace went on, "if my important work had not been interrupted by you! It is God's will that I have being doing, remember that! Cleaning the world of dirty, loud, wicked women who will not be quiet when they are told to be quiet!" He attempted and again failed to retrieve the bookmark. "I would make one from your wife's pretty hair," he said, "as well as from that witch McCroy and that little slut Janet Murray. That would teach her to hit me. I think I would strangle her. I should like to feel the life ebbing out of her. That is always such an interesting moment. Perhaps," he said, turning and addressing Felix, "your surgeon friend Mr Carswell would like to hear my observations on that interesting moment? Lady Rothborough, now – that was most instructive. To see the poison taking hold of her. She was so afraid of me. It was really quite amusing."

His words hung in the air like a noxious smell.

"I'm extremely sorry to tell you, Mr Wallace," Major Vernon said, "there will be no more amusement for you. It's all over. Your wicked games are over, and what is remarkable is that the one person you would really like to have destroyed is very much alive! She will be glad to be rid of you, Mr Wallace, that I can tell you with great certainty."

~

"Mrs Wallace is here," said Sergeant Gibson. "She wants to speak to you, Major Vernon."

"Show her in," said Giles. He was now on the edge of utter exhaustion, but he knew he must see her. "I'm glad you're here," he said to Carswell.

"Let me talk to her," said Carswell. Giles nodded.

The lady was shown in. Carswell found her a seat and said, "I was intending to come and see you shortly to explain matters."

"The constable who came to the house yesterday said Mr Wallace was under arrest," she said. "Are you going to release him? What has he been arrested for?"

"I'm afraid this is going to be rather distressing," Carswell said. Mrs Wallace glanced at Carswell and then at Giles as if trying to interpret their expressions. "As it now stands," Carswell went on, "your husband will be taken to Perth tomorrow and charged with the murders of Mrs Black, Mrs Gowans and Lady Rothborough, and the attempted murders of Mrs McCroy, Miss Janet Murray and Major Vernon."

Even before he had finished this dismal list, she had covered her mouth with her gloved hand, attempting to disguise her shock.

"Truly?"

"Yes, and he has admitted to them, at least partially."

She sat in silence, breathing hard.

"All those women? Are you sure?" she said, after a while.

"Yes."

"Mrs Black – did you say Mrs Black?" Giles nodded. "You have found her?"

"Yes."

"That was not long after we came here," she said. "It was the talk of the place. I spoke to some of her friends and her daughter about it. It was shocking. But you have found her. Where? How?"

"Her remains were in a small ravine beside that path from the Smithy to the Castle Cottages," Carswell said. "She had been violently attacked and then pushed down into the ravine.

The undergrowth hid her body from view."

"Not at the Pass of Vorlich, then?"

"No," said Carswell. "Here in Pitfeldry."

"He said –" She broke off and looked down at her fingers, which she had twisted together. "He told me she must have slipped from the path at Vorlich."

"Mr Wallace told you so?" prompted Giles.

"He seemed so certain. It surprised me at the time. Of course, I did not say anything. He had already had been so cross with me because I asked him to go to the forge and fetch the new poker I had ordered. He does not like being sent on errands. I was silly and I did not ask him the right way."

"A poker?" said Carswell.

"Yes. He thought I was being extravagant. Perhaps I was, but I think it is useful to buy something from all the tradespeople in a place like this, to establish goodwill. One never knows when one might need the smith."

"No, indeed," said Giles. "So he brought home this poker on the day she disappeared?"

"Yes, and he insisted on keeping it for his study," she said. "Do you really think he had something to do with her death?"

"Yes."

"And all these other women?"

"Yes, I'm sorry – this must be very hard for you to hear," he said.

She nodded and attempted to control her tears.

"Has he ever been violent with you, ma'am?" Giles asked.

There was a silence and then she said, "It has never quite come to that, but sometimes I have been afraid that..." She began to rub her pregnant stomach. "What am I going to tell this one?" she said, in a piteous tone. "If what you are saying is true – and I fear, it may be – oh, God help me! God help us!" She broke down and wept for some minutes.

"Excuse me," she said, mastering her tears. "It is the

shock of it. I must not give way to this. I shall not, for the sake of my child. Might I speak to him?"

"Are you sure you want that, ma'am?" Carswell asked.

"He will be gone tomorrow. It would help me, I think, to see him, if it is allowed? I have brought his linen and some supper. And his Bible," she added, indicating the basket she had brought with him.

Carswell left the room to make the arrangements.

Some minutes later, Wallace was brought along the passage, escorted by two constables.

They took him into MacDonald's office, where Mrs Wallace had laid out the contents of her basket on the desk.

"I have brought you some food," she said.

"Oatcakes and cheese?" Wallace said, looking at them. "Was there no meat in the larder?"

"I thought cheese would be better."

"Keeping the meat for your supper, no doubt," he said.

"I'm not sure I will be hungry," she said.

"Then why did you not bring me some meat? Perhaps you think I don't deserve it, eh?"

"There is a bottle of sherry as well," said Mrs Wallace. "And I have brought you some clean shirts and a flannel waistcoat. It will probably be rather cold."

"In prison? Yes," he said.

"What am I supposed to say?" she said. "I'm not the one who has been brought to this."

"They" – he turned to Giles – "are mistaken. Now, listen to me, you will write to your cousin Robert in Glasgow. He can find a lawyer for me, someone who will prove this is all entirely nonsense! I will be vindicated, soon enough."

"After what you have said to us, in front of witnesses, Mr Wallace, I think that highly unlikely," said Giles. "And the physical evidence will affirm it."

"I spoke under compulsion!" said Wallace. "Mark that, Agnes! If you can get anything into your foolish fat head, mark that: I was made to speak under compulsion. This is a travesty. Write to your cousin, and come to Perth, as soon as you can. You can make yourself useful, for once!"

"I'm not sure I ought," she said. "I think..."

"What you think is not relevant," he said. "You will do as you are told."

"No, I don't think I can," she said. "I can't believe that you would have been brought to this if there was no truth in it. Why would you not let me see the poker?"

"The poker?" he said.

"The poker I asked you to fetch from the smithy. I wanted to see it and you took it off to your study without letting me see it. It was the day that Mrs Black vanished, you see – I remember that the next day everyone was looking for her. Mr Carswell has told me she was attacked and pushed down the bank by the smithy, and that is nowhere near where you said she had probably fallen, is it? And I keep thinking about that poker now. Did you –"

At which he lunged at her with his cuffed hands, the constables rushed forward to restrain him. They wrestled him into a chair, and held him there.

"Oh, you wicked, wicked man!" she said, staring at him as he struggled and protested.

"I would do it again," he said. "And again!"

Then suddenly she stepped forward, reached into the folds of her skirts and before Giles realised what she was about, he saw the glinting blade of a little pair of scissors in her hand. An instant later she had plunged them into her husband's left eye.

Wallace screamed and Giles, finding a last reserve of strength, jumped up and pulled Mrs Wallace away from him before she could consolidate her attack. She did not resist, but rather collapsed into his arms in a state of utter wretchedness. He manoeuvred her out of the room, to the dire accompaniment of Wallace bellowing and cursing as Carswell attempted to remove the blade.

In the passageway he dumped her unceremoniously on a bench, too exhausted to do anything more, and she gazed at up at him, her face contorted with anger and distress. But at length she composed herself, and looking down at her blood-spattered hands, said, "You will think me foolish. But I have wanted to do that for some time."

Chapter Thirty-nine

"So he was hiding behind the screen in her room all that evening?" said Lord Rothborough. "When I and the girls were speaking to her?"

"We think he must have come in while you were all at dinner," said Felix. "We last laid eyes on him at the Manse at about seven. He shut himself up in his room. He must have left later and come in through one of the back doors. Probably the door on the west façade."

"Which is never locked," said Lord Rothborough.

"But why should it be?" Felix said. "This is Pitfeldry. A locked door is an insult."

"But I let him into the house!" said Rothborough. "And I approved him for the living in the first place. Dear God, what a devil!"

Felix could only concur.

"I'm sorry that there is nothing very comforting to tell the girls," he said. "She must have suffered somewhat."

"There is a certain comfort in knowing the truth, albeit of a raw kind, and they are all strong, in their own ways. But when any of us will ever be at peace over this, who can say? His poor wife – to be moved to such an act! I do hope that the Sheriff has the sense to dismiss any charges against her."

"Or that his counsel does not use it against us," said Felix. "He will make a dramatic sight in the dock. There was no repairing that eye, although I did my best."

"His counsel will need a strong stomach," said Lord Rothborough. "Truly, when the evidence is out, who will have any pity for him? He is a monster, and most likely they will see his wife as a heroine." Getting up from his chair, he went and contemplated the fire. "Oh, poor Frances! What would I give for ten minutes more with her, just to tell her that I am sorry for it all."

"It would have meant nothing if she had not accepted it. Anyway, I think you did say it to her often enough."

"But not with sincerity," said Lord Rothborough. "I may have done it for convenience, to placate her. My feelings were always well locked up in regard to her. At least she is beyond my petty cruelties now. There is something to be said for that," he said, turning away from his study of the fire. "I must go and tell the girls."

"I'll come with you."

"No, no, there is no need for that," he said. "You should go back to Eleanor. By the bye, is Mrs Gowans' child still at the Rectory?"

"Mary? Yes."

"We must do something for her."

"My parents would agree. I suspect they would be happy to keep her, and not with a view to her going out into service. My father seems quite attached to her."

"That is something," said Lord Rothborough. "One could not wish for a better answer to the matter."

Felix was on the verge of leaving the house when Maria came running out to say goodbye to him. She was flushed with tears, but he sensed the relief in her as she embraced him.

"And Major Vernon is quite safe?" she said.

"Yes, but extremely tired. Have you heard from Sir Mark?"

She shook her head. "Perhaps tomorrow," she said. "Now, go home, Felix, and good night," she added, kissing him twice. "One of those is from Charlotte." And she pushed him gently away towards the door.

"I may get one from Augusta yet!" he said.

"We shall work on her, yes," said Maria, and waved him goodbye.

~

On returning to the Rectory, only his father was still up, sitting as he often did by the fire in his study.

"It's very quiet considering we have so many guests," said Felix, coming in and sitting down opposite.

"Yes, all those young people!" said the Rector. "Very delightful but quite exhausting."

"I will have to talk to Mary in the morning," Felix said. "She deserves to know what happened to her mother."

"Not in any great detail, I think," said the Rector. "She is too young and too innocent for that. She already understands that justice will be done on her mother's behalf, and that a sinner will be put before God for judgement. We may only pray that he repents, sooner rather than later."

"I don't think any sort reflection, let alone repentance, is in his nature," said Felix. Amadeus was lying on the hearth, his belly turned to the fire, gloriously insensible. Felix crouched down and began to caress him. "We should have taken notice of your opinion, boy," he said. "He knew that he was not right. Remember how he growled at him, Papa?"

"Yes, indeed he did," said Mr Carswell. "That was most curious."

"And you sensed it too," said Felix, "that something was not right here."

"I do not like to speak with hindsight," said Mr Carswell. "But I think I can date it to that man's arrival here. That sense of unease. And how skilful he was to make me think of witchcraft as the source of evil! For I am sure he has encouraged these notions in us all. He has stirred matters up to hide his own nefarious purposes."

~

Felix went upstairs and found Eleanor was sitting up in bed, reading.

"What is that?" he said.

"A life of Marie-Antoinette," she said.

"Ah, my mother's favourite. I've never quite understood the appeal."

"But it is utterly tragic, and she was so abused."

"Perhaps with good reason," said Felix, starting to undress.

"How can you say that? She was a prisoner of her circumstances."

"Milking cows into Sevres buckets and pursuing sapphic friendships? Hardly," said Felix.

"What are sapphic friendships? What do you mean?"

"I don't suppose it will be in that book," said Felix. "But it was alleged that she had inappropriately close friendships with other women."

Eleanor had laid down the book and was looking at him with great interest.

"Inappropriate?" she said. "In what way?"

"Well..." he began, and found himself laughing. It was as if all the long trial of the day had contrived to make him light-headed. The thought of explaining such a matter to Eleanor, with her mixture of innocence and high animal spirits, felt both delightfully corrupt and extremely piquant. "It is when –"

"What is so amusing?"

"Oh, heavens," he said, sitting down, now helpless with laughter. "I can't begin to –"

Then he remembered something that made him laugh even more, and Eleanor grew disconcerted, to the extent that she got out of bed and came and crouched down beside him.

"Felix, what is the matter with you?"

"Come with me," he said, staggering to his feet, and picking up a candle. "I want to see if..."

In his stockinged feet, he led her along the passageway to

his old bedroom, which he had been using as a dressing room. He carefully shut the door behind them.

"What are you doing?" she said.

"Shush," he said, going to the built-in press in the corner and opening it. He crouched down and pulled out some large books. They were expensive, educational texts, no doubt sent by Lord Rothborough. He had put them away when he had outgrown the engravings of exotic animals and landscapes and the irritating didactic text that accompanied them.

At the age of fourteen, not long before his departure for Edinburgh, he had, by chance, discovered three extremely improper and most exciting prints, tucked inside an atlas of South America in the Castle library. He had been so entranced by them that he had been moved to purloin them. The old books in the press had made a good hiding place, so good that it seemed that they had not been disturbed since he last returned them there.

They were from the last century and displayed all the splendid frankness of that era. One showed the Prince of Wales having congress with an actress, while the second was a detailed brothel scene. Both of these were cheerfully crude and stimulating in their way, but the final picture was quite a different matter. It showed the Queen of France and Madame de Polignac, or at least the inscription in French said that was who the ladies were. Two beautiful young women were locked in a passionate embrace, their hands straying where they should not, their soft flowing clothes either falling away to reveal a breast or shoulder, or clinging so tightly that little of what was beneath was left to the imagination.

"Voila!" he said, and handed it to Eleanor. He held up the candle so she could examine it.

"Oh, but that is lovely," she said, and traced her finger across the figures. He could see her chest rising in excitement. "My...!"

He for his own part could not quite imagine that this moment was anything but an idle dream. To be standing in his old room, with a beautiful woman dressed only in her nightgown, her hair falling down her back, showing her an image that had so often stirred him – it made him tremble with desire.

"How could anyone call that inappropriate?" Eleanor said.

"No, quite," he said.

"I must show this to Jenny," she said.

"I'd rather you didn't," Felix said. "It is not for everyone's eyes."

"But –"

"Can we not keep it as our secret?" he said, kissing her bare shoulder. "I'd rather you didn't show her. You would have to tell her where I got it."

"Which was?"

"I'm ashamed to say I stole it from the Castle library when I was a boy," he said.

"And you've hidden it here all these years?"

"Yes."

"What if your parents –"

"I don't know what they would have said. I'm not sure what they would say now, to be honest. Nor Miss King. I'd rather she didn't know. She would lose any respect for me that she might have."

"She can keep secrets," she said. "And she does respect you. She is always telling me so."

"She does?"

"She thinks you are quite the model husband and tells me how lucky I am to have you."

"Then this will disabuse her, so please don't. It's far more interesting if it's our secret. I have never told a soul about this before."

"Not even Major Vernon?" said Eleanor.

"Goodness, no."

"But you and he are regular confidantes, surely?"

"We are frank on many points, but there are some things –" He might have added that he was sure the Major would have thoroughly appreciated the engraving.

She broke away from him and went across the room to his desk, where she laid the print down carefully.

"Jenny and I talk about everything," she said.

"Everything?" he said.

"Everything," she said. "She has helped me. She is so sensible. Surely you see how much better I am? I am improved, I think. I'm not such a silly child now, am I?"

That there was some truth in this, he could not deny. He nodded.

"So you must trust her," Eleanor said, taking the candle from him and putting it on the mantelpiece. "As I do." She returned to him and laid her hands on his shoulders, and gazed up at him.

"If you insist," he said. He could hardly demur.

"I do," she said, and pressing herself against him, allowed him to kiss her. As his lips brushed over her neck and his hand began to explore her warm and alluringly-scented body, he was inflamed by the thought of Eleanor sharing his pleasure in the forbidden pictures. He guessed she wanted him to imagine her wantonness with another woman, and in this sweet and powerful fantasy, the crisis of their passion was as intense as he had ever known.

It was strange that they were here, on the narrow bed where he had endured all his boyhood frustrations, but he was too preoccupied with the pursuit of pleasure to care. When their labours were done and they had both caught their breath, he fell asleep in her arms and was quite beyond the reach of speculation and self-reproach.

Chapter Forty

"May I come in?" Mrs McCroy said.

Giles was sitting propped up on his pillows.

"Of course. If you are looking for the cats, they are here," he said. They had stolen in and were lying in the sunlit patch at the corner of the bed.

"Ah, yes, I hope they are not in your way. That is a favourite spot."

"I feel honoured to have them here," Giles said. "How are you?"

It was three days since the incident at the Witches' Pool.

"Better than I could have hoped. And you?"

"Still rather weak, and perhaps a little bruised," he said, laying his hand on his chest where Carswell had pressed him back to life. "But I'm in good order and remarkably alive, thanks to Mr Carswell!"

"I was just thinking about what he did. I did not know that was even possible," said Mrs McCroy.

"Nor I," said Giles. "He tells me that the idea was invented here in Scotland about a century ago. A quick-witted surgeon used such means to rescue a miner who had been drowned, but the idea has not been propagated much outside of the mines and port cities. My feeling is it ought to be much better known. I shall get him to teach it to me and then to our constables. It should be common knowledge."

She nodded.

"I will need to ask you, at some point, for an account of what happened that day," he went on. "But only when you are ready."

"I am ready now," she said. "If you are ready for it."

"I am. I am not good at idling. Please sit down."

She did so, and said, "I ought to have said something a while ago. I'm conscious of that, but it is a matter of trust, you see. There are things of which I cannot speak lightly."

"Yes?" he said, intrigued by her tone. He reached for his notebook, at which she frowned, so he laid it to one side and put up his hands.

"Thank you," she said. "Where there are facts that can be recorded, then I have no objection, but – well, hear me out, and then see what you will write or not write."

"As you wish."

"I have to be cautious," she said. "These terrible events have only proved it. I have learnt to see the world in a way that many people find hard to accept, which perhaps you have guessed at."

"A little," said Giles.

"And I think you might be interested to know how I came to this understanding?"

"Certainly."

"My father was a collector of rare and esoteric books," she said. "But I never knew that until he died and they were left to me. I never expected to inherit anything from him, but both my brothers had died, and so I was left with his library and his furniture. I was a new bride at that point, and my husband had recently been called to his first parish. A library of strange books did not seem quite right for the shelves of our first manse, so I left them in their boxes in the attic and did not think much more about them. Then Mr McCroy was called to a parish further north from here, nearer his own family. Naturally, wanting to help him in his work, I went about visiting and trying to be of use to the women of the parish. They were good Christian women, of course, but I soon learnt that there was a great deal more that they believed in. They told me of the Fae and the Wild Hunt, and the good lady of the moon, who will come to the house and spread a feast if you leave her a cup of milk on the threshold, and many other such wonderful things. I heard them speak of this all with utter sincerity. It confused me, and then I realised I had been allowed to glimpse something not ordinarily understood. So I went back to my father's books and I began to study the matter for myself, and I realised that he, in his turn, had begun to speculate on the nature of these things."

"A difficult position for a clergyman's wife," Giles said.

"Yes, but I came to feel that none of it was incompatible with the Gospels if read correctly. I had a great mentor in an old woman, who lived in the humblest circumstances but who had great gifts, and she taught me how to apply these things practically, and then I found I had a gift for the craft. My father had bought some very rare old grimoires and there were methods detailed in those books that were of great use to me –" She broke off. "It occurred to me that what Mr Carswell did to you might seem very fanciful and not at all liable to bring a drowned person back to life, but it worked. In those old books there is a sort of forgotten wisdom that can be usefully revived."

"I have heard Mr Carswell say something similar himself," said Giles, "that old recipes for remedies should not be dismissed out of hand."

"I'm glad to hear that," she said.

"And my own mother," Giles said, "was not beyond consulting a certain old woman in our village, rather than sending for the apothecary from Alnwick. I have often wondered about that. May I ask you something else?"

"Of course."

"When does a simple remedy become a spell? For there was a spell involved, I understand, in finding Mrs Black?"

"There was," she said, after a moment. "But your first question I cannot answer. It is something for you to pursue for yourself if you are interested, and I think you are."

He nodded.

"Tell me, then, what occurred between Wallace and yourself? He obviously had some notion of this."

"Yes, unfortunately. And, to my shame, it was my doing, for I was indiscreet. I chose my pupils badly. Effie Haynes, you see, was my servant at one time, when she was about seventeen, and I found her clever and agreeable. It was not long after my only little girl had died, just after we came here, and I missed her so badly that I took more care over Effie than I ought. She was quick to learn, but she was wild and passionate and very foolish. She left me, and it was only when she came back here last year and began to practise a travesty of all that I had taught her, as well as a lot of other wicked nonsense, that I knew my mistake. I tried to reason with her, but she had worked the craft for money when she was in Glasgow and got into bad habits. And then, of course, there was Janet – she is so intelligent, I could not resist teaching her."

"So you gave her lessons?" Giles said.

"Not many, for I decided it would be dangerous for her to continue. She is intelligent, yes, but so fragile. It was a grave error on my part, because then she turned to Effie, which of course did her no good at all." She sighed. "I very much regret doing so. I hope she will forgive me."

"What were your impressions of Wallace?" Giles said.

"That he was a man without a soul. I think you know what I mean by that. In your profession, you will have had the misfortune of meeting such people before." Giles nodded. "But I had no notion until that day that he meant to kill anyone."

"What happened exactly?" he asked.

"My conscience got the better of me about Janet, and I decided I would go up to Westerlochan and speak to her. When I saw her in the village outside the church in the rain, looking so utterly lost and miserable, it seemed like a sign that I might indeed be able to put things right with her. So we went into the Church and talked and it was very curious indeed, how frank we could be with one another. We were both crying over it all when he came into the Church. I asked him to go and find Mr Carswell if he could, as Janet struck me as quite unwell, and he agreed, and left again. Then we heard him lock the church door, and it was then we began to be afraid. And after that he came back with a knife. He threatened to cut Janet's throat if we did not obey him. And so we did. What else could we do? Why I did not understand until that moment what he was, I do not know. I have been so foolish. I thought I had learnt so much, that I had some degree of wisdom, but it seems I have learnt nothing at all."

"It is easy for good people to underestimate danger," Giles said. "You could not have known what he was. Such thorough wickedness cannot be predicted, unfortunately. We can only see the pattern when it is too late. I nearly missed the signs myself."

~

The following afternoon, in the shelter of the ancient yew trees, Isabella Gowans was laid to rest in the churchyard of Holy Trinity. There was a good turnout from the village, all watching in great solemnity as the party of foresters who had found her carried her from the church to her grave. There was a piper and all was done in the best Highland style. Mr Carswell gave a short address at the graveside, reminding everyone of her many small kindnesses to her neighbours, her scrupulous adherence to her principles, and lastly of her sincere and abiding love of her Saviour, with whom he was sure she was now at rest. It was impossible to ignore the emotion in the Rector's voice as he spoke, and then, when he was done, the humble stillness in his audience as they absorbed what he had said.

Afterwards, when everyone had left for the Rectory or gone to The Brodie Arms – where Lord Rothborough had paid for a funeral feast – Felix noticed Major Vernon lingering by the open grave. He had insisted on going to the funeral.

He saw him take some items from his pocket, crouch down and throw them in. Then he walked towards Felix, and said, in answer to his inquiring expression, "A bundle of herbs and a flat stone. From Mrs McCroy."

Felix might have asked more questions, but there was something in Major Vernon's manner that suggested he would not have got any straight answers from him. They walked towards the Rectory in silence for some minutes, and then Major Vernon said, "What arrangements are they making for Lady Rothborough? Will she be buried here as well?"

"Yes," said Felix. "There was a fear that she had left instructions in her will that she should be interred in Sussex with her parents, but I understand that when she was in Italy, Augusta persuaded her to excise the clause. It is a pity she did not manage to persuade her about the money as well!"

"I don't think Maria will be thinking about that very much."

"No, I suppose so, and I must try and let my annoyance at her go. The poor woman is dead and that must be an end to it. But one does not like to see those one cares for hurt, and it is a struggle, for me at least, to forgive those who hurt them, even if they are dead!"

"She was not an easy person, that's true enough," said Major Vernon.

"My father is wretched over this," said Felix. "And nothing I say seems to help him. He feels responsible, which is ridiculous. I hate to see him like this!"

"Of course," said Major Vernon. "But you must let time do its work, which it will. That is all that can be said."

They went into the Rectory and were greeted by the sight of Mary Gowans sitting with Lord Rothborough in the hall.

They were engaged in deep conversation. He had even provoked a smile from her, and then, seeing Felix and the Major, he beckoned them over.

"We are making plans," said Lord Rothborough, "for a public garden for the village, with a bowling green, a rose garden and perhaps some sort of building for village gatherings. There is that half-acre to the west of The Brodie Arms which would be very suitable, don't you think? It has a good aspect."

"That sounds an excellent notion, my lord," said Major Vernon. "It would be much appreciated, I'm sure."

"Mrs Gowans was fond of roses, as was Lady Rothborough," said Lord Rothborough. "It seems fitting. But then there is the matter of Mrs Black. We do not know what she liked, do we, Mary?"

"No, my lord."

"Then that will be your task to find out. You must go and see her daughter and then you will write to me about it, and all can be set in motion."

"Yes, my lord, of course I will," the girl said, looking both awestruck and pleased at being given such a task.

"Now, I have kept you too long," he said. "Go and find some cake before it is all gone." When she had left, Lord Rothborough said, "That was all Charlotte's idea – I can't take any credit for it."

"Perhaps we should find some cake, too," said Felix. "And something stronger. I asked Mrs McNeill to send some decent sherry from the inn. The wine in this house is indifferent, to put it politely."

"My brother-in-law has spoilt you," said Major Vernon.

"Undoubtedly," said Felix. "But I'm not sure even Mrs McNeill's best sherry will be up to his standards."

"Canon Fforde is certainly rather exigent in that area," said Lord Rothborough getting up. "Speaking of that gentleman, the most sensible letter from him arrived this morning.

There is great art in writing a letter of condolence, and he has that rare skill. I found it extremely helpful."

Felix was glad to hear this, and was about to take them into the dining room where the wine and cakes were laid out, when there was a banging at the front door. He went and opened it, to find Sir Mark Hurrell standing on the step, looking dishevelled and travel-stained.

"Ah, Mr Carswell! How good to see you," he exclaimed. "They told me at the inn to come here, that you would all be here!" He swept off his hat, catching sight of Lord Rothborough behind Felix. "My lord," he said with a bow, putting out his hand. "Forgive my appearance. I have been on horseback for three days. How are you, sir? I came as fast as I could."

Before Lord Rothborough had a chance to answer, the drawing room door opened and Charlotte and Maria came out.

Maria gave a cry of surprise and delight, and ran into Sir Mark's embrace, and he enfolded her in his arms and kissed her.

"Oh, now I can begin to be happy again!" she exclaimed.

Epilogue

May 1842

Pitfeldry was ready for a wedding. The hawthorns unfurled their white blossoms and the sun shone over the walk from the Castle to the church, although the air was still sharp that morning, and the ladies were well wrapped in their shawls. The bride herself, in the plainest white muslin, was swathed in a cloak of white cashmere, a present from her bridegroom, and her cheeks were crimson from the cold and the emotion of the moment. She shared that tendency to flush noticeable in Lord Rothborough and his children, and Giles observed it now in all of them.

Even the new Countess, dressed in a spectacular mourning outfit, her bonnet heavy with the black lace beloved by her late mother, seemed overcome by the simple graces of the occasion. While Maria and Sir Mark made their vows so cheerfully, she sat scarlet-faced and openly weeping. Emma, who had declared the moment they entered the church that she was certain she would cry and would be quite unable to prevent it, was moved to murmur to Giles when they departed to sign the register: "My lady Dunbar is perhaps feeling it a little too much. I know it is unkind of me to say so, but –"

"To me she looks like a tragic heroine," said the Prince, who was sitting with them. "I never saw her look more handsome or more authentisch. I suppose it is from having constructed her own bedding, though."

"You are quite right," said Emma. "I should not have said that. Poor soul, it does seem she cannot help herself. The Earl does not look at all sympathetic. I do hope things are not too wretched for them."

"From what Mr Carswell and Lord Rothborough have said," said Giles, "it's not quite as tragic as it might seem. She will not stand any nonsense."

"I hope you are right," said Emma. "Ah, here they are again! Oh goodness, I think Sir Mark has been crying as well! This church will be flooded. But these tears are the best kind. We need them."

She was quite right. It had been a weary few weeks. Wallace may have been in chains and unable to do any more tangible harm, but the effects of his actions were a festering sore. His conduct at trial had been singularly repellent and he had worn his guilt like a crown of thorns. He had showed no remorse, only a sort of braggart pleasure in the attention it brought to him. He had been found guilty and sentenced to hang, but Giles felt little relief when the verdict came in. He had found himself struggling with low spirits and often questioning his fitness for the work. Even when he slept, he found Wallace simpering at him in strange dreams. Emma, he knew, had also been suffering nightmares, and it was good to see her in such a state of unguarded happiness that morning. Her handkerchief may have been soaked through, but her spirits encouraged his own.

After the service was over, the couple left the church and were showered with petals and rice by Sophy and Hamish, who had been recruited as attendants. According to Hamish, the rice-throwing was the most important part of the whole procedure, and he was bitterly disappointed that hurling old shoes at the carriage had been declared unnecessary.

The wedding breakfast at the Castle was less lavish than it might have been in ordinary circumstances, but there were liberal quantities of champagne for the toasts and enough elaborately constructed food to provoke the amazement of the guests: there was a tiered bride-cake decorated with the coats of arms of the bride and groom and a huge, gilded pie, apparently the speciality of the Castle, with battlements, windows and a spun sugar portcullis. To finish the effect it was stuck with paper flags.

"The last time one of these was made was when Charlotte was born," said Lord Rothborough.

"And what is inside it?" said the Prince.

"That is a question one does not like to ask," said Lord Rothborough. "I suspect it is for looking at and not eating. But it is a charming tradition." He reached out and plucked one of the flags from the pastry battlements, and added it to his buttonhole.

"Do you have any such traditions in your family, Your Highness?" asked Giles.

"I do not think so," said the Prince, with a frown. "I am beginning to find my own country rather lacking in these matters. The Scottish have such a talent for the picturesque. I think we do not."

"Surely it is a question of cultivation," said Lord Rothborough. "It was never much thought of here until Sir Walter Scott showed us how to cherish what we had. Perhaps you need a poet to do the work."

"Perhaps the Prince is a poet himself?" said Giles. "Mrs Vernon mentioned something about some verses."

"Oh, those," said the Prince, looking embarrassed. "Those were nothing. I only wanted to divert her. I hope you do not mind, sir."

"No, of course not," Giles said, who had been most amused that his prophecy had come to pass. "She was delighted with them, but she would not translate them for me."

"You should be worried, Vernon," Lord Rothborough said, laughing.

"No, it is because I have foolishly said I would try and learn German," Giles said. "It is to encourage me."

"Yes, yes, that is it, quite," said the Prince, a little

flustered now. "And I assure you, Major Vernon, there was nothing in them that anyone would –"

Giles made a dismissive gesture.

"I think I would write poetry to Mrs Vernon," said Lord Rothborough, "if I had the wit to do it. She is the sort of woman who properly appreciates these things."

Giles said, "And she, poor woman, is married to a man who can scarcely find a rhyme, let alone write verse for her. She is lucky to have friends to supply the lack."

The Prince smiled at that, made a bow and excused himself, leaving Giles alone with Lord Rothborough.

"It would not have been disagreeable if Charlotte had liked him," Lord Rothborough said, watching as the Prince crossed the room and went to talk to the bride and groom. "He has a stout heart, I think. But he would have taken her away from me, and that I cannot quite contemplate at the moment. It is quite enough to have two of my girls suddenly not girls any more, but wives!"

~

Having left the drawing room, Felix found that Charlotte had deserted the company and was in the long hall, playing ball with her little dog, Otto.

"He is desperate to go out," she said, "and so am I! Oh, this is very hard work – I am exhausted from smiling."

"It's probably because we are all out of practice," said Felix, sitting down. Charlotte gathered up Otto and sat down next to him.

"Did Papa tell you we are going to London?" she said.

"He did mention it."

"It will be rather quiet, necessarily," she said. "Which is for the best, but it will not stop people coming to stare. All

Mama's friends will want to come and say their piece to me." She gave a shudder. "I've already had some letters that I can scarcely credit! How can people send condolences and use the occasion to abuse Papa? I think some of them truly believe that Wallace had nothing to do with it. They would like to hang Papa."

"You ought not to let them into the house, then," said Felix. "What obligation have you to see them, after all?"

"I feel I owe them something, I suppose," she said. "But then again, there is only so much unpleasantness one can bear. Perhaps I should keep the gates locked against them."

"You may see only whom you choose, now," Felix said.

She smiled. "How strange – that is something I did not have before. A strange thing to inherit. It is the last thing she would want, of course, but I cannot live in her shadow. That much is clear. No one should. And then, what if Papa were to remarry?"

"Do you mean Mrs Martinez?" said Felix, surprised at her directness.

"Who else would he marry?" Charlotte said, releasing her now struggling dog. He went clattering across the floor. "I know what he feels for her, although he has never told me directly so. But I know he writes to her every day. What is she like? Would I like her, do you think?"

"I think so," Felix said, after a moment.

"I should certainly like to know her," said Charlotte. "Do you write to her?"

"I do – I'm a pitiful correspondent, as well you know, but she writes to me. But it is strange – we do not quite know how we ought to be with one another. So we are careful in what we say – somewhat guarded, I suppose. But I think she would be an excellent person to turn to for advice. She has seen a lot of the world."

"He ought to marry her," said Charlotte. "We should encourage it. After a decent interval has elapsed, of course. But really, it is ridiculous that they should not be married, don't you think?"

"I've scarcely thought about it," said Felix. "It would be the talk of the world. She may not want such attention on her."

"She was married to a president, was she not?" said Charlotte. "How different can that be from being married to a prime minister?"

"Do you think he still wishes that?" Felix said.

"Do you doubt it?"

"I don't know. He would probably say that the moment may have passed when it was possible. He would be the first to admit that the party is not fond of him, and after all this –"

"Perhaps," she said, after a moment. "Oh, dear me, how everything has been set on its head! That we can even be sitting here, having such a conversation about Papa, all because that man decided to do what he did. But did he decide? Is that how such evil minds work? Is it even so rational?"

"I wish we knew. It would make our work a great deal easier if there were some sort of model – then we could identify those who were likely to cause havoc. But I do not believe in phrenology, by the by – I can see no evidence at all for that as a predictor of criminal behaviour. You will hear that touted all too often. It is a great deal more complicated than what shape your ears might be. In fact, Major Vernon has a theory that there may be certain patterns of behaviour that may be observable in those individuals that have a taste for killing."

"Ah," said Charlotte, "and he will be the one, no doubt, to make the great advance in the subject, given his talents."

"It's highly possible, although he would be the first to deny any credit for anything. But Vernon's 'Criminal Behaviour' will one day be the standard text, if I have anything to do with it. I mean to make him do something with his theories, certainly," Felix said, and then found himself laughing.

"Although he might object to the phrasing of such a title. Perhaps 'The Behaviour of Criminals' might sound better."

"You had better put that to him."

"I shall," said Felix.

"It must be curious," she said, after a moment, "to be in such close association. You are more like brothers than colleagues. Does he –" She broke off and got up, going again to play with the dog. "Has he said anything to you about –? Perhaps you know what a fool I am on this subject!"

He got up, retrieved the ball from beneath a stool and handed it to her.

"You're not a fool," he said. "These things happen. It's in our nature to be rather warm-hearted – is that the right way to put it? Perhaps it is too kind to call it that. But it is something in our blood. If you had any idea how I have indulged myself –"

"You?"

"Last winter, when Eleanor's mother was with us. I think you have met her?"

Charlotte nodded, and then laid her hand on his forearm.

"Truly?" she said. "Goodness."

"I don't know what came over me, but I could not have prevented it." She nodded again. "And I have worked out a way to excuse myself, of course," he added.

"Which is?" she said.

"To imagine that it is the inverse of being a man like Wallace," he said. "His whole being inclined to hatred. It drove him to destroy. But to be driven by love – and with sincerity, not just out of animal need, then there must be something good in that, something we ought to cherish, surely? What if one never felt anything or only felt hatred? That would be a real affliction. This is – well – something good will come of it, for you, I'm sure, and you will find someone – just as he has."

She leant forward, and putting her arms around him, kissed him on the cheek.

"That is a great comfort," she said. "Thank you. And I'm happy for him, although it hurts me. When I see him with that lovely little boy – I ache with it! Oh, but how good to say that! Thank you," she said, and kissed him again, her tears flowing freely now. "What a wretched, happy day this is – I think Maria will be the happiest of us all. She has such a talent for it!"

The door opened and Miss King came in.

"Oh, here you are, Mr Carswell!" she said. "Eleanor is – well, you had better come and see for yourself."

It seemed that Eleanor had fainted. Felix found her sitting in an anteroom, sniffing at a flask of smelling salts, and grimacing at the stench. She looked flushed, dishevelled and to Felix's eyes extremely beguiling. She threw her arms about him.

"I never faint!" she exclaimed. "You know I never faint. I think Stevens laced me too tight this morning."

"I shall just be outside," said Miss King, going to the door.

"Oh, don't go, Jenny, please –" Eleanor said, stretching out her hand to her.

"You must tell him," said Miss King, and left the room.

"What must you tell me?" said Felix.

"I can't," Eleanor said. "Oh, Felix, I'm so sorry."

"For what? What is going on?"

"It has happened. The thing that we didn't want – I certainly didn't want, and I know that you don't! I am so, so sorry. What were we thinking?"

Felix began to understand her. Over the last few weeks they had thoroughly indulged themselves. It had been an absolute necessity with him, and she had never demurred. Her eagerness had matched his own.

"It's not your fault. If anyone is to blame, I am," he said. "And it may not be certain. You only fainted."

"Oh, it is," she said. "I am two weeks late. I began to get an inkling of it when you went away to Perth. And Stevens could not lace me as usual today. I'm already fat as a pig and I am so sore," she added, touching her breast. "Jenny says that is a certain sign."

"It might not be the case," said Felix, feeling a curious mixture of emotions rising up in him. He realised he would be sorely disappointed if she were not with child. All those nights of careless pleasure now seemed to make sense beyond the moment of blissful release. It was the height of spring, after all – the earth was cracking open with fresh, tiny shoots of green, and despite death being all around them, or perhaps because of that, there was a determination for new life. They had simply fallen into the great cycle of nature, and the result was entirely predictable. The oddest thing about it was how satisfied he felt. "But if it is, then –" He broke off to kiss her on the lips. "So be it. To everything a season!"

He swept his hand over her warm forehead and smoothed her hair. She stared up at him with her lips parted and he felt he could have ravished her there and then, on that sofa in the anteroom, expressly with the intention of getting her pregnant. It was strange to feel oneself on the level of a ram being brought down to the tups, or a prize stallion taken to stud, but at the same time, what good did it do to agonise over such things?

He did recollect where he was, however, and detached himself from her with some effort and went to fetch Miss King.

She looked at him enquiringly as he came out of the room.

"I hope you won't desert us," he said, "if our circumstances change."

"No, never," she said. "You have my word."

~

It had been decided by the family that there ought not to be dancing, and yet it seemed that because it was a wedding, dancing could not be avoided, especially when a party of fiddle players arrived to play for the bride and groom. It was late in the afternoon, and a beautiful spring light filled all the rooms, and when the musicians began to play their reels and strathspeys, it reminded Giles of the fiddle players of his own childhood in Northumberland. It was impossible to resist, and almost everyone who could took to the floor for an impromptu ball. Even Dunbar and his Countess proved their northern ancestry, by running as blithely through the steps of a reel as any of them. The champagne had not ceased to flow, and as some of the servants and other family retainers joined the party, it was supplemented by beer and whisky. The dancing grew wilder, the figures more elaborate and the older members of the party, including Giles and Emma, began to elect themselves observers. They sat down on a sofa and watched, not without amusement, as the others – especially the young men – flung themselves about with varying degrees of abandonment.

"Given he is a novice, Sir Mark is doing very well," said Emma, "and he has beautiful bearing. But I think the crown has to go to Mr Carswell, don't you think? He looks blissfully at home with all this. I do wish he would wear the kilt, though."

"I should not have sat this one out," said Giles. "The man gets two partners at once – very agreeable – a sort of Scotch seraglio set to music. Perhaps not so pleasant for the ladies, though."

"No, I can imagine fearful rivalries," Emma said.

"Unless," Giles said, watching Miss King and then Eleanor weave about Carswell in a figure of eight, "it is not a seraglio, but something quite different again."

"Such as?"

"I'm not sure. Miss King and Mrs Carswell – what do you

make of them?"

"In what respect?"

"They strike me as very close. There is something intense about it. One might say as close as sisters."

Emma was silent for a moment, and then said, "I think they're charming together."

He glanced at her, chastened by her tone. "I need some coffee. Would you like some?"

~

The party was breaking up. The bride had gone to get changed. They were not going far that night, only to a small property belonging to the Castle, up the Glen. Felix noticed Lord Rothborough had taken Sir Mark to one side, and was talking to him earnestly.

"They are probably talking about the fishing," said Major Vernon, who was holding a cup of coffee.

"I think not," said Felix, remembering a similar moment at his own wedding. "It will be a beautifully judged mixture of advice and threats. More of the latter, I dare say, as Maria has always been his favourite."

"That is unjust," said Major Vernon. "My observation of him is that he has always been scrupulous in that regard. Look how well he has settled with the Countess."

"Yes, that's true enough," said Felix, reaching for a champagne bottle and refilling his glass. The reels had made him thirsty. "Ye Gods, Dunbar is a lucky fellow, is he not? I saw the proposed settlement – and they are going to London after all, with a house as a wedding present! Do you not want some of this?" he added, gesturing with the bottle.

"I will stick to coffee. I have drunk myself stupid already," said Major Vernon.

"You had an entire half a bottle, then?" said Felix with a smile.

"More like two," said Major Vernon.

"Goodness," said Felix.

"The champagne was too good. I have a decided weakness for it."

"It is most seductive," said Felix, sipping his own wine. "Come, are you sure will not have another glass? I have a toast to make."

"If you insist," said Major Vernon.

Felix found another glass, drained the last of the bottle into it and handed it to Major Vernon.

"God knows, we deserve this," he said. "Given all that has happened."

Major Vernon nodded, sipped his wine and said, "What are we drinking to, then?"

Felix raised his glass and considered his words.

"Holidays interrupted to good purpose?" the Major said.

"No," said Felix. "Not that, though we should. My mother said it was providential that we were here."

"I have an idea about that," said Major Vernon, "which disconcerts me. I cannot help wondering if we did not provoke Wallace in some way. I was very short with him that first day, after which he must have gone after Mrs Gowans. Then, having enjoyed himself and seeing us running about, he set out to do more damage. Is that possible?"

"It may be, but we cannot be responsible for anything he did," said Felix.

"It just strikes me – and I think I have observed it in other cases – that these people like to be recognised for what they have done. In place of remorse, there is a need to brag. Otherwise, he would just be a dreary clergyman whom no one liked. Now, he will be remembered as a notorious monster."

"That is a good argument against public executions."

"One of the many," said Major Vernon. He took a

mouthful of champagne. "The end of that would be worth a toast."

"One day," said Felix. "No, I wish to drink to marriage, of course, and the fruits of marriage. You see, it may be that soon enough, Eleanor and I will be parents."

"Ah!" said Major Vernon, smiling and raising his glass. "That I can drink to, and with the greatest pleasure. Yes, I do hope so, Carswell, for nothing could be better for both of you. May you be blessed, and soon!"

"It is a strange thing," Felix said. "I have resisted the idea so long, but now it seems to make perfect sense. A challenge, of course, but one that I should no longer avoid."

Major Vernon nodded, and put down his glass.

"It does make one wonder how our opinions are formed," he said. "We are all far more open to suggestion than anyone imagines. The subtlest directions can set us on courses we never predicted. There is such a power in quiet words and small gestures, if done with intention. I find it curious."

"Ah! Is that the real power of witchcraft?" Felix said. "An imperceptible nudge that causes a desired chain of events, good or bad? And have we come to Pitfeldry to be bewitched, as a reward for our help?"

Major Vernon shrugged at this fanciful notion, and glancing through the open door said, "I think they are leaving. We should go and see them off."

Felix turned and saw Maria kissing her sisters. He followed the Major and they joined the party at the door to the castle, where two pipers struck up to see Maria and Sir Mark into their carriage. Favours were thrown to the waiting crowd of villagers and then the carriage departed, turning up the avenue of rustling, fresh-leaved beech trees into the fading light of the afternoon. Felix noticed Major Vernon was looking up at the sky where a silver crescent, the first showing of the May moon, was now visible.

The two men fell into a companionable silence, staring

into the waning light and contemplating for a while all that had happened, and what it meant.

~ THE END ~

Dramatis Personae

Mrs McCroy's house

Major Giles Vernon: Chief Superintendent, Northminster Constabulary

Emma Vernon: Major Vernon's wife

Hamish Gordon: Emma's nephew, aged 9

Sophy Gordon: Emma's niece, aged 8

Alexander 'Sandro' Gordon: Emma's nephew, aged 2

Mrs Patton: Emma's maid

Greene: nursemaid to the children

Mrs McCroy: widow of a former minster of Pitfeldry and hostess to the Vernons

Jean: Mrs McCroy's servant

Pitfeldry Rectory

Felix Carswell MD: consultant surgeon to the Northern Investigation Office, natural son of Lord Rothborough

Eleanor Carswell: Felix's wife

The Rev Mr James Carswell: Rector of Pitfeldry and Felix Carswell's adopted father

Mrs Carswell: Felix Carswell's adopted mother

Miss Jenny King: companion to Eleanor

Jacob: Felix's manservant

Miss Stevens: Eleanor's maid

Grizel and Johnny: servants to the Rector and Mrs Carswell

Pitfeldry Castle

Lord Rothborough: Felix's natural father

Lady Rothborough

Lady Charlotte Haraald: the Rothboroughs' eldest daughter

Lady Augusta Haraald: the Rothboroughs' middle daughter

Lady Maria Haraald: the Rothboroughs' youngest daughter

Franz-Friedrich: Prince of Schwarzenburg-Meckleninghen

James Bodley: manservant to Lord Rothborough

Mrs Parsons: maid to Lady Rothborough

Blair: steward to Lord Rothborough

Mr MacDonald: Lord Rothborough's factor

The Manse, Pitfeldry

Mr Adam Wallace: the minister

Mrs Wallace: the minister's wife

Pitfeldry Village

Mrs Bel Gowans: shopkeeper

Effie Haynes: Mrs Gowans' sister

Mr Gowans: husband to Mrs Gowans

Mary: daughter of Mr and Mrs Gowans

Mrs McNeill: landlady of The Brodie Arms

Lord Dunbar: a guest at the inn

Donnie Anderson

Kirsty Macdonald

Mrs Shairp

Angus Lowndie

Mr Finlay: the Sheriff-Substitute

Sergeant Gibson

Westerlochan Farm

Mr Murray

Mrs Murray

Janet Murray

Jessie Murray

Agnes Murray

Animals

Star: a three-legged collie

Amadeus: a Scottish deerhound, resident of the Rectory

Flora and Margaret: Mrs McCroy's cats

Otto: Lady Charlotte's spaniel

About the Author

Harriet Smart was born and brought up in Birmingham. She attended the University of St Andrews, where she read History of Art, and married a fellow student. She now lives with her husband in an eighteenth-century house in Northumberland.

Harriet has an M.A. in screenwriting. She has published twenty novels as well as helping to design the creative writing software Writer's Café and the e-book editor software Jutoh.

She has been writing the Northminster Mysteries since 2010.

You can follow Harriet at www.harrietsmart.com and BookBub.

Printed in Dunstable, United Kingdom

68601840R00231